WHISPERS
of the
BAYOU

MINDY STARNS
CLARK

HARVEST HOUSE PUBLISHERS

EUGENE, OREGON

Cover by Dugan Design Group, Bloomington, Minnesota

Cover photos © Corey Hilz / Rubberball Productions / Getty Images; Rebecca Floyd / Graphistock Photography / Veer

This is a work of fiction. Names, characters, places, and incidents are products of the author's imagination or are used fictitiously. Any resemblance to actual persons, living or dead, or to events or locales, is entirely coincidental.

WHISPERS OF THE BAYOU
Copyright © 2008 by Mindy Starns Clark
Published by Harvest House Publishers
Eugene, Oregon 97402
www.harvesthousepublishers.com

Library of Congress Cataloging-in-Publication Data
Clark, Mindy Starns.
Whispers of the bayou / Mindy Starns Clark.
    p. cm.
ISBN 978-0-7369-1879-4
1. Louisiana—Fiction. I. Title.
PS3603.L366W47 2008
813'.6—dc22

2007039825

Printed in the United States of America

09 10 11 12 13 14 15 16 17 / LB-SK / 17 16 15 14 13 12 11 10 9

This book is dedicated with much love to
Alice Clark.
Your Christian walk inspires me,
your wonderful personality delights me,
and your kind and selfless actions minister to me.
Thank you for all that you do!

ACKNOWLEDGMENTS

Many, many thanks to...

John Clark, my superhero.

Emily and Lauren Clark, my precious angels.

Kim Moore, the most dedicated editor I have ever known.

Betty Fletcher and all of the other amazing folks at Harvest House.

Kay Justus, brainstorming partner extraordinaire.

Ned and Marie Scannell, my dear and generous hosts who
always come through when I need it most.

My amazing assortment of illustrious experts, including:
Tracy Baudoin, Don Beard, Cheryl Berrios, Brandt Dodson,
Mark Mynheir, Vonda Skelton, and Jennifer Lee Whitt.

The gracious and helpful Janice Kollar of Janice Kollar Fine Art Restorations.

The best medical advisors in the world: Ron Berrios, CRNA; Michael
Jacoby; Keith Lehman, MD; Lamar Lehman, MD; Richard Keller, MD;
Robert M. Starns, MD; D.P. Lyle, MD; and Ronda Wells, MD.

My delightful online group Consensus, whose input and honesty help me
to shape every story. (Visit *www.mindystarnsclark.com/newsletter
.php#resource* for more information or to sign up.)

My FVCN small group, for boundless prayer, friendship, and support.

ChiLibris, as always, for everything.

NOTE TO READER

All epigraphs are taken from *Evangeline: A Tale of Acadie* by
Henry Wadsworth Longfellow, from the 1893 Cambridge Edition
(originally published in 1847).

ONE

Dreamlike, and indistinct, and strange were all things around them;
And o'er their spirits there came a feeling of wonder and sadness—
Strange forebodings of ill, unseen and that cannot be compassed.

The man appeared in the doorway of my studio unannounced, with a brown paper package tucked under his arm. He was younger than he had sounded on the phone, thirty at the most, with dark wavy hair, mottled skin, and a narrow caterpillar of a mustache along his upper lip.

"Miranda Miller?" he asked in what sounded like a thick Long Island accent. "Jimmy Smith. We spoke this morning?"

I was elbow deep in plaster and not in a position to shake hands, so I just smiled and told him to come on in. Ready for a break, I extricated myself from my project and rinsed off my arms and hands at the utility sink. I usually didn't see private clients, but he had been so persistent over the phone—and he had dropped enough important names, names of people who funded some of our grants—that I had made an exception. Now that he had unwrapped the picture and was holding it up, however, I was sorry I had relented. Even from a distance I could see I would be wasting my time, not to mention his money.

"Tell me again where you got this painting?" I asked as I slipped on a pair of handling gloves.

"At a flea market in the East Village. Only two hundred dollars! I'm thinking it was a real steal."

I crossed the room, noticing as I got closer that the top of the man's head barely came to my nose. At five nine I was tall for a woman, but next to this guy I felt like an Amazon. I took the painting from him and turned around to lean on the deep windowsill, the late-morning sunlight warming my shoulders. The painting in question was an 11 x 14 canvas framed in mahogany, a poorly done oil of a busy village market scene. The piece wasn't nearly as dirty as he had described, just a bit dusty, especially around the edges. I'd be happy to clean it up for him, but it didn't seem to need any restoration and I wasn't going to charge him for my trouble. He'd already paid more than enough to get it—many times more than it was worth.

"So whatcha think?" he asked.

"Looks like it just needs a little cleaning," I replied as I stood and carried it over to the work area. "No soot or stains or mildew. Just dust. And not even old dust. It doesn't need restoration. I believe you could easily have taken care of this yourself."

"I mean about the picture."

I glanced at his eager face, hesitant to be the bearer of bad news.

"I'm not an estimator," I hedged. "Just a restorer."

I flipped on the light box and set the painting down on top of it. With the beam projecting through the image, I quickly scanned the canvas for irregularities. Satisfied that there were none, I turned off the box, moved the piece to my worktable, and clicked on the lamps there.

"You have surely had experience with enough fine art to know a good piece when you see one," he said. "So at two hundred, was this a steal or what?"

Or what, I thought as I scanned the canvas again for problems, this time with overhead and directional lighting. Finding no real issues, I flipped the picture so that it was facedown and extracted a soft watercolor brush from the tool bucket nearby.

"Again, I'm no estimator, but 'steal' might be the right word for it."

"I thought so!"

"Unfortunately, I'm sorry to say, you were probably the one who was robbed."

Hoping my words weren't too harsh, I pulled the Genvac hose from the wall and clicked on the machine with my foot. It sprang to life with a low humming noise, the suction through the flannel-covered hose just strong enough to gently draw away the dust I was loosening with the brush. When I finished cleaning the back, I carefully flipped the painting over, glancing at the man's face as I did so. I was surprised to see that he didn't seem disappointed or upset by my bad news. In fact, he looked just as enthusiastic and intrigued as before. The guy was probably rich, considering the names he'd dropped on the phone, not to mention the huge gemstone in the ring that adorned his pinky. Perhaps he regularly used C-notes as kindling or tissues or something, in which case a couple hundred tossed away on a piece of junk at a flea market was no big deal.

"Valuable or not, it's a nice scene, don't you think?"

"Hmm," I mumbled, trying to avoid the question. "This will just take a minute."

I gave the piece my full attention as I worked my way from the top down, brushing the dust loose with the brush and then sucking away that dust through the special hose. I liked silence to concentrate and I was used to working alone, but my guest turned out to be a regular chatterbox, asking questions about the frame, the paint, the artist. I would have thought he was just making conversation if he hadn't been so eager about the whole thing, nervously crinkling the brown paper wrapping he still held clutched in his hands.

"I've been so curious about this scene," he was saying as I finished and clicked off the vacuum with my foot. "Whatcha think that man is selling there?"

I looked where he indicated and shrugged, unable to muster the enthusiasm that he was obviously feeling.

"Tomatoes? Apples? Some kind of red produce, anyway."

"And this architecture behind them. I can't quite place the scene, but it looks European to me. A town square? Late seventeen hundreds, maybe?"

"Maybe."

I slid the hose back into its holder and dropped the paintbrush into the tool bucket.

"What about this symbol here?" he prodded. "What do you make of that?"

I looked where he indicated and saw a strange shape painted in black on the back of a man's overcoat. I was ready to send this fellow on his way and get back to my work, but something about that shape was intriguing. From the tool bucket, I removed a magnifying glass, and then I adjusted the light and bent over the painting to study it more closely.

The symbol appeared to be an elaborate sort of cross either inside the shape of a bell or an upside-down shield. I would have passed it off as a simple embellishment if something about it hadn't made me pause.

"I've seen this shape before," I said, though I couldn't quite place it. "I don't know where, but it's awfully familiar."

"Really?" he whispered, and from the corner of my eye, I could see him licking his lips, the caterpillar undulating.

"It was painted onto this picture later," I added, not bothering to explain the subtle differences between the surface of the symbol and the texture of the surrounding area. "Looks like someone dabbed it on with acrylic. The rest of the work is in oil."

"Ah."

He was finally quiet for a moment, so I took the opportunity to scan the rest of the painting with the magnifying glass. Nothing else about it jumped out at me, and no other irregularities were present.

Finally, I returned to the symbol to take one last look. I had a mind for shapes, but the origin of this image eluded me. Finally, I stood up straight and tucked the magnifying glass away, determined to put it out of my mind. I had been working in art restoration since graduate school, and now by the age of thirty-two had probably seen thousands of symbols and shapes. It stood to reason that one or two had faded from my memory.

"If I had to take a guess, I'd say it's probably a family's coat of arms. That would explain why someone painted it in later. They probably bought this picture and then decided to have it personalized. Like their own little private touch."

"A coat of arms?" he replied doubtfully. "You say you've seen this symbol before?"

I reached for a cotton swab and a jar of mineral spirits.

"I think so. It looks kind of like a cross inside a bell," I replied, dipping the swab into the liquid and then touching it along the bottom of the frame. Pleased with the response, I tossed the swab into the trash, reached for a rag, and dabbed it more liberally. "I can't remember where I've seen it, but it'll come to me later, I'm sure."

Using mineral spirits on the rag, I wiped the wood in a circular motion, explaining to him that I was removing the buildup of several year's worth of furniture polish.

"The frame's not bad," I said as I worked, still pained at the thought of this guy paying two hundred dollars for a twenty-dollar painting. Truly, the mahogany frame was worth far more than the "artwork" inside it. "Most people use a silicone-based polish on fine wood, which is a big mistake. Just regular weekly wiping with a dry rag will do."

He didn't seem interested in a lecture about ongoing care, so I stopped explaining and just finished the job of sprucing up the frame, following the mineral spirits with a fine layer of carnauba wax. By the time I was done, his inferior work of art looked as good as it possibly could.

"We'll let it sit for a few minutes while the wax sets," I told him, peeling off the gloves, "and then you can wrap it up again and take it with you. Should be as good as new."

"I'd like to let it sit longer, if you don't mind," he said, glancing at his watch. "I'll come back later. In the meantime, see if you can remember where you've seen that symbol."

"Oh, don't bother leaving it. Just take it with you now," I said. "It'll be fine." I wondered if he had even heard me say that the painting was essentially worthless. Either that, or he had but didn't care.

"Really, I'd rather come back. I have an appointment," the man said, and then, before I could stop him, he had tossed the brown paper wrapping into the trash and raced out the door. I called after him, but by the time I reached the doorway and looked out into the hall, he had already disappeared from sight.

What an odd man.

It was just as well. I had an appointment myself, a lunch date with my Aunt Janet—or "AJ," as I called her—and if I didn't hurry I would be late. I put away the materials I'd been working with before the man arrived, and then I removed my smock and grabbed the change of clothes I kept in a drawer and headed for a quick cleanup in the bathroom.

My aunt was pure Southern gentility, born and raised in Louisiana, and though she had been living in Manhattan for the past thirty years, she still maintained that a lady never went out in public without full makeup and hair, not to mention perfectly dressed. I did the best I could when I knew I'd be seeing her, but between a demanding job and a five-year-old daughter at home, I rarely bothered fixing myself up these days unless it was to schmooze a museum benefactor or dutifully play the corporate wife at one of Nathan's business functions.

Nathan. Refusing to rehash this morning's discussion in my mind yet again, I focused on freshening up instead, rinsing the last traces of plaster and the scent of mineral oil from my arms and hands. I dried off with some paper towels and then changed into black slacks and a blue top, both of which I'd paid a small fortune for at a travel store because they were virtually unwrinkleable and perfect for keeping stashed in the desk. After adding a chunky silver necklace and bracelet—mementoes of a trip with our curator to Ixtapa—I dabbed on some lipstick, blush, and mascara before letting down my clipped-up hair and running a brush through it.

Once I was finished I stepped back from the mirror, pleased with the result. I was nothing if not adaptable. If I could just get through this lunch without the intuitive AJ pressing me to tell her what was wrong, I'd be fine.

I returned to the studio, thinking that sometimes I wished I was the type of woman who could just bring her problems out into the open and talk about them, especially with my wise and loving aunt. It wasn't that I had trouble with deep, soul-level discussions, it was that I had trouble with deep, soul-level discussions about myself. Friends always said I was

WHISPERS of the BAYOU ✤ 11

such a great listener, but I don't think it ever dawned on them that with me they never had to listen in return—and that's how I liked to keep it. The fact that my husband was unhappy in our marriage was between him and me. I just needed to find a way to work things out, and that I could do by myself. AJ would simply have to mind her own business.

I shoved my work clothes into the bottom drawer of the desk, gathered my purse and keys, and turned off the light. Weaving my way through the yellow maze of hallways that formed the network of museum administration, I continued down the hall until I reached the desk of our new receptionist, a museum studies grad student who was filling in while our regular receptionist was out on maternity leave. I explained to her about the man with the painting, his abrupt departure, and his promise to return.

"If he gets back before I do, just go get the painting from my studio and bring it out to him, would you?"

"No problem. I'll take care of it."

"And in the future, please buzz me before you send someone back. My department doesn't take visitors unannounced."

Her face turned bright red.

"Oh. Sure. Sorry."

"It's a security issue," I explained, feeling bad that I had embarrassed her. "We can't have strangers wandering around back there. It's not your fault. They should have taught you that on your very first day."

"Got it," she replied, smiling gratefully.

I thanked the girl and left, pushing open the door to step out into the warm June sunshine. Joining the flow of people on the sidewalk, I thought how good it felt to stretch my legs after a morning spent working in one position for far too long. I was ready for a break and looking forward to my standing Friday lunch date with AJ.

The restaurant wasn't far, and I covered the first three blocks quickly. To avoid the heavy pedestrian traffic of the square, I took my usual shortcut down the alley I had fondly come to think of as "odor row." Sandwiched between a seafood store and an Italian restaurant on one side and an Indian fast-food place and a dry cleaner on the other, the alley's cement walls caught and held all the smells of all four places, making it a veritable stink fest, a gauntlet of olfactory overwhelm. Though it wasn't the most appetizing way to get to lunch, it was worth the trade-off in avoiding the bottleneck at the intersection.

I was just past the stench of eau-de-fish and about to walk into cloud-of-curry when a flash of movement off to the side caught my eye. Before I could even turn to look, a man was behind me, with one of his strong hands clamped over my mouth and the other pinning my arms to my waist. He pushed me through a narrow doorway into a small, dark cement room where a second person closed the door behind us and then joined in the struggle to force me to the floor. I fought violently against them, but to no avail. Other than landing a few solid kicks to what were probably shins, I was no match for their strength or their carefully laid ambush.

When they finally had me pinned to the floor, I felt a hand grabbing for my shirt, ripping it upward from my back, and I thought I knew what was about to happen next. Somewhere in the back of my mind I tried to divorce myself from the moment. There was a safe place in my head somewhere, if only I could find it soon enough.

Beyond the terror of what might happen next was also a desperate need to breathe. The hand was still clamped about my mouth and nose, blocking all air. With desperate force, I was able to shake my head free from the hand, but as soon as I took a breath to scream, something else went into my mouth, a wide strip of fabric which was tied roughly off at the back of my neck, gagging me so that I could breathe but not speak or scream.

I inhaled frantically through my nose, ignoring the stench as I desperately struggled to catch my breath. As I did, I realized that the room was no longer completely dark. At some point they had turned on a flashlight, and the shadows it created were dancing wildly along the cinderblock wall.

What happened next left me stunned and confused. After having pulled my shirt all the way up to my shoulders, they suddenly left it alone and grabbed the bottom hem of my pants leg instead, pulling it upward to reveal my ankle and calf. The flashlight beam jerked wildly up and down my lower legs, and then one of the men let out a low, frustrated growl. They did the same with the other leg then, and they ripped off both shoes and socks, an act which was followed by more noises of frustration but no words.

Their final move was the strangest of all.

Leaving my bare feet alone, they next grabbed a fistful of my hair. While one of the men pressed my face onto the cold, slimy cement floor to hold it still, the other man kept running his hand back and forth through my hair as he played the flashlight against the back of my head.

"Wait!" said the one holding me down. "Go back."

Reversing the direction of his fingers, the other guy moved back a few inches and then gasped.

"That's it!" he cried.

Except for slight movements of his fingers in my hair, both men were perfectly still for a moment, as if they were studying something back there. Even the flashlight stopped moving around. I waited in silence, terrified of what might come next, the stench of the floor under my nose telling me we were in an empty garbage holding area—and that I was now intimately acquainted with the juices that had recently oozed out of the garbage bags.

"Got it?" the one holding my head said finally.

"Yeah."

Finally, the guy with his fingers in my hair simply gripped a handful by the roots and leaned down to put his lips next to my ear.

"Thanks for your cooperation," he whispered. "Sorry it had to be like this."

With a final, sharp tug of my hair for emphasis, he let go. Then the door opened and they both took off, their footsteps sending a telltale echo through the alley as they ran away.

TWO

What their errand may be I know not better than others.
Yet am I not of those who imagine some evil intention.

 I suppose they expected me to lie there in the filth, traumatized and immobile, a weak and shivering victim.

Don't think so, fellas.

With the sound of their footsteps still echoing in the alley outside, I pushed myself up and took off after them barefoot, adrenaline pumping through my body so fiercely that it never crossed my mind to wonder what I'd do if I actually caught up with them.

From the sound of things, they had run off to the right, so that's the way I went too, tearing the gag from my mouth as I ran. When I emerged at the end of the alley, I looked up and down the street in both directions, but there were no men running away, no men doing anything that would identify them as my assailants. Either I had misjudged the sound of their footsteps as to the direction they had gone, or they had planned their escape as well as they had planned their ambush.

The front of the Indian restaurant held a cluster of sturdy plastic tables and chairs, all of which were occupied at the moment. Heart pounding, I cupped my hands around my mouth and yelled.

"Did anybody see two guys come running out of the alley just now?"

No one responded, though most of the people stopped eating to stare at me. I looked down to see that I was covered, top to bottom, in the green-and-brown slime of aged restaurant refuse.

"I was attacked," I added defensively to a nearby woman who was gaping at me over her plate of tandoori chicken. "In the alley."

"I did. I saw something," a man said finally, waving to me from a nearby chair that would have given him a perfect vantage point. "I think. I wasn't really paying attention."

"What did you see?"

"I don't know," he told me, adjusting the baseball cap on his head. He was about forty years old, dressed young for his age in a sports jersey and faded jeans. "Just a minute ago. I was reading the paper. Two guys came running out right there and jumped into a waiting car."

"Two men come running out of an alley," I demanded, "and it doesn't cross your mind that something's fishy?"

"Nah, they were laughing. Until you showed up, I didn't think anything of it at all."

The impact of the incident finally hit me. I felt my knees growing wobbly, and so I grabbed the nearest chair and sat, gripping the table in front of me for support. Then I began to shake so violently that the table rattled against the pavement. That was when the brown-skinned restaurant manager appeared and listened to my tale of attack and pursuit.

"You wait here?" he asked the man in the baseball cap. "You wait for cops?"

"I ain't leaving. I ain't even got my food yet."

"Good. Good," the manager said. "You wait."

"Okay, but you'll have to throw in extra chapati if it takes too long."

The man sat down and went back to his newspaper as the manager ushered me inside to call the police. Whether from kindness or to get this stinky person out of his restaurant, he then handed me over to an old woman in a sari, who led me to a tiny room in the back crammed with a desk and papers where I could sit. Though she didn't speak a word of English, she brought me some hot tea and patted my hand, and her quiet presence slowly helped me regain my composure.

The police personnel who came were polite and professional, though not much help. They didn't have an explanation for the nature of the attack and no record of anyone else having been accosted in this way. They didn't seem to think there was much they would be able to do, especially considering that I had not seen the faces of my attackers nor even heard them utter more than a few words. We walked down the alley to the scene of the crime, and there I made some guesses as to the men's heights and builds. Otherwise, all the police had to go on were the various smears and markings on the grimy floor, not to mention sticky shoeprints that headed in the same direction I'd thought they had gone. The police snapped photos and took the report and gave me a card that explained how to check back with them in a few days.

"What about the witness?" I asked. "The guy who saw them run out?"

"The man eating out front here? Yeah, that didn't pan out."

"What do you mean?"

"The manager told us to talk to him, but the guy was gone. The people sitting nearby said he got up and left about a minute after he promised to wait."

I gasped, wondering if that meant he'd been in on it too. I explained my theory to the cop, saying that maybe he had lied about what he'd seen to derail my pursuit and then disappeared as soon as he could afterward.

"More than likely, the guy just didn't want to get involved. A lot of people in this city are that way."

"But—"

"He could have all sorts of reasons for walking out of here so he wouldn't have to talk to us. Distrust. Outstanding parking tickets. Immigration issues. Who knows? I wouldn't put too much stock in his leaving."

As far as the cop was concerned, the subject was closed.

The policeman offered to call an ambulance for me, but I insisted that I was fine, just filthy and a bit rattled. I asked him to call AJ instead, who came running over from the restaurant where she'd been waiting two blocks away. She arrived within minutes, and as she came around the corner she burst into tears at the very sight of me.

I was feeling calmer by the minute, almost as if that brief period when I prepared myself to be violated had actually worked, that I had been able to protect my mind, if not my body, from assault. Assessing my condition, I knew I was shaken but not really injured, violated but not raped, angry but with no target for that anger. Except for an occasional tremble, the only remaining signs of my trauma were the slime that still coated me from head to toe and a hole in the knee of my very expensive non-wrinkleable pants.

When the police were finished, AJ insisted that I come home with her to get cleaned up, but I said no thanks, that I really needed to get back to work for our weekly staff meeting. I was late as it was.

With that, AJ simply put a hand to her cheek and gave a sympathetic groan.

"Oh, Miranda," she said, shaking her head. "Honey, snap out of it. You're not going back to work today. Stop trying to be so strong."

What I didn't tell her was that I wasn't *trying* to be strong. Like so many other times in my life, I found strength by virtue of the fact that I had simply managed to go numb.

Still, an agitated AJ was a force to be reckoned with. To placate her, I called in a message to my boss and apologized, saying that I'd had an emergency at lunch and might not make it back in this afternoon. I went along with AJ to her apartment, though it wasn't until I saw myself in the mirror that I understood why she had been so insistent. I was a mess, my hair was disheveled, and the stench of that grimy cement floor had been ground into my clothes and body.

I took a long shower, letting the hot water wash it all away. Afterward, swathed in AJ's robe, my damp hair towel dried and combed out, I emerged to find my aunt in the kitchen, where she was just putting a hastily assembled lunch onto the table. I stood in the doorway, unseen, and watched her toss a salad, thinking what a comfort she was to me, albeit a beautiful and elegant comfort. Always fond of vivid, voluminous fabrics, AJ was still dressed for today's outing in a gauzy shawl printed with bright pink cabbage roses on a field of neon green. On anyone else, the outfit would have looked ridiculous, but on her it was simply stunning. She

turned and spotted me, and that's when I realized that tears were streaming down her cheeks.

"Hey," I said, moving closer. "Hey. It's okay."

I wrapped her in my arms, inhaling the familiar scent of her perfume,
knowing how hard it must be to see someone you love get hurt. I might
not be the most intuituve mother in the world, but if someone had dared
to attack my daughter, Tess, as I had been attacked today, I knew that I
would move heaven and earth to find the culprits and see that justice was
done.

"I haven't been able to reach Nathan," she told me when we pulled apart.
"But I've left messages."

"You shouldn't have done that," I said as I took a seat at the small table.
"I'm fine. Really."

She set a bowl of tomato soup in front of me, shaking her head.

"He's your husband, Miranda. He should be with you."

"Why? There's nothing he can do at this point. And he has a lot going
on at work right now."

AJ pulled up a chair and sat across from me, her lovely features shrouded
in sadness.

"Miranda, honey, you've got to soften up a little. Husbands need to be
needed, especially at a time like this."

"He's *not* needed," I replied, and then seeing the shock on her face, I
added, "I mean, I love him. I enjoy him. In some ways, I depend on him.
But I don't need him. I can take care of myself just fine, thank you."

"Did you take care of yourself in that alley today?"

I set down my spoon, my appetite suddenly having disappeared.

"I'm sorry, I'm sorry," AJ said. "I just hate to see you handling this...
trauma...the way you handle everything else. Like it's no big deal. Like
you'll be just fine on your own."

"This is who I am," I said, thinking that AJ was starting to sound an
awful lot like Nathan. "You—and Nathan—can take it or leave it."

Despite the fact that I was no longer hungry, I focused on the meal in
front of me and ate. After a moment AJ began eating too, the only sound
the clink of our silverware and glasses. Finally, she landed on more neutral

ground by talking about Tess. I answered her question and she replied with another until we were chatting over lunch, ignoring the obvious, pretending that nothing had gone wrong, that two men had not dragged me into the dark just an hour or two before and done whatever it was they had done to me.

From the subject of Tess and preschool and the overwhelming fixation she'd had with *The Lion King* ever since AJ took her to see the show on Broadway, we moved on to the topic of AJ's work as a director at a modeling agency and mine as senior preparator at the museum. I told AJ about the rich man from Long Island and his ugly painting and the strange symbol that seemed so familiar. She found the story amusing until I grabbed a pen and paper from beside the phone and doodled the image for her.

"It looked like this," I said, holding it up to show her. "Like a cross inside a bell. It's driving me crazy that I can't remember where I've seen it."

The smile left her face, her rosy cheeks suddenly fading to white.

"What? What is it?"

AJ swallowed hard and shook her head, as if to shake away her thoughts.

"No," she said, pushing her chair back. "No, no, no."

She rose and began pacing in the tiny room, one hand on her stomach, the other held to her forehead.

"AJ, what's wrong? Do you know what I'm talking about? This shape, have you seen it?"

"This man with the painting, could he have been one of the ones who attacked you?"

"No. They were both tall and muscular. He was short and slim."

My response did not change the expression on her face.

"But they were connected," AJ cried, her eyes wild, her hands now frantically waving in the air in front of her. "However they were connected, this is all *my* fault!"

She began pacing again, her hands still moving in front of her, as if she was trying to grab hold of something ephemeral and elusive, some truth. AJ had served as a mother to me since my own mother died when

I was just a child. In all these years, I had never seen her like this, never seen her so out of control. I felt unnerved, as if the ground underneath me had shifted.

"I was hoping it would just go away, all of it," she continued. "I didn't know this would happen. I didn't know!"

I was thoroughly confused, not to mention frightened for her sake.

"AJ, calm down," I commanded. "Talk to me. What's going on?"

She stepped toward the table and held onto the edge for support, just as I had done earlier at the Indian restaurant.

"Miranda, I've been keeping something from you that I shouldn't have. Just promise you won't hate me or think I'm the most awful person in the world. I didn't know all of this would happen. I couldn't know." Though AJ was in her mid-fifties, for a moment she looked like a little girl—a very guilty little girl.

"AJ, I love you," I said. "I could never think badly of you. Just tell me what this is about."

She nodded, swallowed hard, and told me to come to the living room. Ignoring the dishes, I followed her through the doorway into the living room of the small but elegant apartment.

"Wait here," she directed.

As I sat down on the sateen mauve couch, AJ disappeared down the hall to her bedroom. My mind was still racing, so I took a deep breath and inhaled this home's familiar, calming scent, a mix of fresh gardenias and Givenchy perfume. AJ wasn't gone for long. When she came back, she was carrying a small stack of envelopes. She sat in the seat to my left, her hands once again trembling as she opened the top envelope and pulled out the letter from inside.

"This came for you, about three weeks ago," she said.

"For me? Here?"

"Yes, it was from Charles Benochet, the attorney who handles your inheritance in Louisiana."

I was unsure about what this had to do with all that was going on, but at least I understood why she had opened a letter addressed to me. AJ handled the details of my inheritance, interacting with the Louisiana attorney on my behalf. The legalities were complicated, but basically I owned a house and some land that had been left to me by my paternal grandparents in their will. The way I understood it, the property was already technically mine, but it wouldn't actually come into my possession until the death of their old caretaker, a man named Willy Pedreaux, to whom they had given a life estate or, as they called it in Louisiana, a "usufruct."

Considering that Mr. Pedreaux was in his seventies and Tess was five, we had always earmarked the inheritance to fund her college education. We planned to sell the place, probably sight unseen, and use the proceeds to help her get through school. If the man survived into his nineties, we'd simply go the student loan route and use the money to pay off the debt after the fact, whenever it eventually came into our hands.

"According to Charles," AJ continued, "Willy Pedreaux has been suffering from a lung condition called pulmonary fibrosis. They don't expect him to live much longer."

"Oh."

Of all the things I expected to hear, this wasn't it. From a purely financial standpoint, this was beneficial for me, of course, though considering that a man had to die for me to inherit, I didn't feel happy about it at all. The poor guy, here he was set for the rest of his life in a nice home with no mortgage payment to worry about, and his life was being cut short by a fatal illness.

"That's so sad," I added. "But what does this have to do with anything?"

"Bear with me," AJ said, handing me the letter and gesturing that I should read it for myself.

I skimmed the page of correspondence, which was written mostly in lawyer speak. From what I could tell, this was a courtesy note, written to inform me that I would be coming into my inheritance within a month or two, far sooner than anyone had expected. Then I got to the last paragraph, which added something of a twist:

I'm writing at Willy's request, to see if you might find it in your heart to come down to Louisiana and meet with him

before he passes away. He wants very much to speak with
you. If you can come, please let our office know and we'll be
happy to make the necessary arrangements.

> *Sincerely yours,*
> *Charles Benochet*

I looked up at AJ, feeling inexplicably sad.

"The poor man," I said, "he probably wanted to tell me all about the house and his memories of it and everything. He must not know that I plan to sell it."

"This letter showed up about a week later."

AJ pulled out the second letter and handed it to me. Again, it was from Charles Benochet, but this time his request for me to come down was a bit more insistent:

> *Willy Pedreaux is urgently requesting that you come down so*
> *that he can speak to you. Please consider making the trip, if*
> *for no other reason than allowing this very sick man to find*
> *some peace in his final days.*

"Sounds like this fellow really wants to talk to me." I held a letter in each hand, looking at AJ for more clarification. "But I still don't see what—"

"Miranda," she interrupted, her eyes on the envelopes still in her lap. "Go with me here. After that, there were three more letters, a few e-mails, and several phone calls, all from Charles, all asking you to please come down and meet with Willy."

She handed me the three letters, which I read, and each one sounded even more urgent than the one before. The most recent one even contained a generous check from the estate to cover the cost of airfare.

I realized that AJ had been hiding all of this from me, keeping it to herself despite the desperate tone of these letters.

"Is this guy still alive now?"

"As far as I know, yes."

"Then I don't understand," I said, folding the letters and putting them all back into their envelopes. "If he's this desperate to see me, I'd be willing to go down there and talk to him just to give him some peace of mind. I feel terrible about this. Why didn't you share it with me sooner?"

"Oh, Miranda, it's so complicated. You know I don't want you going to Louisiana. I don't want you to have anything to do with those people."

And there it was, the age-old elephant in the corner she had been avoiding for years. The truth was that I knew very little about my family in Louisiana or even my own late mother—and it didn't help matters that I had not one single memory from the part of my childhood when I lived down there myself. All I knew was that my mom died in a tragic accident when I was young and that AJ, her sister, had subsequently been given custody of me, her five-year-old niece. AJ had come down to Louisiana for my mother's funeral and then brought me back with her to her home in New York. I had never returned to Louisiana since.

AJ never wanted to talk about my mother's death or why my father had essentially given me away afterward, nor about the grandparents and other relatives I had been forced to leave behind. I always wondered about it, but over the years I had learned to stop asking. It certainly hadn't seemed to matter to my father; he had moved to Arizona soon after I was gone and eventually started a new life of his own.

"I tried to be a good mother to you," AJ said now, tears again filling her eyes. "I did the best I could."

I put down the letters and scooted forward on the couch so that I could take her hands. She had sacrificed so much to raise me, serving as both mother and father to me for most of my life. Truly, I couldn't have asked for a better parent.

I tried to tell her as much now, assuring her that I knew she always had my best interests at heart. More important in this moment, I said, was for her to explain why she was so upset and what any of this had to do with what had been going on here today.

AJ nodded, tears welling in her eyes and spilling down her cheeks.

"That man who came to see you at your office, I have no idea who he was or what he really wanted. The men who attacked you, I don't know who they were either."

"Okay..."

"But both things have to do with the symbol, the one in the painting. That cross-in-a-bell has shown up before. In two places, actually."

"Two places?"

"Yes," she whispered, meeting my eyes. "The man...the attack...the symbol...I don't know how it all ties together, Miranda, but I do know they all have one thing in common."

"What?" I asked, almost afraid to hear the answer.

She studied my face gravely and then held out one more letter.

"They all come back around to you."

THREE

As the sunset
Threw the long shadows of trees o'er the broad ambrosial meadows.
Ah! on her spirit within a deeper shadow had fallen.

"This last letter came yesterday," AJ explained, "but it was addressed to me, not you. Rather than one more note from the lawyer, this one is from Willy Pedreaux himself, the fellow who is dying."

I took the paper from her and unfolded it to see large letters scrawled in pencil. The handwriting was uneven and deeply slanted, as if it had been written by someone ill and lying in bed.

The message it contained was brief. It said:

> *Dear Ms. Greene,*
>
> *Please let her come. It's time.*
>
> > *Sincerely,*
> > *Willy Pedreaux*

Under his name he had drawn a single symbol: an elaborate cross inside the shape of a bell.

A chill slid under my skin.

"What do you think this means?" I whispered.

"I'm not sure."

"But you have some idea," I persisted, looking up at her.

"Yes, I do. Sort of."

In all of my imaginings, nothing could have prepared me for what she did next. Now it was her turn to take both of my hands in hers and fix her eyes on mine.

"Miranda, honey, do you trust me?"

"Of course I do."

"Then you have to let me do what I need to do with no objections. Okay?"

"Um...okay."

We stood and she led me down the narrow hallway and into the master bathroom, pulling out a white wrought iron chair from the vanity and indicating that I should sit. I did.

From the cabinet under the sink, she took out a pair of scissors, a razor, shaving cream, and some bobby pins, setting them all on the gray marble countertop. Positioning herself behind me, she began fooling with my hair, using the bobby pins to secure various sections to my head. I couldn't fathom what she was doing, but my eyes widened when she reached for the scissors.

"What's going on?" I asked, leaning away from her.

"You have to trust me, Miranda."

Trust her? I didn't want a haircut, but it also seemed that I had no choice. Relenting, I sat up straight again and let her do what she needed to do. From behind my head, I could hear the distinct sound of a snip, and when I looked down at the ground I could see a long shank of my dark hair falling to the tile floor.

Startled, I reached back and felt my head with my fingers.

"Good grief, AJ!" I cried, realizing that she had cut away a good two square inches of hair, almost to the scalp, from the very center of the back of my head.

What she did next came as even more of a shock, but by this point I was too confused to resist. Pushing away my hand, she used a washcloth to wet that square of my head, dabbed on some of the shaving cream, and shaved it down to the scalp with the razor. I closed my eyes, hoping that at least some artful hairstyling might be able to hide the damage she was now doing until my hair grew back in.

"Okay," she said finally, dropping the razor into the sink, a tangle of dark hairs clumped on the blade.

"Does this have something to do with my birthmark?" I asked as my mind raced, trying to decide what possible reason she might have for shaving a part of my head—the same part my attackers had studied with the flashlight. I tilted my chin away from the mirror, but I couldn't see far enough back to glimpse what she had done.

"It's not a birthmark, Miranda. I only told you that when you were young, so you'd have a answer for anyone who might accidentally run across it—like a hairdresser, or maybe one of your little friends if you were doing each other's hair."

Over the years I had been asked "What's that?" a few times, usually during my misguided attempts to have foil highlights added to my dark hair. Otherwise, the mark stayed completely hidden and unnoticed. I rarely thought about it, and as far as I knew even Nathan wasn't aware that it was there.

"I don't understand," I said. "If it's not a birthmark, what is it?"

Again, I reached back to touch the area on my scalp—only now it was strangely naked, the skin perfectly smooth and hairless.

"It's a tattoo," she said.

"A *tattoo?*"

"I have no idea where it came from or what it means, but it's been there since you were small. I found it when you about six or seven and you wanted me to braid your hair. When I called and asked your father what it was, he had no idea. Only your grandmother seemed to know what I was talking about, but she wouldn't tell me anything. She just said that we would be told eventually, when it was time."

"Time? Time for what?"

"I don't know. She wouldn't elaborate."

I started to protest, but AJ shook her head, looking at me in the mirror.

"Your grandmother was a tough cookie, Miranda. You really wouldn't understand unless you had known her."

My fingers rubbed furiously at the bald patch of my scalp.

"She tattooed a little girl? That's practically child abuse!"

"That's what I said. When I threatened legal action, she told me that if I did anything about it at all, they would countersue me to get back full custody of you. I didn't know if they could win, but I couldn't risk the chance of losing you, so I had to let it go. After all these years, truly, I had almost forgotten about it until the letter came yesterday from Mr. Pedreaux."

Without any further words, AJ reached into the cabinet under the sink and pulled out a heavy silver hand mirror. I stood and turned as I took it from her, my stomach in knots. It took a moment to adjust, tilting the glass so that I could see the back of my head in the reflection of my reflection. Once I did, I gasped, for there it was: a tattoo on the back of my head, about an inch in diameter, etched into my scalp in dark purple ink. The shape had obviously been distorted a bit as I had grown, but the image was unmistakable.

It was an elaborate cross, tucked neatly inside a bell.

Now it was my turn to fall apart. The mirror slipped from my hands, though AJ was so close in the small room that she managed to catch it before it crashed to the ground. Suddenly, the scene seemed to grow hazy before me. Gasping for air, I ran back to the living room where there was more space to move around and breathe, the whole scene playing out again and again in my mind.

Those men had been looking for this tattoo. They had ripped up my shirt to check my back. Tugged up my pants to check my legs. Pulled off my shoes and socks to see my feet. Finally, they had thumbed through my hair to check my head, and there it was. Why those places specifically, rather than just stripping me down and looking all over? Why did they know to look where they did? And once they found it, why did they simply stare for a moment and then run? Were they trying to memorize it?

"I should call the police and tell them I know what those men were doing," I whispered to AJ, who was standing nearby and looking as if she was ready to catch me should I start to fall down. "That might help them connect the dots to some other incident."

"You probably should," she replied. "I'll get the card that policeman gave you. It's in with your dirty clothes."

From the pocket of my torn pants, AJ retrieved the NYPD contact information. I reached the fellow who was in charge of my case and presented a simplified version of what I'd learned, saying that I realized what my attackers were looking for was a tattoo on the back of my head. I described the symbol and explained that someone else had also approached me today about the same symbol, though not in such a violent manner. The cop listened to my tale, but by the end he merely sounded a bit disdainful, as if I was either grasping at straws or completely making it up. By the time the call was over, I knew three things: the symbol of a cross inside a bell was of no significance to the NYPD, there had been no other reports of mad tattoo-hunting attackers, and the man in charge of my case now thought I was nuts. On top of all that, he refused to send someone over to the museum to retrieve the painting in question because, as far as he was concerned, it was not connected to any crime.

I hung up the phone and described his side of the conversation. "Honey, it's not surprising he acted this way," she assured me. "Even in New York City, that's probably not something they see every day, a beautiful young woman and respected professional with a creepy symbol tattooed in the middle of her head."

I walked to the window and looked down at the streets, half expecting to see Jimmy Smith or my faceless attackers or even the witness from the restaurant looking up at me.

"Call him," I said.

"Who?"

"This guy who's dying down in Louisiana. Ask him what it means and what he wants. If he won't say, tell him what happened to me today."

Without another word AJ used the phone for directory assistance and then was connected to the number of the dying Willy Pedreaux. I listened as she spoke to what sounded like the man's wife and then the man himself. AJ spoke politely at first, but soon her voice grew angry and then downright furious. Still, the people on the other end wouldn't budge. Willy refused to tell me anything over the phone, but he said if I came down there to see him right away, all would be revealed.

I grabbed the phone from her and tried myself, but the weary male voice on the other end began to cry, begging me to come, saying this was the only way I could learn the truth before he died. Hearing the whimper of his ill and aged voice, I felt myself growing sick to my stomach, confused and guilty about the whole situation, even though none of this was my fault. As I disconnected the call, I told AJ that as far as I could see, I had no choice. I needed to fly to Louisiana as soon as possible, whether she was happy about that or not.

Before she could reply, I told her to wait, that there was an urgent call I needed to make first. AJ sat and stewed on the couch as I dialed the receptionist at the museum to see if the man had come back yet for his painting. The girl said that he had not, so I had her transfer the call to my friend Bill, who was the head of our museum's security department. I explained the strange situation to him as simply as I could, saying that a suspicious man had left a painting in my office today and that shortly afterward I had been mugged in an alley while walking to lunch.

"The police suspect that the two events are connected," I hedged, "so it's very important to handle the situation correctly if the man returns."

Bill was infuriated at the thought that I had been attacked, and he promised that if the man I described showed up at the museum he would be detained and that the police and I would be contacted immediately. I thanked Bill for his help and ended the call. Hanging up the phone, I looked across the room at my aunt. Her expression was somber, her hands carefully clasped in front of her.

"What is it?" I asked warily.

"Until today, I didn't think I'd ever have to deal with this, with the thought of you going back down to Louisiana."

She seemed so upset that I actually felt bad for her. I may not have known the reasons why she had always kept so much from me, but I had no doubt that she'd thought it was for my own good.

"This isn't that big of a deal," I said gently. "I'll just go down there, meet with this man, and come home. End of story."

AJ leaned forward, pressing a delicate hand to her cheek.

"It's not that simple, Miranda," she said. "Going down there and revisiting your past can only stir up memories and feelings that have long since been put to rest."

"Why would that stir things up? It's not like I remember anything about it anyway."

"But you will. I'm afraid if you go back there, you will."

"So what if I did? Would that be so bad?"

She didn't answer me at first but simply stood and began pacing.

"When I brought you back from Louisiana as a child, Miranda, you were completely traumatized. I didn't know for sure why, and no one down there would give me a straight answer, but my guess was that among other things, you must have witnessed your mother's death. That's something that no child should ever have to see. Even though you're an adult now, remembering that sort of trauma could have all sorts of repercussions. Emotional repercussions."

I watched her pace, thinking how odd it was to see her acting this way.

"AJ, aren't you being a little dramatic? This isn't like you to be so over the top."

She simply paced faster, her hands working nervously together in front of her. Finally, she came to a stop, looking at me and studying my face.

"You didn't talk for almost a year after your mother died. Did you know that?"

"I...what?"

I sat on the nearest chair, my eyes wide.

"When I brought you here, all you would do was sit in the corner and rock back and forth for hours on end, perfectly silent. Never made a sound. It scared me to death. I was afraid you'd never come out of it, never come back to me."

The skin on my arms raised into goose bumps just picturing it.

"I...I didn't know."

"It was horrible to watch. Horrible that I couldn't seem to get through to you no matter what I did."

AJ began wringing her hands, and as she talked I could imagine her as she must have been then: A beautiful young woman, her life filled with promise, suddenly saddled with the full-time care of her dead sister's child— and a crazy child at that. My mind filled with shame at the thought of it, even as my chest swelled with gratitude for all she had sacrificed for me.

"Finally, I took you to a psychiatrist," she continued, "who did a full evaluation. He put you on medication, tried play therapy, all that sort of stuff. When you finally started making sounds, it was almost as though you had to relearn how to talk. By the time you had worked your way back to normal speech, it was obvious you had no memory of what had happened at all. The doctor's recommendation was that I focus on the future, on showing you that you were loved and safe and not in any way responsible for what had come before. As far as your past went, he told me that your brain was simply protecting itself in the best way it knew how, by letting go of the memories that were so traumatic. He suggested that when the situation came up I should give you just enough facts to answer your questions, but never so much that the memories would actually come back. I thought it was good advice, so that's what I have tried to do your whole life."

Gently, I affirmed her efforts but reminded her that psychological practices had changed significantly in the past twenty-seven years. With all of the advances made in the field, I said, in retrospect that man's advice might not have been all that good.

"Not to mention that I am an adult now," I added, "and in a very different place emotionally. I wouldn't worry if I were you."

"Despite the fact that you're an adult now, Miranda, you tell me: Can you remember anything about the first five years of your life? As far as I know, you have not one single memory prior to the age of six. Isn't that true?"

I shrugged.

"But that's not unusual, AJ. A lot of folks can't remember that far back."

She shook her head, coming to sit on the couch to meet me eye to eye.

"They could when they were young, honey. At six, they could still remember four. At eight, they could recall being five. You never did. It all disappeared, like erasing a slate, and nothing has ever come back. I'm sorry, but that's not the same thing as 'a lot of folks' who just can't remember, not at all."

"So what are you saying?" I asked. "That I shouldn't go?"

She let out a long, slow breath, shaking her head from side to side.

"I'm saying that we need to proceed with caution. I'm saying that if you get too much information too fast, you might completely fall apart. I can't even predict what kind of an effect a trip like this could have on your mental health. I know you're a very stable person, Miranda, but there are truths in life that can rock the most solid foundation so hard that nothing will ever be the same."

I bent forward, placing my elbows on my knees and my head in my hands. I understood her position, but she obviously didn't understand mine. A strange man came to my work today for reasons I couldn't begin to understand. Shortly after, two men dragged me into the dark and searched my body for a tattoo I didn't even know I had. A dying man was begging me to come down to my old family home to hear what he wanted to say from his deathbed and using as his calling card the same symbol as the one in my tattoo. I'd say those facts trumped the potential for mental fallout. It was time to act.

I'd worry about the consequences later.

FOUR

Something there was in her life incomplete, imperfect, unfinished;
As if a morning of June, with all its music and sunshine,
Suddenly paused in the sky, and, fading, slowly descended
Into the east again, from whence it late had arisen.

With my hair pulled up in a ponytail to hide my new bald spot, I left AJ's place in borrowed clothing. Feeling skittish, I took a taxi rather than the subway, rattling out the address to my apartment as I slid into the back of the vehicle and shut the door. Halfway there, however, I changed my mind and told the driver to take me to the New York Public Library instead. Once I was safely inside that grand structure, I went on a symbol search, poring through reference books and the Internet, slogging past countless images of symbols, insignia, heraldry, emblems, hallmarks, satanic icons, and more, all in search of a cross inside a bell or an upside-down shield. In the end, I had managed to come up with nothing even remotely close, not one single indication of what the symbol meant or where it had originated.

After two hours I finally gave up and signed onto an Internet computer to check flights to New Orleans. There was nothing left for today, so I bought a ticket for the first flight out in the morning, pressing the final "Buy Now" button with a surge of defiance—defiance against AJ, against the various forces that were at work here, against helplessness. Using the e-mail address from the printouts AJ had given me, I sent a copy of my itinerary to Charles Benochet, the lawyer who handled my inheritance, along with a quick note that said to please tell Mr. Pedreaux that I was coming. After arranging for a car rental, I went onto an Internet mapping site and pulled up directions from the airport in New Orleans to my destination about an hour west of there, to the estate known as Twin Oaks.

With my plans made and my work here done, I gathered up my things and made my way downstairs to the majestic front entrance of the library. On the way I passed a bank of pay phones and stopped to make a call, as the battery on my overused cell phone had run out.

Dropping coins in the slot, I waited for the tone and then dialed my daughter's nanny, Rosita, who always brought Tess over to her house on Fridays to stay until bedtime, so that Nathan and I could each work late and get caught up for the weekend. Actually, Nathan had started the tradition a year before so that he and I could have a weekly date night. That had lasted only a few months, however, until we began once again to drift apart and let our busy schedules get in the way. Eventually our child-free Fridays had turned into an anything-*except*-a-date nights.

When Rosita answered the phone I could hear laughter and voices in the background, and with a surge of jealousy I could picture her big extended family all gathered around the kitchen, rolling tamales and slicing vegetables as they basked in the glow of their love and connection. I'd never had anything like that at all in my life, though I was glad at least that my daughter was able to experience it on a weekly basis.

I told Rosita that I needed her to bring Tess home a half hour earlier tonight than planned because I was leaving on a trip tomorrow and I wanted to spend a little time together before she went to bed. After hanging up I thought about calling Nathan, but I decided I'd rather talk face-to-face once he got home. He had a huge work-related event coming up on Sunday, so I knew he'd be putting in extra time tonight in preparation. That meant that Tess and I could have our nightly half hour of quality time, and then I could put her to bed and get packed for my trip in the peace and quiet of an empty bedroom. Nathan would probably show up just about the time I was ready to turn in. We would have to discuss the logistics of what I needed to do and how we could make this work then.

It was getting dark by the time I came out of the library, so again I guiltily hailed a taxi. Sitting in the black vinyl womb of the backseat, I thought about the conversations Nathan and I had been having lately, and a knot of fear tightened in my gut as I pictured the set of his jaw from this morning. Standing in the bathroom doorway in his pajamas, watching me brush my teeth, he couldn't have laid things out any clearer, though I suppose he could have been less cliché: *No man is an island, Miranda, even if that's how you'd rather live your life.*

According to Nathan, he was tired of being married to a woman who wasn't a "team player," who wasn't "emotionally available," who never let him "in." Though I could clearly see the hurt in his eyes, I couldn't help but feel that he was grasping at buzz words and catch phrases, trying to create that picture-perfect marriage he thought people were *supposed* to have. Still, I wanted to understand, so after I rinsed my mouth and put my toothbrush away, I followed him into the bedroom and pressed him for specifics. He couldn't come up with anything tangible, and that's where the conversation had ended. *It's just an attitude, a way of living and being,* he had said, which made no sense to me at all. *My way of living and being is married,* I had replied, *and how could you be more of a team player than that?*

Now, as I watched the reflection of the city lights roll along in front me, I played his words back again and again in my mind. There was a solid, Plexiglas shield separating me from my driver, standard equipment for all New York taxis, which I assumed was there to provide a layer of safety for the man at the wheel. But as a passenger that divider always made me feel safer too. I liked interacting through something clear but solid, me in my space and them in theirs. I wondered now if that's what Nathan meant, that I lived life that way: Looking but not connecting, seeing but not feeling, emotions through Plexiglas, to everyone including him.

The vehicle pulled to a stop in front of my building, so I put those thoughts out of my mind for now. After paying the driver, I looked from side to side and then opened the car door and got out. For the first time ever, I regretted that we didn't live in a place with a doorman. Steeling my nerve, I walked briskly to the door of our building, opened it, and stepped into the empty lobby. I felt safe enough in the elevator, but when the doors slid open on our floor, I half expected at least one of the men I had crossed paths with today to be standing there waiting for me. My hands were trembling as I fumbled with the lock in the key. Once inside, I quickly closed and locked the door, breathing a sigh of relief that I was safely home and at the same time mad at myself for being so unglued.

Until I felt a warm hand on my shoulder.

Spinning around, I swung my purse as hard as I could, realizing just before the moment of impact that I was about to bean my own husband. Though his upraised hand deflected most of the blow, my bag still managed to clip him on the ear and raise a big red welt almost immediately from his cheek. I yelled at him for scaring me; he yelled at me for having disappeared for two and a half hours. Then we both just stood there, catching our breath and trying to calm down.

"I'm sorry," I said finally, wincing at the redness of his cheek. "Does it hurt?"

"My gosh, Miranda, you've had me worried to death," he exclaimed, ignoring my question and his injury. "I've been calling your cell phone, calling everywhere, trying to find you, but nobody knows anything."

"I'm sorry. My battery died. What are you doing home so early anyway?" I walked farther inside and put my purse and keys away. "Didn't you have to work until ten?"

"Yeah, sure, until I got a message from AJ and called her back and found out what happened to you. Did you think I would stay there after that?"

"Didn't AJ tell you that I'm okay?"

"You're my wife, Miranda!" he yelled, the vein in his temple throbbing. "Whether you're okay now or not is beside the point."

"But tonight was important for you," I said, realizing with a sinking feeling that if the situation had been reversed, I might not have left a big event connected with my job for him, not as long as I knew he was all right. Then, seeing the look on his face, I remembered our discussion from this morning, not to mention AJ's words from a while ago, that husbands needed to be needed, especially at a time like this. Somehow, though I tried to see Nathan's concern as reassuring, to me it just felt stifling. I couldn't play the "needy" game he and AJ wanted me to play.

"I'm sorry, Nathan," I said, going to the kitchen for something to drink. "I didn't mean to worry you. I was at the library, trying to find out more about—" Feeling a flash of shame about the tattoo, I stopped talking and turned to look at my husband, who was still standing near the door, watching me. "Did AJ tell you everything?"

"We talked at length," he replied, his eyes moving to the side of my head, as if he could read my mind. "She's incredibly worried about you. So am I."

I left him there and went to the kitchen, pulling a bottle of water from the fridge. I couldn't explain it, but between my aunt and my husband, what I wanted most to do right now was leave them both behind, race off to the airport by myself, and simply fly down to Louisiana to get this whole thing taken care of.

Returning to the living room, I looked at Nathan, who was standing in the same spot, hands on hips, his straight blond bangs falling forward to cover one eyebrow. Even when he was being difficult, I couldn't help but be struck at how handsome he was, the angular set of his chin so strong, the deep blue of his eyes as piercing as ever. Once upon a time, I had fallen in love with those eyes and the man behind them. I still loved him very much, but these days it seemed that was no longer enough.

Swallowing my pride, I put down my water and stepped toward him, and that was all the signal he needed. Suddenly, he had crossed that space that separated us and swept me into his arms, hugging me so tightly I could barely breathe. I surrendered to the moment, letting him hang on, knowing he must have been nearly as rattled by what had happened as I was.

"I've been going nuts," he whispered into my hair, "thinking about those men and what they did, what they could have done..."

"Shhh," I said, pressing a finger to his lips and then following it there with my mouth.

I kissed my husband deeply, wanting to connect, wanting to make him understand how much I loved him. When the kiss ended, he placed a gentle hand on each side of my face and tried to look into my eyes. Instinctively I looked away, moving back out of his embrace.

"Okay. Anyway, I need to get packed," I said, suddenly feeling awkward and embarrassed.

I headed for the bedroom, but behind me I knew that he was still just standing there, watching me.

"Does anything ever reach you, Miranda?" he asked hoarsely across the widening distance between us.

I stopped walking and let out a long, slow breath.

"Not again, Nathan," I said tiredly, turning to look at him, surprised at the anguish in his eyes.

He didn't reply. Instead, he simply met my gaze for a long moment before turning and walking in the other direction. He moved down the hall to his study and then quietly closed the door.

The rest of the evening was difficult, to say the least. With my hair still in a ponytail, I managed to make dinner, even though cooking was not my forte and meals were usually Nathan's job. As soon as Tess got home, chattering happily about her adventures of the day, I was sorry I had asked Rosita to bring her back early. In theory, quality time always sounded good, but in reality, it could be incredibly distracting.

Nathan remained in his study a full hour, until I knocked on the door and pushed it open. He was sitting at his drafting table, pencil in hand, his expression cold and remote.

"Yes?"

"Supper's ready."

"Thanks, but I'm not hungry."

I stepped inside and closed the door behind me.

"We need to discuss logistics," I said, trying to keep my voice light. "I booked a flight to New Orleans in the morning."

He sat back in his chair and looked at me.

"What's to discuss?" he asked finally, a shadow passing behind his eyes. "Tess and I will be fine. Have a good trip."

With that he pointedly returned to his work, so I left him to it, walking back to the dining room to sit at the table with my daughter. She wasn't hungry either, having already eaten at Rosita's. I didn't feel like talking, but that didn't seem to matter to Tess, who talked enough for both of us as I ate.

Halfway through the meal, I got an idea, so I told my daughter to wait there and I went down the hall to her room, where I retrieved paper, crayons, and colored pencils. Back at the table, I told her that playtime and dinnertime were going to have to be done in combination tonight, because Mommy was leaving on a trip in the morning and I still needed to pack.

"Are you going on an airplane?" she asked, reaching for a piece of paper. "Will you bring me back a toy?"

Tess chattered on and on, and I answered her endless questions as simply as I could without really listening. Though we often drew and colored together at playtime, the picture I began to draw now had nothing to do with quality interaction for my child and everything to do with creating a good likeness of Jimmy Smith, the man who had come to my office with the symbol in the painting. I wanted a likeness to give to the police and to museum security, not to mention to bring down and show Willy Pedreaux. On the phone, he claimed not to know who the man might have been or what he wanted, but maybe if Willy saw a picture of the guy he would recognize him. As all of this symbol business was connected somehow, I thought it couldn't hurt to try. I only wished I had caught a glimpse of my attackers in the alley so that I could draw them too.

I sketched the face for a while then traded out the black pencil for brown, disappointed that it wasn't as easy as I had thought it would be to capture on paper the likeness of a man I had seen in person only once. I kept erasing, redrawing, shading, and erasing again, and as I did I gained a whole new respect for police sketch artists. When I was nearly finished, I just stopped and stared at it for a moment, knowing I hadn't gotten it quite right but that it was the best I could do. I glanced at Tess's picture, which featured an elaborate series of different-colored scribbles.

"That's good, honey," I said. "Very colorful."

"Thanks, Mommy," she replied, glancing at mine. "I like yours too. But why did you draw the telephone man?"

My hand paused in midair, my heart suddenly in my throat.

"What?" I asked, trying to sound casual.

"That's the man that fixes the telephones."

"Here in our apartment?"

"Yeah."

"All the time?"

"No, just once."

"When?"

She paused, trading a pink crayon for purple.

"I don't know. Six or seven years ago, maybe."

"You mean days? Six or seven days ago?"

"Or ninety-two. I'm not sure."

Heart pounding, I pushed back my chair.

"Was it this week, Tess?"

"Yeah, I think so."

"How long was he here?"

"I don't know, Mommy. Like for the whole *SpongeBob*."

"What did he do?"

"He just went around fixing all the phones. I don't know. Why are you asking so many questions? Did I do something wrong?"

"No, baby. You're not in trouble."

"But you have an angry face."

"I am angry, but not at you. I'm upset with Rosita. She knows she shouldn't have let a stranger into the house when the two of you are home alone, that's all."

"Is she in big trouble?" Tess asked, looking at me with a gleam of excitement in her eyes. Someone getting into "big trouble" was usually Tess's favorite thing to watch—as long as it was someone other than herself.

"Kind of," I replied, moving to the charging station near the door and grabbing Nathan's cell phone. "You stay here, honey. I'll be right back."

Letting myself out of the apartment, I padded down the hallway to the elevator area, where I stood as I dialed Rosita's number. Once I had her on the phone and explained why I was calling, she confirmed that a pale man with a skinny mustache had indeed shown up at our door on Thursday in a uniform, carrying ID and a work order, so she had let him in. She said that he had stayed about fifteen minutes and then left.

"Is there a problem?" she asked.

I wanted to scream at her for being so stupid, so careless. But I tried to put myself in her place and had to admit that ID and a work order politely offered by a man in uniform could be convincing if done well.

"Do not ever let *anyone* into our apartment unless we have told you to expect them. Understand?"

"*Si*, Miranda, I understand. Did something happen? Is everything okay?"

"It's hard to explain, Rosita. Bottom line, that guy was not from the telephone company. We don't know who he was or what he wanted, but he wasn't here to fix the phones."

She launched into a panic-filled monologue, trying to guess at what his real intentions had been. Despite the parts that were in Spanish, what I picked up was that she thought he was a robber, there to case the joint; or a rapist, looking for a victim. Thinking of my own brush with violence today, I waited for her to calm down and then had her explain to me exactly what rooms he had gone in and what he had done. She hadn't kept a real close eye on him, she said, but from what she could remember, all he did was go into the kitchen, fool with the telephone in there for a while, and then leave.

"Was he doing something with the phone," I asked, "or the wires?"

"The phone itself, I think."

I didn't know much about telephones or electronics, but I had seen enough spy movies to know that definitely sounded like he was placing a bug. A real telephone repairman wouldn't have messed with the phone itself at all, just the lines.

Rosita offered up such profuse apologies that by the end of the call I was actually apologizing to her for upsetting her so. Turning off the phone, I returned to the apartment, set the phone back on the station, and headed down the hall to Nathan's study, to tell him that the same man who had come to the museum with the symbol in the painting had also been here, inside our apartment. Just picturing that creepy man with his pinky ring and his caterpillar mustache in my home, alone with Tess and Rosita, made me so nauseous I thought I was going to be sick.

Nathan's reaction was equally intense, and he was dialing the police before I had barely finished telling him the news.

While we waited for them to arrive, I gave Tess a quick bath and got her settled on the couch with some of her favorite picture books. Rosita and her husband came over as well so that she could give her statement about the fake repairman and his entry into our home. I was concerned that the whole brouhaha might frighten Tess, but she took all of it in stride, merely excited to see what big trouble was brewing now.

The police stayed long enough to hear what we had to say, take a copy of my sketch as evidence, and do a cursory examination of the telephones. Almost immediately they found something they told us was a "drop out relay," a cheap little bugging device that could be bought at almost any electronics store for under twenty dollars. They bagged the device as evidence and suggested that we hire a security company to come in and do a full bug sweep in order to find the receiving end of the drop out relay system and to check for other listening devices in the apartment.

In the end, they agreed to circulate my sketch of the suspect, though they doubted it would do any good. If caught, the guy could be charged with stalking, criminal mischief, and possibly even burglary, even though nothing seemed to have been taken. We were advised not to keep our hopes up, however, as the chances of finding him were slim. Being Manhattan, a nonviolent, nontheft problem like ours wasn't exactly going to be top priority. Strangely, the cops never asked us what we thought the intruder might have been hoping to hear by bugging our phones. I was glad it didn't come up, as I had no good answer for that question myself.

Rosita and her husband left with the police, and as Nathan shut the door behind them, I couldn't help thinking how quiet our apartment suddenly seemed. Tess was finally tired and fading fast, so Nathan scooped her up and carted her off to bed with barely a protest. Once she was asleep, he and I moved to the bedroom where we sat side by side on the bed and wrote notes back and forth, hashing out plans for how to proceed from here. Afraid there might be other bugs in the place, we spoke as little as possible.

Obviously, the specter of danger hovered over us no matter what plans we made, and in the end it was decided that Tess would fly south with me to go and stay with Nathan's parents in Texas. With her safely out of harm's way, I would meet with Willy in Louisiana; meanwhile, Nathan would stay here to coordinate the bug sweep of the apartment and generally keep an eye on things. I insisted that he also continue to get ready for Sunday morning, when he would be representing his architectural firm at the grand opening of a megachurch in Connecticut that he had helped to design. He had worked so hard, I hated the thought that these problems might mess that up.

Just in case there were more bugs here, Nathan went to a neighbor's apartment to use their phone and make arrangements with his parents. While he was gone, I packed bags for myself and Tess and then went onto the computer to see what I could do about flight arrangements. My intention was to detour through Houston, where Nathan's parents lived, and drop Tess off with them there. But I was still struggling to find something available when Nathan returned and handed me a bunch of scribbled notes, one of which said that if I couldn't get us routed through Houston, his sister Quinn could actually pick up Tess in New Orleans. Quinn was driving home tomorrow from Florida State and could easily detour through the city on her way. Unless I wanted to wait two days for an available flight to Houston, that looked like our only choice. I added Tess to my flight to New Orleans in the morning, printed our itinerary, and shut down the computer. Using the printer, I also made a few more copies of the sketch I had drawn of Jimmy Smith, one for Nathan to take to Bill at the museum and the rest to bring along with me on my trip.

In bed I finally got up the nerve to actually let Nathan see the tattoo on the back on my head. As I took down my ponytail, I was afraid he would be repulsed, but instead of recoiling away he simply reached up one finger and gently touched it.

"I just can't believe it was here all along and we didn't even know it," he said softly. "To me, that's the most bizarre part. I thought I knew every inch of your body."

His warm hand moved down my back, caressing it. I could feel the invitation in his hand, not to mention in his voice, but with all that was going on, I simply wasn't up to what he had in mind. I lied and told him that after today's assault in the alley I felt a bit too vulnerable to be physical with him just yet.

"Oh, gosh, of course," he said, sounding so remorseful that I instantly felt guilty myself. "What was I thinking?"

"It's okay, really," I assured him, turning off the lamp and trying to make up for it by snuggling against him.

He wrapped his arms tightly around me, kissed my forehead, and relaxed. Soon he was lightly snoring away. Next to him, I lay awake for a long time, eyes open to the darkness, thinking again about the Plexiglas divider of the taxicab. Maybe Nathan was right. Maybe I did live my life separated and apart. I didn't want to be that way, necessarily, but it was all I knew. Even with my own child, I had always felt less than connected, less than adequate as her mother. I tried, but I simply couldn't find it within myself to form the sorts of bonds that most people took for granted.

Carefully extricating myself from Nathan's slumbering embrace, I scooted across the wide bed and turned to my other side, facing away from my husband. My eyes filled with tears as I thought of today's conversation with AJ. Maybe when I lost all of those memories of my first five years, I also lost my ability to bond. If that were the case, I realized now as one tear slid sideways from my eye to the pillow, then there was no hope for us as a couple. Nathan wanted a true partner, not a roommate. In theory, I wanted that too.

In reality, there was a wall of Plexiglas between us so thick I doubted anything could ever take it away.

FIVE

Art thou so near unto me, and yet I cannot behold thee?
Are thou so near unto me, and yet thy voice does not reach me?

The limo service came on time the next morning, just as I was hurrying Tess to finish her cereal.

"Come on, T-square," Nathan said, swooping in to urge that last spoonful into Tess's mouth. "It's time to roll."

He turned his back to her and squatted down so that she could get on for a piggyback ride. Once aboard, she squealed with delight as he swayed side to side, pretending to lose his balance. He grabbed the suitcases and I picked up the carry-ons, and to the sound of our daughter's giggles we made our way to the elevator. I gave my husband an appreciative nod as we moved inside and pushed the button for the lobby, grateful for his attempt to keep things light this morning and make our daughter believe that this abrupt change in plans was simply one big adventure.

We emerged from the elevator to find the driver standing near the intercom, waiting to take our luggage. Handing the bags over, we followed the man outside and watched as he began loading them into the back of his blue-and-yellow van.

"I thought we were going in a limousine," Tess said, the laughter suddenly gone from her face.

"A limousine *service*," I corrected as I dug in my bag for a tip. "It's just an expression."

"All right, T," Nathan said, sliding Tess from his back to the ground. "Make sure you watch out for alligators while you're in Louisiana. You know what their favorite snack is, don't you?"

"What?"

"Five-year-old girls!" Nathan cried, kneeling down to her level and pretending to make a snack of her arm.

She giggled some more as he got her settled into the seat and safely buckled up. After a hug goodbye, he emerged and turned to me. Our farewell was much more subdued, a simple exchange of brave smiles followed by a lingering hug and kiss.

"Don't worry. This will all be over soon," he whispered as we pulled apart. "Then we can concentrate on us."

I knew he meant for his words to be encouraging, but as I climbed inside and buckled my own seat belt, I couldn't ignore the surge of panic that rose up within me.

How could we concentrate on us when the problem with us was me?

Tess talked all the way to the airport, a nearly nonstop monologue that continued as we made our way through check-in, security, and even onto the plane. Once we were in the air, though I wanted peace and quiet so I could think, I forced myself to focus on my child and listen. I knew that she was excited and nervous, and that chattering was her way to process this sudden, unexpected trip. As she prattled on, I was just glad we had the row to ourselves so that her talking wasn't bothering anyone else but me.

I dug through Tess's carry-on bag to find something to distract her, finally pulling out her favorite puzzle, a brightly tacky piece of King Tut memorabilia I had bought for her in a last-minute purchase at a museum shop while on a business trip. On the open tray table in front of her, Tess quickly took apart the sarcophagus and put it back together again, saving the jeweled headpiece for last, as always.

"He has pretty eyes, like Daddy," Tess said, running one tiny finger across the Egyptian's face. "I miss Daddy."

"I know you do," I replied lightly. "But you'll have lots of adventures to tell him about when we get home."

Tess grew bored with the puzzle and asked for her favorite storybook instead. I put the puzzle away and pulled out *Garamond and the Gator*, a beautifully illustrated Cajun folktale that Nathan had given her last Christmas. Tess absolutely loved the book and had made us read it to her at least twice a day for months. Secretly, I wondered if the story appealed to some basic instinct inside of her, that portion of Cajun heritage that had come down from my paternal grandmother. As I read the story to Tess now, letting her find for the millionth time the crab, the spider, and the crawfish that were hidden in the elaborate drawings on every page, my hand reached absently for the French twist at the back of my head that artfully hid the bald patch.

What kind of family tattoos a child?

Maybe it was a Cajun thing, a right of passage or a ceremonial ritual. At the library yesterday, as a part of my search for an ornate cross inside a bell or an upside-down shield, I had gone down the path of every country and heritage for which I could find literature, studying their symbols and icons, both modern and ancient. I hadn't found a match for my tattoo anywhere, but perhaps much of Cajun history and icons were more verbal than written anyway. It wouldn't be the first time an entire offshoot culture had preserved its history in oral form.

"Turn the page, Mommy," Tess scolded me now. "You're not paying attention."

I did as she instructed, reading the next page of text with extra enthusiasm.

What kind of family tattoos a child? I wondered again after I finished reading and waited for her to find the crab, spider, and the crawfish. Had my mother done this to me while she was still alive? If she had, wouldn't AJ have known about it?

According to AJ, she and my mother had been extremely close their whole lives, best friends as well as sisters. They had grown up on the "wrong side of the tracks," as AJ put it, though both had escaped their humble beginnings—AJ by running off to New York City to try her hand at modeling, my mother by marrying the handsome and wealthy Richard Fairmont, who brought her to live in his family home across town. That was the same home I was heading to now, the one that had been left to me by my grandparents.

"Do you see the crawfish, Mommy?"

I pointed to the tiny lobsterlike creature peeking from behind a bucket, knowing that even when AJ and my mother lived a thousand miles apart they were in constant touch; AJ said the two of them had written letters almost daily and spoken via long distance once a week. *We knew each other's details,* was how she had explained it to me yesterday, *and nothing in her life or yours or your grandparents, for that matter, ever indicated anything strange or unusual, at least not until I found this tattoo.* Strange and unusual was right.

"Read, Mommy," Tess commanded with a groan.

I took a deep breath and kept going. I had hoped Tess might nap on the plane, but I realized now that she was obviously nowhere near sleep, feeling her usual morning peppiness times ten. I gave up on having any quiet time for my own thoughts and focused on her energy and enthusiasm instead. We interacted for the rest of the flight and somehow between the puzzles, picture books, and toys—not to mention a welcome soda and snack from the flight attendant—we managed to get through the next few hours.

It wasn't until I felt a shift in the airplane, a slight downward tilting of the nose, that I realized we were getting close to our destination. I glanced out of the window over Tess's head, shocked at how drastically the landscape below us had changed. Gone was the sprawling suburbia of the northeast corridor, gone were the rolling fields and red clay of the Southeast hill country. We were in the Delta now, the land vast and green and flatter than any flat I had ever seen.

For some reason, at the sight of the unusual terrain my heart felt as though it had flipped. It began to pound furiously in my chest, air whooshing from my lungs as if someone punched me in the solar plexus. The sound of my heartbeat roared in my head: *Boom! Boom! Boom!*

"What is it, Mommy?"

Tess followed my shocked gaze to look out of the window herself. Right behind her, I felt sure I was having some kind of attack. All sound left my ears save for the pounding *boom boom boom* of my heart. I opened my mouth wide and gasped in another breath, refilling my suddenly aching lungs, and wondered why I had thought this trip would be no big deal, just another voyage in a lifetime of travel. I had not one single memory of here, not of the people or the houses or the land, but somehow the downward tilt of the plane and the sight of the unfamiliar topography outside caused my heart to race and my lungs to ache and my eyes to well with sudden tears.

What was wrong with me?

Squeezing my eyes shut, I swallowed hard and sucked in more air and tried to calm my pounding chest. Clearly, this wasn't a heart attack. It was a panic attack, something I had heard of a million times but had never experienced before.

As I clutched the armrest and tried to get a breath and waited for my heart to explode, all I could think was that AJ had been right.

We weren't even there yet, and already I was off the deep end, fragmenting into a thousand pieces.

SIX

Thus ere another noon they emerged from those shades; and before them
Lay, in the golden sun, the lakes of the Atchafalaya.
Water-lilies in myriads rocked on the slight undulations
Made by the passing oars, and, resplendent in beauty, the lotus
Lifted her golden crown above the heads of the boatmen.

"Ooo, look," Tess cooed, oblivious to my condition, her little voice muffled against the clear portal. "The grass is all sparkly!"

Boom, boom, boom!

I counted to ten, willing my heart rate to slow down, praying they wouldn't have to take me off of the plane either sedated or in a straight-jacket.

Suck it up, Miranda! my mind screamed. *Calm down!*

Boom! Boom! Boom!

Through sheer force of will, I slowly succeeded in making myself relax, resisting the urge to gasp for air. Instead, I kept my eyes closed and just breathed, in and out, in and out, in a steady rhythm. It took nearly a minute, but finally the slamming of my heart against my chest became less all consuming, both in sound and feeling. Eventually, the urge to gasp for air dissipated as well and I continued to breathe steadily: in, out, in, out. Finally, I opened my eyes and wiped my face with the back of my hand, frustrated at the drama of it all.

Why was I reacting this way, all breathless and teary-eyed over some *place*, some stupid scenery spotted from an airplane window? Was this strange reaction just a visceral response to the idea of coming home? In theory at least, if not in memory, this region was indeed my home.

"Mommy, answer me!" Tess was saying, though thankfully her eyes were still focused in the other direction, out of the window. "Why is it sparkly? Is that diamonds?"

Twenty-seven years. That's how long I had been gone from here. Twenty-seven years since I must have witnessed the same terrain from the sky, though flying in the opposite direction. Maybe I had a memory of it, lodged somewhere deep inside. Maybe seeing this place again had tapped into feelings that had been buried ever since. AJ had warned me, and I hadn't listened—either that, or the warnings themselves had caused me to overreact. I wasn't sure which it was.

I forced myself to sit up and look out again, hoping the scenery wouldn't set off another bout of panic. Blessedly, it did not. I scanned the view more calmly this time, breathing deeply as I did, noting that the ground far below seemed marshy, with glints of light sparkling from among the grass.

"It looks like water that's making it sparkle," I replied, finding my voice. "That must be swampland."

"It is!" Tess said, nodding sagely. "I can see alligators."

We were still too far up to see cars clearly, much less alligators, but I wasn't going to be the one to tell her.

"Can you count the alligators?" I prodded, hoping to keep her attention focused out of the window a while longer, at least until the heat left my cheeks and redness faded from my eyes.

Tess counted as high as she could and then threw in some extra numbers for good measure. As she did, I pulled out a tissue, wiped at my face, and blew my nose. By the time she grew bored with counting, I seemed to have myself pretty much under control. At least I could breathe now, and the tightness in my chest was gone, though I still felt shaky and light and clammy.

I stole another look out the window. The empty marshland was now sprinkled with farms and towns. I was amazed again at the flatness of it all, the greenness. The Louisiana landscape was utterly foreign and yet somehow completely familiar to me, though I doubted that my familiarity was based on anything real. Maybe I had seen pictures or something. Maybe I just wanted to think I could remember.

"Look, Mommy. Houses."

Knowing we would probably reach the ground in about ten minutes, I told Tess it was time for us to straighten up and put all of her things away.

"This was fun," she said emphatically as she gathered together her dolls and their tiny clothes. "Mommies almost never just play."

Ouch.

"I play with you all the time, honey," I replied evenly, trying not to sound hurt. Good grief, I made a point of sitting down with her nightly, no matter how tired or stressed I was from work, giving her a good half hour of undivided attention between bath and bed, to read or draw or play any game she wanted. "We almost never miss a night."

"Yeah, but that's because you have to," she said, cramming the dolls into her carry-on bag. "I like it better when you want to."

I let that one roll around in my head for a while without comment as we finished putting our things away. Even today on the plane, I hadn't *wanted* to spend so much time playing with her. I had done it just because I'd had no other choice. Was that one of the reasons I struggled so with parenting, because I interacted out of obligation while other mothers did it simply because it was something they enjoyed? Not having any close friends who were mothers themselves, I had no answer for that question.

"You're right. That was fun," I said finally, wishing I really meant it. "Maybe we can get something new to play with on the flight back."

"Okay!"

I tucked our bags under the seats in front of us. As we angled toward the treetops, I placed an arm across Tess's chest and looked out the window, noting how the rows of dark roofs were punctuated here and there by bright blue tarps. In the row behind us, I heard a man explaining to his seatmate that the tarps were there to cover the roofs that still awaited repair after Hurricane Katrina.

"We made it," I said, pulling my arm back as we taxied to a stop at the gate.

As we waited for the airplane doors to open, I took a deep breath, thinking about my shocking anxiety attack and the fear that I would have to be carried from the plane in a straightjacket. I didn't know what that whole thing had been about, but as the doors opened and Tess and I got in line to file off, I decided that for now at least I really was okay. My body and mind were back to normal and under control.

After going downstairs and retrieving our bags, we moved away from the chaos of the baggage claim area and watched for Nathan's sister, Quinn, who was supposed to be meeting us here. I also had an eye open for Mr. Benochet, who had called me first thing this morning, as soon as he saw my e-mail. He insisted that I cancel the rental car and let him take me to Twin Oaks. When I had protested that I would need some sort of transportation while I was in town, he said that there were several cars out at the house, any one of which I could use while I was here.

"Miranda? Miranda Miller?"

Tess and I both looked to see an older, silver-haired distinguished gentleman, in an elegant suit and tie, coming toward us. He was gazing at me with curiosity, studying my face. I reached back to pat my pinned-up twist and met his eyes, nodding as I spoke.

"Yes?"

"I'm Charles Benochet. Are you Miranda?"

"Yes."

"I knew it was you, *cher*," he cried, slapping his knee as he broke into a broad smile. "Somethin' about the way you carry yourself, and that dark hair. You remind me so much of your *mamere*."

"My who?"

"Your *defante mamere*, your late grandmother. You look so much like her. And this must be your daughter, bless her heart. She looks like she takes after her daddy with those blond curls."

He gave a little wave to Tess and she smiled shyly.

"Do you know my daddy?"

"No, I don't," he said, "but seeing as how there aren't any blue-eyed blondes on your mama's side of the family, I have to guess that you got all that from him." He knelt down to Tess's level. "What's your name, honey?"

"Tess," she answered, hiding halfway behind my legs, thumb suddenly popping into her mouth.

"Cass?"

"*Tess,*" she repeated. "T-E-S-S."

"Got it. Tess. Like, tess-ting one, two, three."

She giggled, and he stood up straight again, grinning.

Since my grandmother's death six years ago, I had spoken to Charles Benochet several times on the phone, always to discuss some detail of the estate that AJ needed my input on. In my mind's eye, the man on the other end of the phone hadn't been nearly so distinguished, so dapper. Maybe it was the South Louisiana accent, but I had pictured someone far less...cosmopolitan. Shaking hands with him now, I realized that I had judged this man unfairly just because of his country accent. Shame on me.

I explained that Tess would be leaving with my sister-in-law, who was supposed to be meeting us here. Unfortunately, there was still no sign of her, so I pulled out my cell phone to call. I had turned it off on the plane and as it sprang to life now, I saw that there was a message waiting for me. I dialed in to pick up that message and listened to Quinn apologizing profusely, saying that she'd been delayed at school. Apparently, she hadn't realized that she had to fulfill several more duties in her job as a resident assistant in the dorm before she was free to leave town and head home. She promised to call me tomorrow once she was on the road, saying she expected to arrive in this area by two p.m. at the latest.

Hanging up the phone, I swallowed down my anxiety about having Tess tag along with me between now and then. All things considered, she should be safe; then again, I had thought I was safe yesterday cutting through an alley in Manhattan, and I had ended up facedown in slime.

Swallowing my anxiety for now, I told Tess about the change in plans. She took it better than I expected, seeming merely disappointed rather than devastated. We headed for the parking garage, Tess and I holding hands as we walked alongside Charles, his driver rolling the bags ahead of us. Stepping outside, we encountered air so thick and hot that I felt as though a steaming wet washcloth had been slapped over my face. I had known that Louisiana in June would be warm, and I had certainly been to a number of humid places in my life, but I had never felt a combination of heat and humidity quite like this, at least not in my memory. The air was unbelievably oppressive. It didn't help matters that my beige linen jacket and brown short-sleeved top formed layers that were no doubt holding in the heat, and the chic rope-and-ceramic-bead necklace I wore felt like a scratchy wool scarf.

But, thankfully, we were climbing into the air-conditioned comfort of the long black limousine a few moments later. Captivated by the television, bar, built in cooler, and other bells and whistles of the fancy vehicle, Tess became frustrated with me for making her wear her seatbelt when what she really wanted to do was jump around and explore. I finally got her to settle down by buckling her directly across from the DVD player, next to the window and within reach of the little fridge. I sat beside her, in the center of the back, and Charles took his place facing backwards on the seat across from us. Needing for her to be quiet and settle in for the ride, I pulled one of her favorite DVDs from her bag and handed it to Charles, who put it into the player. As the driver started up the car and drove us out of the airport, Charles got the DVD started and then made a big deal of letting Tess hold the remote control and showing her how to use it. Soon she was deeply engrossed in a show and we were away from the airport and pulling onto an elevated highway, Charles and I making polite conversation as we went.

The afternoon sun was strong, the blue sky dotted with white and gray fluffy clouds. To our right, a waterway suddenly opened up into a lake that stretched all the way to the horizon, its gentle waves sparkling in the sunlight. In the distant heavens, a bank of clouds slowly slid in front of the sun, dimming those sparkles, but then gradually the light refracted through the clouds into sunbeams, illuminating the entire lake with brilliant stripes of light. The sight was breathtaking, a moment in nature frozen for our pleasure.

The rocking of the car caused Tess to fall asleep, her head growing heavy on my thigh. I pressed the mute button on the remote and turned my attention to the man across from me. He glanced at his watch and then settled back in his own seat, his expression solemn. With Tess conveniently asleep, Charles and I needed to talk about more serious concerns, that was for certain.

"I'm sure I don't have to tell you that you got here in the nick of time," he said, stroking his chin between two fingers. "Your grandparents' old caretaker, Willy Pedreaux, is within days of his death."

"Is he in the hospital?"

"No, he's home with a private nurse. And his wife. The two of them are making him as comfortable as possible, considering. And they've had some help from a local hospice group. He should be able to remain there until the very end."

I shuddered, wishing the man hadn't chosen to die at home, in the house that I owned.

"So why does he need to see me?" I asked. "What is this all about?"

Charles looked at me, surprise evident on his face.

"Well, Miranda, I'm sure I don't know. I was hoping you could tell me."

SEVEN

Beautiful is the land, with its prairies and forests of fruit-trees;
Under the feet a garden of flowers, and the bluest of heavens
Bending above, and resting its dome on the walls of the forest.
They who dwell there have named it the Eden of Louisiana.

"I know far less than you do," I said, trying not to sound irritated at the lawyer's ignorance. "I only learned about the situation yesterday. My aunt showed me your letters and e-mails, and that's it. We tried calling, but Mr. Pedreaux wouldn't tell me anything on the phone. He insisted I come down, so here I am. End of story."

Charles pursed his lips and let out a low whistle.

"Well, I tell you what, Willy wanted you here so bad he was willing to do almost anything to make it happen. I've never seen anyone so frantic. In the past few days, they've had to sedate him twice just to get him to calm down. As much as I've been pestering you to come, Willy's nurse has been bugging me even more. One thing is for certain: Willy's not going to go gently into that good night until he has had a chance to speak with you, face-to-face. I know you didn't have to come, but it was kind of you, considering the situation."

A flash of white caught my eye, and I turned in time to see a broad, beautiful bird lift up from the water and take flight.

"I would have come sooner if I had known," I said. "Unfortunately, my aunt chose not to tell me about any of this until yesterday afternoon." Afraid my voice sounded bitter, I looked at him and added, "I mean, she thought she was doing the right thing. We don't—we kind of cut ties with Louisiana years ago. If she had her wish, things would have stayed that way."

Charles spotted a loose thread on his cuff and gently tugged at it.

"Oh, I know. Janet and I go way back. She's a lovely woman who cares for you deeply. I'm sure she thought she was acting in your best interests. If Willy hadn't been so insistent, I would never have pressed the issue myself."

I reached back to check the bobby pins in my hair, wondering if Charles had seen the letter Willy sent directly to AJ. Surely not, for if he had, he would have asked me about the symbol specifically.

"Let me ask you a question," I said, reaching into my bag and pulling out the drawing of Jimmy Smith. "Do you know this man?"

I handed the picture to Charles and he studied it for a moment.

"No. Should I?"

"Not necessarily," I replied, avoiding an explanation with another question. "How about this?" I asked, using a pen to draw the symbol on the top corner of the paper. "Have you ever seen this shape before? By any chance, do you know what it means?"

Charles took the paper from me and again studied it carefully. He didn't recognize it, either, but rather than explain why I wanted to know, I simply folded the paper and tucked it back into my bag, saying that I had a lot of weird questions like that for Willy, silly things that had to do with my past and my family.

To change the subject, I asked about the dying man's wife.

"Has she made any plans for what she'll do after he dies?" I asked. "I hope she knows that's she's welcome to stay on at the house for as long as she needs. We'd never sell it out from under her."

"That's right kind of you, but trust me, Deena Pedreaux is counting the days until her husband is gone and she can start packing her bags. All she talks about is moving to the retirement community in Florida where her sister lives. Frankly, it's an embarrassment to behold when she does it in front of her husband. It's downright cruel."

"That's just a coping mechanism," I objected, thinking how hard it must be for her to watch the man she loves die. I might want to murder my husband sometimes, but I would never, ever wish him dead! "It must be very hard for her to cope."

"Cope, schmope. Deena's a real piece of work. A very bitter woman. She hates Twin Oaks and always has. She calls it the millstone around their necks."

"But why?"

Charles shrugged.

"That much land, that much house, it's a lot of work. Being given a life estate in such a massive place like that can be a mixed blessing. The electric bills alone are astronomical. Considering that the house is in the Louisiana Historical Registry, a certain level of care must be maintained. Willy has worked hard at it for many years. As the trustee, I've been in a difficult position as well, balancing the need to keep the house in good repair with the fact that it's currently inhabited by a couple who doesn't own it or pay rent to live there. I'm afraid since Katrina I've only done the minimum, just to keep things from getting worse. But you'll see, it needs some work. A lot of work, actually, before you would want to put it on the market."

Astronomical electric bills? The Louisiana Historical Registry? For the first time, I began to wonder if maybe I had been underestimating the size of my inheritance. I knew the house was large, but I had never gotten any real statistics on it, nor did I know how much acreage came with it. Somehow in my mind I had been picturing the ramshackle house from Green Acres reruns, tucked away on a couple of woodsy rural acres along the bayou.

"The place is...big?"

Charles just looked at me, a mixture of surprise and something else, something like pity, on his face. He leaned forward, his elbows on his knees.

"You really don't know anything about your old family home, do you, Miranda?"

For some reason, his question made me catch my breath. There it was again, though to a much less degree, that same surprising onslaught of emotion that I had experienced on the airplane when I realized we were getting ready to land. Tears filled my eyes, and with an embarrassed apology, Charles handed me some tissues from the console and then discreetly turned his head toward the window as I dabbed at my face and pulled myself together. I was glad it was just tears this time and not the racing heartbeat and the difficulty breathing I'd had on the plane. Still, I felt like an idiot.

"Don't apologize," I replied softly, my voice hoarse. "The truth is, I know less than nothing. For all of these years I have been at the mercy of my aunt, who wasn't willing to talk about this place or the people here. If not for Willy's urgent pleas, I don't think I ever would have come back."

"Not even when it was time to sell?"

"No. I was just going to let your office handle all of that."

"You mean just sell it on your behalf and mail you a check?" he marveled. "Without even coming back to see your family home? That's so cut-and-dried."

I nodded.

"AJ, uh, my Aunt Janet has always been opposed to my connecting in any way with my...with the people here."

"But *why?* I mean, I understand when you were younger. The situation was complicated and very tragic. She did what she thought she had to do. But you're a grown woman now. I can't imagine she still expects you to stay away."

I swallowed hard, reluctant to tell him about my emotional state as a child or the psychiatrist whose advice had guided AJ's actions with me ever since. Suddenly, despite all of that, I felt a wave of anger sweeping over me, anger at AJ for keeping me in the dark for so long. Charles was right: She had no right to expect me to stay away forever.

"So you've never had any contact with your relatives here?" Charles prodded. "Ever?"

I shook my head.

"My family consists of Tess, my husband, Nathan, and Aunt Janet.

That's been enough for me. Nathan's parents and brothers and sisters in Texas are all the extra relatives I need."

"What about your heritage?"

"My heritage?"

"Pardon my saying, but you're Louisiana born, Miranda, descended from Louisiana gentry on all sides, not to mention a grandmother who was full Cajun. There's bayou water running through your veins, girl, and jazz music framing out the cadence of your words. I don't know you that well, but it's not hard to see that you've got the dark eyes and beautiful features of your *mamere,* and I would imagine the intelligence and resourcefulness of she and your *papere.* You might not recognize it, Miranda, but there's more of you here than you can imagine."

He words hung between us, the weight of them palpable to me. I felt a stirring deep inside, the awakening of an ache that had been hibernating for decades.

"But my Aunt Janet—" I protested weakly. "Out of respect to her—"

"What about respect for all of the others, for those who have passed, for those who are still alive? You've got an uncle here, Miranda, and some cousins, not to mention your other grandmother, your mother's mother, up in Ruston."

"None of whom I have spoken to or heard from since I was the age that Tess is now. To be honest, Charles, I have no recollection of my time here at all. It's hard to miss people you can't even remember. AJ and I started fresh the day she took me away to live with her in Manhattan."

Charles glanced almost tenderly at my sleeping daughter.

"So you're telling me this place and these people having nothing to do with you and who you are? I'd venture to say they're probably at least *half* of who you are. Just because you don't remember doesn't mean it isn't so. Think of your own child. Would you erase every day of her life up to now and tell her she's better off starting fresh, that the past five years don't matter? That's the most ridiculous thing I've ever heard."

Before I could form a reply, his cell phone rang. He excused himself to take the call, and I was glad because it gave me the chance to think about all that he had said. I turned my body toward the window on my right, stroked Tess's hair in my lap, and gazed out at the landscape. It was utterly foreign to me, the open water having been replaced by swampy, tangled jungle. The road was still elevated, but now we were driving along the treetops, with another big, white bird skirting the tips of the leaves off to our right.

Bayou water in my veins? My grandmother's dark eyes? Again, those eyes filled with tears for a reason I couldn't begin to understand. Part of me felt defensive of my Aunt Janet and her stance against this place.

The other part of me hungered for it, hungered for something I couldn't even put into words.

EIGHT

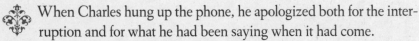

Over their heads the towering and tenebrous boughs of the cypress
Met in a dusky arch, and trailing mosses in mid-air
Waved like banners that hang on the walls of ancient cathedrals.

When Charles hung up the phone, he apologized both for the interruption and for what he had been saying when it had come.

"Before your aunt took you away from here, your family suffered
immeasurable tragedy," he told me, the passion now withheld from his
voice. "I have no right to act as if that wasn't relevant to all that's happened
since. Your aunt did what she thought was best in the raising of her late
sister's daughter. It's presumptuous of me to impugn her character without
taking that into consideration."

I shook my head.

"You don't have to apologize, Charles. My aunt did the best she could.
But perhaps you're right. Maybe keeping me completely in the dark about
my past and isolated from family here was a mistake."

At least I hoped it was a mistake. Despite some misgivings, suddenly
what I wanted most in the world was to see these people again and find
out more about them—and about my own past, the past I didn't know.

As for my mother's death, I had always been told it was a terrible accident, but I had my suspicions that it was a suicide. When I was about ten,

I found a letter from Louisiana hidden in my aunt's closet, which referred to my mother's "death by her own hand." I knew no other conclusion I could draw from that.

Now, after a lifetime of conjecture, of knowing nothing about what had really happened here, nor about the relatives we had left behind, I felt a sudden and insatiable hunger to learn. I wanted to ask Charles a thousand questions, but even as those questions formed in my brain I remembered the warnings of AJ to take it slowly, not to mention my panic attack on the plane. Perhaps my brain wasn't ready to learn everything all at once. But I couldn't resist throwing out one single question, the one that had been rolling around in my mind for years.

"Charles, how did my mother die?"

He met my eyes, pity again evident on his face, and I felt embarrassed that I'd even had to ask that question. What kind of person doesn't know the details of her own mother's death? *Uh, maybe the same kind who doesn't know she has a tattoo hidden on the back of her head?*

He took a deep breath, obviously trying to form his words with care, and then he gave up and said it like it was.

"She hung herself."

My pulse surged.

"So it was a suicide?"

He nodded and then said, "You mean you didn't even know that?"

"No," I replied. "All I was ever told was that she had died in a 'tragic incident.'"

"Oh, it was a tragedy. She was so beautiful, so young. Her life was filled with promise. That funeral was one of the saddest affairs I have ever been to. The family couldn't take much more."

I turned to look out of the window again, trying not to picture the scene as it must have been the night she died. Was she in her nightgown? How long did she hang there, dead, before someone found her? Did she leave a note?

The most important question, of course, was why did she do it—why, when she had a little girl who needed her?

"Was she..." I hesitated, afraid to ask if she was somehow mentally unstable, especially in light of what I now knew about my own childhood craziness. "Did she suffer from depression?"

Charles shrugged.

"It was a very sad time, yes. No one could blame her, if you know what I mean."

I didn't know what he meant, but suddenly I felt the vague stirrings of panic again, that distinct pressure at my diaphragm. Hoping to ward off another attack, I clasped my shaking hands and took a deep breath and changed the subject, asking Charles about the region in general and the beautiful but unusual terrain.

He seemed to welcome the change of subject too, and his face lit up as he answered my questions and pointed out various sights and talked about this place he called home. He was winding up a story about "bayou life," as he called it, when he interrupted himself to point out the town we were passing through.

"This here is Oak Knoll proper," he said. "You can't see the water from where we are now, but the town sits right along Bayou Serein."

We were on what looked like the main drag, and though it wasn't exactly New York City, it didn't seem as out-and-out rural as I had expected. There were a few strip malls, a library, a post office, and more.

"If you need anything while you're here, this is your closest bet," Charles said, waving his hand toward the stores that lined the road. "My secretary printed out some maps and basic directions for you. I'll give 'em to you soon as we reach the house."

"Great. Thanks."

We continued down the road a bit further, where the stores thinned back out to an occasional bar, an auto body shop, and a dusty, run-down motel with a faded sign that labeled it as the Stay-Bay-ou Inn. We made a left turn and passed clusters of modest brick homes, the yards growing more expansive the further from town we went. As we drove I found myself getting used to the scenery, even thirstily drinking it in. We were almost there. Almost home. I half expected to see something familiar, to feel the spark of a memory, but nothing registered at all. Perhaps that was for the best, at least for now.

The houses also were bigger and nicer as we continued, though some couldn't be seen at all, save for a fancy entrance gate through which passed long driveways that wound out of sight in the distance. Occasionally, breaks in the trees revealed glimpses of the houses themselves, and from what I could see they were beautiful.

"Before we turn in," Charles said suddenly, "I almos' forgot to warn you 'bout the trees."

"The trees?"

"The twin oaks, after which the estate was named. As you may recall from the report I sent you a few years ago, Hurricane Katrina hit pretty hard around here. One of the oaks was struck with lightning. We did everything we could to save it, but I'm afraid in the end it was lost. We had to have it taken down jus' a couple months ago."

I wasn't quite sure how to respond. With so many huge trees around here, I couldn't imagine how one less tree could make that big of a difference.

"I understand," I said finally, though I really didn't.

The driver turned on the blinker and slowed to make another left onto a wide, paved driveway between two beautiful stone columns that were joined by an arching wrought iron header curving high above the driveway. The welcoming stone-and-iron structure looked quite old, and I stared at it for a long moment, trying to see if it brought back any sort of memory from when I lived here as a child. It did not.

Still, it was a beautiful introduction to the estate. The house number was engraved into the column on the left, the street name into the right, and the iron arch revealed the words "Twin Oaks" in an elaborate script across the top.

Very impressive.

We pulled forward slowly, following the driveway as it curved off to the right. As we did, we rounded the stand of trees that had blocked the house from the road, and suddenly the view unfolded before me in its full magnitude. I gasped as the scene was revealed: acres and acres of gracious, wooded lawn; and in the distance a house that looked like something from an "Antebellum Homes of the South" calendar. Across the front were four big columns flanking porches on two levels. The house was an imposing white, its windows highlighted by black shutters, and across the front, on each side of the cement stairs, were banks of pink and maroon blooming bushes.

Closer, off to our immediate right, was a massive tree, the most beautiful I had ever seen, its limbs so fat and huge that they literally rested on the ground like tired arms at the elbow, only to rise back up again to extend more branches toward the treetop, forming a massive canopy of leaves that covered the driveway and the surrounding grass in shade. From the limbs hung lacey gray clumps of threads that I realized must be Spanish moss.

"That was the lucky one," Charles said, nodding, then he pointed to the other side of the driveway. "That's the one that didn't make it."

I looked to where he pointed on our left. All that remained now was a giant stump, the last remaining trace of what had been the other oak, the twin.

"That's so sad. Kind of throws the whole place out of balance."

"Not to mention, the name 'Twin Oaks' no longer applies."

"We can plant another," I said, surprised by my feeling of possession, of protectiveness. Somehow, I wanted to make things right.

"Sure," Charles replied. "It'll only take 'bout a hundred years 'fore it's as big as the one that was lost. Imagine that, a hundred years of history snapped clean by one single mighty act of God. I guess worse things could've happened. At least the main house is still standing, and no one here got hurt."

Charles pressed the button to lower the opaque glass separating us from our driver.

"Emmett, pull on around to the garage. We'll go in the back way."

My eyes were wide as we continued along the driveway, going straight rather than curving left to pull in front of the house. From a distance, the house had been huge and imposing and beautiful, but the closer we got the more I could tell that it was in a terrible state of disrepair. Paint was peeling from under the eaves, the banister along the front porches were missing half of their ornate spindles, and the surrounding shrubbery was nearly overtaken with vines and weeds. Within the curve of the front driveway sat a crumbling, cement circle, which I had to assume was a dormant fountain.

"I'm afraid Willy hasn't been keeping up with things very well since he got sick. He was diagnosed with a lung disorder just a few months before Katrina, and by the time the storm had passed he was having a lot of complications and in no condition to make the kinds of fixes that were needed. At least you had good insurance, so my office took care of the most important things, like the section of the roof that got ripped off and the windows that were blown out. But the dock's never been repaired, and a couple of the outbuildings were either completely destroyed or damaged so badly that they could no longer be used. That's when Willy and Deena moved into the house proper, after the caretaker's cottage was torn up so bad in the storm."

I just shook my head, dismayed that the damage had been left to sit like this for so long.

"Why were they living in a little side cottage when this big house was completely at their disposal?" I asked, thinking of the terms of the life estate. My understanding was that once my grandparents were both dead, Willy had been given free reign of the entire property for the rest of his life.

"Willy's tightwad wife," Charles said with a wink. "Shoot, Deena rubs those nickels so hard, the Indian rides the buffalo."

"Excuse me?"

"It's just an expression. She's cheap, *cher*, so tight with the pennies that when they finally moved into the house she only let them live in a little part of it in the back. Except for Willy's room, she keeps the air conditioner at 'bout ninety. Otherwise, she's got the house completely sealed off. Like I said, she'll be happy when she's done with this place and can get out of here."

I could only shake my head in wonder. How could she want to leave such a magnificent place? How could anyone?

My heart full of an emotion I could not name, I looked down at my daughter, touching my hand to her hair. She was sleeping soundly, her chest gently rising and falling with each even breath. I may not be the best mother in the world, not even close, but I knew that I loved her, that I would do anything to keep her safe, to make her happy. AJ had been acting out of love for me when she swept me away from here and kept me away, of that I had no doubt. But seeing the beautiful house and grounds and understanding now what we had left behind was simply heartbreaking to me. This would have been a perfect place for a little girl to grow up.

Had AJ really taken me away from here out of love?

We pulled around the side and came to a stop between the house and a long row of garages. Craning my neck to take it all in, I could see that the house was even bigger than it had looked from the front. Dotted around the back of the property were other, smaller buildings, though most were in various states of disrepair.

"The bayou's that way," Charles said, noting the direction of my gaze, "though it's so overgrown right now you can barely see the water from here. You can take a look at it later."

I nodded, my heart in my throat. Did I remember this place? Was the sight of this looming house burned somewhere deep in my memory, not gone but merely tucked away in some hidden fold of my brain?

I didn't know. I didn't feel as though I was home. I just felt...I wasn't sure what I felt.

"Miranda, if you want to let your daughter keep sleeping, Emmett can stay here with her while we go inside."

I didn't want to insult either Emmett or Charles, but I wasn't about to leave my baby with someone I didn't know and hadn't even met until today. After all that had happened in the last few days, I felt safer keeping her as close to me as possible.

"That's okay. She needs to wake up anyway," I said, reaching down to give Tess a gentle shake. "Otherwise she'll never be able to get to sleep tonight."

Tess wasn't happy about being awakened, but at least she stopped whining as soon as we got out of the car and I picked her up. She was petite for a five-year-old, and though I couldn't carry her around all the time, I didn't mind doing so for now.

Tess rested her head on my shoulder as we followed Charles to the house. He raised a hand to knock, but before his fist struck the wood, the door swung open and we were face-to-face with a woman in her late sixties or early seventies, with short choppy hair, deep frown lines, and dark circles under her eyes.

"Deena," Charles said. "How is he?"

"Still dying. This her?"

Ignoring her rudeness, Charles graciously swept his hand toward me. "Deena Pedreaux, this is Miranda Miller. And this is her daughter, Tess."

The woman looked me up and down, sizing me up, taking in my crisp slacks, my tailored blazer and top, my pulled-back hair. Apparently unimpressed, she focused her pair of brown beady eyes on my face.

"'Bout time you got here," she snapped, and then she turned on her heel and walked away, leaving the door open behind her.

Charles gave me an apologetic look and gestured for me to follow.

Coming through the back door into a dark and stuffy kitchen was a rather unceremonious way to enter the house of my youth and get a look at my inheritance. As we walked, I decided not to pay much attention to our surroundings but to keep a sort of tunnel vision instead. I decided I would focus on the task at hand for now. There would be time and opportunity later for looking around and forming a true first impression.

We walked from the kitchen down a long narrow hallway that ended in a cramped living room. It was even stuffier in there, with no windows and protective covers on the upholstered furniture. I felt a surge of pity for the dying Willy, and I was glad Charles had told me that his bedroom had its own air conditioner.

"I'll wake him up and tell him you're here," Deena said, motioning for us to wait. She walked to the end of the hallway and softly knocked on a door. Opening it, she slipped through and closed it behind her.

"I don't like that lady, Mommy," Tess said in a loud whisper. "She's mean."

"She's just tired, honey. You know how people get cranky when they're tired."

Tess didn't reply, but for the second time today she slipped a thumb into her mouth, an old habit that Rosita had assured me had been broken. I started to pull Tess's hand away from her mouth, but then I thought better of it and pretended not to notice. With everything else going on, the last thing I needed right now was for her to throw a tantrum.

The door opened again, but this time another woman appeared and waved for us to come up the hallway. She looked to be just a little older than I was, quite petite and exotically pretty with almond shaped eyes and light coffee-colored skin. Her black hair was woven into an intricate set of braids which were pulled back from her face by a wide headband. She wore a nurse's uniform, and though she also didn't smile or give us a warm greeting, she didn't seem mean or angry, just solemn.

"You're Miranda?" she asked as we reached her, her black eyes locking in on mine. I nodded. "You came in time. I'm so glad, for his sake. Maybe now he can speak his mind. Then he'll be able to die in peace."

NINE

And in the flickering light beheld the face of the old man,
Haggard and hollow and wan, and without either thought or emotion,
E'en as the face of a clock from which the hands have been taken.

"Is somebody gonna die, Mommy?" Tess asked, popping her thumb out of her mouth and lifting her head from my shoulder. "Who?"

I wasn't sure how to answer, but Charles saved me by interrupting.

"That's just an expression, *cher,*" he assured her. "Miranda, do you mind if I come in with you? I'd like to speak to Willy myself."

"Please," I replied, suddenly feeling claustrophobic. I had come a long way to be here, but at that moment I wanted to be anywhere *but* here.

The young nurse stepped back and held the door open, and we had no choice but to move inside. At least it was blessedly cool in there, a large air-conditioning unit humming from a window nearby. It was also bright, with no drapes to block the afternoon sunlight pouring in through numerous windows as well as a pair of French doors at the far end. Looking through those doors, I could see a small brick patio with a grill just outside. A stone walkway meandered away from that patio alongside a tall hedge.

The room was large and beautiful, with a stone fireplace to our left flanked by a grouping of furniture. Judging from the books and plants that lined the walls, I decided that before it had been converted into a bedroom for the dying man, it must have been a solarium or a library. At the far end, blocking a window, was a single hospital bed, surrounded by adaptive devices and other medical equipment. At an angle to the bed were two chairs with a low table between them, the surface cluttered with magazines, needlework, and a few paperback books, obviously diversions for the passing of time as the man's wife and his nurse attended to him in his final hours.

"Come on in. He don't bite," Deena snapped at me.

I stepped forward at her command, and it wasn't until then that I allowed myself to focus in on the patient himself, a slight figure covered almost entirely by a white sheet, his face and hands nearly as pale as the linens.

Tess wiggled to get down, but I resisted, keeping her captive in my arms lest she bump into a piece of medical equipment or step into hazardous body waste or something.

"Willy, how are you?" Charles asked, approaching the bedside. Slowly, Tess and I followed suit.

"De´pouille," quaked a weak voice from the bed.

"Aw, o-ye-yi," Charles replied sympathetically in what I had to assume was Cajun, the two of them sounding as though they were from another planet.

"Thanks so much for...bringin'...Miz Fairmont here," Willy said to Charles, switching to English, his deeply accented words punctuated by ragged breaths. "I can't tell you...how much...I 'preciate it, me."

The poor thing, he seemed very much near the end of his life, weak and small and still. Despite the trouble he had breathing, he was quite calm, and as he looked at me I could see that there was a sparkle of life yet in his eyes. He attempted to give me a smile, but it came out as more of a wince.

"Little Miranda Fairmont," he rasped. "Long time no see."

I don't know what I had expected, but this wasn't it. This man didn't seem hysterical or agitated at all. Instead, the wife standing next to him was the agitated one, wringing her hands and looking at me with a mixture of suspicion and irritation.

"Her name ain't Fairmont no more, you idiot," Deena barked to her husband. "Accordin' to Mr. Benochet, she's married now."

"Fairmont's fine," I said to Willy, ignoring her. "Or, um, Miller. Miranda Miller."

"Whatever her name is, she's here now," Deena said. "Go ahead and tell us whatever it is you need to say to her."

As if in great pain, the man turned his head and looked at his wife with a withering glare, one that must have sucked up every speck of energy he possessed just to manage.

"When I'm...good and ready...Deena...not a minute...sooner."

Blinking, the woman matched his hateful glare with one of her own.

"Well, considering that you're going to be dead soon," she hissed, "you'd better hurry it up."

She had trumped him, apparently, winning the duel. He visibly withered, taking his eyes away from her face and sinking further into the covers. After a moment he coughed wearily and closed his eyes.

Whether this was their usual dynamic or not, I was extremely uncomfortable having Tess witness such a brutal exchange. Nathan and I had certainly been known to argue, but rarely with such venom and never in front of our child.

"If you people will excuse me," I said, summoning up my nerve, "I'm going to have to find someone to take care of Tess so that I can come back here by myself. This really isn't appropriate..."

"I don't want a babysitter, Mommy," Tess whined, clutching my hips with her legs in a death grip. She always went to others easily, but I knew right now she was in unfamiliar territory and feeling on edge, as was I.

"Mr. Benochet, you're good with kids," Deena said in a voice that had suddenly switched from vinegar to sugar. "Why don't you take the child out front where she can take a set on the swang?"

"Tha's good idea," Willy added weakly from the bed, his eyes closed. "Y'all go...play a lil'...*pain pee po.*"

"I'd be happy to, Willy," Charles replied. "But I'd like to hear what you have to say first. We've all gone to a lot of trouble to get Miranda here so that you can talk to her."

Willy opened his eyes and looked around at those who were surrounding his death bed, ending with me.

"What I gots to say...is 'tween me and her. I wants all y'all out."

Charles looked quite disappointed that he wasn't going to be able to stay and hear the words that I had been brought here for, whatever they were, but he recovered quickly, rubbing a hand across his face and then flashing Tess a warm smile.

"Well, how 'bout it then, *Boo?*" he said to Tess. "You wanna come wit' me for a little *pain pee po?*"

"I don't need to go potty," Tess objected, which brought a laugh from Charles and Willy.

"No, *cher.*" Charles explained with a grin. "Playing the *pain pee po* jus' means going out and doing something useless but fun. Like hanging out."

"You want to play with me?" Tess asked him. "I have some dollies in the car."

"Either that or we could go try out the swing. They got two swings, actually. One is a rope swing in the front yard, hanging from a big ol' tree, and the other is a bench swing on the gallery, hanging by chains from the rafters. From what I recall, they're both pretty dandy."

Tess peeked at me, warming up to the idea once I gave her an encouraging nod, and she wiggled her way down to the floor. I wasn't in the habit of sending my child off with a man I had just met, but Charles wasn't exactly a stranger. After all, he'd been a trusted advisor and friend to my Louisiana relatives for more than forty years—not to mention that I instinctively felt that he was a good guy.

"Please keep a very close eye on her," I said.

"Not to worry. I won't let her out of my sight for a moment."

Charles took my daughter's hand and led her through the French doors that led to the patio area, joking easily with her as she giggled in return. Once he closed the doors behind them, I watched through the glass as they moved past the grill and around the high hedge until they disappeared from view.

"Deena...go on," Willy rasped to his wife. "We need to be alone."

Deena hesitated, pointing a crooked finger toward the nurse. "What about her?"

"Lisa can stay."

Ouch. Visibly shamed, Deena harrumphed, speechless, and then finally turned on her heel and marched from the room, going out through the door where we had entered and slamming it loudly behind her.

As soon as she was gone, tension seemed to melt from the room. Willy exhaled a ragged breath and apologized for his wife's behavior, pausing for another breath every few words.

"It ain't been...easy for her here," he whispered. "She never wanted...to live in...Louisiana...and I was never...willing to leave."

I reserved comment, afraid that I might say something terribly rude about the woman's cruelty.

"Can I get you anything?" the nurse asked, reaching for a pitcher of water on a table by the wall. I thought she was speaking to me and I was about to decline when I realized that she was addressing Willy.

"Jus' a...coupla sips," he replied, letting her slip a bendy straw between his lips and then put a hand under the back of his head to raise it slightly.

As he drank, I took a deep breath to try and relax, but that was a mistake. My nostrils filled with the piercing stench of antiseptic and sweat, along with a faint trace of urine. I blew the air back out through my nose and after that made a point of inhaling only through my mouth.

Willy continued to slurp through the straw for a few more moments, finally pushing it out from his mouth and closing his eyes. Again he spoke, squeezing out words between labored breaths.

"Forget...whatever you've heard...on the...subject, ladies, dying ain't... no fun at all."

Lisa smiled at me, and with a soft motion of her hand waved me forward.

"Come closer," Willy added, opening his eyes in time to see her gesture and second it. "Lisa, *Boo*...raise the bed...a little...would you?"

The nurse pressed a button on the bedrail and with a grinding sound the whole head of the bed slowly raised up at an angle, inching upward until Willy told her to stop. She helped him shift his body a bit, fussing with the pillows until they were both satisfied.

"I don't know...what I'd do...without this girl," he said, patting the nurse's arm fondly. "She takes...such good...care of me, her."

"Just doing my job," she replied modestly, but then a look passed between them, a gaze of deep affection I couldn't begin to decipher or understand.

"So...Miranda," he said, turning his attention to me, passing a papery dry hand across his pale lips. "Last time...I seen you...you was 'bout...the size...your *pischouette* is...now."

"Pee-schwet?"

"Your little girl."

I swallowed hard, nodding.

"Yes, I was five, same age as my daughter."

He closed his eyes, as if remembering.

"Your grandparents...they 'bout died...of grief...from missing you after you...lef' here," he wheezed. "I don't...think they...never got over it."

He coughed, a hacking mess that sounded disgustingly productive. As Lisa helped with a tissue, I turned my head and considered what he had just said.

They missed me after I was gone?

This was news to me. To hear AJ tell it, my grandparents hadn't been able to get rid of me fast enough once my mother died. I grew up assuming that they hadn't missed me for a moment, nor given me another thought ever again.

"Mr. Pedreaux, is that what you brought me here for?" I asked, my voice strained. "To tell me that?"

He grunted no and shook his head, the action causing him to cough again, which then led to full-out choking. Lisa quickly propped him up and whacked him squarely on the back between the shoulder blades until he had recovered.

"You okay now, Uncle Willy?" Lisa asked.

"*Uncle* Willy?" I blurted without thinking.

"Lisa's my *Boo*, my sweet niece," Willy cooed.

"My mom is Creole, married to his brother," she added, which explained their mutual affection—not to mention the difference in skin color.

"Anyway, Deena's...right. I best...get down to...business, 'cause I ain't got much...time lef', me."

I hated to say that I agreed with him, but it was obviously true. Wanting to get on with things as well, I reached for a nearby chair, scooted it close to the bed, and sat.

"Thank you for...coming, Miranda. It do my heart good...to see you... again. You know, you the...spittin' image...of your *pauve defante mamere*, your poor sainted grandmother."

So he and Charles both thought I looked like my grandmother. Having never seen of picture of her, I didn't know if that was true or not. Willy was looking me over with his rheumy eyes, as though he was seeking out evidence of the generations of forebears that lent their various features to my appearance. I resisted the urge to look away and instead met his gaze with my own.

"What did you need to tell me that was important enough for me to fly down here, Mr. Pedreaux?"

He swallowed several times, blinking, as he seemed to gather his thoughts.

"Now dat you here," he said. "I ain't...quite sure...how to begin. It's a long story...and I'm a...an old man. My mind ain't...it ain't so clear these days..." his voice trailed off. I glanced at his niece, who winked at me in return.

"You might be having a little trouble with your breathing, you old goat, but your mind is sharp as a tack. Go ahead. Spit it out. Stop keeping everybody in suspense." She looked at me and added, "He's been making me wait to hear what he has to say until you got here. For some reason, he wants to tell us both together."

"What if I hadn't come?" I asked.

"We've been taking it day by day," she replied. "I guess there would have come a point where he had no choice, but so far he wasn't willing to go there."

"It's time now...to bring it all...into the light," Willy rasped. "There's been...too much darkness...for too long."

The room was silent for a long moment after that, and finally he looked at me again, eyes full with tears. He blinked, sending twin lines of liquid down each withered cheek. In response, Lisa's smile faded. Quietly, she reached for another tissue and dabbed at his face to wipe them off. He didn't even seem to notice.

"How do I...begin to explain...what I done?" he finally implored between breaths, in a voice thick with emotion. "To make...you see my...actions was...justified? To be sure...that everything will be...taken care of? To be sure that...the secret, it don't...die wit' me?"

"Secret?" I asked, glancing at Lisa, who seemed intrigued.

Summoning his strength, Willy lifted his head from the pillow and spoke more clearly and emphatically than he had since I came in the room.

"I'm sorry for what I done, Miranda...for what the circumstances made me do. I hopes one day...you can find it in your heart to forgive me."

I started to respond but had to hold my tongue as he kept going.

"More importantly...you mus' learn the reason *why* I done it. The secret...it cannot die wit' me, no. It cannot! I swore that I would take the responsibility...Now it's time for the two of you to do the same."

The effort of speaking so intensely sent him into a new round of coughing, though he resisted this time when Lisa tried to help, holding up one spotted, bony arm to keep her at bay. Finally, when his coughing spell was over, he put his head back against the pillow with his eyes closed, sweat beading along his pale and wrinkled forehead, despite the chilly air that filled the room.

"What secret, Mr. Pedreaux? What do I need to forgive? And what kind of responsibility do you want us to swear to?"

"I'm sorry..." he whispered, his voice so soft that we could barely hear him. Lisa and I both leaned even closer to the bed. "It was for...the angelus. We had to be able to get to the angelus."

He exhaled in a ragged, sour breath, his eyes still closed.

"What's the an-*jell*-us?" I asked.

"It's a prayer," Lisa replied. "You know, the Hail Mary? You're supposed to say it three times a day."

"No." Shaking his head, Willy opened his eyes and looked up at Lisa. *"Pas la prière."*

"Not the prayer?" Lisa asked him. "What, then?"

"My *Boo*...Don't you know the *chucotement du bayou...*'bout *l'angelus?*"

Lisa shrugged.

"I don't know, Uncle Willy. Maybe. Why?"

"L'angelus!" he cried, the urgency apparent in his voice. "Is not a *chucotement de bayou* at all! Is *la vérité!* And I am the last surviving *gardien.*"

I looked to Lisa for a translation, but she was leaning toward Willy, focused on him.

"Uncle Willy, we'll say the Hail Mary for you, the Angelus, whatever you want. Do you want me to call in a priest? We can probably get one here pretty fast."

Poor Willy looked as though he might explode. He started shaking his head, eyes bulging,

"No, no, no," he cried. " *L'angelus! Ne pas la prière, la cloche!*"

"What's he saying?" I asked Lisa.

" 'Not the prayer, the bell.' "

The *bell.* My eyes widened as my hand flew up to the back of my head. The gesture was not lost on Willy.

"Miranda, you know what I'm talking about...You were *marked* for this...*destined* for it..."

"Who did this to me?" I demanded, pulling the clips of my hair so it could fall loose to my shoulders. "And why? What does it mean?"

"We had to make sure you would return...We had to make it clear...the... enormity...of the task..."

Lisa looked at me.

"What is he talking about?"

Feeling a surge of anger, I turned my back to the nurse and lifted the top part of my hair. She reached up and helped move it out of the way, gasping when she saw it.

"Uncle Willy! It's like yours."

"Like his?"

She dropped my hair, reached for the covers, and lifted them from Willy's feet. She pushed up the leg of his pajama pants, and there on his skinny white calf was the same tattoo, though not distorted from growth like mine.

At the sight I felt panic stir in my chest and bile rise in my throat. I *had* seen this symbol somewhere before. The memory of it popped vividly into my mind: It was on skin. As a tattoo. Not the white, shaven skin on the back of my head. Not the hair-covered skin of an old man's leg. Somewhere else, on lovely skin, on skin that was soft and sweet-smelling and kind. I closed my eyes, swallowing hard, envisioning my own hand, a tiny hand, reaching out to trace the image with my finger.

"Stop!" I cried, standing up to pace, my hands clutched at my ears. Was this it? Was this my first childhood memory dredged up from what was supposedly that blank slate inside of my head? I wanted to see more, remember more, but as hard as I focused, the scene faded away, sliding into black. The more I tried to pull it up again, the further away it felt. Finally, I just stood there, eyes closed, and waited for my racing heart to slow down.

I had done it. I had remembered something. Though it hadn't sprung full blown into my mind until now, stirrings of the memory had probably begun yesterday morning, the moment I first pulled out my magnifying glass and spotted the tiny version of the symbol that had been painted into the busy street scene on Jimmy Smith's canvas. On someone's skin. That's where I had seen it before.

"Miranda, are you okay?" Lisa asked.

I opened my eyes to see the concern on her face. Behind her, Willy was watching me as well, but with curiosity, not necessarily compassion.

"Willy, who else had this tattoo?" I demanded, stepping toward my chair. "It was someone I loved very much."

He nodded, his eyes twinkling. "Your *grandmere*. On her left shoulder." Stunned, I sat, my breathing under control. Again I had averted a full-out panic attack. Though I wanted to keep going, I was also scared.

Suddenly, more than anything, I wished that Nathan was there by my side, holding my hand, keeping me strong.

TEN

Sometimes a rumor, a hearsay, an inarticulate whisper,
Came with its airy hand to point and beckon her forward.

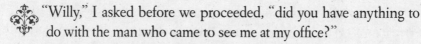 "Willy," I asked before we proceeded, "did you have anything to do with the man who came to see me at my office?"

"What are you talking about?"

"Jimmy Smith. The guy with the painting." I turned to Lisa. "This weird guy came to my office yesterday under the pretense of having a painting restored. This cross-inside-a-bell symbol had been painted into the scene, and he was asking me questions about it."

Reluctantly I went on to explain about the subsequent attack in the alley and how the two thugs searched my body looking for the tattoo.

Willy pushed himself up from the bed, gasping for air.

"Oh, *cher*, I don't believe it. Did...you tell them...anything?"

"What could I tell them? The symbol looked familiar, but I wasn't sure why. I didn't even know this tattoo was here until later in the day, when my aunt showed it to me."

Willy made me repeat my story, going through the full sequence of events. When I was finished, he collapsed back against the covers, air whooshing out of him like a deflating air mattress.

"Who were they?" I pressed.

"I don't know. There could be so many...This ain't good. Not good at all, no."

Lisa held up both hands, palms outward as if to call a stop to the conversation.

"Is Miranda in danger?"

"I don't know. I have to think about this. I don't know."

"Then let's deal with that in a minute," she said. "Right now, tell us more about the symbol."

Willy stared at the ceiling for a long moment, as if to pull his thoughts together again.

"What does the tattoo mean, Uncle Willy? What does the symbol stand for?"

"It is the mark of *Le Serment*," Willy said slowly, almost proudly.

"*Le Serment?*" I asked, looking to Lisa, but she looked as though she was as lost as I was.

Willy looked back and forth from Lisa to me, pleading in his eyes.

"The two of you...it's your time...your turn to take *Le Serment* and carry it forward for a new generation. There's always two, you see, in case one die, the other will still be alive to do what must be done. For many year, it was me and Ya Ya. When she got the *fou*...I found another...to replace her. He was younger than I wanted, but I was desperate. Then he die...in Katrina...All them Guidry boys die together, trying to ride out the storm...on their...shrimp boat, the stupid *têtes duré*...Now the only Colline d'Or left that can do this is me and the two o' you. Since Katrina, I been so scared...what if I die without never telling you...or explaining why I done what I done...*Pour les gens de Colline d'Or...*"

"Look, I'm having a lot of trouble understanding your words," I said. "And you're speaking a lot of French or Cajun or whatever it is. Maybe I should go get Charles to help translate for me."

At that, Willy's eyes opened wide.

"No!" he cried, stirring up his lungs into another spasm. "Charles ain't *Colline d'Or!*"

He clutched at his throat, coughing and gasping for breath. This time he didn't resist as Lisa lifted him and whacked him firmly on the back.

Once she got him through it and set him back against the pillow, she asked him if he wanted to take a break and let us try this again a while later.

"No," he whispered. "There's not enough...time...to wait. We mus'...do this now."

"What's ko-lean-door?" I asked, thinking of what he'd said about Charles, wondering if I should be concerned that my daughter was off somewhere with the man right now. "Is my daughter safe?"

"There's nothing wrong with Mr. Benochet...'cept he ain't from Colline d'Or...it's a place."

Feeling utterly confused, I let out a slow breath and wished there was just some way to pull the words out of this man's brain without him having to use his mouth and lungs.

"Uncle Willy, how can we make this simpler for you?" Lisa prodded. "I really don't think you're up to this."

"The two o' you," he rasped, "you gots to take *Le Serment* first, and then I can tell you everything."

I looked at Lisa, who seemed to be running the word through her brain.

"*Le Serment*..." she mused, squinting in thought. "Oath? You want us to take an oath?"

He looked from her face to mine, nodding his head, his rheumy eyes filling with tears. If this poor old man, for whatever reason, had brought me all the way down here just so I could make some sort of stupid pledge before he died, then I only hoped we could get through it before his final ragged breath, lest I have nightmares of him being tormented throughout eternity, his final piece of earthly business left undone.

"The *Serment*, she's long," Willy said, "and *en Française*. But we can't get to...the next part of...what I have to tell you till that's done."

"Maybe we could save your voice by having you write it down instead," I suggested.

Lisa nodded.

"What do you think of that, Uncle Willy?" she said. "You think you'd be able to write the oath down?"

He grunted in frustration.

"Is not 'posed to be writ down...ever. Is all up here, *dans la tête*."

"Yeah, but desperate times call for desperate measures," Lisa said.

Willy hesitated, and then he reluctantly gave his assent.

"I'll do it...but den you gots to burn it. Promise you'll burn it, soon as we done here."

"We promise," Lisa and I said in unison.

She hopped up and went to the nearby table, looking in the drawer for pen and paper. As she did, Willy continued speaking.

"I never had no childrens of my own, you see," he said to me tiredly, "but I didn't worry cause them Guidry boys was all...young and strong... trustworthy...And I knew sooner or later...you would be back, Miranda... if I sent the message to your aunt. Then after Katrina, everything change. Them Guidry boys was dead and I was so sick, so fast."

I glanced at Lisa, who had procured the pen but was now digging around elsewhere for a blank sheet of paper.

"The two o' you," Willy continued, "you gonna be good *gardiens*. Lisa, I don't know Miranda's heart, but I'm praying she's got...her *mamere's* good sense, her noble character. And Miranda, I knows my Lisa is *honnête, aimable*..."

Lisa found a spiral notebook and flipped it open to a fresh page.

"But Lisa, you mus' promise me, not a word a dis to Junior. Not one word. To the day you die."

"Here you go," Lisa said, ignoring his comment, handing the notebook to him along with the pen.

"Don' act like you not hearing me," her uncle scolded as he took it from her. "That boy is a *bon rien*, yah. *Canaille*, he is."

She sat in the chair and adjusted her headband with strong brown fingers, finally agreeing to his request. Watching her, I remembered my own loose hair and reached up to return it to the French twist.

"You either, Miranda," Willy said tiredly as he began to write. "I don't know your husband, but this has to stay between Lisa and Miranda and no one else. No husbands. Just one Pedreaux and one Saultier, both Colline d'Or."

I was so lost, but at that point I was willing to say or do almost anything to move the conversation along. Lisa and I both waited in silence, the only sound the urgent scratching of Willy's handwriting upon the page. He managed to scribble down a few lines before he stopped and closed his eyes, exhausted from the effort.

"Is this it?" Lisa asked, leaning forward to read what he had written. "That's not so long."

"No, I have barely begun," he said. "There's jus' so much..."

"Can't we just skip this part, Uncle Willy?"

Willy opened his eyes and looked at me, his expression grave, and he spoke between labored breaths.

"I did not...give my life for this...only to fail in the end. We will...do it right or not at all."

He picked up the pen and again continued writing, speaking as he did. "Once you both take *le Serment des gardiens de l'angelus*...then I can tell you...where to find it."

At that, a sob caught in his throat. He looked at me, something like guilt mixed with panic in his eyes.

"Then you will know the terrible thing I did, Miranda," he cried, barely able to suck in one more breath. "And once you do, I jus' pray God you will forgive me!"

Willy's outburst sent him into a new coughing spasm, this one so severe that even Lisa's whacking him on the back didn't help. He could barely bring in any air at all, and when his face began to turn blue, Lisa changed tactics, twisting the knob on a big oxygen canister behind the bed and placing a clear mask over his mouth and nose.

"Can I help?" I asked. "Should I go get Deena? Call a doctor?"

Lisa didn't answer but merely shook her head as she remained focused on her patient, checking his pulse, adjusting the knobs on the canister. After a moment, he stopped struggling, and then his body relaxed as he just lay there, eyes closed. Soon, the bluish tint of his skin gave way to a more normal pale pink and the sound of his breathing became regular and strong.

"I think he just needs to take in some oxygen and rest a bit," she said finally. "He needs a break. This is hard work for him."

Lisa grabbed the notebook from his lap and read what he had written so far, which looked to me to be in French, and barely legible at that. She translated it for me slowly, struggling to make out his handwriting.

"'As a guardian of the angelus, I promise to...protect it with my life, um, care for it against harm—and hide it from evildoers until'..."

"'Until' what?"

"That's where it ends. Until."

I sat back, as stumped as I had been before. Hide it from evildoers? Certainly, I had encountered more than one evildoer since all of this began.

Lisa gently placed the notebook, facedown, on Willy's chest, looking as frustrated as I felt. Had I flown all this way just to say some ancient French oath and learn that my tattoo really was in the shape of a bell? I pinched the bridge of my nose, closing my eyes, and went over the entire conversation in my mind. If only his words hadn't been so confusing, with so many in a language I didn't understand.

"So basically, what do you think he was saying?" I asked, opening my eyes to look at Lisa. She didn't answer right away but instead sat there for a while, watching the slight rise and fall of Willy's chest as he was breathing.

"Something about an old myth being truth," she answered finally.

"What? How'd you get that?"

"He asked me if I remembered the *chucotement du bayou* about the *angelus*. A *chucotement du bayou* is an old Cajun folk tale, like a myth."

"So what's the myth of the angelus?"

She shook her head.

"I have no idea. I don't remember one having to do with an angelus—not the prayer or a bell."

She stood and retrieved a stethoscope from the other side of the bed and leaned over her uncle to listen to his chest, deep frown lines forming around her eyes. Finally she removed the black tubes from her ears and set them onto her shoulders.

"Listen," she said, "those old bayou tales are just dumb stories, like how the alligator got a long snout, or where the sun goes after it sets."

"Tall tales you mean, just for fun?"

"Yeah, but I don't know which one Uncle Willy was talking about. The one about the angelus? I just don't know. It sure doesn't ring a—" She stopped and then smiled at me, and we both finished her sentence together by saying "bell."

"I don't know why someone would hide a bell," I said. "Maybe it's not a real bell but something else called a bell. Or something hidden in a bell."

"Like what?"

"I don't know, maybe he's got some sort of ancient scroll," I mused, "like, the actual angelus prayer written down somewhere, and that's what we have to guard. It could be hidden inside some bell. Are there any bells at this house?"

"Not that I know of. Just a doorbell."

I thought for a moment, going back over the conversation in my mind.

"So who died in a shrimp boat?" I asked. "I think his name was Teddy Ray?"

Lisa thought for a moment and then chuckled.

"Not Teddy Ray, *têtes duré*. It means hardheaded. There were three of them, actually, three hardheaded brothers who died riding out the hurricane in their boat instead of evacuating."

"Did you know them?"

"Around here, everybody knows everybody. We weren't exactly friends, but they were nice guys, distant cousins actually. Cajun good ol' boys, you know. The kind that smell like seafood, their hands rough and fingernails black, always got a dip of chaw under their bottom lip? The kind of guys I specifically left behind by moving to California. Of course, just my luck, who do I meet there and fall in love with? A Creole boy from New Orleans! Junior may not win husband of the year, but at least he doesn't dip chaw or smell like fish."

Being from New York, I didn't know a lot of people who carried "chaw" around under their lip, but I could imagine what she was saying. No wonder she had wanted to expand her horizons!

"There were so many tragedies in Katrina," she continued. "The Guidry boys were just one more story for the papers. Their mother was already a widow, and then in one bad storm she lost her three children as well. So sad."

"You think they would've had enough sense to come in out of the rain."

Lisa glanced sharply at me, her eyes suddenly dark and angry.

"You weren't here. You don't know anything about it."

For some reason, my comment had stepped on her toes. I waited a beat and then tried again, leaving the touchy stuff alone.

"How about this place Willy mentioned, this Colline d'Or? Where's that?"

"Never heard of it. I have no idea."

We were both silent, lost in thought.

"Wherever—and whatever—the angelus is," I said, "I think its hiding place has something to do with me. Something that's going to make me angry and require my forgiveness."

"Yeah, apparently."

"What's the last thing he said before he started choking? That once we took the oath, we'd learn the 'terrible thing' he did?"

"Something like that."

I looked at the man's face, nearly obscured by the mask, and suddenly felt angry. What right did he have to bring me all the way down here just to tell me some sort of horrible news? Was it something that could be undone? If not, then what was the point? There were already enough dark clouds in my life right now, from the state of my marriage to the unknowns in my childhood. Did I have to deal with a dying man giving me some sort of deathbed confession and more than likely touching on facts that I knew nothing about anyway?

"Lisa, what kind of man is Willy?" I asked as I stood up, feeling the need to stretch my legs. "I know he's your uncle and all, but what's he like? Has he ever done anything, um, bad? Illegal, even?"

Lisa put away the stethoscope and shook her head.

"Gosh, no. He's just a good ol' boy too. Till he got sick, he worked hard, played hard. Cajuns love a cold beer, love their music, love to go fishing. He did all of the above as often as he could."

"From what I understand, he took good care of the house and grounds until he got sick."

"Absolutely. This place used to be gorgeous. I'm sorry it's…I mean, it's too bad that it needs so much work now. If you could restore it, it would probably be worth a fortune."

"If I had a fortune to fix it up in the first place."

"Yeah, but there's so much stuff here, paintings and artifacts and antiques. You could probably sell off some pieces and get enough money to pay for the fix up. Aren't you some kind of artist? You'd probably be good at that."

"I'm in art restoration," I explained. "I'm senior preparator for a museum."

"See? That works."

I realized again that I hadn't even seen the rest of the house. We had been ushered directly through the back entrance and down the long hall-way into here. What a weird concept for me to grasp, that as soon as the man in front of me died, this whole place and everything in it would be mine. All mine. Had I known the magnitude of my inheritance from the beginning, I would have done things a lot differently.

"You seem kind of restless," Lisa said. "Why don't you go take a walk? You can check on your daughter. I can come and get you as soon as he wakes up. Knowing Willy, he could sleep for an hour."

She was right. I was restless, and I did want to check on Tess.

"What if he…what if he doesn't make it?" I asked. "What if he dies and we never get the rest of that oath, much less the rest of the facts of whatever it is he's trying to say?"

"I'm not worried. His will to live is strong…at least until he has finished saying all that he has to say."

I hoped that she was right.

"Go on," she prodded kindly. "I'll come get you as soon as he starts to stir."

"You're sure?"

"Yes, I'm sure. I think the swings are up that way, around the corner of the house."

She pointed in the direction Charles had taken Tess. I thanked her and let myself out the French doors.

ELEVEN

Deathlike the silence seemed, and unbroken, save by the herons
Home to their roosts in the cedar-trees returning at sunset.

Once again the hot, humid air took me by surprise. This time, however, the heat felt good, a welcome relief after being in such a chilly room. Moving past the old-fashioned barbeque grill, I followed the path around the hedge and alongside the house, taking in its massive presence, as I went. How I yearned to get inside and explore, walking in through the front door this time, and making my way from room to room until somewhere, somehow, hidden in some dark corner or secret alcove, I could find another spark of a memory. It had to be there, some trace of the first five years of my life.

My walking slowed as I tried to imagine it, and then I stopped, the scene so vivid in my mind that I swore I could hear laughter, the sound of a child's laughter. It seemed so real! I stood frozen in place as my mind raced, listening, knowing it must be the laughter of my own childhood self. I tried to picture it: me, as a little girl, running down shiny wood hallways and skipping across the lawn.

Then, suddenly, I realized that what I was hearing *was* real: It was the sound of my own child, squealing in delight from the front yard. I sped up my steps until I came around the corner to see my little baby swinging high up into the sky, Charles Benochet standing wide-legged upon the lawn under a big tree, grinning up at her as he braced for the next push.

"Whoa, that's kind of high there," I said, moving toward them, my heart leaping into my throat.

"Mommy! Look! I'm flying!"

I ran closer, my arms lifting from my sides, ready to catch my child when she plummeted to certain death.

"Relax, Mama. She's fine," Charles said as the swing reached its high point and began falling back the way it had come.

"Please get her down," I said under my breath. "She's only five years old."

He did as I asked without comment, slowing the swing until the pendulum had wound itself down to a mere arc across the bare spot in the grass. By that point Tess was on the verge of tears, and suddenly I wished that her babysitter Rosita was here, or Nathan. They would know how to handle this, how to distract her from the situation and make it all okay. The best I could do was put my hands on my hips and try to look unbending. I may have trouble standing up to my own child in many areas, but not when it came to her safety.

"You never let me do anything fun!" Tess accused me as she sat there balanced on the swing, her toes scraping in the dirt as she slowly moved back and forth. Then she pulled out the big gun: "I want *Daddy!*"

"I never let you do anything *dangerous.* You're going to break your neck on that thing."

"Mister Charlie said you used to swing on it when you were a little girl."

I glanced at Charles, who was helping Tess down.

"Your mama used to love the swing on the gallery too," he told her as she let go of the rope and stood on solid ground. "That one was better, in a way, 'cause then the two of them could go on it at the same time. Come on, I'll show you."

He reached for her hand and she weighed her options: stand here yelling at Mom or go with this new plan. She chose the latter, shooting me one last, irritated look before taking off across the lawn. With a pang, I felt the familiar sensation of being the third wheel around my own child. Between Nathan and Rosita, it was a feeling I was used to. One of these days, I still hoped to grow into motherhood, a role that was as ill-fitting on me now as a wool coat that had been run through a hot washer.

I fell into step behind them, pausing at the front porch as they mounted the steps and crossed to the bench swing hanging from the rafters near one end.

As they settled down on the wooden slats of the seat, Charles on one side, Tess in the middle, I was trying to imagine myself as a child, standing here, looking up at my own home, the home of my parents and grandparents and great-grandparents before them. The porch was graceful but worn, the front door one massive single panel framed in elaborate molding. Soon, I knew I would be able to open that big door, step inside, and see if I felt that I had come home.

For now I crossed to the swing and sat down on the other side of Tess, glad to see that the steady rocking was lulling her into a calmer state. After a moment Charles cleared his throat and then spoke softly to me over her head.

"So was it worth the trip?"

"Excuse me?"

"What Willy had to tell you. Was it worth coming all the way down here for?"

"Oh. We're not finished yet. He needed to take a break. He's having trouble talking and breathing at the same time."

"Ah," Charles replied, and then we swung back and forth for another minute. "He must have a lot to say."

I knew he wanted to ask me what I'd learned thus far, but I didn't think it would be right to tell him—not that I had learned all that much yet anyway. I was glad that he didn't come right out and ask me, though he came pretty close.

"Whatever it is," Charles said, "I just want to make sure you know I'm glad to help you out with any legal matters. And, of course, anything you tell me will be held in complete confidence, protected by the lawyer-client relationship."

"Yes," I said, feeling awkward. "That's good to know."

We were silent again for a moment, but this time our silence was broken by the appearance of Lisa the nurse, who came walking around the corner of the house, the frown lines between her eyes now gone.

"There you are, Miranda," she said. "He's awake now. Doing better."

"Good." I scooted forward to stand, and then I thought twice and looked at my ad hoc babysitter. "Charles, are you going to be okay with Tess just a little longer?"

"Oh sure, we're fine. I wonder if I could run to the rest room real quick first, though. I need to speak with Willy for a second anyway, so lemme do that and then I'll be right back."

"Take your time."

Charles told Tess he'd return in a minute, and then he hopped up from the swing, bounded down the steps, and walked briskly around the corner. As he went, I studied Lisa, wondering what kind of person she was and what this was going to be like to share some bizarre secret with her, something that Willy said only she and I could ever know.

Lisa made no motions to leave but instead remained there, hands on her lower back, stretching. I wondered if she got claustrophobic sometimes, spending all day in that sick room, enjoying the outside scenery through the glass. I knew I couldn't do her job. I was happy that I worked with tools, not people.

"Does Willy seem okay?" I asked Lisa once Charles was gone.

"He's good. When I left he was busy writing away."

"Thank goodness."

Lisa climbed up the steps and stretched again and smiled down at Tess.

"So what's your daughter's name?" she asked.

"This is Tess," I said of my semi-hypnotized child. "She's five."

"Mommy, I'm hungry," Tess said, popping out of her lulled state.

I glanced at my watch and realized we had never eaten lunch—and it was nearly two o'clock. Considering the emotions running through my mind today, it didn't surprise me that I wasn't hungry, but how had I managed to neglect my child? So much for all of that mother-daughter bonding we'd shared on the plane; if I couldn't meet her basic needs, what good was I?

"I've got an apple and some crackers in my carry-on bag," I said to Tess. "Why don't we go around back and see if the car's open?"

"I want *real* food, Mommy. I want macaroni and cheese."

I started to reason with her, but Lisa intervened.

"We don't have any macaroni and cheese, but we can sure do better than crackers," she said. "Why don't we go to the kitchen and see what we can dig up? Maybe a sandwich? Miranda, how about you?"

"I, uh, I'm not hungry, thanks. But a sandwich for Tess would be great. Are you sure it's not an imposition?"

"Imposition? It's Southern necessity! How could we bring you here and not even offer you food or drink?"

She smiled, her teeth pretty and white in her dark face. Somehow, out here in the hot afternoon sunshine away from her dying uncle, she seem younger, less burdened.

"Come on, sweetie, let's go to the kitchen," Lisa said to Tess. "Miranda, since you're not eating, maybe you could go sit with Willy and come get me when he's finished writing."

"Is that mean lady going to be in the kitchen?" Tess asked, and I could feel my face flush.

"She might be," Lisa answered with a smile. "But I'll protect you. She doesn't dare mess with me."

Tess slid off of the swing and hesitantly walked toward Lisa. Together, the three of us went back around the way we had come. When we reached Willy's room and opened the door, we were hit with a blast of cold air, like stepping from an oven into a freezer.

When we were back inside, Willy and Charles were talking, the pen clutched in Willy's hand, the notebook resting facedown on his chest. Charles was standing at the head of the bed, his back to us, but at the sound of Tess's voice, he turned around, his grim expression quickly changing to a smile.

"Mister Charlie!" Tess cried, as if she were meeting a long-lost friend. I wasn't proud of it, but from somewhere deep inside I felt a surge of jealousy.

After ten minutes apart, she greeted him with as much enthusiasm as I got from her at the end of a long day.

"Hey, Miss Tessie Wessie," Charles replied. "Too hot out there for you?"

Lisa explained that they were just passing through on their way to the kitchen to put together a late lunch.

Tess was tugging on my pants, and I glanced down to see her little hand cupped beside her mouth.

"I don't like this room, Mommy, it smells bad," she said in her classic stage whisper.

Feeling a flush heat my face, I was about to reply when Lisa spoke.

"Let's keep going, hon. Do you like ham? I think we have some ham for a sandwich. And if it's okay with Mom, maybe we'll introduce you to sweet tea."

"Tea?" I asked doubtfully, thinking of the caffeine rush that might plague us the rest of the afternoon.

"She's a little young for tea," Charles corrected before I could reply, "but I bet they got some lemonade. I could use a glass of that myself. Willy, will you be okay here for a minute?"

"I'm staying with him," I said.

"Okay, *cher,* see y'all in a bit then."

Lisa, Charles, and Tess left the room together to head back up the long, hot hallway to the kitchen. Alone with Willy, I took my seat and focused on breathing through my mouth, the smell of sickness and death nearly palpable.

"Your *pischouette* is a beauty," Willy said.

"Thank you."

"You named her Cass, I see. How nice."

"No, Tess, not Cass," I replied, wondering if it was our accents—or lack thereof—that kept confusing people. "Short for Tessera, which is an artist's term. My husband is an architect, so his pet name for her is T-square. It's their little private joke." I was babbling out of sheer nervous energy. Hating the sound of my own voice, I forced myself to shut up. "But don't let me bother you. You keep writing."

In the silence that followed I looked around the room and finally allowed my eyes to meet Willy's. I thought he would be writing again, but instead he was just gazing at me.

"It ain't jus' your face...your hair...your height," he told me. "It's the way you carry yourself...something about the gestures you use..."

His voice trailed off, but when he saw my confusion, he added, "Your *mamere*. Everything about you remind me of Ya Ya."

"Ya Ya?"

"Sorry, I mean Miz Portia. Your grandmother. Ya Ya's short for Portia. When you grow up like we done...crawfishing together in the canals... poling through the swamps...it's hard to let go of the old nicknames. She were like a sister to me. Once she married your *papere* and became a lady...we all had to call her Miz Portia in public. But when it was just the two of us...it was always Ya Ya. She was a fine woman, her."

I stared at Willy in wonder, realizing that was probably the most I had ever been told about my grandmother in one sitting! I knew I had Cajun blood in me and that it had come from my paternal grandmother, but in a million years I hadn't pictured her crawfishing or poling or anything like that. Somehow, my image of her centered around fancy dresses and tea services and impeccable manners.

"If she grew up in the swamps, how did she end up here?" I asked, gesturing at the grandeur that surrounded us.

"Love. Beauty. Your *papere* caught sight o' her one day...and that was it. He was gone..." Willy chuckled, cleared this throat, and then shook his head self-consciously. "But you don't want to hear an old man reminisce."

"Oh, please," I urged. "Go on. If you feel up to it."

It was probably more important to keep him pressing toward the ultimate goal. But as he relaxed against the pillow, his eyes retreating to some distant time, I couldn't help but wish he would just talk to me forever, filling in all the blanks of my life.

"I was young...had just started working for...the Fairmonts when my mama she die..."

"I'm sorry."

"Now Mister Xavier...he knew I didn't have no time...to take the bus all de way home...and I didn't have no car...So he droved me hisself all the way to Bayou Teche...so I could bury my mama. When we gots there, Ya Ya was on the swing...out in the yard waiting for me to get there...not a day more than eighteen...the mos' beautiful woman in Iberia Parish, her. When I see her, all I see is a sister...but Mister Xavier, he took one look at her...and he say...'Willy, I don' know...who dat girl is...but if she taken...I gonna kill myself.'"

Willy laughed, which stirred up another cough, a deep one. I stood, wondering if I should go get Lisa, but he waved me back down and after a moment seemed to recover. Remembering her actions from before, I pulled some tissues from the table and held them out to him, glad when he took them from me and held them to his own mouth rather than make me do it for him.

"Please go on," I said, knowing he needed to keep writing the oath but also wanting to hear more about my grandparents.

"The res' is history...Mister Xavier, he decide to stick around...for the whole weekend...took him a room at a motel in town...and spent every minute...pretending to help with the funeral arrangements...but really he was jus' trying to...charm Ya Ya."

I leaned forward, listening to his labored breathing, willing him to keep talking, *keep telling*, like a thirsty man praying for a faucet to flow.

"He was older than her, and people talk...thought she married him for...for his money...but I knew de truf. I seen her fall...in love wit' him too. She love him for real. She love him so much eventually she give up...everyting...her home...her fambly...her ways. She tell 'Ya Ya' goodbye to become 'Miz Portia Saultier Fairmont'...lady of the manor. I tell you what...goin' from the swamps to this big fancy house...she had a lot to learn, her."

"How did she do it?" I asked. "Did she go to charm school or something?"

"Nah. The things that are harder to learn, she already had those inside a her...the grace...the posture. So Mister Xavier, he ask his mama to take his new bride...under her wing. Old Missus Fairmont, she the one teach Ya Ya...how to be a real lady. After while, if you didn't know Ya Ya's past...you would never guess she ain't growed up dat way. Thas' how much she become a proper lady."

"Wow."

"Only when they was alone...or when she was wit' me or de kids...did she turn back into...who she really were. Sometime Mister Xavier, he ax me...to take them in the boat...down the bayou, out to the swamps...Them was the bes' times, yeah...just relaxing on the water, the whole family and me...fishing...poling. Your daddy and his brother...they was jus' boys...they loved them days...they adored their mama. Them times was when...she really let herself...smile...feel so happy...jus' like when we...was growing up together."

"I'm confused," I said softly. "My grandmother was your sister?"

"By blood, jus' cousins. Distant cousins at dat. But she was raised over to my mama and them...so in de heart...we was brother and sister...from day one."

He smiled, his old eyes twinkling.

"I done cried at that wedding...almos' as much as the mother of the bride. I was jus' so happy...two of de best peoples I know...joining together in matrimony. Not to mention...now I wouldn't feel so...far from home. 'Cause part of home...was now gonna be here with me."

"That's a lovely story," I said, feeling suddenly guilty at the thought of Lisa returning to find that her uncle hadn't written another word.

"That's why there's two swings out front...I give 'em the one on the gallery as my...wedding present. Then Mister Xavier, he say...put me a rope swing...up in the pecan tree. He used to watch Ya Ya...out the window...playing wit the boys on that swing...and remembering how they met."

His eyes filled with tears. "I miss 'em both, so much..."

I had no comfort for this dying man, no words that I could say to make him feel better.

"At least I'll be seeing 'em soon..." he added, trying to cheer himself up. "They both be waitin' for me at the pearly gates, I jus' bet. They probably got my fishin' pole already done hooked and baited for me!"

He smiled at the thought of it, the happiest I had seen him since we met. But then the smiled faded from his lips and features, as if a shadow was passing over his face.

"What is it?" I asked.

"In heaven...all is revealed," he said simply. "That means they already know...the whole truth...of what I done. I had a good reason." He was quiet for a moment and then added, "But maybe...they won' be waiting at them...pearly gates...after all."

TWELVE

Moody and restless grown, and tried and troubled, his spirit
Could no longer endure the calm of this quiet existence.

As if sensing the urgency of the situation, Willy remembered the pen in his hand. Grabbing the pad without another word, he wrote furiously, pausing every minute or so to rest his hands and close his eyes.

After one particularly long break, I realized that he was asleep. Seizing the opportunity, I stood and peeked at the pad, to see that for all his efforts he had barely made it halfway through the second paragraph.

I was leaning over him like that when the door swung open and his wife strode in.

"What are you doing to him?" she demanded.

"N-nothing," I replied. "He's writing me a note, and I was just looking to see if he was finished."

She came over to grab the pad from his hands before I could stop her.

"Do you speak French?" I asked, my heart pounding, wondering if I should grab it back. After all, if Willy wanted his wife to have this information, he wouldn't have sent her out of the room in the first place.

"Speak it some," she replied. "Don't know how to read or write it, though."

She tossed the pad back onto her husband's chest, which woke him up.

"What's going on?" he slurred, a tight grimace coming over his face at the sight of his wife.

"Time to empty your bag," Deena snapped. "'Less you want it to spill all over the floor."

"It can wait," he told her.

"The kid says it stinks like a bathroom in here. That means it's full."

I was mortified, knowing by "the kid" that she meant my daughter. Quickly, I moved out of the way.

"I'll come back," I said even as Deena was already fooling with the bag of urine that had collected near the floor.

Neither of them replied, so I strode toward the inner door and let myself through, pausing as the door closed behind me so that my eyes could adjust to the dark hallway.

I worked my way down the winding hall in the reverse direction that we had come in, then the sound of laughter drawing me toward the kitchen. There, I found Lisa, Charles, and Tess sitting around the table, enjoying chips, sandwiches, and lemonade.

"Oh, no," Lisa cried when she saw me, bursting into fresh laughter, wiping tears from her eyes. "Did she really go back to dump his bag?"

"Yes. Why? What did Tess say to her?"

"She said, 'That man's room smells like the bathroom in the train station!'"

She and Charles both howled while Tess sat between them looking proud of herself though not quite sure why.

"Tess, that wasn't nice," I said, stifling a smile. "You don't say things like that to people. Where are your manners?"

"Don't fuss at her," Charles scolded me in return. "She was just being honest. Just being a kid."

"I'm sorry to encourage her," Lisa added, again wiping at her eyes. "But I get a quiet satisfaction whenever anybody gets Deena's goat."

Moving to join them, I sat in the fourth chair and joined their conversation. Though I was glad to get to know these people better, I couldn't help wishing Deena would hurry up. Here at the end of Willy's life, we didn't have a minute to spare!

"Boy, it's warm in here," Charles said, sweating even more than the glass of lemonade on the table in front him. He reached around to the suit jacket which hung from the back of his chair and pulled out a folded handkerchief, which he dabbed along his forehead.

"It's a good thing poor Willy has an air conditioner," I said.

Lisa and Charles gave each other pointed looks, and then they obviously decided to share what they were thinking with me.

"Last fall," Lisa said to me, lowering her voice, "Willy was a little more mobile than he is now, but he collapsed on his way to the bathroom. Deena found him unconscious and had to call nine one one to get him to the hospital."

"No, wait," Charles interjected, also in a whisper, holding up a finger to pause her tale, "she called her insurance company first, to make sure the ambulance would be covered. *Then* she called nine one one."

"That's right. Anyway, it was a really hot day. When the EMTs got here, they were appalled at the temperature of Willy's bedroom. Turns out, it was a hundred and ten degrees. He'd passed out from heat stroke."

"Oh, my."

"At the hospital, the doctor was going to report Deena to protective services, but she bargained with him and promised to put in an air conditioner and bring in hospice care. Ever since, Willy insists on keeping that room at about sixty degrees, just out of spite. It makes her nuts, but there's not really anything she can do about it without getting in trouble again."

Lisa and Charles both chuckled conspiratorially, but I merely smiled to be polite. I didn't think the story was funny at all, just sad. Maybe because of the problems in my own marriage, I was feeling particularly sensitive to the cruel games unhappy husbands and wives could play with each other.

Deena finally emerged from the back of the house just as Tess was asking to go back outside. I washed her plate at the sink, thanked them for the food, and then Charles led Tess out the back door to play while Lisa and I returned to Willy's bedside.

As we came back into the room and pulled the door shut, I felt an urgency to the situation again, a desperate need to focus on the task at hand and get some answers. Willy was writing when we got there, so Lisa and I took our seats and waited quietly. He stopped every minute or two to close his eyes and rest, but finally he stopped and held out both pen and paper toward Lisa.

"I give up," he said wearily. "It's too hard...too slow...we gotta go back to speaking instead of writing."

Lisa and I huddled together looking at the papers while she went through and translated it for me line by line. On the bed, Willy closed his eyes, but he was listening intently just the same. Essentially, this part of the oath dealt with our responsibility in choosing the next *gardien* when the time would come that we could no longer serve. Apparently, a *gardien* had to be someone of good character, discrete and trustworthy, who had descended from Colline d'Or. Once chosen, they had to recite this oath "and remember it always."

I took a deep breath and let it out. So not only was I going to have to say this thing in French, I was going to have to memorize it too? I just hoped Willy wouldn't insist on waiting for it to be memorized before he moved on to the next step, which was to tell us exactly what the angelus was and where it was hidden.

"You sure that's not the whole thing, Uncle Willy?" Lisa asked, looking up. "It sounds complete to me."

"No, *Boo*," he replied, shaking his head. "There's more, but we can start with this. You gots to make your oath."

He told us to raise our right hands, but as I did I realized that I wasn't taking this oath thing seriously at all. I was only paying it lip service for his sake, not to mention for the sake of learning more about the symbol on my head. Maybe I'd feel differently once I learned what this was all about, but in my heart I really wasn't going to swear an oath until I knew exactly what it was that we were protecting. As if he could read my mind, Willy hesitated and told us to lower our hands.

"Lisa, *Boo*...you gots to run get something first...from the parlor."

"What?"

"Bring the picture that hangs...over the piano."

"Right now?"

"Yes, but go quick, and be quiet. You don' want Deena to start yellin'."

"Can I come too?" I asked her, jumping up. I would have like'd to stay there with Willy and talk, but suddenly I couldn't resist the opportunity to glimpse the rest of this house.

"Yeah, sure," Lisa replied, opening the door to the hallway to peek out. "Uncle Willy, you hang tight. We'll be right back."

The coast was clear, so she waved me along and together we tiptoed halfway up the hall. She stopped and turned to the right, silently opening a door I hadn't even realized was there. Together we slipped through and shut it behind us, and then I followed her as she moved through the shadows of the front half of the house, weaving from room to room in and among dark lumps of furniture. My heart was pounding in my throat, and I was feeling like a thief in my own home. Finally, Lisa reached her destination and reached for a framed photo hanging on the wall above a sheet-covered piece of furniture, next to a window that had been boarded shut from the inside. Carefully, in the light that peeked from a gap along the bottom of the wood, she pulled the frame from the wall and tucked it under her arm.

"Why would Deena get mad if she knew we were up here?" I whispered as we began to make our way back.

"Nobody's allowed to come up here," Lisa replied. "She says it's so she doesn't ever have to clean, plus she's afraid someone might leave a light on by mistake."

"Makes sense."

Lisa grunted as she bumped into a large chair. She sidestepped it and kept going.

"But I think the truth is she's scared of it. I think she thinks it's haunted."

At that, she held a finger to her lips, and we went the rest of the way in silence. When we reached the hall it was again empty, and we were able to slip through and back to Willy's room, our mission accomplished without being spotted.

He was asleep when we got there, but this time Lisa didn't wait for him to wake up on his own. Instead, she put a hand on his shoulder and gave him a gentle shake.

"What?" he said, pulling out of sleep.

"We have it," she announced. "What's next?"

Willy ran a bony hand over his face, obviously trying to gather his faculties.

"Give it to Miranda."

Lisa handed me the framed photo, and as I took it from her, I was surprised to see that it was an old black-and-white image of a couple standing between two saplings, each young tree not much taller than they were. The picture was very old, the faces blurred but everything else clear, their clothing in the style of the turn of the century.

"That's your great-great-grandparents on the Fairmont side...standing between the Twin Oaks."

I was stunned, the frame suddenly heavy in my hands, as if I was holding the weight of generations. In the background, I could see only a wide, grassy expanse where this house would soon be built.

"It would be three generations before a Saultier...would come to live here," he continued. "But the good Lord He know...what He was doin'. He was preparing the way...the opportunity...the location..."

Willy's voice trailed off and I looked at him, even more confused.

"This oath...she's serious business, Miranda. She is the weight...of all that come before...of all that will come after. You mus' understand that...if nothing else."

I still didn't understand, not at all, but at least somehow I now grasped the gravity of this moment. Without a word, I set down the picture on the table, returned to Willy's bedside, and raised my right hand. After a moment, Lisa moved closer beside me and raised hers as well. Together, we promised to protect the angelus—whatever that was—with our lives, care for it against harm, and hide it from evildoers until we could take one of two steps. In periods of safety, when we could no longer serve, we would choose another guardian for the angelus, a man of good character, discrete, and worthy of confidence, descending from the village of

Colline d'Or. We would pass along the responsibility to him, and in turn, he would have to memorize the oath and swear it as well.

"Perfect," Willy said when we were done.

He opened his eyes and smiled.

"We almost there," he said softly. "Now you jus' have to repeat after me...for the second half."

I didn't press for a translation this time. I just heard the words and said them back to him, assuming that the second half of the oath ran along the same lines the first.

"*En temps de grand...danger,*" he said.

"*En temps de grand danger,*" we repeated.

"*...je serai dans...l'obligation...*"

"*...je serai dans l'obligation...*"

He coughed once then continued.

"*...de reveler...le lieu...*"

"*...de reveler le lieu...*"

"*...où...se...trouve...*" he paused, coughing.

"*...où se trouve...*"

His coughing didn't stop, so finally Lisa broke her position so that she could move behind him and whack him on the back. She was able to get him through it, but the cough started up again as soon as he tried to speak.

"*...où se trouve l'angelus...et...le presenter...à...*"

He couldn't get any more of it out without bursting into a furious coughing spasm. As he had done earlier, he had so much trouble catching his breath that finally Lisa had to reach again for the oxygen mask. I watched as she did so, feeling more confident this time as to the rhythms of his care. Next, his skin would turn from blue back to pink, then he would relax, then his breathing would return to a more normal rhythm, and then he would take a little rest.

At least that's what was supposed to happen.

When she put the mask on his face, however, his skin didn't turn pink at all. Instead, it grew more blue, then a very odd shade of purple. Lisa kept looking at the tank, twisting the dials, checking his vitals. Then all of a sudden she ripped the mask from his face and lunged at his chest, slamming her hands against his diaphragm and pressing with all of her might.

"We need help!" she commanded. "Call an ambulance!"

Stunned, I just stood there, frozen.

Lisa put her hands to Willy's mouth, pressed hers to it and exhaled loudly.

"Miranda! Now!"

At that, I jumped into action, running toward the door.

"Use my cell phone!" Lisa cried, and I looked back to see her gesturing toward the table with her head, counting loudly as she again pressed into Willy's chest.

I threw open the door and yelled for Deena. Then I ran back to Lisa's phone, picked it up, and with trembling hands tried to turn it on. Though it took mere seconds to come to life and prepare itself for dialing, by the time I was able to press in nine one one, it felt as though hours had passed.

"Willy's in trouble!" I told Deena as she came rushing into the room. "I'm calling for an ambulance!"

Rather than heading for her husband, however, Deena ran toward me and ripped the phone from my hand, pressing the button to end my call before the connection even went through.

"No you're not!" she cried. "He's DNR! He's under hospice care!"

She shoved the phone deep into her pocket and only then turned to see the state of her husband. He was a deep bluish purple, as lifeless as if he were made of stone despite the fact that his eyes were wide open. With a guttural yell, she rushed at Lisa and pushed her from her husband's body.

"Leave him alone!" she cried. "He doesn't want this!"

"Yes, he does," Lisa defended angrily. "He wasn't finished. He didn't say all that he had to say."

The two of them argued over Willy's lifeless body, Deena accusing Lisa of being selfish and cruel, Lisa accusing Deena of being cheap, of refusing to call an ambulance just because at this point it wasn't covered by Medicare or insurance. Both women were adamant, both were furious.

Neither seemed to understand that it was a moot point now anyway. Willy was already dead.

From the looks of things, no matter what anybody did, I had a feeling he was going to stay that way.

THIRTEEN

*Sweet was the light of his eyes; but it suddenly sank into darkness,
As when a lamp is blown out by a gust of wind at a casement.*

The next hour passed in a blur of activity and emotion. When Lisa finally saw the situation for what it was and understood that Willy was gone for good, she broke down and sobbed. Deena's grief was more internal than that, though I could tell that for all her blustering and cruelty while he was alive, she was devastated as well now that he was gone.

I couldn't imagine how they must feel. I just tried to stay out of the way, a quiet figure against the wall, as they both said their farewells to the lifeless figure in front of them. Listening to their grief, their sobs and whispers, I thought of Nathan. For a moment I wished I was with him, just holding him, holding on as tightly as I knew how. How cold and final death was! It left no room for second chances.

When I thought I could hear Charles and Tess coming up the hall, I quickly excused myself to catch them before they came into the room. As I stepped into the hot hallway and pulled the door closed behind me, I gave Charles a look so that he knew to turn around and go back the way they had come. When we reached the kitchen, I told him what was going on.

"Willy has, uh, passed," I said, glancing at Tess to make sure she didn't know what I was talking about. "Just about ten minutes ago."

Charles looked surprised. He sat, landing tiredly in the chair.

"Well, that's a shame. Though probably a blessing, considering how sick he was."

"Deena and Lisa are both in there now, saying their goodbyes."

"Was he able to finish telling you everything he wanted to say?"

"No," I replied. "Not at all. We were barely halfway through."

I didn't know much about the way that hospice worked, but I assumed that someone needed to call in and make some sort of arrangements about the body. When I mentioned this to Charles, he nodded and said that he would go to the ladies and help do what needed to be done.

"With Willy gone, I'm not sure what you want to do next, logistically speaking."

"Don't worry about us," I said. "Right now I'd just like to get out of the way. If you can tell me where to find one of those spare vehicles you mentioned, Tess and I will help ourselves to a car and maybe run to town for a while."

I didn't add that what I most wanted to do right now was get to a library where I could look up the Cajun myth of the angelus.

"All right," Charles replied. "I understand. But remember Deena's got a bedroom ready for you here at the house when you want to come back."

Charles went to the door and called out for the driver. He was sitting in the shade of a big tree near the limo, and I felt bad that he'd been stuck outside all this time without air-conditioning—not that coming inside this house would have been all that cooler.

"Emmett, did you pick out a vehicle for the ladies?" Charles said.

"Yes, sir, I sure did. It runs fine, and I got it all cleaned up and waiting over there."

He gestured toward an old blue Buick that was parked along the driveway under a shade tree.

"It's not exactly new," Emmett said to me, "but it was a real nice car in its day. Has all the bells and whistles, power windows, power brakes. I just had to give it a jump start and ride it around a bit. Should be fine now."

"Thank you."

Charles instructed his driver to give us the maps and directions, and then he told me he would be in touch later. Outside, the driver gave me the information I needed to make my way around town. After showing me the maps, he gave me a key ring that was full of keys, which he said were for the car, the house, and every single one of the buildings on the property.

I felt the weight of those keys in my hand, thinking how weird it was to look around and know that I *owned* every single door they opened; in fact, I owned every bit of buildings and land within sight. Incredible, especially for this city girl.

I buckled Tess into the backseat, started up the old car, and drove away, glad to leave behind all of the grief and sadness inside Twin Oaks, at least temporarily. Using the map, I headed back to town and straight to the library, which turned out to be a cute brick building tucked on a shady street near the municipal complex. The place wasn't huge, but it was well organized, with a nice kids' section and a row of Internet-access computers. I got Tess settled with some books on an orange vinyl bean bag chair, and then I signed up at the desk for a library card and logged onto a computer.

For a while I simply gathered information, searching for websites that could tell me more about Cajun myths, Colline d'Or, and, of course, the word "angelus." According to an online encyclopedia, an "angelus" was either a prayer or a church bell. The bell was so named because in many places it was rung three times a day to remind people to say the angelus prayer. That made sense to me. When I searched for "angelus" and "Cajun myth" together, all sorts of hits came up that I could slog through, but in the end none of them seemed relevant to my search.

After forty-five minutes Tess was bored and whiny and ready to go, but I still had found nothing useful at all. I was about to throw in the towel when a woman came in with two children, sent them over to the kids' section, and headed straight for the romance novels. Like a moth to flame, Tess forgot her whining to me and made a beeline toward the little girl and boy, eager to make new friends. My child was nothing if not gregarious.

Heeding the librarian's warning that they would be closing in fifteen minutes, I switched from the Internet to the card catalog and actually had what I hoped was a little luck. In the end, I checked out seven different books on Cajuns, myths, and local lore, hoping that surely I would find something of help inside one of them, something about the Cajun myth of the angelus. Now I just needed to go somewhere quiet and safe where I could pore through these books and find the answers I sought.

I was afraid that I would have trouble prying Tess away from her new friends, but fortunately the mom finished her transaction at the counter and was ready to go when I was. We all walked out together, she and I smiling at each other over the heads of our chattering children.

"Mommy, that girl got her face painted," Tess said, tugging on the hem of my blazer. "It's a butterfly."

"And we had cotton candy," the boy added. "And pony rides."

"Where'd they do all that?" I asked Tess as we headed down the sidewalk.

"At the booty festival," Tess replied.

The mother laughed and corrected her.

"The boo-*dan* festival, honey. B-o-u-d-i-n." To our blank expressions, she added, "Boudin is a sausage. Y'all must not be from Louisiana."

"We're from New York," Tess replied.

"Well, in that case, you should definitely take in the festival. It really is a lot of fun."

Directing her comments to me, she described how to get to the location of the fairgrounds, which were about fifteen miles outside of town. I listened just to be polite, knowing a country fair was the last thing on earth I had time for what was left of this day.

"Mommy, I wanna go ride a pony and get a butterfly on my face!" Tess cried, her plea tinged with a whine.

"I think it runs till nine," the woman added as she unlocked their car. "But if you go, try to get there in time for the fais do do, which is a kind of a Cajun dance. I think that starts at seven."

A Cajun dance.

I thanked her and waved goodbye, thinking who else would be at a Cajun dance but some real, live Cajuns—maybe even one who could tell me the Cajun myth of the angelus? If we went, might we also find someone who recognized the symbol or my drawing of Jimmy Smith, my mystery visitor in New York City?

Feeling a small surge of hope, I buckled Tess into the car, started it up, and then dialed the number for Twin Oaks to see if Lisa might want to go with us to help us ask around. She declined, sounding subdued and sad.

"If you're going to the festival, you'll probably be getting back here kind of late," she added, saying that I should call her when we returned so that she could let us in and show us to our room and get us settled for the night. Though I had a key to the house, I accepted her kind offer anyway, because once we were inside I wouldn't have known where to go.

As we drove out of town, I tried calling Nathan just to check in, but he didn't answer the phone at his office or at home, so I left a message at both places, telling him only that we'd made it to Louisiana and that things were "fine" on this end. With Willy dead and so many questions still unanswered, that wasn't exactly true, but I could give him the details later. Disconnecting the call, I knew I could have tried his cell phone as well, but I had a feeling that he was probably on the job site, and I didn't want to disturb him. Driving down the straight, flat Louisiana road, I thought about tomorrow morning back home and the important event I was going to be missing.

Nathan was a junior architect in a big city firm that had been heavily involved for the last eight or nine months in the creation of a megachurch in Connecticut. Nathan's boss had been in charge of designing the massive multilevel balcony system for the sanctuary, but halfway through the project the man had suffered a heart attack and had had to take a leave of absence from work. Seizing the unexpected opportunity, Nathan had asked the owners of the firm if they would allow him to step up and take charge in his supervisor's stead. Skeptical that one so young and relatively inexperienced could handle such an important job, the owners had nevertheless given him the green light—albeit in a heavily monitored fashion—whereupon Nathan had managed to exceed everyone's expectations.

The church was finished now, the balcony system even more elaborate and impressive than the original design, and word in the industry was that Nathan was a true rising star. Some of his superiors had been surprised by the depths of the skills he had demonstrated when given the opportunity, but not me. A big part of what had attracted me to Nathan when we first met in college was his intelligence, his creativity, and his architectural vision. Someday, I had no doubt, he would have his own firm, and his talents for concept, design, and execution would be legendary.

In any event, tomorrow was the big reveal, the church ribbon-cutting ceremony, and Nathan had been invited to go as representative of the firm and even say a few words to the congregation on their behalf. Though I had been looking forward to being there with him, I couldn't be in two places at once. As I pictured him attending to those final details by himself and preparing to attend the ceremony all alone, I felt a deep sadness envelop my heart. He wanted a wife who was in the cockpit with him, but right now we were both flying solo.

Ignoring the loneliness that rose up inside and began to gnaw at my stomach, I continued to drive toward the festival, the late afternoon sun just dipping below the trees in the magnificent, multicolored Louisiana sky.

FOURTEEN

Gayly the old man sang to the vibrant sound of his fiddle,
Tous les Bourgeois de Chartres, and Le Carillon de Dunkerque,
And anon with his wooden shoes beat time to the music.
Merrily, merrily whirled the wheels of the dizzying dances
Under the orchard-trees and down the path to the meadows;
Old folk and young together, and children mingled among them.

On an ordinary evening, in an ordinary situation, the boudin festival would have been delightful. As it was, the longer we trudged around and flashed the drawing and tried to find out something, anything, the more I just wanted to go home, curl up into a ball, and cry.

Tess tried to be a trouper, but she was at the end of her rope too, cycling through pouts, tantrums, and tears at will. Just to keep her quiet and distracted and moving, I bought her whatever she wanted, every treat, every souvenir. The praline candy with a snowball chaser was not my finest hour as a mom.

Not one person recognized the symbol or the fellow in the drawing or knew the Cajun myth of the bell, though many of them looked at me strangely when I asked. One man patted my shoulder kindly and said that if he spotted the guy in the picture, he'd be happy to snap a coon trap 'round his ankle and keep him there until he paid me every red cent of the child support I was owed. Taking my cue from him, I made that my story whenever Tess wasn't listening, until half of the people on the fairgrounds thought I was a poor, abandoned single mom with a no-account runaway ex-husband. That led to several good-natured passes from eligible men and one short, stout lady to quip, "Honey, husbands usually leave their wives for women who look like you, not the other way around." I wasn't sure whether to take that as a compliment or an insult.

The fact that no one recognized the sketch was only half the problem. Making matters worse was the slow realization that although boudin was a Cajun sausage and a fais do do was a Cajun dance, the place wasn't exactly crawling with Cajuns—at least not from what I could tell. I didn't hear a trace of French spoken, and every booth or display that had the word "Cajun" in it seemed to be using the term merely as a brand or marketing tool, not a description of its vendors. Serving at the counters were mostly all-American teenagers or helmet-haired steel magnolias.

Near the bandstand I finally found a clump of old men speaking a guttural French among themselves, and when I asked if by any chance they were Cajun, one gentleman, the accordian player, acknowledged that yes, they were indeed. Excited, I tried to strike up a conversation, but his answers were mostly monosyllabic, and none of the others would even look me in the eye—not even when I said I was a transplanted Cajun myself, descended from the Saultier line.

They hardly glanced at my drawing. Ignoring me, they began tuning up their instruments, getting ready to play for the dance, so finally I decided they were distracted and busy with that and not in a position to have a conversation with a stranger. I told them to break a leg and walked away, rejected by my own kind. Only when their music began a few minutes later was I able to shrug off my hurt. Their zydeco beat was infectious, the strange combination of washboard, accordion, and fiddle positively electrifying. I stood and listened, wondering if the music was tapping into something deep in my soul handed down through the generations. But then I looked around at the crowd and realized that everyone else had the same stupid smile on their face that I did. It was the music itself, the universal language of a delightful art form, regardless of heritage.

The songs lightened our step for a while as we continued to make our way around the fairgrounds, the moon rising on this hot sticky night. Eventually weariness once again overcame us. When Tess and I finally reached the face painting booth, I told her that it would be our last stop and then we could leave. I was exhausted and frustrated, so while Tess got in line to get a butterfly on her cheek, I sat at a picnic table nearby and just let my eyes scan the crowd, wishing I had some way to look into everyone's mind and find that one person who might give me the answers I was looking for.

It wasn't a regular habit, but I was very near praying for help when my eyes landed on a booth just ten feet away. It was a nice display, professionally designed, with an elaborate header advertising the Louisiana Museum of Art and Culture. Two women were manning the booth, both of them in their forties and, judging by their elegant clothes and jewelry, obviously moneyed. Keeping one eye on Tess, I went to the counter where they were giving away free literature and struck up a conversation, asking if their museum had any information about Cajun myths.

They were both very nice, saying that yes, there were indeed several resources at the museum that I might find helpful. Unfortunately, it wouldn't be open on Sunday, but I could come and take a look first thing Monday. I asked how I would get to the museum driving from Serein Highway in Oak Knoll.

"Is that where you live?" one of them asked, her head snapping up.

"Um, well, my family home is there."

"Get out of town," she cried with a smile. "That makes us neighbors."

It didn't take long to figure out that not only were we neighbors, but her house was next door to Twin Oaks. Once that connection was made, I received the distinct impression that I had just earned a best friend for life—whether I wanted one or not.

"Honey, you gotta take over here," she said to her coworker. "This lady and I are going to the food court to have ourselves a cup of coffee and a long chat."

"Actually," I said, "my daughter's in line to get her face painted."

I pointed out Tess, and the lady gave her a wave and squealed at "such a lovely, lovely child."

"I'm not surprised she's such a beauty," she added with sheer Southern flattery as she extricated herself from the booth. "Her mama's pretty enough to be a model."

The woman suggested we sit at the picnic table instead, and she brought along two bottles of waters from her booth. As we got comfortable, she introduced herself as Olivia West Kroft.

"You can call me Livvy," she added.

"I'm Miranda. It's a pleasure to meet you."

Conversation flowed easily, though I was disappointed to learn that Livvy hadn't known my family. She was from Vicksburg, Mississippi, and had only lived on Serein for two years. She called her husband Big Daddy and said that he had swept her off her feet and brought her down here to live at his estate, "Little Tara." She now had two stepdaughters, Melanie and Scarlett, which right there kind of told me everything I needed to know about life with Big Daddy.

As she talked I realized that in a way this woman was a caricature of a wealthy Southerner, from the immoveable, perfectly frosted hair to the tiny magnolia blossoms that had been hand painted onto the tips of each of her fingernails. Still, there was something likeable about her. From her precisely tailored appearance, I would have expected her to be uptight, but instead she was relaxed and gossipy and dangerously funny.

As Tess finally reached the front of the line and her face painting began, I steered my conversation with Livvy to where I wanted it to go by saying that I was hoping to do some genealogy research while I was in town, particularly on the Cajun line that had come down through my grandmother.

"The whole reason we came to this festival tonight was to meet some real Cajuns," I said, "but there don't seem to be very many around."

"No, I guess not," she replied. "Cajun country is at least two parishes west of here—and a few more than that to get to the heart of it."

"I thought Cajuns were everywhere in Louisiana."

"Well, sort of, but you'd have to look at a map to understand. There are about nine parishes that are densely Cajun. Once you get outside of those, they're more scattered. We have a few Cajun scholars who do research at the library, but that's about it."

"That's a shame," I said, my heart sinking. My bright idea for getting some Cajuns to tell me the myth of the angelus was going to be more trouble than I thought. "I tried talking to the guys in the band, but they weren't very friendly."

"Cajuns never are."

I looked at her wide eyed over the bottle as I took a sip of water.

"I mean, you'll never meet a more decent, hardworking group of people," she added, seeing the surprise in my face, "but they don't let outsiders in easily. It's a whole mentality, you understand. The way it has been explained to me, Cajuns usually judge folks by their character, not by appearances or social graces or wealth or prestige. Once they see your character, once they understand you're a good person, then you're in. When that happens, you'll find them to be very warm and welcoming. It's just not an instant process."

"Even if they know I'm part Cajun myself?"

She shrugged.

"It's less about the blood pumping through your heart, hon, than it is about how that heart leads you to conduct yourself toward others."

"I see," I said softly, understanding now why I had been rejected by the band; it was nothing personal, just a cultural thing.

Still, this news made my search even more difficult, considering that I needed to get into a Cajun "inner circle" as soon as possible, to find out about the myth. I said as much to Livvy, and she suggested that I go the friend-of-a-friend route.

"We've got a couple of Cajun families in our church," she said. "I'd be happy to introduce you. They'd probably be glad to help you with your genealogical research."

"That would be great," I told her, watching from the corner of my eye as Tess wiggled impatiently, getting the last finishing touches on her facial art.

"In fact," Livvy added, "we could probably get them to do lunch tomorrow. Where are you going to church?"

Not *are* you going to church but *where* are you going to church. So Southern. Stifling a smile, I hedged a bit, saying I wasn't sure yet.

"Oh, honey, then why don't you come with us to ours? I'll round up a group afterward, and we can all go out to eat at the Firelighter. You can pick their brains to your heart's content."

"Do you think your Cajun friends will come along?"

"Are you kidding?" she laughed. "No self-respecting Cajun would ever turn down a good meal and good company. They'll be there, for sure."

Sitting through a boring church service seemed a small price to pay for the right conversation. I agreed to go but declined on her offer for a ride and wrote down the directions instead.

Tess came running up to us just as I finished, a bright blue-and-purple butterfly shining from her cheek. I introduced Tess to Livvy, who seemed utterly captivated by my adorable child. Excited by the face painting, Tess forgot to be cranky for a few minutes, so I decided to seize the opportunity and get out of there before she ruined a good first impression.

I reached out to shake Livvy's hand as we parted, but she merely pushed my hand aside and swept me into a hug instead.

"Oh, Miranda, I'm just so tickled to meet you. You have no idea," she said in her charming Southern drawl. I wasn't sure whether she really meant it, but her words certainly sounded sincere.

Our visit made a nice end to a rotten evening, so much so that by the time Tess and I joined the stream of people moving toward the parking lot, I realized I was smiling. There was something to be said for a warm welcome from a stranger—especially when that stranger quickly became a friend.

The smile faded from my lips as I remembered other strangers who had recently come into my life: the man who had invaded my home and my work, the thugs who had mugged me in the alley. Looking nervously around, I pulled Tess close and began to move faster.

When we were almost to the car, I felt a hand at my elbow, but when I spun around, ready to strike, I realized that it was the accordion player from the Cajun band. He was leaning close as if to whisper something in my ear.

"That symbol you been showing around?" he said in a low, raspy voice. "All them questions you got? I wouldn't do that no more if I was you. It ain't safe."

"But I need answers," I said in return.

"Let the wicked fall into their own nets," he said cryptically. Then, just as quickly as he had appeared behind me, he disappeared again into the crowd. Feeling chilled despite the warm night air, I gripped Tess's hand tightly in mine and jogged the last few steps to the car. My heart didn't stop racing until we were buckled in and on the road.

Let the wicked fall into their own nets?

What did that mean? Was that man a friend, trying to help me? Or an enemy, attempting to throw me off course?

I didn't know, but all the way back to Oak Knoll I kept a diligent eye on the road behind us, my white knuckles gripped around the steering wheel like a vise. In the backseat, Tess was awake but too tired to talk, the butterfly resting motionless on her cheek.

FIFTEEN

...at times a feeling of sadness
Passed o'er her soul, as the sailing shade of clouds in the moonlight
Flitted across the floor and darkened the room for a moment.
And as she gazed from the window she saw serenely the moon pass,
Forth from the folds of a cloud, and one star follow her footsteps.

After making a number of detours to make sure we weren't being followed, I turned finally from the empty road onto the long driveway of Twin Oaks. It was nearly ten p.m. and I felt terrible about showing up here so late, especially after such a difficult day. I dialed the cell phone number Lisa had given me, and though it sounded as though I had roused her from sleep, she said she'd be at the door waiting.

True to her word, Lisa was there tying the belt on her robe. She ushered us inside, locked the door behind us, and showed us to the bedroom that was to be ours while we were here. It was down a hall to the left of the kitchen, next to Deena's room, and through the walls I could hear the vague rumble of the older woman's snores. Our suitcases were already there, waiting on the floor between twin beds. The room itself was so cramped and small that there was barely enough space to move around, but it would do, at least for tonight.

"Hey, it's not so hot in here," I whispered suddenly, realizing that cold air was pouring down from a vent on the ceiling.

"Charles put his foot down and made Deena turn on the central air 'cause you're here," Lisa whispered in return, rolling her eyes. "They had a big fight about it until he promised her that he would prorate the gas bill so she wouldn't have to pay for it."

Lisa led us next back up the hall and past the kitchen, to point out the bathroom we should use. She offered to make us a late night snack, but I declined and thanked her for her help.

"See you in the morning, then," she said, and with that she padded off toward her bedroom in the opposite direction.

Leading the exhausted Tess back to our tiny bedroom, I unpacked our nightgowns and toothbrushes and helped her get ready for bed as quickly as possible. After I had tucked her in, I dimmed the lights and headed quietly down the hall to the bathroom where I took a long, hot shower. Tess also needed a bath, but she could take one in the morning.

The pounding water felt wonderful on the back of my neck and head, working out the kinks of this difficult day, smoothing out the aching roots of hair that had been twisted up since morning.

Despite the urge to linger in the hot steam, I finally finished my shower, toweled off, and put on my nightgown. When I got back to our bedroom, I was surprised to see that Tess was still awake, so overwhelmed by her own exhaustion that she couldn't go to sleep. Afraid her whining might wake up Deena, I spoke to her in soothing tones as I unwrapped the towel from my head and rubbed it around on my hair, careful not to reveal the bald patch in the back. Finished, I hung the towel on a nearby chair and quickly ran a comb through my hair.

"Do you remember how we put you to bed when you were just a baby?" I whispered to Tess, knowing that at the tender age of five she already loved stories about her own youth.

"How?" she asked, a tiny pout tugging at her bottom lip.

"Come here. I'll show you."

With a grunt, I reached down, scooped her up, and put her on my hip. I carried her over to the window, explaining softly that when she was little we used to go all over the apartment and tell different things good night. Here in our tiny room, I reached up and parted the curtains, revealing the moon-splashed lawn outside.

"Good night, moon," I said in a singsongy voice. "See you in the morning."

"See you in the morning," my child echoed.

I let the curtain fall closed and walked several steps to the door.

"Good night, doorknob," I whispered. "See you in the morning."

"See you in the morning," Tess added.

I glanced down to see that her eyelids were drooping.

Together, we went around the small room and said good night to the mirror and the lamp and suitcases, slowly calming her toward sleep. By the time we had worked our way back to the bed, her little head was resting against my shoulder. There in the darkness, I just stood there and rocked back and forth for a moment, thinking that sometimes I loved my child so much it hurt inside, like a knife pressing into my ribs.

Leaning awkwardly, I pulled back the covers and laid Tess on the bed. She climbed down and snuggled in as I tucked the sheets around her. I sat on the bed beside her, smoothing the hair from her forehead as she closed her eyes.

"Mommy?" she whispered.

"Yes, baby?"

"Is there a dragon behind the wall?"

I stifled a laugh.

"No, that's just somebody snoring."

"Okay."

Tess didn't speak again, and soon I realized that she was asleep, her breathing even and soft. I sat there for a long time, just watching her little chest rise and fall with each breath.

My baby's cheeks were rosy, her lips almost puckered, and there in the soft glow of the lamp she looked like a tiny china doll. There was so much of blond-haired, blue-eyed Nathan in Tess's features that sometimes I forgot to look for myself in there too. Here in the region of my birth, I couldn't help but wonder not just how much of me was in my child, but how much of my mother, my grandmother? If Tess did have the slope of their chin or a similar wave in her hair, how would I even know? I wouldn't, for I couldn't recall either woman and had never seen any pictures. AJ always said it was better not to look back.

Tess let out a heavy sigh, and I again reached up and gently touched her hair, twining one soft little curl around my finger. I was filled with a surge of love, deep and strong, the kind of love that filled me up and made me more than whole.

Then, in a flash, my mind filled with the image of Willy Pedreaux, dead in his bed, a scrawny lump under white sheets.

With a gasp, I released Tess' curl and pulled back my hand, throat-clinching fear engulfing the love I had felt just the moment before.

I closed my eyes, a surge of dread rising up from deep inside. It wasn't the pulse-pounding, shaking-sweating panic I'd felt on the airplane, but a different sensation entirely, an old, familiar, and disturbing ripple of fear that ran from heart to stomach and back again. I became nauseous with the resurgence of my most deep and secret shame: The truth was that I had spent much of Tess's lifetime preparing myself for the impending inevitability of her death.

Since the day I first learned I was pregnant five years before, I had been plagued with the horrible, persistent conviction that one day my child was going die, maybe even before she was born. I couldn't explain it—I had never told anyone about it—but even after an easy delivery and healthy birth, the fear persisted. Those first few months, I would stand beside her crib for hours, terrified that at any moment she might stop breathing. When she survived infancy and became a toddler, I just knew she would toddle off a ledge one day or fall down a flight of stairs.

By the time she started preschool, I was convinced that the school would be bombed or that a kidnapper or murderer would steal her away when the teacher wasn't looking. Of course, I got through the days by reminding myself that I was being overprotective and irrational, that nothing bad had happened to her thus far, which was good proof that probably nothing ever would. Still, logic was weak compared to the strength of my conviction. I suspected that losing my mother at a young age had gone a long way in creating this fear in me. Despite plenty of evidence to the contrary, the knowledge that Tess could die at any time never completely left my mind.

Even now, as I sat here in this tender moment, rather than relish the precious treasure I had been given, all I could think of was death, of an old man whose lungs filled with a fluid that could not be expelled, whose yellow eyes solidified into twin marbles of nothingness as I stood nearby and watched.

Swallowing hard, I moved to my own bed and got between the sheets, my hand shaking so badly when I went to turn off the light that I knocked something on the floor. Glancing down, I saw that it was a book, a black leather-bound Bible. I leaned down and picked it up, put it in a drawer, and then turned off the lamp.

In the dark, I listened to Deena's snores and the whisper of the air conditioner and the creaks and moans of the old house, and I thought about death and life and my little girl.

"Good night, my baby," I whispered out loud, hoping the sound of my own voice would comfort me. "See you in the morning."

I closed my eyes, overwhelmed with exhaustion, knowing with certainty that truly loving someone required not just selflessness and generosity—two things I could handle much of the time—but also bravery. Loving someone without fear overwhelming that love was an act of immeasurable bravery.

And that kind of bravery was something I had in very short supply—for my child, my husband, or even for myself.

SIXTEEN

And through the night were heard the mysterious sounds of the desert,
Far off, indistinct, as of wave or wind in the forest,
Mixed with the whoop of the crane and the roar of the grim alligator.

"Ooo, Mommy's in big trouble."

I awoke to the sound of Tess's voice. Opening my eyes, I rolled over to see her standing there between the beds, pointing at my head. The room was still dark, but the moon glowed through the sheer curtains, casting a triangle of light across my face.

"Mommy, you let somebody draw a picture on your head," Tess announced, her eyes wide. "In permanent marker! And you cut off your hair!"

Rubbing my eyes, I propped up on one elbow, mad at myself for not thinking to put my hair in a ponytail before I went to sleep.

"I know," I whispered. "Grandma Janet and I were just playing around, trying something new. But it doesn't look very good, and now I'm sorry we did it."

"Grandma Janet says you're not supposed to draw on people or walls, only paper," she said, the words sounding as if they were coming straight from AJ's mouth.

"That's true. It was a dumb thing to do."

Tess reached up and gently pushed my face away so that she could take a closer look.

"What's it a picture of, Mommy?"

"Keep your voice down, honey. It's just a doodle," I told her, trying to act nonchalant. I thought about adding that it was a secret, our little secret. But then I was afraid that might give it too much importance, turning the whole thing into big news, which to Tess was almost as much fun as big trouble. "I'm embarrassed about it," I said instead, "so I think I'll keep it covered with my hair until it wears off."

"Good idea. It looks weird."

Grabbing my watch from the bedside table, I saw that it was a little after five a.m.

"Tess, we have to go back to sleep. It's too early to get up yet."

"I know, Mommy," she replied, smoothing down my hair so that it would cover the tattoo. "But I got scared. Can I get in your bed with you?"

"Um, sure," I said, though there wasn't much room in the narrow twin. I wasn't in the mood for a few sharp kicks to the kidneys—par for the course when sharing a bed with Tess—but I didn't want her to be frightened. I helped her climb over me so that she was wedged between me and the wall.

"There *is* a dragon in the other room," she whispered. "Don't you hear it?"

I explained the cause of snoring and told her that the rhythm of the breathing proved it was a person and not a dragon. That did much to allay Tess's fears, and soon she was sound asleep by my side.

I, on the other hand, tossed and turned for more than half a hour. Though my body was weary, my brain was firing on all pistons, jumping from thoughts of Willy to Nathan to Twin Oaks to my work back home to the symbol tattooed into my scalp. Finally, I decided that I might as well give up on the idea of sleep altogether. It simply wasn't going to happen.

Surrendering to the inevitable, I swung my legs over the side of the bed and sat up, focusing on the small pile of library books I had brought in from the car last night. At least I could get some reading and research done while Tess slept, especially since we wouldn't need to start getting ready for church with my new friend Livvy for several more hours.

First, however, I freshened up in the bathroom and then made coffee in the kitchen, hoping the delicious smell and soft crackling sound of the coffeemaker wouldn't wake anyone else in the house. Back in our bedroom, I made myself comfortable on the bed that had been Tess's, parting the curtains just enough to let in a little early morning light. I stacked the books in a pile next to me, intending to go through them one by one, hoping that I might uncover the myth of the bell or at least find the location of Colline d'Or.

The first book I grabbed was a history of the Cajun people, and though I had intended just to skim quickly through, I was soon drawn into the narrative, spellbound by the facts surrounding *Le Grand Dérangement*, or the Great Expulsion, as it was known—which seemed to be the pivotal event in the history of the Cajuns.

Their story began in an area of Nova Scotia known as Acadia. In the year 1755, the book said, French settlers there were given a difficult choice: swear an oath of allegiance to the British crown or risk expulsion. Up to that point, the Acadians had always focused on farming, trade, and community, remaining as neutral as possible toward the various outside powers that came and went. They refused to take the oath, and as a result they were forcibly detained and then deported in what became the largest ever forced migration of whites in North America. Though many of the Acadian refugees managed to escape to Quebec and other surrounding areas, over the next few months more than 10,000 of them were expelled from the region and shipped off to unreceptive American colonies or to Europe, placed in prison camps there, or simply left on the docks to fend for themselves or die.

I took a sip of coffee and continued to read, moved by their tales of suffering and misery, of starvation and sickness and death. By the end of the Seven Years' War, half had died, and of those that were left, the Acadians were truly a people without a home. Throughout Europe and the American colonies, the Acadian refugees were never really welcomed or accepted anywhere they went—until they made their way to Louisiana. There, the Acadians were greeted with open arms and given tools and land west of the Mississippi, compliments of the ruling Spanish government, who hoped these hardworking people would establish new settlements in the marshes and prairies there. During the next twenty years, more than 3000 exiled Acadians made their way to Louisiana, where families and communities were reunited and allowed to flourish as they learned a whole new way of farming and building and living. Over time, the Acadians became simply "Cajuns," a people known for their hard work and even harder play. I was amazed to read that from those 3000 original Acadians who settled in Louisiana, more than 500,000 had descended! It brought tears to my eyes when I thought about the fact that I was one of the 500,000.

Tess was stirring in the bed, so I forced myself to skim through their more modern history, the ups and downs of an American people group with their own language, music, food, and folklore. It was the folklore that I was most interested in, so I put down the history book and flipped through the other resources, particularly a collection of Cajun folktales. In that entire book, I could find only one story that had anything to do with a bell, a silly yarn about a man who snored so loudly that the ladies in town thought he was the church bell, so they got up, dressed, and went to mass in the middle of the night.

Frustrated, I tossed that book onto the heap and reached for the next one. It was an atlas, and I pored over it in search of a place known as Colline d'Or. I couldn't find any such town in Louisiana, so I also checked Nova Scotia, Britain, and France, all to no avail. As far as I could tell, either Colline d'Or did not exist or it was so small that it hadn't earned a spot on any map.

Tess began to wake up, so I put the atlas away and grabbed the last book, a collection of literature that included the well-know epic poem "Evangeline," by Henry Wadsworth Longfellow. I was skimming through, trying to remember if I had studied the story in college, when the word "angelus" popped out at me. I stopped and reread the stanza, a lovely description of the Nova Scotian town of Grand Pré, just prior to the expulsion:

Softly the Angelus sounded, and over the roofs of the village
Columns of pale blue smoke, like clouds of incense ascending,
Rose from a hundred hearths, the homes of peace and contentment.

My pulse quickened. It might be a long shot, I thought, but perhaps this was the myth of the angelus. Tess sat up and began chatting, but I ignored her, instead continuing to read the sad tale of two lovers, Evangeline and Gabriel, who were separated when British soldiers took Gabriel and the other young men of the village away. In the poem, Evangeline spent most of her life trying to find her true love again. By the end, she had finally tracked him to a Philadelphia poorhouse where he lay dying, and the lovers were tearfully reunited just before he passed away.

I closed the book and put it down, doubting that this story had anything to do with Willy's cryptic words about the myth of the bell. The word "angelus" had appeared in the fictional poem only three times—and hadn't figured into the plot at all. I realized I was grasping at straws. Perhaps talking to Livvy's Cajun friends would help me out after all, because these books, while quite interesting, still hadn't been able to answer any of my biggest questions.

I pushed all of the books aside, realizing that Tess was awake now and talking almost nonstop in an attempt to get my attention. I took her to the bathroom, filled the tub, and left her there with a few toys. Leaving the bathroom door open so that I could hear her playful chatter, I padded down to the kitchen, where Deena was just sitting at the breakfast table, reading the newspaper. After sawing wood all night long, she didn't look very rested, though the puffiness around her eyes could have been a result of crying rather than exhaustion.

She sounded very matter-of-fact as she described the removal of her husband's body yesterday afternoon and the fact that she would be going down to the funeral home this afternoon to finalize plans for the viewing and funeral.

"Otherwise," she added, "I'm just trying to pack up and move out of here as fast as I can. I know you're waitin'."

"Waiting?"

"For me to leave. It's your house now."

I took a deep breath, wondering if this bitter woman had ever experienced a kindness in her life. I would feel more relaxed once she was gone, but I wasn't about to rush her off at such a painful time.

"Deena, you don't have to hurry on my account. Please, stay as long as it takes. Really."

She seemed suspicious of my generosity, but she finally agreed to take me up on it as long as I would let her do the cooking for all of us while we were here.

"That's very kind of you," I said, "but Tess is leaving this afternoon, and I'm not sure how much longer I'll be able to stay, either."

I hadn't let myself think about that, about the husband and the job that awaited me back home, about the life I could easily return to now that Willy was dead. Except for the missing hair, which would grow back eventually, nothing had really changed. Had it?

Of course it had.

Heading up the hall to check on Tess, I had to admit to myself that everything had changed. It had changed with the appearance of Jimmy Smith in the doorway of my office, with the attack in the alley, with my flight to Louisiana, with the limited information Willy had given me, with the oath I had taken, with the man at the fair last night, with my return to this family home that was now mine.

With a surge of determination, I decided that I wasn't leaving here until I found the answers I sought and had set things right again.

SEVENTEEN

So passed the morning away. And lo! with a summons sonorous
Sounded the bell from its tower, and over the meadows a drum beat.

An hour and a half later, with Tess in her nicest dress and me in white slacks and a light blue silk shirt, I found the church in town, a big white structure with inlaid stained glass panels along the sides and what looked like an education center out back. Before leaving the car I stuffed my purse with crayons and paper, hoping I would be able to keep Tess quiet for a full hour. Once we got inside, however, we found Livvy waiting for us in the vestibule and learned that she had arranged for Tess to join the five-year-old class. That sounded good to me. Surely she would enjoy hanging out with a group of kids much more than sitting still next to me in the service, trying to behave.

We got her settled in her classroom and proceeded to the sanctuary, Livvy apologizing that her husband couldn't join us because he was away on business. She did introduce me to her stepdaughters, Melanie and Scarlett, who smiled at me shyly and then excused themselves to sit with the other teens.

As Livvy and I walked in and chose a pew, I thought how funny it was that Nathan was also in a church this morning for his ribbon-cutting ceremony. Except for weddings and funerals, we hadn't been in a church in years, and now here we were both in one at the same time, albeit a thousand miles apart. Like Nathan, I believed there was a God; I just didn't see why it was necessary to go to a church to find Him if He was supposedly everywhere.

Waiting for the service to begin, I leaned over and asked Livvy if she had ever heard the expression, "Let the wicked fall into their own nets," thinking of the words the old Cajun man had told me at the festival last night. Livvy nodded, but rather than telling me what it meant, she simply picked up her Bible and started flipping through the pages. With a flush of heat to my face, I got the point: This was church time, not chatting time, and I needed to shut up.

The service began with a few songs followed by announcements. I didn't pay much attention until a woman about my age got up and put in a plug for their young mother's group. As she talked about their summer picnic, play dates, mom's night out, and more, I found myself feeling isolated and even kind of lonely. How I wished there was something like that near us in Manhattan. Probably there was, but I just hadn't taken the time to find it. I should look into it, I thought, certain that I could learn to be a better mother if I had friends who were also mothers. Our lives were so busy and our schedules so packed that except for AJ our social circle consisted mostly of professional acquaintances, workout partners, and occasional friendly conversations in the elevator with neighbors.

When the woman went to sit down, Livvy slid her Bible onto my lap, her finger pointing to a passage.

"Here it is," she whispered, and with another flush of heat I realized that she hadn't been ignoring me. She'd been flipping through her Bible for the answer to my question.

Bending my head, I read the words on the page, which had the heading "Psalm 141." The passage was a prayer, and it ended with those words: "Let the wicked fall into their own nets."

The next fifteen minutes of the service were lost on me as I sat there and read and reread the passage, trying to decipher the words. From what I could tell, it was a prayer for protection against bad people, describing what fate awaited them:

...my prayer is ever against the deeds of evildoers;
their rulers will be thrown down from the cliffs,
and the wicked will learn that my words were well spoken.
They will say, "As one plows and breaks up the earth,
so our bones have been scattered at the mouth of the grave."
But my eyes are fixed on you, O Sovereign Lord;
in you I take refuge—do not give me over to death.
Keep me from the snares they have laid for me,
from the traps set by evildoers.
Let the wicked fall into their own nets,
while I pass by in safety.

Last night, had it been the man's intention to let me know that God had my back, so to speak? Or was he being more literal, trying to pass along some sort of clue about the information I sought? If that were the case, then I would have to look everywhere from cliffs to graves to snares in my search to find the angelus, whatever it was. A clue this vague really didn't help at all.

Feeling disappointed, I decided to let the words roll around in my subconscious mind for a while, thinking maybe there was something here that I was missing. The choir was just finishing a lovely, inspiring number, and I forced myself to focus on that instead.

Following the song was a sermon, an interesting twenty minutes or so about brotherly love. I wasn't paying a whole lot of attention until the preacher began to talk about the Lord's plan for fellowship, companionship, and even marriage. In almost a direct echo of Nathan's recent words to me, the preacher said that God did not want us to go through life alone but to join with others in our walk, learning to give and to receive in kind.

"'Though one may be overpowered,'" the preacher said, "'two can defend themselves.' And three? Well, folks, 'a cord of three strands is not quickly broken.'"

I thought that was a lovely way for him to put it, especially when he explained that that third strand was supposed to be God. As the man moved on to his conclusion, I wondered if maybe that was the missing element in my troubled marriage, that third strand that right now wasn't intertwined in our rope at all. If Nathan and I chose to "invite God" into our union, whatever that meant exactly, would we be bound more tightly? Would we finally be able to connect on the level that Nathan desired? I didn't know, but it was an interesting train of thought, one I hoped to come back to later.

By the time church was over and Livvy had finished rounding up a group to go to lunch, I was starving. I took my own car to the restaurant and listened to Tess talk nonstop about her Sunday school class the entire way. Not surprisingly, she had loved every minute of it and was now the proud owner of a lion's den made out of macaroni noodles. At the wheel, I was mostly consumed again with thoughts of Psalm 141 and the hidden message I simply knew it must contain.

True to her word, Livvy had found two Cajun families to join us for lunch. I forgot most of their names after the introductions, but it didn't seem to matter. Mostly, they referred to each other—and to me and Tess, for that matter—as Boo or Cher or Ton Ton. One of the teenagers was named Ya Ya, and when I said that that had been my grandmother's name, I was informed that Ya Ya was common for any name that ended in an "a." Hence, my grandmother Portia had become Ya Ya.

The meal was delicious, Louisiana seafood prepared to perfection. Even Tess enjoyed the shrimp and fish—two things I could never convince her to eat at home. Once I felt comfortable with the group, I broached the topics I had come there for, starting with the question of whether anyone was familiar with a placed called Colline d'Or. None of them had ever heard of it, at least not in Louisiana. One guy said that Colline d'Or translated to "Hills of Gold"—though apparently the only hills of any real significance around here were the man-made rises at highway overpasses. Perhaps there were hills in Nova Scotia, I thought, deciding that I would get a different, more detailed map and try there again.

Next, I brought up the subject of Cajun myths. One by one, they each launched into their favorite *chucotement du bayou,* though when I asked if there was one about an angelus or a bell, no one could recall what it might be. Tess enjoyed the story of *Le Pont du Nez Piqué,* about a massive bridge that turned out not to be a bridge at all but the back of a gigantic alligator who would rest during the day but get up and roam the countryside at night. She laughed in delight as the man next to her told the tale, though I had to wonder if she would ever look at any bridge the same way again. Given my warning at the festival, I decided to hold back on showing the drawings I had made. I also didn't want to arouse Livvy's suspicions. She still thought I was simply asking all of these questions for the sake of genealogical research.

Though I received no hard answers while there, about the best thing to come of the meal was a better understanding of the complexities of the Cajun mystique. Everyone at the table agreed that most people's stereotypical idea of a "Cajun" was far too simplistic. Many Cajuns did live as trappers and shrimpers in rural carefree poverty, they said, but many also became scholars, poets, and well-paid professionals. Many Cajuns kept to themselves and spent their free time drinking and dancing, giving no thought to what the rest of the world thought of them, but others lived mainstreamed lives and worked hard to change the perception of a vastly unappreciated and underserved people group. They said that despite the differences, most Cajuns were extremely secure in their ethnicity, proud of their heritage, and filled with an uncommon zest for life. The more they talked, the more I began to feel something stirring inside my own heart, a sense of pride for that part of myself that I had never given much thought, my Cajun blood.

I asked if there was any history of tattooing among the Cajun people, but they just looked at me quizzically and said no more so than in the general public.

By the time the check came, my head was spinning from all I had learned. Grateful for their input, I insisted on picking up the tab. When they tried to fight me for it, Livvy just laughed and told them to let me have it, that I was an heiress now and could well afford a meal out. I smiled as I looked over the bill, thinking that the total cost for the entire group was less than dinner for four at the Plaza.

"I may be an heiress," I said to Livvy as I handed the waitress the check along with my credit card, "but I'm afraid the house I've inherited needs more work than I can afford."

"You should talk to my brother Aaron," she replied. "He's a carpenter and general fix-it man, and he's staying with us for the summer. His rates are very reasonable."

"Oh, do, Miranda," one of the others added. "Aaron's great. He really knows his way around construction."

That sounded like a good idea, even if he just came over to give me an estimate of some of the more urgent repairs. I probably wouldn't start on anything yet, but if we were eventually going to put the house on the market, there was certainly some work to be done first, however we ended up paying for it.

Outside, Tess and I said our goodbyes and thank-yous to everyone except Livvy, who walked us to the car. On the way, she asked more about our life in New York and my work there. When she learned that I was an art restoration expert, she became very excited, saying she had some paintings that had been damaged in Katrina that she'd love to hear my opinion on. I wanted to take a pass, but considering how kind she had been to set up this lunch for me, I felt obligated and agreed to take a look if I had time while I was in town.

"I'll bring a couple of them over to Twin Oaks tonight," she persisted, and for a moment I thought of Jimmy Smith and his insistence that I look at his stupid painting as well. *Wouldn't it be bizarre,* I thought, *if Livvy's artwork also had the symbol painted into it?*

At least she seemed to know a bit about art and the restoration process. As she talked, I got the feeling that she had seen her share of masterpieces, particularly in her work with museums. It was fun to talk with someone who knew the trade. By the time we reached the car, gave some air kisses, and parted ways, I realized I was again smiling, just as I had last night. It had been a long time since I had made a new friend.

Steering the Buick out of town, I drove along Serein Highway and slowed as we neared Twin Oaks, once again savoring the grandeur of the iron-and-stone entryway. I turned onto the driveway and proceeded up and around the bend, to where the house and grounds suddenly came into view past the stand of trees. What a sight! I could only imagine how my grandmother must have felt when she saw it for the first time, the beautiful, backwoods Cajun girl coming here to meet her fiance's wealthy family. She must have been terribly intimidated.

I parked around back, in the shade of a tree, and as we got out of the car I noticed Lisa out in the yard, ahead and to the right, walking toward a small gardening shed and then stepping inside. We strolled over to join her, reaching the building just as she emerged from the doorway with a shovel in her hand. She jumped when she saw us.

"Sorry, we didn't mean to startle you."

"That's okay," she replied, running a hand across her sweating brow. "What's up?"

She was wearing a T-shirt and shorts, both smeared with dirt, and in her other hand she held a bottle of water. Strewn on the grass nearby were several more water bottles, all empty, and a smattering of lawn tools.

"Are you digging a hole?" Tess asked, pointing to the shovel.

"Nope, just doing a little gardening," Lisa replied. Then to me she added, "Working the dirt is how I handle grief and stress."

Being a city girl, I didn't know much about gardening, but it seemed an odd choice for the hottest part of the day.

"Come on around the back of the canning shed. I'll show you."

Rather than leading us to the area in the yard that had obviously at one point been the formal gardens, she simply led us around behind another outbuilding where the earth had been turned over in preparation to receive a flat of flowers that sat waiting nearby.

"Willy always meant to plant something here," Lisa explained, "so I figured I'd put in some impatiens in his honor."

"That's nice," I said, remembering how hard Lisa had worked to keep Willy alive, not to mention how deep her sobs had been once she realized he was gone. She must be feeling the loss quite strongly today.

"It's supposed to rain tonight," she added, "which will be good for them."

"Can I dig a hole, Mommy?" Tess asked, greedily eyeing the shovel.

"Not in that pretty dress," I replied.

"Okay," she said and then she simply reached down, grabbed the hem, and pulled the dress off over her head. She handed it to me and reached for the shovel, wearing nothing but her panties and a white cotton undershirt.

Lisa burst out laughing, and I had to admit that it was pretty funny. Glancing at my watch, I saw that Quinn could be here soon, so I decided we could stay outside for the time being and let Tess work off a little steam before starting the long drive to Houston.

"I'll be right back," I said, and then I took the dress to our bedroom and exchanged it in her suitcase for a shirt and shorts. Thinking better of my own white pants and expensive blouse, I made a quick change into jeans and a button-down shirt tied loosely over a white tank top.

By the time I got back outside, Lisa had put away all of the tools except for a small trowel, which Tess was now using to poke in the dirt. I made her pause to put on the clothes and then apologized to Lisa for interrupting her gardening.

"It's getting too hot to work right now anyway," she said. "And we need to talk. I'm glad to take a break."

She gestured toward a shady spot on the lawn not far away. Together, she and I walked to it and sat on the grass, chatting softly as we watched Tess play in the dirt.

"Oh yeah, I guess we need to do this," Lisa said, reaching into her pocket. She pulled out a pack of matches and a folded piece of paper, which I quickly recognized as Willy's scribblings from yesterday.

"I forgot all about that," I said, feeling terribly guilty that the promise we had made to burn it had completely slipped my mind.

Lisa did that now, holding it up as she caught it on fire and finally letting it drop to the grass when the flames nearly reached her dark fingers. The fire sputtered out when there was only an ashy triangle left, but just to be safe Lisa doused it with a splash of her bottled water.

After that she and I talked about all that Willy had said yesterday and all the questions that had been left unanswered by his death. I told her how I'd spent the time since, from our trip to the library to the boudin festival last night to our lunch with the Cajuns today. I showed her the drawing of Jimmy Smith, which she studied for a long time.

"You took this around at the festival?"

"Yeah."

"And not one person recognized him?"

"Nope. Do you?"

She shook her head.

"I'm sorry, Miranda, I don't. But it's a good idea. Can I keep this and maybe take it around later to some of the places Willy used to go? You know, like the bars, the hardware store, the barber shop..."

I told her of the old Cajun man's strange warning, but she said she'd only show it to people she knew and trusted.

As Lisa talked I watched Tess, lost in her own imaginary little world, and from what I could tell she was now setting the stage for her own version of *The Lion King*. She was wandering back and forth between the dirt and a pile of sticks under a nearby tree, carefully choosing the ones that would best suit her purposes for building a lion's den. She noticed me watching and waved, a stick in each hand.

"Look, Mommy, I'm Scar!" she cried happily.

"I see that," I replied loudly, then under my breath to Lisa added, "though why she wants to be the evil villain in the story rather than the hero is beyond me."

Lisa smiled.

"She's precious, your daughter."

"Thanks," I replied, agreeing wholeheartedly.

I asked Lisa about her family and she told me about her husband, Junior, a mechanic who worked on an oil rig out in the Gulf of Mexico.

"It's an odd life," she said, "three weeks on, three weeks off. I miss him so bad when he's gone, but after he's been back for a week I'm ready to get rid of him again!"

We laughed. I thought about telling her about my own marriage woes but thought better of it. Between grieving for her uncle and trying to solve the mystery he'd left behind, she had enough problems already; surely she didn't want to hear about mine.

"Junior won't be back for another ten days," Lisa added, glancing shyly at me, "so I was wondering if maybe I could stick around here till then to see if I can figure this whole thing out."

"But how?" I asked miserably. "I don't even know what step to take next."

Lisa shrugged.

"I could talk to people, like I said, and maybe offer to help Deena by packing up Willy's papers. There's a chance he left something behind in some document or something that might clue us in."

"It's worth a try," I mused, suddenly feeling quite hopeless. "You're welcome to stay if you want."

"Thanks. At least this way you can go back home and I'll keep you posted from this end."

I opened my mouth to tell her that I wasn't leaving just yet when my daughter let out a bloodcurdling scream. Stunned, I looked up to see her frantically clawing at her legs, jumping back and forth as though they were on fire. In an instant I was on my feet and flying across the yard, praying to God she hadn't been bitten by a rabid animal or a poisonous snake, ready to kill with my bare hands whatever it was that had dared to hurt my child.

EIGHTEEN

Meanwhile had spread in the village the tidings of ill, and on all sides
Wandered, wailing, from house to house the women and children.

"I just don't understand why you didn't warn us," I said angrily to
Lisa as my child sat on Deena's kitchen counter, whimpering.
"I'm sorry. I thought everyone knew about fire ants," Lisa replied.

She was mixing a paste made of meat tenderizer, baking soda, and
water while Deena searched the bathroom cabinets for Benadryl. I stroked
Tess's hair and spoke soothing words to her, trying not to wince at the welts
that had raised up in about ten different places on her legs.

"I don't like fire ants," Tess said through pitiful tears. "They hurt,
Mommy."

"I know, baby," I said, wishing I could take all the pain away.

I was just grateful that the cause of her screams had been ants and not
something horrible or maiming or deadly. Lisa brought over the bowl of
paste and made a game of dabbing it onto each welt, slowly teasing the
pout from Tess's lips. Deena emerged from the back moments later with
a half bottle of Benadryl, which she handed to me.

"Thank you so much," I told her. "She might need more again later,
so if I can just keep the bottle, that would be great. I'll pay you for it, of
course."

"What kind of person do you think I am?" Deena asked, but before I could answer she said, "You can subtract ten percent because it's partially used."

Not bothering to reply, I measured out a dose for Tess. She was just swallowing it down when there was a knock on the door.

"Come in!" Deena shouted, making the rest of us jump.

The door slowly opened and then Nathan's sister peeked her head inside.

"Miranda?" she asked, blinking as her eyes adjusted to the light. "Oh my gosh, is this whole joint really yours? It *rocks!*"

My face burned with embarrassment as I invited her in and made the necessary introductions. Not only had Quinn's greeting been inappropriate, but she had interrupted what was not one of my finest moments as a mother. At least Tess was instantly cheered at the sight of her aunt, the painful stings nearly forgotten in her excitement.

Though it was hard to think of my daughter leaving, I didn't have much time to spare either, so after dispensing with the introductions, I quickly cleaned Tess up and got her ready to go. Outside, we put Tess's suitcase and carry-on into Quinn's little hatchback, and I resisted the urge to lecture my young sister-in-law about safe driving as she prepared to hit the road. What could I say about safety anyway, considering that I had allowed my own child to be stung so badly in the yard less than an hour ago? In the backseat, Tess had a glazed look in her eyes, and I realized that the Benadryl was kicking in and she would probably conk out very soon. I told Quinn as much, saying in a way it was good because Tess might sleep halfway to Houston.

For some reason, I got tears in my eyes as I told my daughter goodbye, which was strange considering that I frequently traveled for business and was used to our partings. I chalked it up to the emotion of the last few days. This hadn't been an easy time for any of us, not at all.

I gave Quinn the bottle of Benadryl and the leftover paste in a paper cup and told her to call me immediately if the bites started to look worse or if she noticed any sort of allergic reaction in Tess, such as shortness of breath or a runny nose.

"No prob," Quinn said, taking the proffered items and tucking them between two bags on the passenger seat. "I'll keep an eye on her, but I'm sure she'll be fine."

Leaning into the backseat, I double-checked Tess's seat belt, fixed the pillows around her so she could comfortably go to sleep, and then hugged and kissed her again, holding my emotions in check as we said goodbye. I stood and waved until they disappeared from sight around the bend of the driveway, and then a sob burst from my lungs once the car was out of sight. Standing there, I let myself cry, not even sure which of my current traumas I was crying about. Probably all of them. Finally, I wiped my face and took a few breaths, forcing myself to calm down.

As I turned back toward the house, I was suddenly overwhelmed with a feeling of apprehension. Though it would have been nice to have the house to myself, to fling it wide open and explore from top to bottom, to search out memories and feelings from my past without anyone else around to get in the way, a big part of me was glad that I wasn't here alone. The two women who were currently serving as my housemates were also unwittingly my protection. As the preacher had said, though one may be overpowered, two can defend themselves—and a cord of three strands could not easily be broken.

Still, at the moment I didn't want to have to make conversation or be with anyone else. When Lisa poked her head out the door to make sure that I was okay, I told her I thought I might take a little walk around the property and explore.

"Good idea. If we're gone when you get back, we're just down the road at the funeral home."

"Okay."

"Don't go into any of the outbuildings. They have some structural damage. And for goodness' sake, watch out for fire ants."

"I will, thanks."

Taking her advice, I started my walk by returning to the place where Tess had been stung to see what a fire ant pile really looked like and make sure I didn't land on one myself. Glancing up at the sky as I went, I realized that clouds were moving in. Lisa had said it was supposed to rain tonight, so maybe this was a good time to walk around anyway, before the grounds became muddy.

Behind the building Lisa had called the canning shed, it wasn't hard to find the spot where my baby had been stung. Judging by the footprints, she had stepped squarely in the middle of the ant pile, a mound about eight inches high and maybe a foot across, made up of particles that resembled gray, uncooked cream of wheat. The mound was currently swarming with angry ants, and I took a step back, lest a few wanderers find their way to my legs. Nearby were the two sticks Tess had been holding when it happened, both lying where she had dropped them on the ground near the ant pile.

Something about one of those sticks caught my eye, and even though it had a few fire ants on it, I moved closer and leaned down to get a good look. With a shiver I realized why in today's version of *The Lion King* Tess had decided to play Scar. Scar was the evil uncle who lived in a cave surrounded by the gnawed carcasses of animals. I sucked in a breath, understanding that this particular stick wasn't a stick at all: It was a bone.

To the best of my limited knowledge, it was a human bone.

I ran to the house, resisting the urge to scream, but when I flung open the back door both women looked up at me with dismay, assuming that I, too, had been bitten by ants. By the time I explained what I had found and brought them back outside to see for themselves, neither one of them seemed to be exhibiting any sort of alarm or excitement.

"This is the country, Miranda," Deena said, planting her feet widely in the green grass. "Animals die out here all the time. Doesn't take long for the insects and other animals to pick the carcass clean."

"In rural areas, finding a bone isn't that unusual," Lisa agreed.

"But this isn't an animal bone," I insisted. "I had a lot of anatomy and physiology in college, I studied the human body inside and out as a part of my art curriculum. I'm not a doctor, but I think I know a human bone when I see it."

I glanced at Lisa, who was summarily unimpressed.

"You're a nurse, Lisa," I cried. "Don't you agree that it's human?"

"I have no idea," Lisa said, shaking her head as Deena snorted derisively. "You'd probably have to ask an anthropologist or something."

"Forget an anthropologist, I'm calling the police."

Against their objections—and ignoring the roll of Deena's eyes—I pulled out my cell phone and dialed nine one one. After giving the operator my location, she patched me through to the appropriate station. The man who took the call was as unexcited as Lisa and Deena had been, repeating their objections almost word for word.

"But I'm almost certain it's a *human* bone," I said, and then I proceeded to explain my educational background just to make him understand that I knew what I was talking about.

His answer to that surprised me.

"Yes, ma'am," he said, "it very well could be a human bone. That wouldn't be all that unusual."

"What do you mean?" I demanded, wanting to scream. Out of regard for the newly widowed Deena, I took a few steps away, lowered my voice, and hissed into the phone. "Don't people in Louisiana use caskets to bury their dead? Or do they just toss the bodies out in the woods where the animals will pick 'em clean? What's wrong with this picture?"

The line was silent for so long that I was afraid the man had hung up on me.

"Uh, ma'am," he said finally, "maybe you don't realize that Hurricane Katrina did a number on many of our graveyards. We've had cemetery ornaments and bodily remains and human bones popping up in all sorts of places. South of here, there were entire caskets floating down the street. Chances are, that's some fellow's shin bone that got blown out of one of the graves in town. Or, just as likely, it could be a piece from some old lady's rib that rode the wind all the way here from Grand Isle or something. A hurricane is a mighty thing, ma'am, and Katrina was one of the worst we've had in a while."

I took a deep breath, still irritated but also ashamed. I had no experience with anything remotely similar except for Hurricane Gloria, which hit the Northeast back in the '80s. I had been nine years old at the time, and all I could recall about it was the excitement of watching the wind whipping around the trees in Central Park.

"So you're not going to send someone out about this?" I asked, feeling defeated and embarrassed.

"I can't any time soon," he replied. "Though if you'd like to bring the bone into the police station and drop it off, I'd be happy to get it to the coroner and have him take a look. He might have some thoughts on the subject. I guess it wouldn't hurt for you to mark the place where it was found, just in case."

"Fine. We'll mark the spot and bring it in."

I hung up the phone but didn't have to explain the outcome to my two companions as they were still standing there and had heard most of the call.

Trying to soothe my embarrassment, Lisa offered to drop the bone at the police station when they went into town.

"You never know. You probably did some grieving family a favor," she added. "I wouldn't want the bones of somebody I love to be scattered around by the wind."

Without another word, they headed toward the house, Lisa's face blank but Deena's still carrying an expression of amused scorn. I felt sure that as soon as the door closed behind them they would start whispering and giggling about stupid Miranda and her ignorant Yankee ways.

Feeling churlish and irritated and in no mood for anything but solitude, I decided to continue my walk. Considering my options, I looked around and finally veered off to the right, beyond the garage and toward what must have been the gardens once upon a time. They were mostly a tangled mess of weeds and vines now, but beneath all of that overgrown foliage were rosebushes filled with blossoms and buds, beds of flowery perennials run wild, and even what had likely been neat little rows of vegetables at one point.

I strolled around the structures and half-structures that remained on the estate, thinking about the paperwork I had seen back when my grandmother died and AJ told me about the will and Willy Pedreaux and his life estate. From what I could recall, this had originally been a working sugarcane farm with a tremendous amount of acreage, though parcels had been given out and sold off over the years, including the part of the land that had held all of the sugarcane fields. Back when I read that paperwork, my impression had been that Twin Oaks had essentially been whittled down to almost nothing by the time it came into my hands, which was why I had always assumed my inheritance was relatively insignificant. To my mind, I had hoped that an old house and some rural acreage would be equal to about four years' college tuition. While that was nothing to sneeze at, it wasn't even close to the reality of this estate's true value—which probably equaled eight or nine times that much, if not more.

Walking closer to the bayou that edged the property, I studied the one building that still seemed to be mostly intact. Constructed of steel beams interspersed with wood panels, it stood perfectly straight—unlike some of the more slanted all-wooden structures nearby—and it towered over this area of the yard at nearly three stories tall. Shading my eyes, I tilted my head back and looked up, feeling the stirring of some sort of memory. This was just one more building where they had either stored or processed sugarcane, but for some reason I was both simultaneously drawn to it and repelled by it, as if this building represented danger—but a danger I wanted to be a part of.

With a shudder I stepped back, noting that a big window on the top floor had obviously been sheared away by the hurricane's high winds. Now only a big hole remained, leaving that part of the building empty and exposed, like a giant eye looking out over the grounds of the estate. No doubt, that whole room had been enjoyed ever since by birds and other wild creatures, probably even bats.

Losing the traces of whatever memory the sight of this building had tried to bring up, I realized that I could hear a trickling sound nearby, the gentle current of Bayou Serein. Sure enough, peering through the thick tangle of bushes next to me, I could catch glimpses of it not ten feet away. I wanted to get to it, to kick off a shoe and dip in a toe, but there was so much brush between me and the water that I had to walk alongside the tangled growth for a good thirty feet before it finally cleared to make way for a path.

There were three paths, actually, heading in three different directions, with a lovely stone bench centered in the clearing where they all began. The bench faced in the direction of the middle path, a short walk that led straight to the water. I ran down it quickly and stopped at the dilapidated dock that jutted out from there.

Thrilled with the sight, I wanted to pull off my shoes and socks and step in, but for now I contented myself with kneeling there at the land's edge and dipping my hand into the warm water instead.

The scene was breathtaking.

All around me was pure wilderness, the foliage on the far banks so overgrown that vines and moss hung nearly down to the water, creating mirror images of the same. The waterway was wide and slow moving and surely the most peaceful thing I had ever seen.

There's bayou water in your veins, Charles Benochet had said to me, and as I stood back up and looked out on the dark, shining surface, I finally understood what he meant. This place felt so right, so normal, so...*familiar.* Was it possible that this also was a memory, a whisper of some long-lost moment that tickled at the edges of my brain? I couldn't recall standing on this bank, looking out at this scene, but surely as a child I had, and it felt incredibly familiar to me now. For a moment, I closed my eyes and just listened, inhaling the sweet scent of pine and honeysuckle. Nearby, the wind rustled through the reeds along the bank, and when I opened my eyes again, it was to see a huge white heron slowly sweeping down directly across the waterway from where I stood. I watched as it came to a landing on stick legs. Then it put its entire head into the water and came up with a small fish in its mouth. The beautiful bird tossed its head back and swallowed, and then it paused, perhaps sensing my presence. It didn't fly away but instead just stood there, frozen, as if waiting for me to make the next move.

NINETEEN

Faint was the air with the odorous breath of magnolia blossoms,
And with the heat of noon; and numberless sylvan islands,
Fragrant and thickly embowered with blossoming hedges of roses,
Near to whose shores they glided along, invited to slumber.

A dark cloud passed in front of the sun, reminding me of the passage of time and the oncoming rain. Finally, regretfully, I bid the heron farewell and moved away, startling it into flight as I walked back up the path. I promised myself I would return to that spot as soon as I could, even if it was just to sit on the bench and watch the water flow by. I couldn't imagine how amazing this place would be if we could clear away enough brush so that the bayou could be seen from the house.

When I reached the bench, I looked toward the house and realized that the nearest room was the very one in which Willy had died. It sat at the perfect vantage point for a view, and I decided that was probably why the room had so many windows, so that one could sit there and look out and enjoy the magnificent scene of the bayou. Oh, how I wished I could remember how the house and grounds looked when they were in their splendor, long before the doors and windows were all boarded up and the banks of the bayou had become so overgrown that the view was obscured.

Inhaling deeply, I decided to continue my meandering, choosing the path to my left. It led me through high trees and thick woods until it shifted down to the water and ran alongside the bank. It made for a pleasant walk, passing under the giant boughs of waterside trees and moving through the shadows cast by the tallest farm building, the one that had given me that strange feeling of danger just a little while earlier.

I continued to walk, hoping I wouldn't encounter any stray dogs or snapping turtles or swamp hermits as I went. I quickened my pace, curious where this path would lead. It didn't take much longer to find out. As I came around the bend, I could see the end of the tree line ahead, and beyond that the site of a house. I walked closer to get a better view, even though by this point I probably wasn't on my own property. Stepping out from among the trees, I found myself looking at the back of a beautiful antebellum home, one that seemed very familiar. I wondered if my brain was trying to dredge up yet another childhood memory when I realized why I recognized it, and I had to laugh: This house wasn't from my past, it was straight out of *Gone with the Wind!*

Even from the back, I could tell that this must be Little Tara, the home of Livvy and Big Daddy Kroft. The place seemed lovely, if a bit grandiose, but what I couldn't help noticing was how perfect it all was, from the white exterior with crisp green shutters to landscaping so manicured it was as if someone had gone around with a pair of fingernail clippers. Somehow, knowing Livvy, that didn't surprise me.

I turned and headed back the way I had come, feeling embarrassed for the contrast of Twin Oaks, which was torn up and dirty and weary looking. I appreciated Willy's dedication through the years, not to mention Charles' diligence in handling the bigger issues, but the sad truth was that no one had done anything beyond the most necessary of repairs for some time. I remembered Livvy's offer of her carpenter-brother, and I hoped he'd be able to come over and take a look at the place soon.

When I reached the bench at the trailhead, I went ahead and took the third path, curious to see if it led to a neighbor on the other side. As I walked, I found myself growing more comfortable with my surroundings, less apprehensive about what scary thing might be lurking around the next bend. The smell of honeysuckle was all around me now, and I inhaled deeply and then let my breath out, wishing suddenly that Tess was still here with me so that I could show her how to pick the blossom and pull out the stamen, bringing with it a single drop of the nectar inside. I froze, shocked at how vividly I could recall the taste.

How did I know that? Was there honeysuckle growing in New York? Had AJ taught me to get the nectar from a blossom and let it drop onto my tongue?

Or had I been younger, much younger, only a child, perhaps right here on this very path, when someone else taught me and let me taste, that moment forever embedded into my brain?

Deep in thought, I forced myself to keep walking, wondering just how many memories might come back if I continued to explore. I wasn't paying much attention to my surroundings until I heard a strange noise off to the right, a rhythmic clanging, almost like a metallic drum. Slowing, I continued forward until a man's voice joined the clanging, yelling out angry commands. I didn't think he was shouting at me, but I wasn't sure—and I didn't feel like sticking around to find out. I turned to go back in the direction I had come but soon passed a break in the trees where I could see what was going on. I stopped, ducking down to observe, stunned at the bizarre spectacle in front of me.

In a clearing beyond the trees sat a man in a wheelchair, his back to me. He held a pot in one hand and a big metal spoon in the other, and he was banging the spoon against the bottom of the pot and yelling nonsense phrases, such as "Get a move on there!" and "Watch for the hot spots!"

From what I could tell, there were no other people nearby. There was, however, one other creature present, and what I saw nearly broke my heart: It was a dog, balancing on what looked like a makeshift seesaw, a plank on top of a metal cylinder. The dog seemed terrified, and I very nearly marched right out from my hiding place in the brush to rescue him. Instead, my heart racing in my chest, I simply gathered my nerve and ran toward home. I went as fast as I could, desperate to get some authorities out here to rescue that poor, abused dog.

I was fully out of breath by the time I reached the house, but this time

Lisa and Deena were gone. I pulled out my cell phone and dialed nine one one for the second time today, cringing when I recognized the voice of the officer on the other end from my earlier call.

Halfway through the description of what I'd just seen, I could tell he recognized my voice too. Sounding very skeptical, he nevertheless took down my address and said he'd send someone right out.

I paced in the driveway for ten minutes, desperate to help that poor dog. Finally, a police car came up the drive, but as soon as a uniformed officer climbed out of the car, I could tell he'd been warned by the dispatcher that I more than likely had a screw loose.

Ignoring the bemused expression on his face, I thanked him for coming so quickly.

"We got a report of animal abuse?"

"I'm afraid you'll have to follow me," I said. "It's down a path, through the woods a ways."

"Just tell me where it is, ma'am. You'll need to wait here."

"Okay, but I have to show you which path."

I led him to the trailhead near the bench and pointed it out, saying he should go along it about fifty yards and then follow the banging sound. I described what he would find once he got there, but as soon as I said the word "wheelchair," the officer broke into a knowing smile.

"Don't laugh at me," I said. "This guy could have a gun. Maybe he's not even handicapped. I had every reason to run."

"I tell you what," the cop replied, "why don't you come with me after all?"

We walked briskly up the path, the sound of banging soon evident up ahead. When we reached the break in the trees where I had stood watching before, the cop surprised me by stepping forward into the clearing, giving a loud whistle and then a wave. The man in the wheelchair turned, surprise evident on his bearded face.

"Stay there!" he said to us, holding up one hand. Then he returned his attention to the dog, clicked his tongue, and the dog stopped her sudden barking, though she remained balanced on the bucket watching us warily.

"Hold," the man said to the dog in a calm voice. "Bubba, do that whistle thing again. Hold."

To my surprise, the cop let out another whistle. This time, the dog did not bark or respond at all. We all waited for a moment, the cop glancing at me with a bemused expression, and I was torn between rage and embarrassment.

Did he know this guy?

Finally, the man in the chair gave two tongue clicks. At that, the creature jumped off of the bucket and ran to him, receiving effusive praise and a good rubbing behind the ears.

"Thanks for your help, Bubba," the man finally said, looking up at us. "What're you doing way out here in the woods?"

"Sorry to sneak up on you, Spinner," the cop said as he stepped forward and gestured toward me with his thumb. "We had a report of animal abuse."

The man in the wheelchair focused in on me then, his eyes sparkling from under bushy eyebrows.

"Ah, I see," he drawled. "Don't be embarrassed, darlin'. You're not the first person to see me doing my job and think I'm being cruel."

I looked at the dog, just sitting there, her tongue lolling out of the side of her mouth as she breathed heavily.

"Maybe one of you would like to explain?" I said, looking from the man to the cop.

"This is Duchess," the man in the chair said, reaching out again to stroke the dog behind the ears. "I'm testing her out to see if she has the makings of a canine aid."

"Canine aid?"

"Ol' Spinner here is an expert," the cop said. "He works with breeders and pounds and organizations all over the country, evaluating dogs to see if they're fit for service and, if so, what kind."

"I don't understand."

"Everything from guide dogs and search and rescue to K-9 units and therapy," the man in the chair elaborated. "By the time a dog gets to me, he's been evaluated for health, intelligence, and general temperament, but then I take it from there, to see what type of fit might be best, if at all. Duchess here is looking pretty darn promising for S and R."

"S and R?"

"Search and rescue. Her balance is excellent, and she passed on distractibility too. Didn't you girl?"

Focusing on the dog, he put extra effort into rubbing her neck, and she actually closed her eyes with pleasure.

"Why the banging pot?" I asked doubtfully.

"You ever been in a search and rescue situation?" he asked. "They're noisy as all get out. The dogs have to be able to balance and focus without being bothered by outside distractions."

The dog opened her eyes then and looked up at the man, who spoke a few more words of praise.

"She wants to come say hello," he told me. "Do you mind?"

"Um, sure," I replied, taking a few steps closer.

With a flick of the man's wrist, the dog happily bounded toward me, pausing to lick the hand of the cop and then coming to a stop right in front of me. I knelt down and petted her, thinking she had the prettiest brown eyes I'd ever seen.

"I appreciate your concern for a helpless animal," the man said, putting his hands on each wheel and rolling in my direction. "But as you can see, she's just fine." He gave the cop a wink and continued. "Though now that that's settled, I suppose I ought to ask you what you were doing way out here in the woods on my property."

"Your property?" I asked, standing. "This is my property."

Clearly amused, he glanced again at the cop.

"Oh? And who might you be?" he asked, barely holding back a smile.

"My name is Miranda Miller, formerly Miranda Fairmont. I just inherited the estate known as Twin Oaks."

Suddenly, all expression drained from the man's face. His skin paled, his eyes widened, and in a voice barely louder than a whisper he said, "Miranda? You're little Miranda?"

There was something in his gaze, an intensity, that made me uncomfortable.

"Not so little anymore," I said warily. "Did you know me when I was a child?"

"Know you?" he asked, and then he began to roll toward me again, tears suddenly filling his eyes.

"Miranda, I'm Holt Fairmont. Spinner's just a nickname."

"Holt?"

"Yes," he said, coming to stop. "Miranda, I'm your father's brother. I'm your Uncle Holt."

TWENTY

Ripe in wisdom was he, but patient, and simple and childlike.
He was beloved by all, and most of all by the children

The cop left soon after, obviously aware that uncle and niece needed some privacy during this very surreal moment. Holt invited me back to his house, which he said wasn't too far away. Heading there, we passed all sorts of training equipment in the yard, including some ramps, a slide, and what looked like a bridge, though there was nothing underneath it except grass.

Soon we came upon the back of his home, a big log cabin that sat on a broad curve of land along the bayou. There was no undergrowth to hide the water here, and as Holt led me around front and up the ramp to a wide, inviting front porch, I couldn't get over the beautiful view.

I also couldn't get over the surprise of meeting an uncle I hardly knew anything about. I was aware that my father had a brother named Holt and that he lived in Louisiana, but I had no idea he lived so close or that he would be so glad to see me. I kept stealing glances at his face, trying to see if there was a family resemblance. I thought he might have same jaw line and high cheekbones that my father and I shared, but it was hard to tell with so much beard in the way.

Holt seemed nervous, but he tried to be a good host, offering me tea and asking if I wanted to go inside where it was cooler.

"No, thank you. I'm fine out here," I said, nervous myself. "It's just so beautiful."

"Thanks. I like it."

He gestured toward a rocking chair and so I sat, watching as he dumped the dog's water bowl over the side of the porch and refilled it from a tap near the door. I asked if he needed help, but he said no, he was fine. He was able to get around really well, considering that he was in a wheelchair, and I wondered what the story was about all that.

"I hope I'm not making you uncomfortable," he said, his eyes on mine as he finally rolled himself to a stop a few feet away, "but I just can't help staring at you. Man, you are such a Fairmont! You look like my mother, your grandmother. The same black eyes, the same face shape. So beautiful. My gosh, Miranda, I haven't seen you since you were five years old."

"I'm sorry that I don't know very much about you," I replied, figuring I might as well lay that out up front. "Aunt Janet never talks about the family here, so there are a lot of gaps in my knowledge. I mean, I knew you existed, but that's about it."

He studied my face, nodding.

"To be honest, I don't know all that much about you either, Miranda. I talk to your dad about once a year and he catches me up, but obviously that's not enough."

I didn't mention that I, too, only talked to my dad about once a year, usually on Christmas Day, and more than likely at the urgings of his tightly nipped-and-tucked Arizona wife. She wasn't exactly my dream of a stepmother, but her vague notions of family obligation at least prevented him from being able to forget about me entirely—which would probably have been his preference.

"Anyway," Holt continued, "I hope you'll be around long enough for us to fill in some of these gaps on both sides. I'd love to get to know you better."

"Me too. I mean, I'm not sure yet how long I'll be here—with work and everything, I can't stay too long—but I hate to race back home with so many questions left unanswered. Either way, now that we've met, I would love to stay in touch."

"Cool!" he said, excusing himself to go inside and get a pen and paper so that we could exchange phone numbers and addresses. As he came back out and handed me the paper with his information scrawled on it, I felt as though he were handing me the link for a chain that had long ago been broken.

Writing out my information for him, I wondered if it would be possible to put that chain back together again.

"I'm just so excited to see you. You have no idea," he enthused as he folded my info and tucked it into his shirt pocket. "Here you are, all grown up and everything. How old are you now, if you don't mind my asking?"

"I'm thirty-two."

"Thirty-two," he marveled, once again tears forming in his eyes. "So many years, so much lost time. We really need to become more than just strangers meeting in the woods, you know."

He grinned, revealing two rows of straight white teeth under the beard.

I was silent for a long moment, utterly dumbfounded by this conversation. AJ had always led me to believe that the people here wanted nothing to do with me, that I was better off never having contact with any of them. Yet here was this man, my own uncle, in tears twice within ten minutes through the sheer joy of seeing me. It made no sense.

"I feel the same," I said, flushing with a mixture of embarrassment and joy. "Being down here after being gone for so long is pretty...intense. It's nice to know that you're so close by." I cleared my throat and continued. "Speaking of that, maybe you should explain to me about the property lines. Where does Twin Oaks end and your land begin?"

"My land starts about twenty feet beyond the training area, where we just were. I've got five acres, but they mostly go the other way, along the bayou. When my parents parceled out my share, they let me pick what I wanted, so I grabbed my favorite section of the waterway—and then I made sure to build up high enough that I wouldn't have to worry about flooding. It's my own little piece of heaven on earth."

"That was good that your parents were willing to do this, to give you such a nice part of their land."

"Yeah, Richard and I were a regular Jacob and Esau, taking our inheritance long before our parents died. Your dad chose money, but I opted for land."

Whether they got it early or not, I wondered why their inheritance was so much smaller than mine, considering that I was a second-generation heir. Holt didn't seem bitter that his niece had been given the lion's share of the estate that had belonged to his parents, something that by all rights should have been split between him and my father. According to AJ, my grandparents did what they had done without explanation or apology. My father carried a chip on his shoulder about it, a chip nearly as big as Twin Oaks, but Holt seemed perfectly happy with his home and land, which was probably a testament to his character, finding contentment in his situation whatever it may be.

"But, hey, regardless of where the property lines fall," he added, "please feel free to come here any time you want—though I hope you won't always find the need to bring along a police escort."

I smiled shyly.

"Yeah, sorry about that."

"Nah, easy mistake."

We both smiled at Duchess, who had finished slurping from her bowl and was now trying to find a place to relax. She walked into the area between us, moved around in a circle, and then plopped herself down on the wooden floor.

"So how long have you been in town?" Holt asked me. "I didn't know you were coming."

"Gosh, even *I* didn't know I was coming until Friday night. The flight was yesterday morning."

"How is Willy doing?"

My eyes widened.

"I'm sorry. I guess you haven't heard. He died yesterday afternoon."

Holt looked quite surprised. Turning his face toward the water, he slowly nodded his head.

"Willy was a good guy. Very loyal to the family. This is selfish of me to say, but I'm glad he outlived my parents. They depended on him a lot. It would've been tough if he'd gone first."

"He spoke very highly of them both, especially his beloved Ya Ya."

Holt smiled.

"Yeah, Willy and Mom were always so funny together, especially when we would go out on the boat and she could really let her hair down. They could have entire conversations with just a bunch of sounds." Holt imitated the two Cajuns talking, alternating in a high and low voice as he said things such as " Kee Yoo!" and "Mais La!"

I laughed, recognizing that the low voice sounded exactly like Willy.

"Anyway," Holt continued, "it was always my understanding that you were going to have Benochet handle the property sale and settlement for you, on your behalf. I'm guessing you changed your mind and decided to come here for yourself?"

"It's kind of complicated," I said. "Willy wanted to talk to me before he died, so I flew down at his request."

"What will you do now? Are you going to put the house on the market?"

His question was a simple one, the answer obvious, yet I was having a hard time bringing myself to say the words or even nod my head.

"Before I do anything," I told him finally, "I just want to get a feel for the place, maybe bring back some childhood memories. But, yes, eventually I'll be putting it on the market." I wanted to ask if that would be hard for him, seeing his family home sold to some stranger, but I held my tongue.

"Was the place familiar to you at all?" he asked.

I looked out at the water, spotting a log as it floated down the bayou.

"To be honest, I don't remember anything about Louisiana. I have no memories prior to the age of six. AJ—uh, my Aunt Janet—says I was traumatized when my mother died and that my mind just erased everything up to then. The late seventies are a complete blank to me."

To my surprise, Holt laughed.

"Join the club!" he said. "Those years are a blank to me too! I was a stone-cold drunk, wasted out of my mind most of the time. In fact, I have more than a *decade* that's just one big blur. It's only through the love of some buddies and the good Lord Himself that I was able to survive and dry out and start my life fresh."

I glanced around at the tidy house, at the satisfied dog at my feet, at the man who sat across from me. He did look a little swamp-wild with the bushy beard and long hair and all, but I wouldn't have pegged him for a drunk.

"I'm sorry," I said. "Were you an alcoholic?"

"*Am.* I *am* an alcoholic. And, sober or not, I will be until the day the Lord calls me home."

I nodded, thinking how ironic it was that my uncle drew a blank on the same years that I did. The reasons were different, of course, but the effect was probably much the same.

"Have you ever tried to get those memories back?" I asked.

"I did what I could, so that I could make amends," he replied. "But the bulk of that time is still pretty fuzzy. From what I've been able to piece together, I pretty much lived out of a bottle from 1976 to 1988."

I wondered what the full story was, why he started drinking, how he got sober, and how he stayed that way. More than that, I wanted to know why he was in a wheelchair and whether he'd been handicapped his whole life or if some illness or accident had put him there.

"Listen, that's enough about me. Tell me about you, Miranda. Your dad says you and your husband are real movers and shakers, living in New York City, doing very well..."

"Movers and shakers. I don't know about that," I said, smiling shyly. "My husband's an architect and I'm an art restorer."

"An art restorer. How fascinating."

I talked about my position as senior preparator for the museum, how it was my job to receive and evaluate new acquisitions, assign to my staff the various cleaning, repair, and restoration tasks that were needed, supervise their progress, and do the highest level restoration work myself. As I heard myself talk I realized that there was a lot about my job I didn't like. Administration and supervision were not fun for me, and neither was all the paperwork that went with sorting, arranging, and classifying the museum's holdings. The only part of what I did that was actually enjoyable was the hands-on stuff, particularly inpainting, which was my specialty. For the first time I wondered if I had allowed myself to be promoted too far too fast. Just because I had the ability to do a job well didn't mean that was the job I should be doing.

"My mom—your grandmother—was an incredible artist. I'm sure you got your talent from her. Is that what you studied in school? Art?"

I nodded, telling him a bit about my education, my internships, and my career, finding myself as eager for this man to know me as I was to know him. He seemed genuinely interested in what I was saying, and I kept thinking, *Is this what it's like to have family? Is this what it's like to have an uncle?*

"You have one child, right?" he asked.

"A daughter. She was here with me, but now she's on her way to Houston to stay with my in-laws."

"Oh, that's a shame. I can't believe I missed her."

"I thought it would be better for her to go so I could...you know, handle the house matters and deal with the funeral and everything."

"Makes sense. How old is she now? I'm thinking four? Five?"

"She's five. Her name is Tess."

He lifted his head in surprise.

"What's her name?"

In the distance, I could hear rumblings of thunder. Looking out at the water, I saw that it wasn't yet raining, but the sky was much darker than it had been before. I turned back to Holt, squinting my eyes.

"Why does everyone around here react that way when I tell them my daughter's name? *Tess.* Her name is Tess. It's not that unusual, is it?"

"Tess," he repeated softly. "I thought you said..." his voice trailed off.

"Cass?" I prodded. "That's what Willy thought."

"I guess, yeah."

The thunder rumbled again, much closer this time.

"Anyway," he told me, looking up at the sky and obviously trying to change the subject, "it looks like I might need to drive you home. I was having some problems with my van's alternator earlier, but I might be able to get her up and running long enough to drive you next door and back."

I glanced toward the old van with the handicapped plate that was parked beside the house. I didn't want to make him have to go to all that trouble. As the sky grew even darker, I knew I could probably make it if I ran.

"I'll be fine," I said, standing. "If the rain starts before I make it back to the house, a little water won't kill me."

"I'm not worried about the water. I just don't want you to get struck by lightning. It would be a darn shame to find you and lose you all in the same day."

He was kidding, but something about his concern was very touching. I hesitated, feeling utterly torn; I wanted to leave, but I wanted to stay.

"I'm sure you'll be fine if you hurry," he added. "But I hope you'll come back real soon. Maybe even tomorrow?"

Hearing the earnestness in his voice, I actually felt a little choked up. He was my uncle, and he wanted me to come back. He wanted to know me, to spend time with me.

"I would love that," I said, meaning it.

Impulsively I leaned down and gave him a hug.

Then I took off for home, running down the ramp and around the back of house and through the training area and up the path to Twin Oaks. The rain started when I was about halfway there, the drops fat and cold on my warm arms and face. By the time I reached the stone bench, the skies had opened and let loose with a downpour so intense that I was fully soaked to the skin within seconds.

My mind was a jumbled mess of thoughts, impressions, feelings—and a strange sort of joy. Relishing the moment, I felt the sudden, irresistible urge to explore the house—the whole giant place from top to bottom. I wanted to open every closet, every drawer, search through trunks in the attic and boxes in the basement and everything else in between. I was ready to see what was hidden in the shadows. I wanted answers—answers about Willy, my mother, my life, my tattoo, *myself.*

Nearly laughing as I ran through the torrent to the house, I wasn't even worried when I saw that Lisa's car was gone and I was here alone. So intent was I on my mission that I didn't see the man standing at the back door until I was almost on top of him.

I froze just a few steps away, a sheet of rain forming a wall of water between us, pouring from the gutter over our heads.

TWENTY-ONE

Urged by a restless longing, the hunger and thirst of the spirit,
She would commence again her endless search and endeavor.

I did not recognize this man, but he was tall and muscular and could easily have fit the description of one of my attackers in New York. Heart in my throat, I glanced wildly around, trying to decide which way to run.

"I'm Aaron West. Livvy Kroft's brother," the guy called out loudly to be heard over the noise. "Are you Miranda Fairmont?"

Relief flooded through my veins. This man wasn't a danger; he was only here to help. With trembling hands, I pulled out the set of house keys, moving to join him in the tight space underneath the overhang.

"Miranda Miller," I corrected as I fumbled through the keys. "My married name is Miller."

"Got it. I'm sorry if I scared you. I walked over on the path, so I guess you didn't realize I was here because my truck is not in your driveway."

It took a few tries to find the right key, and as we stood there huddled together just protected from the rain, I could smell wood shavings mixed with sweat, hear the rat-tat-tat and whoosh of the water above and around us, and feel the heat radiating from his body. By the time I got the door unlocked, my senses were in overdrive—and not in a good way. Simply by virtue of the fact that he was a big strong guy, his presence behind me brought back the terror of my attack.

Once I opened the door and we stepped inside, my fear receded significantly. Continuing around the counter to the kitchen, I grabbed an entire roll of paper towels, tugged off a giant wad, and then tossed the roll to him.

"I came here to give you some estimates," he told me as he pulled off a wad for himself, "but I'd say job number one ought to be those rain gutters."

I dabbed at my hair, making sure the clip was intact and hiding the bald spot, and then I ran the paper towels down each arm while a puddle collected at my feet.

"I'm so sorry no one was here," I said. "I was taking a walk and just happened to run into my uncle, who lives next door."

"That's okay. I meant to come sooner, but I got busy in the workshop doing a project for my sister."

We chatted as we continued to dry off, and I was glad to see that he was obviously knowledgeable about woodworking and home repair.

"I can't believe that much rain can fall that fast," I said, giving up on trying to dry my outer shirt and peeling it away from the tank top I had on underneath. Carrying the button-down top to the sink, I wrung it out. I set my shirt in a wad on the empty dish drainer so it could drip there for a few minutes and turned my attention to my guest, suggesting that he take advantage of the rains to go up and explore the attic for leaks before doing anything else.

"I have no idea where the attic access is," I added, "but I'm sure if we look around we can find it."

He finished wiping the mud from his shoes and turned to me, his face suddenly bright red.

"Don't worry, I'll find it," he said, his eyes quickly moving to the ceiling. "In fact, I'll do that right now."

Without another word, he moved from the kitchen and down the hall. Startled by his abrupt departure, I could hear the sound of doors opening and closing in the distance and then feet pounding up a flight of stairs. I was about to call up to him to wait for me when I caught my reflection in the mirror, and at a glance I understood what was going on: Both my white top and the lace bra I was wearing underneath were soaked through and almost completely transparent. Considering all this guy had seen, I might as well have charged admission and called it a show!

Blushing furiously, I made a dash for my bedroom. I was mortified, and I hoped that Aaron had reason to stay in the attic for several hours—or at least until the blush faded from my cheeks.

I stripped off all my wet clothes and pulled on a whole new outfit of jeans and my baggiest, loosest top. After hanging my wet clothes over the chair rod to dry, I took down my hair, brushed it out, and neatly put it back up again. I was getting so tired of this hairdo, but when I touched the shaved place on my head, all I could feel was a little bit of stubble and a whole lot of bare skin.

When I finally emerged from the bedroom, I was mortified to find that Aaron was back in the kitchen and hovering near the door, cell phone in hand. I knew he knew I knew what he'd seen, and for a moment I debated whether to say anything or just let it pass.

"I can't find the attic access anywhere," he said, all business. "If you don't mind, I need to run right now. I think I'll come back in the morning when it's not raining to look around outside and see if it's there somewhere. We can talk then about whatever other jobs you want done."

"Oh, sure," I said. "Whatever you think."

"All right, then. I'll see you in the morning."

He opened the door and ventured on to the stoop. Moving toward him, I could see that the rain was still pouring down outside in the gathering darkness. I asked if he wanted to wait until there was a break in the weather—or at least borrow an umbrella if I could find one.

"Um, nah, rain won't kill me. And anyway," he said, flashing me a shy grin, "I could use a cold shower. Evening, ma'am."

With that, he ran out into the storm, past the row of garages and the shed, disappearing from view as he neared the path that would lead him home. Relieved to see him go, I closed the door, my mind moving to the realization that I was here alone for the first time.

Alone.

In my own home.

By myself, free to explore to my heart's content without another soul around to watch or distract or pass judgment.

Feeling my earlier enthusiasm resurge, I decided not to waste another minute. Retracing the steps that Lisa and I had taken when we sought out the Bible for swearing our oath, I made my way to the front room where we had found it, flipping on light switches as I went. From there I continued on around the corner and forward a few steps to the main entranceway inside the front door. I turned on the lights there too, but many bulbs were either missing or burned out in the main fixture.

Despite the dust and the boarded up windows and the sheet-covered furniture, as I turned around and took my first real look at the interior of Twin Oaks, I was overcome with a deep sense of awe and connection—connection to my family, to my past. In its prime, the house had obviously been beautiful and gracious and grand, with a massive, curving staircase as the focal point of the entrance hall. To my right was an open doorway that led to a living and dining room. To my left was a large, rectangular mirror mounted on the wall. I paused to look in that mirror, knowing my mother had probably stood here and done the same. Slowly, I raised one hand, and for a moment what I saw looking back at me was not myself as I was now, but myself as a child. Startled, I stepped back and lowered my hand.

I could *see* it.

I could *remember* it—as clearly as I remembered events from last month, last week even. Closing my eyes, I focused, remembering that I was young, maybe four, and I was standing at this very mirror, slowly raising my right hand up and down. Nearby, people were laughing, a happy laugh that for some reason made me feel proud. The memory faded, but this time I wasn't left grasping for some wisp of a feeling. I opened my eyes, knowing I had finally retrieved a real moment from my past, a moment from what was supposedly that blank slate inside my mind.

Feeling suddenly euphoric, I ran from room to room, flipping on more lights as I went.

"I'm home!" I called out to the air as I made my way up the stairs, opening my mind to whatever memories might choose to come flooding back.

At the top of the stairs, I moved forward to one bedroom and then another, each with its door that led to the second story balcony. Also on that level, flanking the hallway, were two sitting rooms, another bedroom, a bathroom, and a screened-in back balcony. Every room held furniture, some more than others, the finer pieces covered with sheets. I tried to decide where my bedroom had been, but nothing here seemed to have been set up for children. Feeling disappointed at first and then a little dumb, I reminded myself that my grandparents had continued to live in this house for many years after I was gone. It was no surprise that at some point they had done away with the child-sized bed and the little bureau or whatever I had had and better utilized the space for themselves.

Finally, I just stood there in the hallway at the top of the stairs, marveling that I had once lived here, that I had moved among these wooden floors in my bare feet, laughing as I ran a stick along the spindles of the staircase to make a clack-clack-clacking sound against the wood. I gasped, realizing that that was yet another memory. In this memory, as with the other, was the sound of laughter, and I hoped that meant that my childhood had been a happy one, despite the tragic way it had been cut short.

Sobering at the thought, I wondered where my mother had chosen to kill herself. With a shudder, I felt the air around me grow clammy, and in the distance, somewhere downstairs, I thought I detected the sound of doors opening and closing.

"Miranda?" a woman's voice called.

For a flash, I thought it was my mother, calling to me from the grave. Then I heard footsteps on the stairs, saw a dark head moving upward, and I realized that it was just Lisa.

"Miranda, girl, what are you doing up here?" she said, reaching the top step and turning toward me.

"Just looking around."

Regretfully, I decided to end my explorations for now. I turned off all of the lights and went with Lisa back down the stairs.

"I brought you some supper," Lisa said as we made our way toward the kitchen, my euphoric mood shrinking back down to size as we went. "Deena and I decided to eat an early dinner in town. The two of us have been tag-teaming Willy's care for so long now, it was weird to both be out and away from the house at the same time—even if we were there to finish planning out the funeral."

In the kitchen Deena was puttering around, straightening up, and musing aloud how I could have used up half a roll of paper towels in an afternoon.

"Our new handyman got caught in the rain and had to dry off," I said, biting my lip. "Don't worry, I'll be happy to replace it with a new roll."

"Good. See that you do."

"Handyman?" Lisa asked, and I explained to them that our neighbor's brother was a carpenter and fix-it man and that I had asked him to give me estimates on some general repairs.

"Not that I'm trying to rush you out or anything," I said quickly to her and Deena. "I just need to get some estimates while I'm here in town."

"Hey, like I told you, it's your house now. Have at it. Doesn't bother me."

Lisa pointed out my meal in a bag on the counter and then bid us both good night. At not quite nine o'clock, it was a little early for sleep, she said, but she wanted to dry off and get into her pajamas before Junior's scheduled phone call.

"You going into the library to talk, like you did this afternoon?" Deena asked her, almost sweetly.

"No, I won't do that again. I'm allergic to dust. With all of those old books in there, I was sneezing for an hour, and I still have a terrible headache."

I hadn't even realized the house had a library, I said, but when Deena explained where it was, I understood why I hadn't noticed it; to get there, you had to walk through the stuffy little sitting area that was down the hall on the way to Willy's room.

I needed to make some calls myself, so I told them I wanted to take a look and would be back in a few minutes. As I walked down the hall, I dialed the number of Nathan's parents, trying to ignore the closed door to Willy's room at the end of the hall.

Nathan's mom answered cheerily, but our conversation was quick because Quinn and Tess had literally just arrived. I spoke briefly to Quinn, who said the trip had been uneventful and that Tess's fire ant bites were no longer hurting, just itchy. I thanked my sister-in-law again for helping out, and repeated those thanks to my mother-in-law when Quinn gave her back the phone. She assured me I was doing them a favor by letting Tess come and visit.

"She's gotten so big since Christmas," she said, "and she talks non-stop."

"No kidding."

I hung up, pausing to take in the sight of the cozy little library. The room was small, no bigger than the average bedroom, but the walls were lined with shelves of books, top to bottom. In the center was a grouping of comfortable chairs around a coffee table. On the far wall was a big window with a padded window seat in front, with luxurious pillows lining the cushions and the whole thing framed with maroon velvet curtains.

As lovely as it was, however, Lisa had been right in saying that it smelled dusty. Breathing through my mouth as I skimmed the book titles on the shelves, I was going to give Nathan a quick call as well, to pass along the news that Tess had been safely spirited away. But I saw that he had left a message for me earlier, just to touch base, saying that he would be tied up for a few hours and he'd try to call me later tonight. He said that in case we didn't connect, I'd probably want to know that the security company had done the bug sweep and that it had come up empty. They had found the receiving device for the phone bug, but there were no other bugs present. Apparently, we were free and clear. Also, he said that his ceremony at the church this morning had gone fine, though from the sound of his voice, there was more there than he was telling me. Knowing I would hear all about it eventually, I called back and left a message for him, just saying that I was sorry about all of this phone tag, but I appreciated the news. I told him Tess was doing great at his parents' house and not to worry about things down here.

When I returned to the kitchen, Deena was wiping the counter. I sat at the table and pulled the Styrofoam box from the bag, eager to see what they had brought me that smelled so good. When I opened it, however, I was disappointed and not at all sure if I was going to eat it.

"What's wrong?" Deena demanded harshly. "Don't you like red beans and rice?"

"I don't know," I replied, eyeing a giant sausage that lay atop a pile of saucy maroon-colored beans. "I've never had it before."

Her scornful grunt was just enough of a challenge to make me give it a try. I unwrapped the plastic fork and took a bite, finding much to my surprise that it tasted even better than it smelled. I dug in, my hunger suddenly awakening with an embarrassing growl from my stomach. Deena continued to busy herself in the kitchen, and I wished she would simply head to bed too.

"You want something to drink with that?" she asked gruffly, and before I could reply she had plopped a glass of milk down on the table in front of me.

"Thanks," I said, glancing at her scowling face.

It wasn't until that moment that I remembered where she had been today: to the funeral home, to make the final arrangements for her husband. A surge of guilt and sympathy rose up in me, and I put down my fork and dabbed at my mouth with the paper napkin. Shame on me for being so self-centered, even if this woman was a bit of a pill.

"How are you doing, Deena? I know today's errand couldn't have been easy for you."

"Ain't like it was a surprise or nothing."

I didn't quite know how to reply, but before I could form the right words, she came and sat across from me at the table. Gruff or not, I had a feeling she needed to talk about it. That she did, just giving the basic details at first—viewing Tuesday evening, funeral Wednesday at noon— and then going on to describe the order of service, the flowers, even the outfit she had picked for the casket.

"Willy and I went over his last wishes a hundred times," she said, folding and refolding a paper towel in her gnarled hands, "but I don't know why I never thought to ask him what clothes he wanted to be buried in. I hope I brought the right choice. He didn't own no suits."

"You know what?" I told her. "If it were all that important to him, I'm sure he would've brought it up before he died."

She peered at me, the crease in her forehead easing just a bit.

"I hadn't thought of it that way. You might be right."

She seemed to relax somewhat, though she didn't exactly turn warm and fuzzy. Instead, she began to complain about everything from the cost of the casket to the rudeness of the florist to the care given to Willy in his final days by Lisa. According to Deena, she just found out that Lisa had misrepresented herself when first coming there to work.

"What do you mean?"

Deena leaned forward, speaking just above a whisper.

"I mean, she took this job saying she was a nurse. Turns out, she weren't nothing of the kind."

TWENTY-TWO

Silence reigned o'er the place. The line of shadow and sunshine
Ran near the tops of the trees; but the house itself was in shadow,

 "What do you mean? It's not like you hired a stranger. Lisa is Willy's niece. Wouldn't you know if she was a nurse or not?"

Glancing down the hallway, Deena continued.

"Yeah, but he hadn't seen her for about five years, not since before she went off to California to try and become an actress."

"An actress?"

"Yeah, she was going off to become a star, but then after she got out there she met up with that Creole boy, gave up acting, married him, and moved back to New Orleans. Next thing we heard, they was living in Chalmette and she was going to school for nursing. I figured she was at Tulane or LSU or something. Turns out, she just went to some Vo-Tec place, taking a three-week course on how to change bedpans."

I sat back, considering this information, thinking how professional and competent Lisa had seemed when working with Willy.

"How did she end up here, caring for Willy?"

Deena shrugged.

"She and Junior lost their home and all their stuff in the hurricane and didn't have no insurance, so they had to move in with her mama and them down in Houma. Pretty soon after that, Junior got a job on an oil rig and Lisa started taking work as a private duty nurse. When Willy got so sick that we had to hire somebody to help out, he told me to give his niece a call and see if she wanted to do her private duty nursing for him over here. Never crossed my mind to ask her if she really was what she said she was."

"So you never actually came out and asked what her qualifications were? Never saw a résumé?"

"Nah. She said, yes, ma'am, she had herself a nursing certificate and took the job right over the phone. Got here two days later and been living with us ever since, 'cept for every few weeks when Junior gets back on shore and she runs down to stay with him at some boarding house in Grand Isle."

I took a bite, thinking about it. Though I understood why Deena felt she had been conned, the situation seemed perfectly innocent to me. I asked what Lisa's hourly rate had been, and when Deena told me the amount I knew that that was her answer right there. No RN or LPN would ever have done home care for that low of a figure. Deena should have known that she was getting exactly what she paid for.

"So what's so bad about her being a nurse's aid?" I asked. "Didn't she do a good job?"

"I guess, but I let her make a lot of decisions that maybe I shouldn't have. I trusted that she knew more about medical things than I did, but now I realize she didn't know squat."

Taking the last bite of my dinner, I suddenly felt bad for Lisa, who was being unfairly judged here. I had a feeling that the only misleading thing she had done was to be so competent at caring for Willy that Deena had made some assumptions she shouldn't have. Having lost her home and possessions in the storm, at least I understood now why Lisa had bristled when I'd made an insensitive comment about the Katrina victims who hadn't had the sense to come in out of the rain. I felt bad about that too.

"So how did you find all of this out exactly?" I asked, running the napkin across my mouth as Deena's cheeks flushed a deep red.

"It's this house," she said finally.

"The house?"

"I found out a while back. It has something to do with the vents."

"What do you mean?"

"If you go stand in the laundry room, you can hear every word that's said in the library. I overheard her on a phone call today, trying to sign up with a home health agency now that her job here is done."

I sat back, glad that the calls I had made from there had been relatively benign, for no doubt Deena had run down the hall to eavesdrop on me too.

"But that doesn't mean you have to go in there and listen," I scolded, thinking that Jimmy Smith with his bug on my home telephone had nothing on her. "Shame on you."

"Hey, your grandma's the one who showed me. She figured it out about ten years ago, when they had some work done on the house. She was in the early stages of dementia then—"

"Wait," I interrupted. "What? My grandmother had dementia?"

"Oh, sure, by the time she died she was completely senile. Anyway, everybody else thought she was just talking crazy when she said there were people living in the new washer and dryer. I told her to prove it to me, and sure enough she did. Turns out, all she was hearing that day was your grandpa and a couple of his friends chatting in the library, which isn't all that close to the laundry room, but for some reason the voices come there."

I tried to digest the news about my grandmother, though it was hard to reconcile the image of a beautiful young woman I had been building in my mind with the picture of the senile old lady I was getting now. Hoping to find out more about that in a minute, I tried to stay focused on the subject at hand.

"So you just happened to be in there doing laundry today when Lisa chose to go into the library to make some private phone calls?"

"Sort of in reverse," Deena replied sheepishly. "I saw her go into the library with her phone, so I decided to do some laundry."

"I see."

"Hey, I don't have to defend myself to you," Deena said, folding her arms across her chest with a huff, clearly sorry that she had taken me into her confidence. "I didn't do nothing your grandma hadn't done."

Trying to smooth over the awkward moment, I invited her to tell me more about my grandmother. Though I was hoping to hear some tales of long ago, like Willy had given me, instead Deena chose to talk about the last few years of my grandparents' life, when my grandfather hired a round-the-clock staff of nurses to care for his wife here at home rather than put her in an institution.

"He moved into a bedroom down here so that she and her caregivers could have the run of the whole second floor. They say by the end all she did was paint those crazy pictures from morning to night, on and on and on, talking 'bout 'history can't repeat itself.' It was nuts."

I felt the hairs on the back of my neck standing up.

"What history?" I asked. "What paintings? Are they still around some-where?"

Deena dismissed my questions with a vague wave of her hand.

"I don't know what happened with all that. Willy took care of it some-how."

I tried a few more questions, but Deena was obviously finished with the subject of Portia Fairmont and ready to talk more about herself. I tried to steer her back, asking questions about my mother and the rest of the family, but finally Deena pushed herself away from the table and announced that she was tired and going to bed. Seeing the look on my face, she must have felt bad for being so abrupt.

"You gotta remember," she told me, her tone softening, "I wasn't never as involved with your family as Willy was. Until about eight years ago I had me a job in town as a secretary. My husband might've spent his time taking care of the house and the grounds around here, but when I was home at night and on the weekends, I mostly kept to myself. The cottage was pretty separate from this house, especially with the garages in between."

"I see."

"Once I was retired, I would come over here sometimes, to help out or whatever, but your grandma was losing it by then, so it's not like we became good friends or nothing. Sorry."

And with that the subject was apparently closed.

Deena went on to bed after that, leaving me alone in the quiet kitchen. If I hadn't been so wide awake, I might have opted for an early bedtime myself. As it was, however, I decided that I had an important task to do first, one that involved paying another visit to the second floor.

Just so I wouldn't have to explain myself, I decided to wait until I could hear Deena's snores coming through the wall before I made my move. In the meantime, I went to my tiny bedroom and retrieved the Bible I had shoved in the drawer last night. My mind had been working on the message from the old man all day, but I still didn't know what his biblical clue had been about. Getting comfortable on the bed, it took a while to find the section called Psalms, but once I had it I read number 141 and then a bunch of the other numbers too, enjoying the poetic cadence of the words but finding no new significance to the phrase he had muttered to me last night.

Finally, when the rumble of the dragon began, I closed the Bible and padded out of my room. I didn't know if Lisa was also asleep yet, but it didn't really matter. Her room was down the hall in the other direction, so I doubted she would hear me anyway. Just to be sure, I walked softly as I went, opening the door to the front of the house as slowly as possible so that it wouldn't squeak.

I flipped on the light once I had shut the door behind me, glad when the room with its creepy shadows was fully illuminated. I didn't know why this felt different now than it had just a while ago, but for some reason I didn't approach this task with the enthusiasm I'd had when I first thought of it.

The paintings, I told myself. *You need to see if you can find the paintings.*

That was enough to get me across the room, around to the entryway, and halfway up the stairs. There, I hesitated, looking up at the darkness, listening to the creaks and moans of the old house above me.

This wasn't that big of a deal, really, just a matter of walking up some stairs, turning on some lights, and poking around in a couple of closets. When I had been upstairs earlier, I had been more concerned with the layout of the rooms and recapturing some memories than with looking for anything specific. Now that I had been told, however, that my grandmother had left something of herself behind—something specific and tangible and possibly even related to the same matters that had obsessed Willy in his final days—I was driven to find them. Somehow, I also knew that holding my grandmother's original artwork in my hands would help me feel that there really was a connection between us, that the skills I possessed actually did have their genesis in my family tree and weren't just some unrelated talent tossed out to me at birth.

Mostly, I wanted her art to speak to me, to tell me things I did not know.

With that thought in mind, I summoned my nerve and walked up the rest of the stairs into the darkness, running my hand along the wall until it found the light switch. With a click, the shadows there were banished and my pulse could return to normal.

It wasn't until I was crossing the hall that I saw the movement, a flash of something filmy and light in the darkness of a bedroom. With a choking gasp, I turned and dared to look again—and that's when I realized that I had spotted my own reflection in a mirror hanging over a dresser. Swallowing hard, I told myself to get a grip, that if I really was this creeped out, I could always wait and do this tomorrow. It's not as though someone was holding a gun to my head.

Taking the plunge, I proceeded for now, moving into one of the front bedrooms and taking a look in the closet there, finding only some discarded lamps and a few wicker baskets. I was hoping to spy a stack of canvases or a box of watercolor paintings or a portfolio case of loose pages, but there wasn't anything of the kind in there. I moved on to the bedroom next door and tried again, searching first the closet and then the bureau.

Still coming up empty, I moved to a sitting room, which had no closet but did have a trunk and a desk. Though I didn't find what I was looking for, it was interesting to see the sorts of items that had been left undisturbed, from the old clothes neatly folded in the trunk to drawers of office supplies sorted in the desk. I found a roll of 12¢ stamps there, and I wondered if that had been the cost of first-class postage the last time this desk had been used.

The back bedroom on the right was completely devoid of anything, so I crossed the back hall to the other bedroom, pausing as I went. There was something different there in the hallway, something wrong or changed or altered. I turned in a circle, looking at the perfectly normal walls that surrounded me, unable to put my finger on what was bothering me about it. With a shrug, I moved on to that bedroom and then the bathroom, coming up with nothing of importance in either.

There was only one room left, and I entered it with a heavy heart and not a lot of optimism. There were boxes in the closet there—including one box of what looked like letters—but no paintings at all. I grabbed it anyway and set it near the doorway to take with me when I went down. Then I moved to the biggest piece of furniture in the room, a beautiful French-Liege wardrobe against the far wall. I reached for the double knobs and pulled both doors open with a loud creak.

I gasped. I hadn't managed to find the paintings but I had discovered the next best thing: my grandmother's painting supplies. There on the neatly hand-labeled shelves sat an assortment of brushes, papers, art tools, and even a few ancient dried up tubes of acrylic paint. Just standing there, I inhaled deeply and picked up the scent of an artist's lair that I knew so well, mixed with dust and aged wood. Carefully, I reached out and lifted a paintbrush from its wooden Winsor and Newton box, marveling at the sable brush that was of such high quality that it still held its spring and point all these years later. Enthralled with my discovery, I hoped to come back up here in the daylight and go through the cabinet more thoroughly.

For now, I closed the cabinet doors, retrieved the box of letters, and left the room. Turning off the light, I moved out into the hallway, disappointed that I hadn't accomplished my main goal, but glad at least that I had found the cabinet.

I was moving past the back bedroom when I spotted a soft glowing light from inside. Stepping backward, I hesitated at the doorway looking into the darkness, and when the light appeared again I realized that it was coming from outside, that I had seen it through the window.

Curious, I crept across the room in the darkness and made my way to that window, standing in the shadows and peeking out between the curtains. Orienting myself, I realized I was almost directly above the room where Willy had died, facing in the general direction of the bayou.

I thought maybe the light had been from a passing boat on the water, but when it glowed again I was startled to see that it was higher than that, shining from somewhere up in the trees, two flashes and then it was done. I stood there and watched, but after several minutes the light did not come on again.

Finally, I gave up waiting and continued downstairs, trying not to assign some sinister or threatening source to what could have a perfectly logical explanation. I would ask Deena or Lisa about it tomorrow. For now, I had some letters to read.

Down in my tiny bedroom, I sat on the bed and opened the box, hoping this was some sort of personal correspondence and not just a cache of business communications.

As soon as I got a good look at the handwriting on the envelopes, I knew who had written them. Flipping through the box, I realized that every single letter had come from the same person, the same place: Janet Greene in New York City. Though they were addressed to my grandparents, Mr. and Mrs. Xavier Fairmont, I assumed they had been my mother's, communications from her sister in the big city. I pulled one letter from the box at random, feeling guilty for invading their privacy—especially on the same night I had scolded Deena for doing the same to someone else—but the temptation was too great to resist. Opening the letter, I began to read.

It didn't take long to realize that I had been wrong. This letter wasn't written from AJ to my mother. It really was written from AJ to my grandparents, several years after my mother had died. It was dated July 1985, and all it contained was a chatty description of a Fourth of July trip AJ and I had taken to the Statue of Liberty. I reached for another letter and pulled it out, skimming to see that it was almost as mundane. Dated January 1987, it discussed my schoolwork and a recent problem I'd had with a classmate—private stuff of monumental importance to an eleven-year-old that I very well remembered having shared with AJ in confidence.

Heart pounding, I took a closer look at the whole box of letters, realizing that they were in chronological order, all from AJ to my grandparents.

Shaking my head, I had to think about this for a minute. AJ's sister Yasmine had been married to their son Richard. Other than that, the only connection that AJ shared with Xavier and Portia Fairmont was the fact that she had been given custody of their granddaughter: me.

With a dark sense of foreboding, I pulled out the very first letter in the box, dated ten days after my mother's death, and proceeded to read four pages of description about our traumatic flight home from New Orleans—which apparently I had spent staring out the window for three hours—AJ's attempts to get me settled into her apartment, and her concerns for my mental health. *She still hasn't spoken a word,* the letter said, *and spends most of her time huddling, rocking, etc., like she did down there, so I have made an appointment for next week with a good psychiatrist. I'll enclose his bill with my next letter. I'm not sure what it will cost, but no doubt you understand the necessity and would approve the expense.*

I looked up, trying to figure out what I had stumbled upon. AJ had never made any secret of the fact that she received money from my grandparents to help her with the expenses of raising me. Because of them, I had been able to attend the best schools in Manhattan, take private art and music lessons, even go on a graduation cruise with AJ and two of my best friends through the Greek Isles. But I always assumed the exchange of money had been a one-time thing, like a trust set up in my name that AJ administrated for me.

Instead, I realized as I read these letters, the money had come to her in various amounts over the years, apparently depending not just on what our current expenses were, but on how much AJ had written in the previous month's letter. Each note started the same, with a thank you for the bank deposit. But as I read my way through the years, I saw that whenever there was an extra long missive, quoting cute things I'd said or one that included photos of me or drawings I had done, then the next month's letter used the words "very generous," as in "thank you for the very generous bank deposit." Even when she was furious at them over the discovery of the tattoo on my head and the resulting custody battle threats, she continued to write each month, reporting the latest news laced with a few jabs about "the hideous mark" that had been inflicted upon me and the "vicious black-mail" they were using to keep her from reporting it.

I might have been able to understand why she had invaded my privacy and sold my soul, for surely a young woman alone in the city with a child needed a lot of money to stay afloat. What I didn't understand was why she had told me for years that the people down here didn't care about me, that they weren't interested in knowing me anymore, and that I should have nothing to do with them. She'd been lying. It was a lie. They *did* care. They *did* want to know. They wanted to know so badly that they were even willing to pay for the information.

I paused in my readings to clear my head. I brushed my teeth and changed into my nightgown, then I got back in the bed, intending to sit there and read every single letter in this box, even if it took all night. As I did, I was astounded at the amount of information and insight they contained, almost like a diary of my life. As angry as I was at AJ, I also couldn't help feeling that at least she had been a perceptive parent to me, relating thoughts and impressions that were frequently dead-on. She described at length my first real boyfriend, sharing her concerns that we were lingering too long in the stairwell when he brought me home and we said good night. When I was a senior in high school, she talked about my single-minded devotion to a career in the arts, dissecting my potential talents as a painter and sculptor with a fair amount of accuracy. Later, near the end of my freshman year in college, she rejoiced over my announcement that I didn't want to be an artist after all but an art restorer instead. She was thrilled, the letter said, as that guaranteed me a much more secure financial future.

Don't you find it interesting, a later letter said, *that Miranda has chosen to go into a field where she will take beautiful things of old that have been neglected and hurt and will lovingly restore them, setting them right again? I have to wonder if deep in her heart she will always want to go back and make things right in her own life—which of course is not an option.*

Several paragraphs down in the same letter, she apologized for being so maudlin, saying that it was the twentieth anniversary of my mother's death, which was making her feel very reflective. *Yasmine has been gone twenty years today*, it said, *and I still expect her to call me on the phone any moment. I still miss her so much I can't sleep sometimes for the ache deep in my chest. Having lost so much yourselves, especially Cassandra, I'm sure you understand.*

It wasn't the first mention of this Cassandra person, whoever she was. All I could gather was that she had died young, and that she had been important to my grandparents. I wondered if maybe she was my aunt, a sister to my father and his brother, despite the fact that no one else had ever mentioned her to me. I had obviously known and loved her myself when I was small, because the earliest mentions of her in these letters were about how I had forgotten everything and everyone from my first five years, even my mother and Cassandra.

It was almost four a.m. by the time I got to the description of my wedding. Through tears, I read about the beautiful ceremony and my gorgeous dress and the way I had gazed at my new husband as we said our vows. After my wedding, the letters grew more infrequent, and I realized that at that point she was no longer writing for money but simply to stay in touch. Her last note was the only one written just to my grandmother, with condolences on the loss of her husband:

> *As you know, I have been very conflicted about you and your husband's actions for many years. Now that he has passed, I think perhaps I have judged too harshly, for what parent wouldn't move heaven and earth to protect their own, regardless of the circumstances? At least I was given the chance to parent Miranda, and for that I will always be grateful to you both, not just for your financial support but for your willingness to come to an arrangement in the first place.*

Tears filled my eyes as I continued reading.

> *Miranda is now pregnant, news that fills us all with great joy as I'm sure it will you too. Despite having made a good life for herself, I don't think she has ever really let anyone past those walls that were so carefully constructed during the*

trauma she suffered as a child. My hope is that when this
baby is born, he or she might finally be the one to open up
Miranda's heart and show her that real love needn't be feared
but embraced, even at the risk of great pain.

With that, I began to cry in earnest, for AJ's hopes had been short lived and sadly misguided. I saw now what she had known all along, that I was incapable of truly loving anyone, even my own child. Holding back my sobs for fear of waking Deena next door, I continued to read that last letter to the end.

I'm sure you are feeling great pain now yourself, with the
death of your beloved Xavier. I can only offer the hope that
you will survive this, and I pray that eventually the joy of
having had him to share your life will outlive the pain of
loss. It is my understanding that you are quite ill yourself and
maybe can't even comprehend the words in this letter. I shall
leave you at this, then, with one thought, that out of much
grief and sorrow also came, in the end, much good. Miranda
Fairmont Miller is a lovely young woman, generous of spirit
and gentle in nature. If you could know her, you would be so
proud. As your only living grandchild, she may not remem-
ber her past, but she carries within her womb the future. And
in the end, that's what matters most, that life goes on, that
hope gives birth to hope.

With love—and yes, finally, with forgiveness—I remain...

    Yours,
    Janet

TWENTY-THREE

Is it a foolish dream, an idle vague superstition?
Or has an angel passed, and revealed the truth to my spirit?

Pounding. Someone was pounding on my door.

I opened my eyes to see that it was morning. I had cried myself to sleep amidst the letters, which at some point during the night had spilled out of the box and were now scattered all over the bed.

The pounding wouldn't stop, and I felt sure it was Deena, rudely waking me up, probably so that she could start complaining about something or gossip more about Lisa, just as she had last night. I threw aside the bedspread and jumped up, not even bothering to dig in my suitcase for my robe. I flung open the door as I demanded "What?"

Deena was not at my door. No one had been knocking.

Instead, several feet away, Aaron West was perched atop an aluminum stepladder, hammering at a place on the wall near the ceiling. He had paused, mid-hammer, the moment I opened the door, and now we stood staring at each other like two idiots.

"I, uh, I'm so sorry," he said, taking in my rumpled hair and my flimsy nightgown. "I didn't realize anybody was in there."

I could feel the heat practically burning through the skin of my face and neck. Quickly, I jumped behind the door and leaned outward so only my head was visible.

"What are you doing?"

"I'm checking for rot. You got a pretty nasty leak upstairs, and I'm trying to figure out how far down the damage goes. But look, I'll come back. I can do this later."

He was halfway down the ladder before I spoke.

"Aaron, wait. Just because I keep unintentionally flashing you is no reason to run away. I'm fine. We can pretend that this, too, didn't happen. I'd rather you keep working."

"You don't, like, go around completely naked at any point, do you? A man can only be a gentleman for so long."

I laughed.

"I promise, from now on, only turtlenecks and burlap sacks."

Smiling, I shut the door. A few minutes later, as I pulled on jeans and a comfortable shirt, the hammering finally stopped. By the time I had the bed made and the letters returned to their box and tucked away beside my suitcase, I opened the door to see that Aaron and his ladder were gone from the hallway. Relieved, I walked down to the bathroom with my toiletries and makeup, where I showered and got ready for the day. With my damp hair in a ponytail rather than a fancy twist or a bun, the first item on my agenda, after grabbing some breakfast, was to make several very difficult telephone calls.

Deena was in the kitchen cleaning out the refrigerator. She greeted me with a grunt, waving toward a plate of bacon and eggs that was sitting on the counter, covered with a paper towel.

"Didn't know you were gonna sleep half the day away," she grumbled, and I glanced at the clock on the stove to see that it was only nine thirty. I wondered what she would make of some of my friends back home, who would sleep until two or three in the afternoon whenever they had the chance. "You'll have to heat that up."

I thanked her for the breakfast as I ran it in the microwave. I realized I would either need to visit a store soon or give her some cash to cover the cost of having me here. No doubt she had already added the two eggs and two strips of bacon to my tab alongside the Benadryl and paper towels. She suggested I make myself some toast as well, which I did, mostly so that I could assemble a breakfast sandwich with the eggs and bacon and carry it outside to eat while I made my calls.

"Deena, I need to ask you a favor," I said as I waited for the toast to pop out. "I wonder if you might be willing to walk through the rest of the house with me later and tell me how it used to be laid out when I was a child. I would like to know whose room was where and so forth."

"Why on earth do you want to know that?" she demanded, emerging from deep in the fridge with a questionable pack of meat in one hand and some wilted lettuce in the other.

"Because I'm curious," I replied, removing the toast from the toaster and putting together my sandwich. "The only other person around here who might know that is my Uncle Holt, but with him in a wheelchair he wouldn't be able to get up there anyway."

She snorted.

"Sure," she said. "Just tell me when. I'll be around, packing all day. Packing and cooking. I hate to see this food go to waste."

I reached for the salt and pepper, asking her about the strange light I had seen last night from the upstairs window. She had no idea what I was talking about, so I quickly changed the subject and asked how well she knew my Uncle Holt.

"Well enough. Why?"

"I just wondered about the wheelchair. What's the story there?"

"Same as a lot of boys his age. Went to Vietnam as a handsome young soldier, came back lucky he was in a chair and not a box."

"Oh," I said, surprised I hadn't calculated his age and thought of that myself. I wrapped my sandwich in a paper towel and set the plate in the sink. "So how come he went to war but my father didn't?"

Deena huffed.

"I don't know," she said. "Probably because your father used every bit of his parents' influence to pull some strings and keep himself stateside. I seem to recall that when Holt was drafted he gave in to the inevitable without as much of a fight."

"I see."

I thanked her for the food and excused myself to go outside, thinking about the two brothers, Richard and Holt, as I walked. Judging by what AJ had written in her letters, they had both been spoiled and indulged by their parents while growing up. Ultimately, I realized, one of the brothers had ended up emotionally handicapped but physically whole, while the other was physically handicapped but emotionally whole, at least as far as I could tell. I wondered what had made the difference, why my father had remained so immature and unevolved while Holt had managed to grow up and become a man of character. Facing his responsibilities as a soldier had probably been a good start.

With my breakfast in one hand and my cell phone in the other, I made my way down to the bench at the trailhead so that I could look out at the bayou as I ate and made my calls.

When I turned on my phone, a message was waiting from Nathan, sent earlier this morning. I dialed into voice mail and took a bite of my sandwich as I listened. He was sorry we hadn't been able to talk last night, but he was glad I had called and maybe we could connect tonight. He went into more detail this time about the ribbon-cutting ceremony at the church yesterday morning, but I could tell from his voice that there was something he wasn't saying. He warned me that the next three days were going to be crazy busy for him as he and the engineer worked to close out the project completely, but that I could call whenever I needed, even if I needed him to come down here.

I erased his message and called back to leave one for him, telling him to focus on his job and not worry about me, though I appreciated his concern. After hanging up, I thought about calling AJ, but I wasn't up to that conversation just yet. Instead, I dialed in to my boss at the museum and explained that I had gone out of town this weekend to visit an old family friend who was dying, but that the friend had died while I was here, so I was going to stick around for the funeral and might not be back in this week. I rarely missed a day of work, but suddenly my job there felt a million miles away and not nearly as important as I had always felt it to be.

After disconnecting I realized I had lost my appetite and tore up the rest of my breakfast into tiny bits and tossed them toward the water, hoping the heron would return.

"Better be careful. You might draw alligators that way."

I turned around to see Aaron West, smiling at me from a few steps behind.

"Are there really alligators in there?" I asked.

"I imagine so," he replied, "but I wouldn't worry about it. I don't know of any that hang out around this part of the bayou."

"That's good. I hope."

He moved forward, his eyes on my face.

"I'm sorry to bother you. I just have a quick question."

"What's that?"

"I finally figured out the problem with the attic. The reason I couldn't figure out where to get up into it was because there's another whole floor, a third story, and then the attic is on top of that."

"What do you mean?" I asked, twisting around to look at the house in the distance.

"You can tell from out here that there's something up there just by looking at those dormers," he said, pointing to the highest, smallest windows of the house that ran just below the roof line. "I had figured those dormers were a part of the attic, not more living space, but I was wrong. They're a part of the third story rooms. I guess the attic is pretty small and doesn't have any windows."

I was stunned.

"You're telling me this house has a third floor of living space?" I asked, heart pounding. "How do you get to it?"

"Apparently there's a flight of stairs from the second floor."

"I never saw one," I said, certain that I had peeked inside every door and closet up there and had come across nothing of the kind.

"I know, me neither. But Miss Deena told me where they are. She said that her husband put up some Sheetrock to hide them a long time ago. She said he had to do it to keep your grandmother from wandering up there after she began to show signs of senility. They were afraid she might fall back down. So he walled them off and after a while she forgot they had been there."

I could just picture it, this poor, senile old woman insisting that she be able to go up and down at will, testing the limits of her caregivers. No wonder they had walled it off. I could only imagine her confusion after that, no longer being able to find something that she felt sure had been there before.

"Anyway," Aaron continued, "I need to get up to the attic, but that means I'll have to take down that Sheetrock to get up to the third floor first. I asked Miss Deena if that was okay, but she sent me out here to check with you."

"This Sheetrock you want to take down," I said, my spine tingling, "is it along the back hall, near the bathroom?"

I was thinking of when I had been up there last night, of the place that for some reason just hadn't looked right to me.

"Yeah, exactly. The stairs are there, behind that wall."

As he said it, I could picture it, but as I did I felt vaguely unsettled, as if taking down that wall would take away a layer of safety as well. A big part of me wanted to go with Aaron right now and watch him break through. But a bigger part said I needed to proceed more slowly, that another panic attack like the one on the plane might be waiting right behind that wall.

Still, that didn't mean he shouldn't prepare the way for the moment when I would feel ready to take a look. I felt a surge of excitement, knowing that there was a chance my grandmother's paintings could be up there.

"Yes, please," I said resolutely. "Tear it down. While you're at it, would you please go through the whole house and take down every board and every plank off of every single window and door? It's time to throw this place wide open."

Judging by his expression, I think he didn't know whether to be amused by my fervor or alarmed by it.

"Sure," he said. "Whatever you want."

He started to walk away but I called after him.

"I don't suppose you could recommend a good local cleaning service, could you? I'm not just ready to bring in the light, I want to get rid of the dust and dirt too."

"No, but my sister will. I was about to call her anyway, so I'll ask and let you know."

With that, he headed back to the house as he pulled a phone from his pocket, leaving me there beside the water to contemplate the call I needed to make next.

It was time to talk to AJ, to tell her that I had flown down here Saturday morning without even telling her. She was going to be concerned about me, of course, but she was also going to feel very betrayed. Last night, when I had been so furious with her, I had felt betrayed as well. But after reading all of the letters and having some time to digest them, my emotions regarding AJ were now in an entirely different place. I felt a lot of things toward her, a little angry, yes, but also embarrassed that she knew me even better than I knew myself. Most of all, I felt indebted. Indebted that she had given up her life for mine, that she had taken me in and loved me like a mother would have and never flinched in carrying out this obligation to her dead sister. How could I repay something like that? It took reading all of those letters before I began to see the full scope of what she'd done for me. In light of all that, this was not a call I wanted to make. It was simply too hard to face her right now with all of these thoughts and emotions rolling around in my mind.

For at least ten minutes, I thought about what I might say, and then finally I dialed her office and was deeply relieved when her secretary said she was in a meeting and wouldn't be out for at least an hour. I hated to be a big chicken, but I knew that gave me the perfect excuse for not dealing with all of this directly right now. I asked the secretary to tell her that I was in Louisiana and for her to call me back on my cell phone when she had time to talk. I hung up after that, ignoring my guilt, thinking that this way AJ could absorb that news first and then we could discuss it later.

I was just standing up to go back to the house when I heard a woman's voice calling to me from off to the right.

"Yoo hoo!"

Startled, I looked up the path to see Livvy marching my way, a great big tote bag hanging from her shoulder and a thick book tucked under one arm. She was followed by a young woman carrying a casserole.

"Aaron said you were out here," Livvy told me. "I'm glad I caught you. I've got some fun surprises."

I had so much to do that I wasn't really in the mood for a visit, but Southern hospitality being what it was, I knew I needed to make her feel welcome even if I had to give her the bum's rush to get her back out of there.

"Hi, Livvy. How are you?"

She gave me an air kiss and then nodded toward her companion.

"Surprise number one. This is Sissy. She's here to clean your house."

My eyes widened.

"That was fast."

"It's your lucky day. Sissy always does my place on Mondays, but Melanie's home sick today with her allergies all flared up. Between the cleaning chemicals and the vacuum cleaner and the dusting, I think all that might make Melanie ever sicker. I was just about to send Sissy home when Aaron called and said you needed somebody. Voila, here we are."

I thanked them both, so relieved to have someone here so quickly that I didn't even ask what it was going to cost me.

"Sissy, you go on ahead and bring that casserole to Miss Deena and ask her where she keeps the cleaning supplies" Livvy directed.

"Yes, ma'am."

As she walked away, Livvy opened the tote bag and showed me the contents. Inside was what looked like a framed canvas, carefully protected by a Mylar sleeve.

"This is one of the paintings that got damaged. I really just need an opinion. Please let me know what you think it would take to have it restored, or if it's even possible."

"Sure."

Next to the painting was something small and black that looked like an elongated flashlight.

"I also threw in a portable UV light I borrowed from the museum. I thought it might be helpful. They need it back by tomorrow, though."

"Great."

"Finally," she said, "the biggest surprise of all. I've only got a second and then I have to run, but I just couldn't wait to show you."

"What?" I asked, relieved that she was about to be on her way.

"You're gonna be happy," she said proudly, picking up the book.

"What is it?"

"I did a little research at the museum this morning, for your genealogical question."

"Oh?"

"I found it, Miranda. I found Colline d'Or."

TWENTY-FOUR

Over the roofs of the village
Columns of pale blue smoke, like clouds of incense ascending,
Rose from a hundred hearths, the homes of peace and contentment...
Neither locks had they to their doors, nor bars to their windows;
But their dwellings were open as day and the hearts of the owners;
There the richest was poor, and the poorest lived in abundance.

Back at the house, once I made sure Sissy was off and rolling with the cleaning, I slipped away to my tiny downstairs bedroom, closed the door, and pulled out the book Livvy had brought me. According to her, the reason I hadn't been able to find Colline d'Or on any map was because it no longer existed. All she'd had to do, she said, was go through some Cajun history books that featured older maps, and there she had finally found it: Once upon a time, Colline d'Or had been a village in the Piziquid Valley region of Nova Scotia.

Livvy had marked the pertinent pages with Post-it Notes, so I flipped to them right away and devoured the information hungrily. The book had several paragraphs about the town, saying that Colline d'Or had been one of the last Acadian villages to have its citizens rounded up by British soldiers in the *Grand Derangement*. Unlike most other villages in Nova Scotia, however, not one of the citizens of Colline d'Or had attempted to escape into Quebec or other surrounding areas. Instead, a deeply religious group who cited the Christian principles of peace and nonresistance, they had gone voluntarily with the soldiers en masse and were eventually shipped off to an English prison camp. Many of these Acadians had died in transit or in the camp, but ten years later, those who were still alive made their way to Louisiana and settled there. The original town in Nova Scotia no longer existed, most of the homes and crops having been burned to the ground by the British.

So much for peace and nonresistance.

I turned the page and found Colline d'Or on the map. Seeing it there was so real, so significant, that I could practically feel the tattoo on my head pulsating. Such a place existed after all, and from what Willy had told us, I felt sure it was the Nova Scotian village from which he and my grandmother—not to mention Lisa and I—had descended. Now if we could only learn what the myth of the angelus was, we might be able to piece this puzzle together.

Feeling hopeful about this for the first time since Willy died, I closed the book and went in search of Lisa. She wasn't home, so I put the book away for now and asked Deena if she was ready to take me through the house and answer my questions about it. I sure felt ready to see it, I thought bravely, even the now-open third floor that Aaron West's efforts had revealed.

Deena lowered the heat under a pot on the stove and took off her apron. She didn't exactly seem enthusiastic, but at least she was willing. We started downstairs as she perfunctorily pointed out the parlor, the foyer, the dining room, and the living room. As we walked up the curving staircase together, I couldn't help but wish I had a more effusive tour guide, as thus far mine was practically monosyllabic!

The maid had already finished one of the front bedrooms and was partially done with the next. Between her cleaning efforts and Aaron having removed the boards from the doors and windows, already it was like a different place up here. I stepped into the clean, sunny room, the bed stripped and the wood furniture gleaming. I crossed all the way to the door, flinging it open to reveal the second floor balcony outside.

Stepping onto it, I inhaled deeply as I looked out over the beautiful, sweeping lawn.

"When you were a child, this was one of the guest rooms," Deena said, following along behind. "The whole left side of this floor was for guests. The right side was for your grandparents."

Moving back inside, I closed the door and walked into the room behind it. This one hadn't been cleaned yet, so the furniture was still covered with sheets, but according to Deena, this was the guest sitting room. I tried to pull some tales from her of visiting dignitaries or colorful relatives, but it was like trying to get blood from a stone. She had no tales to tell, just simple facts that she was attempting to dispense as quickly as possible.

When we finally reached the staircase that had now been revealed by the removal of the Sheetrock, I felt my pulse quicken. Leading the way to the top, I wasn't surprised to hear Aaron clomping around above us in the small attic.

"Your parents lived in the front bedroom here, the same room your daddy grew up in," Deena said, continuing our tour.

She opened the door to reveal a wide, lovely bedroom that had a triangular window at its front. I walked toward it and peeked out to see that we were jutting out over the second story balcony. It was gorgeous up here; no wonder he didn't want to leave even after he got married.

"When they were boys, your Uncle Holt lived in this room over here," Deena said, leading me back into the hall and across it to a door on the left. "But when you lived here, this was the nanny's quarters."

The room was oddly shaped, and judging by the furniture had served a combination bedroom and small sitting room.

"Everybody shared the same bathroom," Deena said as she led me through it to emerge back in the hallway under the attic stairs. "That just leaves these last two rooms, which your mama turned into a bedroom and a playroom."

She opened the door on the other side of the hall, revealing the playroom first. I stepped forward, disappointed that there were no toys or other momentoes present—just a wall of empty shelving, a child-sized table and chair set, and a brightly colored rug on the floor.

"That's the bedroom there?" I asked, gesturing toward the door.

"Yep, that was it," Deena replied.

Something inside of me was nervous about moving on to the last room, but I wanted to proceed. Slowly, I turned the knob, pushing the door open to reveal the pale pink walls of a little girl's bedroom. It was a little less sparse than the playroom had been, with two dolls sitting neatly atop the dresser and matching flowered bedspreads on each of the twin beds, white with pink and yellow roses.

On the wall above each bed was a framed painting of varicolored roses and ivy. Over one bed, I realized the ivy formed letters, spelling out my name: Miranda. Over the other bed, they formed a different name.

Cassandra.

"Deena?" I asked, my voice sounding far away and strange. "Who is Cassandra?"

"What?" she asked, stepping into the room beside me.

I had trouble catching my breath, but I pointed to the wall and said, "There. That name. Who is Cassandra?"

Swallowing hard, I looked at Deena's confused face.

"I don't understand the question," she told me. "Cassandra was your sister, of course. Your twin."

A roaring began between my ears.

"I didn't have a sister," I said simply, shaking my head back and forth as chills began to race up and down my arms.

"Of course you did. You were identical twins, for goodness' sake. Miranda and Cassandra."

I felt myself slipping, sliding away from that place to somewhere else, somewhere different. Somewhere dark.

"And what happened to Cassandra?" I asked, the words bouncing around in my brain like a pinball shot from a cage.

"She died. That's why your mother killed herself. You certainly knew that."

I opened my mouth, trying to answer. But before any words came out, my world went black and the ground rushed up to smack me in the face.

TWENTY-FIVE

Fair was she and young; but, alas! before her extended,
Dreary and vast and silent, the desert of life, with its pathway
Marked by the graves of those who had sorrowed and suffered before her,
Passions long extinguished, and hopes long dead and abandoned.

 When I opened my eyes, I knew two things: I wasn't in the pink bedroom anymore, and I had a terrible headache.

Blinking, I looked around to orient myself and realized that somehow I had somehow gone down one level and to the front bedroom, the one that had been cleaned. Blinking again, I realized that I was being stared at by Aaron and the maid. Before any of us could speak, Deena came into the room with an ice pack that she promptly laid on my forehead.

"Are you okay?" she asked, distinct creases lining the sides of her mouth in a frown.

I took a deep breath, let it out, and said that I thought so but I wasn't sure.

"What happened?" she asked.

I glanced at the other two who were still hovering at the foot of the bed. Sensing my embarrassment, Deena shooed them both away.

"What happened? You were just standing there, talking, and then all

of a sudden, boom, you were down on the floor. Now you got a big ol'
egg on your head."

Opening my eyes again, I focused on her face, wondering how to
explain.

"I guess I fainted from the emotional shock of the moment."

"What do you mean?"

I exhaled slowly, not wanting to give this woman a detailed history of
my psychological makeup. Still, I didn't want to lie.

"It's hard to explain," I said. "But I'm sure you can imagine how it felt
to be reminded of Cassandra."

"I guess so."

"I'll be okay, I'm sure. I just need to get my bearings. Did Aaron carry
me down here?"

She nodded, wringing her hands.

"Yeah, he was gonna take you all the way down to your room, but it
was hard to maneuver the first flight of stairs, so he didn't want to risk a
second time. You're just so tall, he was afraid he might drop you. We put
you in here instead."

"Thanks."

She clasped and unclasped her fingers.

"You should probably drink something," she added. "I have some apple
juice in the kitchen. That might be good for you."

She was hovering so nervously that I agreed yes, that would be perfect.
After she was gone, I laid there on that old bed and stared at the ceiling,
thinking how an entire world can flip upside down in a single moment.
Had I been through an earthquake or transported to another town via
tornado, I don't think I could have felt any more disoriented than I did at
that moment.

I had a sister. A twin. An identical twin.

Her name was Cassandra, and we shared a bedroom and a playroom
and a nanny and a whole family.

I called her Cass.

She was my constant companion.

One by one, things began to click into place, little clues and hints that somehow I had known this all along.

Was that why I had insisted on naming my child Tess, because it sounded much the same? Tess, Cass. No wonder so many people had been confused about the name since we got here.

How could AJ never, ever have told me?

The ice bag began to slip, so I reached up and moved it back into place, finally understanding why she had warned me about coming here. How else could you safely tell someone news that was this big?

How else could you tell someone that truly half of who they were had been cut out of their life in an instant and then erased from their mind?

Holding the ice bag, I rolled onto my side and drew up my knees, a deep overwhelming sadness piercing my heart. I didn't remember Cassandra, not yet, but even so I missed her, not to mention that I selfishly missed that other part of who I was. Tears filled my eyes and slid sideways down my face as I thought of yesterday's memory at the mirror in the hall. How many times as a child and a teenager had I stood at a mirror and looked at myself and felt somehow a little less lonely, a little less alone? I wasn't some pathetic egotist who found pleasure in looking at herself. I was a girl who was trying to bring back someone she forgot she had lost.

I wanted to know more. I wanted to know how she died. I wanted to hear everything, down to the most seemingly insignificant detail. I wanted to learn how life could end for one of us and not the other.

Somehow, still overcome with the shock of the sudden revelation, I must have simply shut down or either drifted off to sleep. I came back to awareness with a start when Deena returned, a tray in her hands, my nostrils filling with the smell of soup. Chicken soup.

I sat up, startled, realizing that something had changed, that the lighting in the room was different than it had been before I closed my eyes.

"What time is it?" I asked. Rubbing my face, I felt frightened, as if I had just been not in sleep but in some altered state, some other reality.

"Almost four. You been sleeping for hours. I was getting worried so I just called my doctor and he told me the symptoms to watch for, in case you got a concussion." She went on to list them—headache, abnormal sleepiness, dizziness, confusion, lack of feeling or emotion, anxiety, blurred vision, and vomiting—concluding with the suggestion that she take me to the hospital.

"No," I said, assessing my state. "Except for the long nap, I don't have any other symptoms. I'm fine, I'm sure."

I didn't add that I *was* feeling a weird combination of confusion, a lack of emotion, and anxiety—but I felt sure that had nothing to do with a concussion and everything to do with the revelation that had come just prior to it.

"Well, at least you ought to eat something," Deena said, placing the tray she was holding on to my lap, a simple arrangement of soup, spoon, crackers, and juice. Though I wasn't hungry, I took a bite of the soup to be polite. "I also got a surprise for you."

"It seems to be my day for surprises," I replied, pulling away the cracker I'd been about to bite into.

"You'll never guess who just showed up at the back door."

"Who?"

She walked to the banister and leaned over the side, calling down for whoever it was to come on up.

"It's your daddy," Deena said, returning to me. "Says he's come to town for Willy's funeral. I didn't even realize he was all that fond of Willy."

Suddenly, my father bounded up the stairs and into the room. I was so surprised to see him that I nearly spilled my soup.

Coming on the heels of my revelations about Cassandra, my father's timing couldn't have been worse. Still, he was here now and seemed happy to see me. He leaned down and placed an awkward kiss on my cheek, telling me how much he missed me, that he couldn't believe our paths had not crossed for several years. I tried to smile in return but wasn't very successful.

Once Deena left the room, my father pulled over a chair and sat near the bed, asking about my fall and the lump on my head. I assured him it wasn't anything serious. We made small talk, me asking about his flight, him asking what I was doing here. I wasn't sure how to explain, so I just said that Willy had wanted me to come down so he could see me all grown up before he died.

Ignoring the suspicious expression on his face, I asked if he'd brought Abby and the kids, but he said no, that he had come alone. To my mind, it was just as well. He had remarried when I was seven years old to an Arizona divorcee with two surly children and a big mansion in Tucson. Though he played the dutiful stepfather to her children, she had no interest in reciprocating with me, though I'd always had the feeling she encouraged him to maintain those ties himself. Eventually the contact between father and daughter had dwindled down to a single, annual phone call on Christmas Day. Considering how very little he and I had to talk about, it seemed to be enough.

Now, in this moment, with me feeling so emotionally vulnerable, I wondered if I dared bring up the subject of Cass. I had so many questions, and I realized that this might be my first real opportunity to connect with my dad in years.

"Can I ask you something?" I said, feeling inexplicably nervous, as I handed him the tray.

"Sure," he replied, taking it from me and setting it on the floor out of the way.

"Would you mind talking to me about Cassandra?"

He seemed startled, to say the least. Eyes wide, he hemmed and hawed.

"I didn't know...I thought...You weren't..."

"You thought I didn't remember," I said for him.

"Yes. Janet always said you had forgotten her and that we were never supposed to bring it up."

"That was true," I replied, "until today."

I went on to explain how I had found out, passed out, and thus turned out with a bump on my head. When I finished, he stood and went to the window, looking as though he'd rather be anywhere but here. He didn't reply for a long time, and as I waited for him to speak, I just sat there and watched him.

Richard Fairmont had always been a handsome and sophisticated man, with a chiseled jaw, perfect hair, and the elegant yet aggressive carriage of someone who knows what he wants and is determined to get it. In the few times I had seen him in the last ten years, he had always been perfectly groomed, a Southwest tan lending a healthy glow to his angular face. Looking at him now, I decided that he was all polish, no substance, a very handsome, sophisticated, empty shell of a person.

"What would you like to know?" he said finally, turning back to look at me.

"Anything," I replied. "What was she like? What were we like? Were we close? Do you still miss her? How did she die?"

"Ah," he said, moving back to sit again in the chair. "Just a few simple questions like those, huh?"

We shared a sad smile and then I sat back and waited for him to speak.

He talked, slowly at first, describing his beloved daughter who had died. He said that we had been mirror image identical twins, which meant that we were the same, but opposite. She was the left-handed one, the aggressor, the braver soul. I, on the other hand, had been much more timid, less gregarious, less verbal. He said that we were together constantly, often living in our own separate world, speaking our own unique language. Our favorite game was follow the leader, with her always the leader and I the follower. We also had another game, he said, a trick of sorts that we were so good at that they would troop us out at parties to entertain the guests.

"What trick?" I interrupted, goose bumps rising up on my arms. "Where?"

"One of you would stand in front of that long mirror near the front door and make some motions one after the other, like raise your hand, wiggle your fingers, stick out your tongue. Then you'd turn around and do more things like that toward the doorway, which was directly opposite. Only that time you weren't doing them facing a mirror, the other one would step out and stand there so that you were doing them facing each other. It was uncanny. No matter how long it went on, it was like each of you knew what the other was about to do and they would match it, movement for movement, so closely that it was just like you were still doing it with the mirror. The first few times, I thought your series of movements was all choreographed and memorized, but then one day I realized it wasn't. You just knew what to do, exactly when the other one did what they did. It was bizarre."

I closed my eyes, the mystery of the mirror in the front hall now solved.

"How did she die?" I asked softly.

"It was so ridiculous, so tragic. Her favorite little nightgown was too long, a hand-me-down from a cousin that she insisted on wearing whenever she could. One night, she must have had a bad dream, because she got up to come in our room or go get the nanny, we were never sure. Anyway, she must have tripped on that stupid long nightgown, because she fell down the stairs to the second floor and broke her neck. She died instantly."

I shook my head, unable to fathom the heartbreak that must have resulted from such a tragic incident. Even now, my father's words sounded removed somehow, like a well-rehearsed speech that he'd learned to give in order to assuage the pain.

"And that's why my mom killed herself?"

"Yasmine was never all that strong of a person anyway," he said, "but after we lost Cass, she really went off the deep end. Her grief was unbearable. I always said it would have gotten better if she just could have held out, but she wouldn't. The very night after the funeral, she went outside to the garden and hung herself from a tree."

I gasped.

"And just like that, in one fell swoop I lost a child and then a wife," he added.

How utterly unsurprising that he'd put it that way in this moment, rather than saying the other truth, which was that in one fell swoop, I had lost a sister and then a mother.

"And so it was," he continued, "like dominoes falling, one tragedy in my life creating another. First Cassandra, then Yasmine..."

"Then me?"

He shrugged.

"In a sense," he said. "For a while at least, you were so far gone you were as good as dead. I didn't know if we would ever get you back."

I sat up straighter, leaning toward him.

"Then explain something to me," I said, the question suddenly filling my mind, pounding out all others. "How is it that after losing your wife and daughter so tragically, you chose to let me go off to live with AJ? Didn't you want to keep me with you? Hadn't you already lost enough?"

He ran a hand over his face.

"I knew how much your aunt loved you. I knew she could do a better job of raising you than I could—especially considering the condition you were in."

"Any other reasons?" I asked, feeling suddenly as though I needed to press him for more, for the self-oriented bottom line that always guided everything that he did.

"Sure, fine," he snapped, rising to the occasion the way I knew he would, "what do you want me to say? That I had lost a child who looked exactly like you? It was easier for me to get over it if you weren't always around, where I would have to see you and remember her."

He left me by myself after that, saying he needed to run an errand in Baton Rouge that might keep him there for the night, but that he would see me at the viewing tomorrow. Errand or not, I knew that his departure was more about getting away from a tense and sad conversation, more about getting away from me.

The story of my life.

TWENTY-SIX

Feeling is deep and still; and the word that floats on the surface
Is as the tossing buoy, that betrays where the anchor is hidden.
Therefore trust to thy heart, and to what the world calls illusions.

I laid there and thought about what I could accomplish with the balance of the day. Though I wanted to search the top floor of the house for my grandmother's paintings, I didn't think I was up to going there again just yet. I needed to talk to Lisa, to update her on Colline d'Or and find out if she'd had any luck asking around about Jimmy Smith or the symbol of the cross in the bell, but according to Deena, she'd left earlier this morning and said she wouldn't be back until dinner.

That left the issue of AJ and the difficult conversation we needed to have, but my cell phone had been conspicuously silent all day.

Thinking of last night's letters and of today's discovery about my twin sister, I realized that most of all I had the overwhelming urge to go back and see my Uncle Holt and maybe talk to him about some of what was going on. We still didn't know each other all that well, but we had made a connection yesterday, and I felt sure that he was as eager to spend time with me as I was to spend time with him. I went downstairs and freshened up, and though Deena wasn't crazy about the idea of me going for a walk in the woods with a head injury, she didn't try to stop me.

Despite the late afternoon heat and humidity, the walk to Holt's house did me good. By the time I got there, my stride was strong and the pain on my forehead had lessened. Were it not for the bruise and slight swelling at my hairline, I might have put the fall out of my mind completely.

Just like yesterday, I could hear Holt before I saw him, though this time there was no banging pot, just his voice. Afraid I might startle Duchess again, I cupped my hands around my mouth and called out the news of my arrival. By the time I reached the clearing, Holt was sitting there waiting for me, his hand on the collar of a massive blond-colored dog.

"Miranda!" he cried, his eyes crinkling in delight. "I've been hoping you'd pop in today."

I gave him a hug and then with his permission greeted the dog, asking about Duchess. He said she'd been sent on her way this morning with a recommendation for search and rescue training, replaced by this new candidate, Sugarpie.

"Sugarpie?" I asked with a chuckle. "For this big lug?"

"Yeah, kind of humiliating, isn't it, especially considering he's a male. Anyway, help me out a sec, would you? I want to try something."

"Sure."

"Hold on here and walk him over to that post, and then on the way back, act like you're losing your balance. I want to see what he does."

Gripping the handle of the dog's harness, I did as Holt instructed. When I started to wobble, I was surprised to feel the dog's big body move right up against me and steady me in place.

"Good," Holt said calmly, though whether to me or to the dog I wasn't sure. "Now do it again, but this time wobble a little longer."

I repeated the steps, walking to the post and then turning around and coming back. This time, as soon as the dog braced against me, I noticed that Holt took a shiny red ball and rolled it along the ground so that it passed right in front of us. Sugarpie whimpered, but he stayed where he was until I finally stopped wobbling and stood up straight. Even then, he didn't dart away, though I could tell he wanted to.

"Excellent. You can let him go."

Sugarpie bounded away, retrieving the object of his affection, and then the three of us headed for the house, the dog carrying the ball in his mouth. Holt said my visit was perfect timing as he was ready to take a break and have something cold to drink.

Soon Holt and I were relaxing on the porch with our cups of sweet tea, looking out at the lazy bayou, and I asked him how he had landed into this whole dog thing in the first place. He said that it started when he was about six months sober and volunteering down at the VA hospital. A patient there had one of the very first "PTSD Dogs," who had been trained to help her owner manage the challenges of his post-traumatic stress disorder. Holt said this dog could do everything from retrieving the guy's medication to crowd control to panic management, and watching her work had inspired him to launch a new career in the field.

Despite his handicap, Holt went back to school to become an animal behaviorist. After graduating, he worked as a trainer, but soon it became obvious that his real gift was for evaluation and placement. Eventually, he founded his own nonprofit organization that did just that. Currently, he had two employees, dozens of volunteers, and a waiting list for his services that could keep him busy around the clock seven days a week, if he let it.

"So do you have this same sort of gift for evaluating people?" I asked.

He laughed.

"I don't know. I never thought about it," he said. "I suppose if somebody stayed here for a week like the dogs do and let me run them through a bunch of tests, I just might."

We both smiled, gazing out at the water.

"If I were a dog, where would you place me?" I asked.

He rubbed his beard, considering.

"Well, let's see, you didn't lick my face when we met," he quipped, which made me laugh, "you take direction well, and you've obviously got the ability to focus."

He had started out teasing, but now he grew more serious.

"You're tall," he continued, "and strong, I imagine, but I wouldn't want to depend on that strength too heavily because you're so slender. I'd say, considering your warm nature, your obvious loyalty, and your high intelligence, I'd start by testing you for medical assistance tasks. Depending on how calm you remain in a crisis, you could work with someone who has anxiety or depression or even a chronic pain disorder. I don't think I'd recommend you as a guide dog because recovery time might be a concern."

"Recovery time?"

"That means how long it takes you to bounce back and get to work when you've been thrown for a loop. Fast recovery is vital for some areas, but you strike me as the type of person who might need to absorb things for a while. Maybe mull them over before you can move on."

I met his eyes and then looked away.

"I'd say," I told him, "that your talents give you insight into both man and beast."

"Thank you," he replied, and then we just sat there, the only sounds the hum of crickets and the gentle rocking of my chair. Finally, he spoke. "So what is it that you're bouncing from right now, Miranda? If you feel like talking about it, I mean."

I did feel like talking about it, and I was so glad he had asked.

As Holt sat and listened, I began to unburden myself, telling him about the letters I had found from AJ to my grandparents, my learning of Cassandra just today, and the conversation I'd had with my father afterward. Holt offered an ear and a shoulder and a lot of wisdom, and as I shared what I was feeling, I decided that it really wasn't all that difficult to be the one on the telling side of a heart-to-heart rather than taking my usual stance as the listener. Holt said he had known about my erased memories, which was why he'd been so surprised yesterday when he thought my daughter was named Cass.

The only time he contradicted me was when I described my anger at AJ for keeping me so isolated from the rest of this family.

"I understand that she wanted to give me a fresh start," I said. "I even kind of get why she never told me that I had a sister, much less one who had been my identical twin. But why keep me from having a relationship with my grandparents? Why keep me from having a relationship with you?"

"I can't speak for her motives with my parents," he said, "but I'll tell you exactly why she kept you away from me. When the two of you left here, Miranda, I was a mess. I didn't deserve to be a part of your life. I was drinking, doing drugs, all kinds of stuff. That's who I was to her at that time. I don't blame her one bit for cutting off that tie."

"But what about later, once you got sober?"

He shrugged.

"I contacted her once, to see if maybe you and I could establish some sort of relationship. She said it was...complicated. In the end, she felt it best if things stayed as they were. I couldn't blame her. She didn't know the man I had become."

I understood what he was saying, but still I didn't agree.

"How did you become that man, Holt? Why are you so very different from my father?"

"Why don't we take a walk? Or rather, you can walk, I'll roll. I'll answer your question as we go."

I wasn't sure what our destination was, but I had a feeling we weren't just aimlessly wandering the countryside. We put Sugarpie on a leash and brought him with us, heading up Holt's driveway for a while and then diverting onto a wide, well-worn path that led us alongside the bayou. As we went, Holt told me his story, how he and my father had been raised with every advantage, every indulgence. Their parents, he said, were experts at getting the two mischievous boys out of trouble. When Richard was drafted, they managed to protect him from going to Vietnam, but two years later when Holt faced the same problem, things had changed, and finding a way to remain stateside wasn't quite as simple. He ended up having to serve in combat, where he fought for nine months before getting caught in an ambush that obliterated most of his platoon and left him paralyzed from the waist down. By the time he got back home, he was a bitter, angry paraplegic with no hope for the future. Regardless of his parents' money or power or influence, the wheelchair was something he knew they would never be able to bail him out of.

Meanwhile, his brother had moved back home, taken a job in their father's company, and married the beautiful Yasmine Greene. Holt tried to figure out how he, too, could create some semblance of a normal life, but that all began to fall apart within a year or two, about the time the perfect couple, Richard and Yasmine, announced they were expecting their first child. Holt had been using drugs since Vietnam, but at that point he turned to the bottle too. By the time Cassandra and I were born, he was such a drunk, in his words, that when my mother brought us home and he held one of us in his arms—he was sorry, but he couldn't even remember which one—he nearly dropped that baby on the floor. Five years later, by the time Cass and my mother died, he said, he was living in an adapted trailer at the foot of his parent's property, either drunk or stoned around the clock and of no good use to anyone.

"That's why you can't blame Janet," he said. "Heck, I even showed up drunk to Cassandra's funeral, a bottle of Jack Daniels in my hand. Your father was so agitated, he actually punched me in the jaw. I was kind of glad. At least then I felt something. Four days later, when they buried your mother, I didn't even bother to go."

His words were rough, but I certainly got the picture.

"I hate to sound like a cliché," he said, "but I really did have to hit bottom and come to the end of myself before I could begin to climb back up."

He went on to describe how an old war buddy dragged him to an AA meeting where he learned about having a "higher power."

"They say your higher power is what you believe it to be, but I knew who that higher power was. His name was God, and He had been waiting to hear from me for a long time."

Holt talked about how he found a church-based recovery group and then found faith, how God dragged him "kicking and screaming" into believing that he could either buy the whole package or none of it at all.

"The whole package?" I asked.

"The Bible. Either it's the true Word of God or it isn't. You can't pick and choose just the warm and fuzzy parts, or just the parts that make sense, and then use them to create your own version of who you wish God was. I realized that I had two choices: embrace the whole thing or reject the whole thing. Period."

"So you embraced it and became some Bible-toting Holy Roller?" I asked, trying to make light of it but feeling stupid the moment the words came out of my mouth.

He was quiet for a moment and I was afraid I had offended him, but then I realized that he was just taking care to form the right words before he replied.

"You know what parts I had trouble with?" he said, his wheels crunching over some branches that had fallen on the path. "The verses about suffering. The parts where these early believers, these incredibly important followers of Jesus, saw their lives get worse, not better, after they believed. Why, I wondered, would you choose to follow someone who was only going to drag you down? 'Take up your cross and follow me'? Please! Trust me, I already have a cross. Everywhere I go, I roll there on a cross. And I want to make things even *worse*?"

I listened to him talk, thinking that if he was trying to convince me not to believe as he did, he was doing a pretty good job of it!

"Then I found what I was looking for," he continued, "the words that made sense—not just for Christianity, but for what had been the problem my whole life."

I didn't reply, wondering how a simple Bible verse could give anyone that much insight.

"It's from Romans," he said. "I have it memorized. May I share it with you?"

"Sure," I replied, tossing a stick ahead of us and letting go of Sugarpie's leash so that he could run for it.

"It says, 'We rejoice in our sufferings, because we know that suffering produces perseverance; perseverance, character; and character, hope. And hope does not disappoint us, because God has poured out his love into our hearts by the Holy Spirit, whom he has given us.'"

"That's lovely."

"Those words, Miranda, those words explained everything to me. In my entire life, I had never had to suffer through anything—not even a class I found boring at school or a punishment I was given by the nanny. My parents bailed me out of suffering, which meant I had never learned perseverance or developed character or found hope. And hope was what I needed most. That's what saved me from myself. That's what finally led me to believe, which in turn brought the Holy Spirit into my life. And that's the most important part of that verse. The suffering which leads to all of those other things wasn't the point. The point was that the suffering doesn't even feel like suffering anymore, because I was transformed the moment I accepted Christ. He came into my heart and changed my life."

It was an interesting story, and I could tell it came from the heart. We continued on, side by side, for a bit longer, and though I was glad to have heard such passion for what he believed in, I didn't know how his experience could apply to me.

Finally, Holt seemed to be slowing down, and I realized we were approaching two stone pillars, almost smaller versions of the ones that flanked the driveway at Twin Oaks.

"What is this?" I asked. "Where are we?"

Holt took a deep breath and exhaled slowly.

"We're at the Fairmont family cemetery," he said. "I thought you might want to visit the graves of your sister and your mother."

TWENTY-SEVEN

No answer
Came from the graves of the dead, nor the gloomier grave of the living.

I don't know what I had been expecting, but this certainly wasn't it.
As we stood at the stone gates, rows of our family graves just inside, I felt my heart thud against my chest like a drum.

"I don't know if I'm up to this," I said. "Not yet."

"That's fine, there's no hurry. They're not going anywhere."

I glanced at him to see that he was smiling.

"You think this is funny?" I asked, poking him on the shoulder. "This is tough for me. Very tough."

"Of course it is. I'm just trying to help."

And he did help. Just having him there helped. Maybe, I thought, this was one demon I could face head-on. At least I wasn't alone.

"Let's go in," I said. "I'll let you know if I need to turn back."

"Sounds good to me."

Moving past those gates, I could see that there were about thirty or forty graves in all, some of them with simple engraved headstones, some with more elaborate statuary and even above-ground crypts. I didn't usually mind cemeteries; sometimes I thought they were quite beautiful. This one was especially so, with Spanish moss hanging down from the nearby trees and a gentle breeze moving through the warm air, the dark water of the bayou gently rolling along in the distance. I wondered if I had ever been here before, and I asked Holt if I had been allowed to come to either funeral, or if they had decided I was too young and instead kept me at home.

"Sorry, but with the condition I was in, I don't remember," he said. "Somehow, I doubt you came. That's a lot to expect of a five-year-old, unless you're JFK Jr. or something."

Holt didn't say exactly where my mother and Cass were located, and I didn't ask. I wanted to find them for myself, something that shouldn't take long in this small family graveyard. Before I started scanning headstones, however, I thought of the bone I had sent off to the police, and I feared that perhaps it had come from here. In my fragile state, I knew that seeing an upturned grave or a wind-disturbed casket might send me over the edge. I told Holt about it, but he just patted my arm and assured me that no, except for a few toppled statues, Katrina had left this particular cemetery unmolested.

"I have a guy come in regularly to do the maintenance. He keeps things up very well. There aren't any missing bones from here."

Thus reassured, I began to walk along the first row, reading headstones. There were names, so many names, but Fairmont was the one that showed up most. The oldest graves I saw were from the 1800s, which gave me again that sense of being one link in a very long chain. That chain came into sharp focus when I reached two particularly beautiful graves, side by side, for Xavier Theodore Fairmont and Portia Saultier Fairmont. My grandparents.

Their headstones were similar, though on hers, under her name, was a quote:

Other hope had she none, nor wish in life, but to follow
Meekly, with reverent steps, the sacred feet of her Saviour.

"I'm guessing your mother shared your faith," I said to Holt as he rolled to a stop beside me.

"No, not really," he replied. "It's a nice sentiment, but just a literary quote."

He leaned forward from his chair and pulled a clump of weeds from the ground nearby. Judging by the clump of green on his lap, he'd been doing it all the way down the row.

"I mean, I can't presume to know the heart of another," he added, "but I can guess. Her religion had a lot of rules, and she followed those rules as best she could. But I think in all that 'stuff' that she missed the point. As the Scripture says, 'These people honor me with their lips, but their hearts are far from me. They worship me in vain; their teachings are but rules taught by men.'"

"But isn't being a Christian all about following the rules?"

He looked up at me with an expression that I could only describe as beatific.

"Being a Christian is about knowing the truth, Miranda, and it's that truth that sets you free."

I thought about that as I moved forward again, Holt lagging behind as he did the weeding, Sugarpie hovering near his chair, sniffing and rooting along the ground and generally enjoying the outdoors. Holt was such a gentle person, and he was one of the few "born again" types I had ever really talked with.

I wondered how that would feel, to have such a strong belief in something that couldn't even be touched or seen. I supposed that for someone like him, it wasn't a bad way to live. At least it gave him comfort and peace—even strength through adversity—and those were all great things he needed and things that made him who he was.

As I reached the end of the row without finding the graves I sought, I took a deep a breath and moved inward along the second row. I didn't have to go far. The moment I saw the tiny above-ground crypt, I knew it was for a child. Stepping closer, I could clearly read the name on the headstone: Cassandra Lynn Fairmont.

My sister, my twin.

I don't know how long I stood there, but it must have been a while. I became aware of the encroaching darkness and of an itchy mosquito bite on my neck. Glancing up, I saw that Holt was still rolling along the perimeter, tossing an occasional stick for Sugarpie and weeding away, and

I realized that the walking space for this row was too narrow and bumpy to accommodate his chair. I was overwhelmed with gratitude that he had kept himself nearby regardless, and I realized that it was getting late and we really ought to go.

I moved on to the next crypt, which was etched with the name of my mother. As I stood there looking at it, I realized that with all of the emotions that were swirling around in my mind right now, above all else I had a deep and abiding sense of guilt. I was thirty-two years old, I realized, my mother had been dead since I was five, and this was the first time I had ever come to see her grave. Had Willy not sent for me so desperately, I would never have come at all. Yet she was my mother.

My mother, who had died.

The feeling started at the tips of my fingers, a tingling sensation that began like small pinpricks and quickly escalated into buzzing stripes of nerve pain. With every beat of my heart, my feet began to feel as if they weren't even on the ground but were instead floating.

Why, my mind hammered, *why have I never let myself feel the loss of her absence from my life?*

Why, my head pounded, *why have I spent all of these years pretending it didn't matter, that being raised by an aunt was the same as being raised by my own mom?*

Had I not come here, I could have gone through the rest of my life ignoring that entire black knot of pain and loss, pretending it wasn't even there.

It was that black knot of pain, though, a churning surge of something dark and horrible that suddenly welled up inside of me, filling my entire being, forcing my hands to sweat and my vision to blur. The horizon became hazy and even as I thought, "Not again!" I was falling toward the ground. This time, though, was almost like slow motion, and instead of the floor hitting me in the head, I felt myself falling against something much softer, much warmer.

My eyes closed, and as they did, my final thought was *I'm sorry, Mama. I'm sorry I forgot how much I needed you.*

TWENTY-EIGHT

Friends they sought and homes; and many, despairing, heartbroken,
Asked of the earth but a grave, and no longer a friend nor a fireside.
Written their history stands on tablets of stone in the churchyards.

Somebody was rubbing a soft, wet washcloth across my cheek.

I raised up one arm to push them away and felt it whack against something furry and large.

Alarmed, I opened my eyes to see a big, blond dog with dopey eyes standing there staring at me. It was Sugarpie, who had saved me from another big bump to the head.

"I'm okay, boy," I said, pushing myself up to a sitting position and draping an arm around his neck.

I looked up to see Holt straining to roll his way closer, one wheel caught against a stone.

"It's okay, Holt. I'm okay. The dog protected me."

Holt turned his face upward and then his eyes met mine, a deep crease running vertically down the center of his forehead. He looked upset, and I felt bad that I had scared him by collapsing in a place he couldn't get to.

Summoning my strength, I got to my feet, walked forward, leaned down, and simply put my arms around my uncle. He hugged me back, fiercely.

"I'm sorry," I whispered. "I'm okay."

He didn't reply, but when we pulled apart, I could see him wiping tears from his face.

"Look at it this way," I teased, dabbing at a tear of my own. "I probably just saved you several days of dog testing."

He laughed out loud, and with my help we made our way out of the cemetery and back toward his home.

Once we were there, I didn't linger. The sun had set and I only had a little bit of light left to get home. We said our goodbyes and then I took off jogging, eaten alive by mosquitoes as I went but making it back to Twin Oaks before it got too dark to see. When I flung open the back door, I startled Deena and Lisa both, who were sitting there at the table, a pot of stew between them. I was glad to see that my father wasn't there also.

"Little late for dinner, aren't you?" Deena snapped.

I glanced at the table. Though Lisa had nearly polished off a full plate of something dark brown and lumpy, Deena's serving sat in front of her, barely touched.

"Sorry," I replied, feeling belligerent and hearing the sarcasm in my own voice. Toning it down, I added, "Time got away from me. I didn't mean to worry you."

Deena huffed, but I could tell that's what had been behind her bossy tone. She'd been concerned.

"It's just so nice to get to know my Uncle Holt," I said, walking to the sink to wash my hands for dinner. "He is a fascinating guy."

"He's been good to us," Deena said in a very uncharacteristically generous statement. "I think he's the only one who really knows what Willy and I sacrificed for the Fairmonts."

"Oh, please," Lisa snapped. "You live in a freakin' mansion. You'll complain about anything."

With that, Lisa dropped her fork onto her plate with a clank and pushed away from the table.

Deena did not look offended, merely amused.

Lisa carried her plate and glass to the sink, dropped them in with just enough force to make a statement, and stomped out of the kitchen.

"We need to talk later," I called to her as she went.

"Come knock on my door as soon as you finish eating Deena's poison."

I joined Deena at the table, apologizing for the interruption.

"She's just being ornery. Eat up, won't you?"

I wasn't very hungry, but I scooped out some of the stew just to be polite. Next to it I added a scoop from the casserole Livvy had brought over. It was tasty, but Deena's stew was terrible. After Lisa's remark about the food being poison, however, I was embarrassed for Deena's sake not to eat both with equal enthusiasm.

"You've barely touched your food," I said.

Deena put down her fork, slowly shaking her head.

"The viewing's in the morning. I just don't know how I'll get through this."

I nodded, recognizing her pain not just in her words but in the defeated slump of her shoulders.

"Uncle Holt says he takes everything one day at a time, sometimes one hour at a time or even one minute at a time. He says when someone has to face something difficult, that's the only way to get through."

"Guess he's right."

I invited her to talk about Willy, asking how they met to get her started. As she reminisced, I continued to eat just enough to make it look as though I had enjoyed the meal.

While her story of he said/I said/he did/I did romance was no doubt fascinating to her, I found myself growing bored and restless and eager to get upstairs and search that third floor for my grandmother's paintings. Finally, when her story drew to a close, I thanked her for sharing and then seized the opportunity to make my exit.

"I think I'm going to move to one of the bedrooms on the second floor," I said as I got up and carried my dishes to the sink. "There's a little more room up there."

"Suit yourself," she replied, watching as I took a few minutes to squeeze out some dish soap, fill the pan with warm water, and wash my dishes along with the others that were there. "I'll get you some sheets for the bed."

"Thanks."

She left the room and came back with a pile of crisply folded sheets, which she set on the end of the table.

"And you got some phone calls," Deena said. "Miz Kroft nex' door, said she was just checking to see if you'd had a chance to look at her paintings, whatever that means."

"I wonder why she didn't call on my cell phone."

"Said she tried but you didn't answer."

I wiped a hand on my shirt and retrieved the phone from my pocket to see that it was dead. Pressing buttons did not bring it to life, and I knew that I had gone too long without charging it yet again.

With a surge of guilt, I realized that AJ might have been trying to call me after all but simply hadn't been able to get through.

"Did anyone else call?" I asked, almost afraid to hear the answer.

"Yeah, the maid that did all that cleaning today. Said she was here for four and a half hours total so you owed her forty-five dollars, and you could just give it to Miz Kroft. I said that was highway robbery, but she said that was none of my business and between you and her."

"Forty-five dollars?" I smiled. "Gosh Deena, where I come from that's what it costs for about one hour of cleaning, not four."

"What a stupid waste of good money."

"Speaking of money," I said as I set the last plate in the dish drainer, "do you want me to go shopping for replacements on the things I owe you? Or since you're moving out, would you rather just have cash?"

"Cash would be fine. I'm trying to get rid of things as it is, not accumulate more."

I went to my bedroom, retrieved my purse, and dug out forty bucks. Coming back into the kitchen, I handed it over and said for her to let me know if she thought it had come to more than that.

She tucked the two twenties into her bra, a twinkle in her eye, and then carried her own full plate to the trash can and scraped the food away, adding the plate to the dishwater so I could wash it too.

After that, Deena went down the hall in the general direction of Lisa's room. I thought she might be going down to talk to her, but as I watched she turned short and went into the living room area instead. After a moment, I heard the television click on.

I finished with the dishes and then hurried to my own room in the opposite direction, packed my suitcase, and lugged everything to the door to the front of the house. Leaving it there, I headed toward Lisa's room. I spotted Deena on the way, watching TV as she packed up a box from the shelves.

Continuing onward, I knocked on Lisa's door.

"Just a minute," she said in a muffled voice, and as I waited for her to open it, I glanced toward the door to Willy's room at the end of the hall. I hadn't been in there since he died, but I was glad they were keeping the door closed. Last night Deena had complained that not all of the medical equipment had yet been removed by the medical supply company, and though I didn't know if they had yet taken away the bed or not, I couldn't stand the thought of seeing it there, now empty, and remembering the sight of Willy's final gasping breaths.

"Yeah?" Lisa demanded, swinging open the door, though when she saw my face, her features softened. "What's up?"

She held her cell phone in one hand and held the fingers of the other over the mouthpiece.

"You're on the phone," I said, "I didn't mean to bother you."

"What do you need?"

"Come upstairs and find me when you're finished," I said. Then I lowered my voice to a whisper and, thinking of Colline d'Or, added, "I have something big to tell you."

I took my things upstairs and settled into one of the front bedrooms, plugging my phone into the charger before I did anything else. By the time I finished getting organized, Lisa still hadn't come up, so I thought I would use the time while I was waiting for her to take a quick look at Livvy's painting. I brought the tote bag down the hall and around the corner to the room that held my grandmother's art supplies. It had a completely different feel tonight with the sheets gone and wood gleaming from the gorgeous antique furniture. Lovely.

In the corner was a drafting table with a work lamp clamped on the side, so I turned it on and carefully unwrapped the painting, for some reason expecting to see a hideous nineteenth century scene of vendors selling fruit and vegetables in a town square, the bell-and-cross symbol painted onto someone's cape.

Instead, I caught my breath as I realized that it was a gorgeous original Horace Pippin, a homey scene of a family gathered around a wood stove. Sadly, the damage was significant. The worst problem that I could see was that the varnish had softened at some point, a result of high temperatures. Once that happened, the dirt on the surface had become permanently attached to the painting.

Beyond that, there were dots of mildew along the bottom, and the canvas had also come loose from its stretcher in several places. Moving the lamp to get some raking light, I was glad that the surface showed no rippling or folds. I didn't have a light box to check for splits or small tears, so I took out the UV light instead, turned off the overhead light and the lamp, and studied the resulting picture in the uniquely illuminated darkness. Slowly pointing the unit across the surface, I didn't spot any other irregularities or surprises other than some cleavage which reflected brightly near the top.

I formed the words of my evaluation in my mind, mentally listing my recommendations for Livvy. The picture could be improved but not returned to its original state. Considering the value and beauty of the work itself, I thought it would certainly be worth the expense of trying, though she had several choices about how to proceed and to what extent she'd be willing to go.

Glad at least that I had had the chance to take a look, I crossed the room to turn on the wall switch, the glowing UV light still in my hand. As I reached up, I hesitated, a strange white glow reflecting back at me from around the switch plate. Looking closer, I saw that the enamel wall paint had simple peeled off a bit, probably worn down and scratched by the repeated motions of people turning on and off the overhead light. The UV lamp was picking up whatever had been underneath that paint. Curious, I moved it closer, shining it on the wall from different angles. Sure enough, there was definitely something there.

Flipping on the overhead light, I turned off the UV light and set it on the floor and then used my fingernails to scrape at the peeling wall paint around the light switch plate. There was something uniquely colored underneath, but it wasn't wallpaper and it wasn't regular house paint.

It was a picture of some kind, and when I had peeled off several inches of the easily-flaking enamel, I was stunned to see that I had revealed the face of something small and white, a little dog.

"What are you doing?" Lisa's voice said from the doorway.

Instead of answering, I merely shook my head and asked her if she would mind going to get Deena.

"You want me to bring that selfish witch up here? No thanks."

"Please," I said. "It's important."

I continued to scrape in every direction that it would let me, breaking two nails in the process. I had gotten as far as I could when Lisa returned to the room, trailed by Deena.

"What do you want? I'm missing my show."

"Deena, what is this on the wall?" I asked.

She looked at the picture my scrapings had revealed, which now included two dogs walking alongside a wooden fence.

"That's one of your grandmother's paintings," Deena said, summarily unimpressed.

"On the wall?" I asked.

"I told you she was nuts. She painted all over the place."

"But I thought you meant on canvas. I thought you said she made a bunch of paintings and you didn't know what Willy had done with them."

"No," Deena replied, looking at me strangely, probably confused by the urgency in my voice. "I told you she made a bunch of paintings and I didn't know what he had done *about* them. I knew they was here, I just didn't know what he used to cover them up."

Stunned, I took a step back and waved my arms in a circle, indicating the whole room.

"Did she paint every wall in here?" I demanded.

"Every wall in here plus practically every wall in the whole upstairs hallway, plus halfway down the stairs."

I wanted to scream! Here I had been searching for a few meager canvases, when the paintings were so much more than that—and all right here under my nose, hidden in plain sight.

"Deena, this is important," I said, stepping forward to look her right in the eyes. "I need you to show me every place my grandmother painted."

"Why?"

"Because I'm going to recover them, and I don't want to waste any time or miss a single one."

Obviously thinking I was also nuts but willing to humor me, Deena walked around, pointing out various places where she thought she could recall having heard my grandmother had painted. I could tell she wasn't happy at the thought that I was going to take down the enamel paint her husband had so carefully put up.

"They had some big fights about this," Deena said after she showed me the final area. "Willy was so upset he could barely talk about it sometimes."

"What do you mean?" I asked, glancing at Lisa, who seemed bored by the whole thing.

"Your grandmother was driven to keep painting, and Willy was just as driven to come up here every night and cover it up. That's why she did it in so many different areas. He'd cover one up so she'd move to some new place and try again. Finally—"

Deena stopped talking, a blush creeping into her cheeks.

"What? Finally what?"

"I hate to say it, because it so wasn't like him."

"Please, Deena. What?"

"Finally, Mr. Fairmont, he heard Willy yelling at your grandmother. Got so mad he told Willy to leave her alone and that he wasn't allowed upstairs again. Drove Willy crazy that she was up here messing up the walls with all her stupid painting. But he had to wait 'til she died before he could get back up here to cover it all up one last time."

TWENTY-NINE

Silently one by one, in the infinite meadows of heaven,
Blossomed the lovely stars, the forget-me-nots of the angels.

I got right to work, using a variety of tools that Deena was able to rustle up for me, including sandpaper, putty knives, kitchen knives, emery boards, a flathead screwdriver, and even occasionally a blow drier.

Lisa offered to help but I wouldn't let her, afraid that too aggressive of a hand would cause irreparable damage to the paintings. She stayed for a while anyway as I worked, keeping me company and listening to what I had learned about Colline d'Or, and describing her own fruitless adventures asking around about Jimmy Smith. We both agreed that we weren't quite sure what tactic to try next, though secretly I hoped that this painting might give us some direction. Finally, she went on to bed, saying that she was tired and she'd see me in the morning.

By midnight, I had managed to get the enamel paint off of one third of one wall while causing only minimal damage to the artwork underneath. Feeling exhausted and vaguely nauseous, I thought it might be a good time to stop for the night. Before I did, though, I wanted to take a step back and observe in its full scope what I had managed to reveal. I walked across the room, turned, and took it all in.

My grandmother was a talented lady, that was for certain. Her painting style was quite charming, though I hadn't uncovered enough of the scene for it to make much sense. Mostly, it looked like a quaint little countryside filled with wood-and-thatch houses, fields in the distance, and thus far no living creatures except for the two dogs.

Though I loved the picture itself, in a way, I was disappointed. After hearing Deena's story about Willy getting so upset, I had hoped perhaps my grandmother had been up here painting out the secrets of the myth of the angelus or something. If that were indeed the case, I had a lot of work left to do before it would make much sense.

I gathered my tools and put them in the cabinet, deciding to clean up the chips of paint that littered the floor in the morning. I didn't feel very well, and as I got ready for bed I was mad at myself for working too long and too hard on an evening when I should have forced myself to take it easy, considering the bump on my head. In the bathroom, after brushing my teeth, I studied the lump on my head in the mirror, glad at least that the swelling was almost gone, though the bruise had taken on a mottled blue tinge around the edges.

I climbed into the bed and turned out the light, only then thinking about how far away I was from anyone else in this big old house. As the wind blew outside I could hear all sorts of creaks and moans, and as I was falling asleep I could almost swear I had heard someone walking around on the floor above me. My nerves on edge, I didn't sleep well, and around two a.m. I sat up, my heart pounding. I had to throw up.

There wasn't time to make it to the bathroom, so I ran for the trash can instead, violently emptying the contents of my stomach. The episode repeated itself several times over the next hour, until there was nothing left to bring up and I merely heaved.

By that point, I was genuinely frightened. Deena's doctor had said to watch for nausea as one of the signs of a concussion. This was far beyond mere nausea, thus I could only conclude that this was far beyond a normal concussion. I was angry at the doctor for not being more aggressive in his suggestions. My biggest concern at this point was being able to get down the stairs and to the back of the house to ask Lisa to take me to the hospital.

I didn't even bother to get dressed but simply pulled on my robe and slipped into my shoes. Borrowing an empty trashcan from the room next door, I carried it with me as I went down, just in case I felt another episode coming on.

By the time I reached Lisa's room, my legs were wobbly and I was sweating profusely. I started to knock on her door when I realized that it was half open. Peeking inside, I could see that her bed was empty. That's when I heard her in the bathroom, running the water. I waited but she didn't come out, so finally I wobbled my way up the hall and knocked on the bathroom door. When it opened, my nostrils were assaulted by the smell of vomit, her vomit.

She and I just looked at each other, and I realized that she was as sick as I was. Though I was comforted by the thought that this obviously wasn't the result of a concussion, that left me to conclude that either we had some horrible stomach bug or we were suffering from food poisoning.

Suddenly, I pictured Deena as she had been this morning, cleaning out the refrigerator and determined to cook up all the food so it wouldn't go to waste. Apparently, she had cooked up *all* the food, even that which should have gone straight into the trash.

"I knew there was something wrong with that goulash," Lisa said.

"Yeah, me too," I agreed.

I explained about my mistaken assumption of the concussion.

"Since I obviously don't need the hospital," I said, "I'm going back to bed and try to get some sleep."

It was a long night, however, and sleep was in short supply.

Mostly, I dozed on the floor next to the trash can, waking every hour or so to go through dry heaves. I tried to drink water, but anything more than a sip would set me off again. I was miserable.

By morning I was at least able to climb back into the bed. There, I slept fitfully, the stomach spasms lessening to once every several hours rather than every hour. I knew I would never make it to Willy's viewing that evening, and I hoped that Lisa was faring better than I was. When I had seen her last, she'd been lucky to make it to the bathroom, much less to the funeral home.

I awoke in the late morning hearing sounds in the room next to mine. Feeling wobbly, I made my way to the door and looked inside to see Lisa slowly making the bed there.

"What are you doing?" I asked.

She looked at me with the wan face and messy hair that said her night had been as bad as mine was.

"Deena refuses to believe it's food poisoning. She thinks we've got the flu. Made me move out of the downstairs so I don't give her my germs."

"I don't blame her," I said. "If I had done this to someone I wouldn't want to take responsibility, either."

Back in bed, I slept until noon, at least when I wasn't throwing up again. At one point, I considered whether I should call my uncle and ask him to pray for me. Somebody needed to because I felt pretty sure that at any moment I was going to die.

My first period of normalcy came after two p.m., when I awoke without the need to vomit. I felt shaky and weak and dehydrated, in need of more than just water, but I knew I was in no condition to go downstairs to the kitchen to get something to drink. I did think I'd give a trip to the bathroom a try, but as I walked out of my room I saw a tray at the top of the stairs. On it was a thermos, a pack of crackers, two bowls and spoons, and two cans of ginger ale. Obviously, Deena had made us some lunch. Judging by the soup in the thermos, it looked like Campbell's from a can, so I decided to risk it. I shared our bounty with Lisa, who managed to keep hers down about as long as I did. At four p.m., I wondered just how much one person should have to suffer before they were simply allowed to die. I didn't think I could take much more—that is, until the police detective came up the stairs and told us that the death of Willy Pedreaux had not been from natural causes.

Willy had been murdered.

THIRTY

Nodding and mocking along the wall, with gestures fantastic,
Darted his own huge shadow, and vanished away into darkness.

At first, I thought maybe I was asleep and had been dreaming. But this guy didn't leave and soon he was joined by another. They needed to interview each of us, they said, though neither man ventured much farther into our rooms than a few feet. Even when Lisa told them it was more than likely food poisoning and not a stomach virus, they still kept their distance.

When it was my turn to be interviewed, they asked me to describe my entire day on Saturday. I was just glad they let me do it from a prone position on the bed. Closing my eyes, I retraced all of my steps, beginning with the arrival of our limo at the house and ending with the sight of Willy lying dead in his bed. They interrupted a lot with questions, trying to pinpoint the comings and goings of all the people in and out of Willy's room. Only when I finished my story did it occur to me to ask how on earth he had been murdered.

"We were all there when he died," I said. "We watched it happen—and Lisa did everything she could to stop it."

"There were some irregularities in the autopsy," one of the cops replied. "Questions with the lungs and such."

"But I saw him die of natural causes with my own eyes."

"Well, it seems that someone helped those natural causes along. He was given an inhalant."

"An inhalant?" I demanded. "The only thing Willy inhaled that day was oxygen."

The men looked at each other.

"Was it the oxygen?" I asked, my mind racing. "Did someone tamper with it or change out the tank?"

The detective seemed to be considering his words.

"The coroner believes that a chemical was added to the humidifier connected to the oxygen tank. Unfortunately, though the tank and tubing are still here, the small plastic tank that holds the water for the humidifier is missing."

I thought about that, remembering how absolutely purple Willy had turned when Lisa had put the mask on his face there at the end. I went back and described how all of that had gone—how his body had responded so well to the oxygen the first time and not at all well the second time. They didn't seem surprised by what I was saying, and I had a feeling that Lisa had told them the same thing.

"Wouldn't that mean," I asked, trying to clear my head despite my illness, "that someone had to have added the chemical between uses? Like, at some point in the hour or so between when he used it once and when he used it again?"

I was just thinking out loud, but the cops looked at each other and said yes, that was why they needed to take a DNA sample from me.

"Wait a minute, *I'm* your suspect?" I asked, sitting up and then, as the room began to spin, thinking better of it and lying back down. "Are you kidding me?"

"It's not just you, ma'am," the cop replied. "We've taken samples from the other two ladies, Mr. Benochet, and his driver. Everyone who was on the premises when Mr. Pedreaux died, with the exception of your little girl."

"Why DNA?" I asked. "What can that prove?"

"There was...evidence. That's all we can say at this time."

They called a technician to come upstairs, who pulled on a pair of rubber gloves and used a long cotton swab to roughly go around the inside of my mouth.

"Can you tell us what you had for dinner last night?" one of the detectives asked when the tech was done.

"Excuse me?"

"Your sick friend seems to think the two of you might have been intentionally poisoned by Miz Pedreaux."

I was about to object, but then I remembered Deena's strange behavior last night, as she pushed her food around on her plate but never really ate any herself. Could she have done this horrible thing to us on purpose? If so, were we going to die too?

Describing the food that had more than likely made us sick, I felt a new surge of nausea. I had a feeling they were going to confiscate what was left and whisk it off to their lab. I asked if they thought we should go to the hospital.

"I'd call a doctor, at least. Better safe than sorry."

I laid my head back and looked up at the ceiling, trying to wrap my mind around the idea that we may have been poisoned.

"There's just one more thing," the detective said, pulling on a pair of gloves himself as his partner brandished a flashlight and a camera.

"What?"

"We need to examine your head."

"My head? Where I bumped it?"

The men looked at each other and back at me.

"You bumped your head?" one of them asked suspiciously. "How?"

I explained that I was upstairs earlier today and that I passed out and fell down, banging my forehead onto the floor. I couldn't imagine what that had to do with anything, but the next thing I knew these guys were both inspecting the bump on my head.

"I don't see any broken skin," one of them said to the other, his breath reeking of coffee.

"Check the rest," the other guy said.

"Ma'am, could you please take your hair down so we can examine your scalp?"

My pulse surged as I looked up at them, mortified at the thought that they would see the shaved part and the tattoo. Was that what they were looking for?

"Is this legal?" I asked, holding a hand to the back of my head. "I don't think it is. I think I want a lawyer before you do anything else."

The cops stood up straight and clicked off the light.

"That how you want to do this? Fine. Let's go down to the station and your lawyer can meet us there."

"I can't go down to the station. I can barely walk."

"Your choice, ma'am."

It was a standoff, one we all knew I was going to have to lose.

"At least can you tell me what you're looking for?"

"Broken skin," said one.

"A cut," said the other.

"Fine," I replied, pulling the ponytail from my hair. "Have at it."

With deep shame, I simply sat up and leaned forward, trying not to recall my attack in the alley as I subjected myself to their inch-by-inch examination of my head. When they ran across the tattoo, as I knew they would, one of them let out a low whistle.

"You live in New York, you said?"

"Yes."

"They do crazy things like this up there?"

"Like what?"

"This here tattoo."

"Of course. It's all the rage, totally in fashion. Don't you read *Vogue* magazine?"

When they had gone over every inch of my head, they snapped off their light and left me alone. Feeling utterly violated, I quickly tugged my hair back into a ponytail.

"Maybe I'll get me one of those," one cop said to the other as they left the room. "Charlene likes me to be in fashion. I could get Elvis. Just not fat Elvis."

After they went down the stairs, I rolled to my side and pulled back the sheer curtains to look outside. With the balcony in the way, I couldn't see down to the ground, so I gathered my strength to get up and walk to the side window and look out there. From where I could see, there were several police cars parked along the driveway, and probably more out back.

Had the whole world turned upside down?

The cops had said they would be searching the house for the humidifier tank, and I couldn't imagine what would happen next if they found it. I thought of Deena and her complaints about how long it was taking the medical supply company to come and pick up the rest of the equipment, and I wondered if she had a reason to be so impatient.

I was trying to decide if I had the strength to go downstairs and see what they were doing now when Lisa appeared in my doorway, still wearing her nightgown. Her brown skin was ashy gray, her eyes blood red.

"Can you believe this?" she said. "It feels like we're in an episode of *The Twilight Zone.*"

We discussed the situation, trying to reason out who could or would have killed Willy. Lisa felt certain that it was Deena, though the only motive she could come up with was her jealousy and anger about being excluded from the conversation he had wanted to have with Lisa and me.

Somehow, as awful as Deena was, I had trouble seeing her as a murderer. For that matter, I couldn't imagine that Charles or Lisa would be capable of something like that either. That left only the driver, Emmett, whom I hadn't really gotten to know at all. As for motive, I couldn't begin to imagine why someone would want poor old Willy dead. The only reason I could think of was to keep him from telling us whatever it was he had been trying to say.

"Do you think we should go to the hospital?" I asked.

"Not just yet. Let me make some phone calls first."

She went back to her room and I drifted off to sleep, only to awake ten minutes later to the sight of Deena, who was standing in the doorway, eyes blazing.

"What were you thinking?" she demanded.

"What?" I struggled to lift myself up to my elbows.

"Those policemen insisted on taking last night's goulash as evidence of a crime! Do you honestly think I poisoned you?" She took a few steps away, to Lisa's doorway and demanded, "Lisa, do you?"

I closed my eyes. I didn't have the strength to deal with this right now. Still, Deena ranted and raved for several minutes, calling us selfish and liars and betrayers—and finally murderers.

"You probably killed him, Lisa, with all your fake nurse knowledge. You're no nurse! Your whole reason for being here was a lie!"

Moving over into my room, Deena pointed a gnarled finger at me.

"And you! I told those cops how I caught you leaning over Willy's body. You was in there all by yourself, long enough to set things up so he would die."

I wanted to defend myself, but I could feel the now-familiar pressure of bile rising in my throat, so I didn't dare speak. Instead, I merely leaned over, grabbed the trash can, and threw up.

Disgusted, Deena marched to the top of the stairs, where she stopped and turned, looking from Lisa's open door to mine.

"I'm leaving this house!" Deena announced. "The two of you can fend for yourselves for all I care."

"I don't think the police will let you get too far," Lisa called from her room.

"Far, schmar, I'm going to my cousin's house in town," Deena replied. "I'll send for my things later."

With that, she clomped down the stairs, slammed a few doors, and then all was silent.

"Miranda, can you hear me?" Lisa called from her sick bed.

"Yeah?"

"I talked to my friend Mike. He's a lab tech. He's going to come over here and take some blood to run a toxicology screen."

"Should we go to the hospital?"

"Let's wait and do this first. I don't know about you, but I don't have any health insurance. And I wouldn't trust my dog to the local charity hospital."

After that, I drifted in and out, dreaming I was in a long line, waiting to check into a hospital. Along the sidewalk were the poor and homeless, all sick or injured or having babies. At one point, I opened my eyes—to see Jimmy Smith standing at the window next to my bed, looking in at me.

Jimmy Smith?

I let out a bloodcurdling scream and he ran away. By the time I got up and threw open the balcony door—not even thinking until after I had done so what a stupid move that might be—there was no one there. I pounded on Lisa's outside door and then ran around the perimeter of the balcony, looking down. There was no sight of him on the lawn. Finally, her door pushed open and she stood there looking as though she had been pulled from a deep sleep.

"Jimmy Smith was here! The man in the drawing! The one who came to my office with the painting!"

She studied my face, probably wondering if I were hallucinating.

"I'm not crazy!" I yelled. "I woke up and opened my eyes and he was standing right here, right outside my window."

I walked to the place where he had stood, but there were no obvious signs that anyone had been there. I examined the window itself, but it did not look as if anyone had tampered with it in any way.

My body was so full of adrenaline that for the moment I felt much better. Still in my nightgown, I pulled on my robe and ran downstairs to get a cop, but was I shocked to find that they were all gone. Every car had left.

Lisa and I were here alone.

I wondered what we could do to protect ourselves. Step one might be to go around and make sure all of the doors and windows were locked. That I did as quickly as I could, starting with the front room so I could grab a fireplace poker to us as a weapon. I checked the doors and windows of the entire first floor, hesitating at Willy's room, which had a yellow tape across it. Summoning my nerve, I twisted the knob and pushed open the door to his room, knowing that there was a good chance the cops had left the French doors to the outside unlocked.

As I stepped in, I was both shocked and relieved to find someone there, a uniformed cop who was standing at those French doors, his back to me. When he heard me enter, he spun around, suspicion clouding his puffy features.

"What are you doing in here?" he demanded, striding forward. "This is a crime scene!"

As calmly as I could, I tried to explain what was going on, that I had woken up to see a man watching me through the window and that since I didn't see any police cars still here, I was going around trying to lock the place up tight, to protect myself. He remained silent through my entire explanation, the set of his chin telling me that he didn't believe a word I was saying. When I asked him to go outside and see if he could find this guy, he just shook his head and told me that he had to remain at his post.

"Where is everyone else?" I demanded. "Where's your car? Are you even a real cop?"

That was probably a mistake. With deeply controlled anger, the man told me to get out of the room or he would arrest me on the spot for tampering with evidence. Quickly, I retraced my steps out of there, but I stood at the threshold, the door still open, and questioned him further until he admitted that his partner had taken the car to get something to eat but that he would be back very soon. Just then, said partner appeared at the French doors, a McDonald's bag tucked under his arm, a prisoner in handcuffs at his side.

"Hey, look what I caught prowling around out there," the cop said to his partner as he walked in.

"I wasn't prowling," the prisoner said in a steely voice.

"Hey, lady, is this the fella you were talking about?"

"No."

The man in custody was not the short and pale Jimmy Smith at all, but instead a tall black man in a T-shirt and jeans.

"I came here at the request of my friend Lisa," the prisoner said tightly.

My eyes widened.

"Are you Mike? The lab tech?"

"Yes. Are you the other one who's sick? I'll be with you in just a moment.

My stuff's outside. This overzealous bigot took one look at me walking up to the door and decided to arrest me."

"You had needles and things," the arresting officer said defensively. "I didn't know what you was gonna do."

"I was coming to draw blood. I'm a phlebotomist."

"Is that something kinky?"

"A phlebotomist works in a medical lab," I explained. "He's here to draw blood for some blood tests."

"Well, why didn't you say so in the first place?" the cop asked with a grunt as he set down his bag of food and uncuffed his prisoner. "You're free to go. But you gotta walk around the other way. This here's a crime scene."

I watched in dismay as the cop then lifted his bag of food, pulled out a pack of fries, and handed them to his partner, spilling several onto the crime scene floor in the process.

I met Mike at the back door, brought him in, and led him upstairs, all adrenaline now gone from my body. In its place was sheer exhaustion, misery, and more nausea. Upstairs, he drew Lisa's blood first and then mine, promising that some of the results would be back quite soon. From the description of our symptoms, however, he said he didn't expect any of it to be positive, that it sounded like good old regular food poisoning to him. On the other hand, he added, if our hair started falling out or our gums began to bleed, we might want to head to the hospital.

After talking a bit with Lisa, who felt sure Jimmy Smith's appearance at my window had been a figment of my delirious mind, I washed my face and brushed my teeth in the bathroom, checking my gums for good measure. Back in my room, I cleaned up all traces of my earlier sickness and began to wonder if maybe she was right after all. Maybe I had dreamed the sight of Jimmy Smith. If he had been there for real, I told myself, there was no way he could have disappeared that quickly. Just to be safe, I hung a blanket over the window so he couldn't see in and propped a chair against the door so he couldn't get in. Then I climbed back under the covers and slept some more, wishing I knew how to pray.

Around dusk, I awoke feeling somewhat better. I was still shaky and

244 ♦ MINDY STARNS CLARK

weak, but the nausea seemed to have passed, at least for now. I was sitting up on the side of the bed, wondering if I should try to eat something, when Lisa came up the stairs, carrying two plates of toast and some ginger ale.

"I'm a little better. How about you?" she asked, setting everything on the table next to my bed.

As we ate and drank, we compared symptoms and rehashed the misery we'd both been through. Lisa said she had hoped to go to the viewing, which would be starting soon, but that she really wasn't up to it. I was surprised that they were still having it as scheduled, considering that Willy had been murdered.

"I called to check, but they said that the body was finally released today, in time for the funeral home people to do what they had to do."

"What's the status downstairs?"

"Cops all gone, house locked up tight. I'm not scared with just the two of us here alone tonight, are you?"

I thought of Jimmy's face looming in my window and nodded.

"Just a little. Maybe I'll go down and get the fire poker just to have as a weapon."

"Suit yourself," she replied, yawning. "I'm turning in."

I was ready to go back to sleep as well. After brushing my teeth one more time, I went and got the fire poker and then for good measure grabbed the ash shoveler and the bellows as well. Back in my room, after making sure that all doors and windows were securely locked and blocked, I laid my weapons within easy reach, climbed under the covers, and turned out the light, feeling about as safe and protected as I could, given the situation.

My fears thus allayed, I reached for my cell phone and opened it up, thinking how Nathan and I had been playing phone tag since I got here. While that was helpful for the general exchange of information, it did nothing for either of us emotionally. For the first time ever, I began to feel the weight of our separateness in a tangible way, and it wasn't a good feeling. I was lonely, bereft, anchorless.

Was that how Nathan felt about us all the time?

For some reason, my fingers were shaking as I pressed in our home number. Listening to it ring so far away, I closed my eyes and swallowed hard and told myself that being vulnerable to another person didn't take bravery, as I had always thought, so much as it took trust.

I could trust Nathan.

There was no good reason not to let him all the way in.

Sadly, once again he did not pick up the phone. I listened to the sound of his recorded voice, tears springing into my eyes. The message I left was yet again merely factual—that I was touching base, that I had gotten food poisoning but that I hoped it would be all over soon, that I would try him again tomorrow.

Turning off the phone, I set it on the bedside table, closed my eyes, and drifted off to sleep. Somewhere deep in the night, I dreamed that I was trapped inside a big Plexiglas box. Everyone I loved was on the outside just going about their day, but they could not hear me and they would not look at me. I kept pounding and pounding on those solid clear walls, screaming to be heard, but no one even saw that I was there.

THIRTY-ONE

Must we in all things look for the how
and the why and the wherefore?

When I woke up the next morning, I felt like a new person, the medical crisis seeming to have passed. Standing carefully, I decided that I was steady on my feet, the nausea completely gone. Lisa was still asleep, but I hoped that when she woke up, she would be feeling as good as I was.

Energetic and alive despite all of yesterday's turmoil, I quickly showered, dressed, and then stripped the bed and carried everything down the stairs and into the back part of the house. There, I found the laundry room and started a load of sheets and blankets on the hottest setting, eager to kill any lingering germs. As the washer chugged away, I grabbed a bottle of liquid disinfectant from the shelf and brought it to the kitchen. I started a pot of coffee, and then I returned upstairs for my germy, bagged trash cans and brought them downstairs and out the back door.

Stepping into the sunshine, I was surprised at how humid the air was this early in the day. There was a neat little hose caddy not far from the door, so I carried the cans over to the grass, set the hose inside one of them, and turned on the water. As it filled, I went back into the kitchen to wash my hands, make some toast, and assemble my coffee.

Fifteen minutes later, the cans were disinfected and shining clean and I was enjoying my breakfast outside on the stoop. Despite my good mood, I knew that there were plenty of somber issues at hand, chief among them being Willy Pedreux's funeral today at noon.

Thinking about his death, I decided to take a walk, going around the outside of the house to his room. The whole patio area outside the French doors was still blocked with yellow crime scene tape, which I chose not to cross. Instead, I just looked through the glass into the empty room and then turned around and directed my gaze toward the bayou.

Considering the accessibility of these doors, I didn't understand why the police were convinced that the killer had to be one of the known entities. It seemed to me that almost anybody could have come here via the bayou, tied up their boat, come up the path, and walked straight to this room to commit murder, practically sight unseen.

I backed up a ways and looked at the house, realizing that there weren't any rooms along this side that had been in use at the time, as both the front half of the house and the upstairs had been closed up tight. If the killer knew that, he would have known he could make this trip without ever being spotted unless someone happened along here outside. Considering that this wasn't exactly a high traffic area, that wasn't very likely, either.

Turning, I walked down toward the water and scanned the shoreline for footprints in the mud. There weren't any, but that didn't necessarily prove anything considering that it hadn't rained until the day after Willy died. Looking toward the house from here, I could see that there were several large bushes between here and there that could have afforded excellent cover for a murderer to watch and wait for the right moment to make their move.

The day Willy died, he had been left alone several times, though never for very long. I tried to remember how much time I had spent around front at the swings with Charles and Tess and then Lisa. Even if it was just for five minutes, could that have given the killer enough time to slip inside, somehow tamper with his humidifier, and then get away? I thought so, if they had moved fast and had known what they were doing. As for Willy himself, he had drifted in and out of sleep. It wouldn't have been hard to accomplish the task without him ever even knowing someone had been there fooling with the apparatus that was behind his head.

Taking my theory a step further, I realized that the killer wouldn't even necessarily have had to come via the bayou. He or she could have walked over from either of the two paths too. I felt sure that neither Holt nor Livvy could be murderers, but who's to say that someone else didn't use one of those access points to carry out their nefarious plan?

A few minutes later, back upstairs, I shared my theory with Lisa as we both got ready for Willy's funeral. I wore a navy Dolce and Gabanna suit with chunky gold jewelry, but when Lisa emerged from her room and I saw that she had on a more casual top and skirt, I switched out the jewelry for a simple chain necklace, afraid I might be overdressed as it was.

We rode together in her car, tossing out various ideas about his death as we went. Once there, Lisa invited me to sit with her and some of her relatives up on the right, but I declined, not wanting to infringe on the section that had clearly been reserved for family.

Standing in the back of the room, I spotted Deena sitting in the front row, near the coffin. I was torn in my feelings toward her: guilty, if Lisa and I had wrongly accused her of poisoning us, self-righteous if we had not. Either way, I felt bad for being here, because I knew my presence would make Deena uncomfortable—and considering that she was here to bury her husband, that seemed unkind of me regardless.

I walked up the aisle anyway, hoping to take a quick look at Willy, pay my respects, and then slip to the back of the room and sit there, unnoticed by the widow. The casket was surprisingly lovely, perhaps the nicest I had ever seen. Willy lay against the tasteful silver fabric, dressed in a striped button-down shirt and black slacks, a small Bible in one hand and a rosary in the other. Considering that he was dead, he looked pretty good.

I turned to walk back and find a seat, but Deena spotted me then and stood, wrapping her bony arms around me. For a second I was afraid she was attacking me, and then I realized that it was a hug.

"I been sitting here trying to figure out who done this kindness," she whispered, "and I finally realized the only one it could be was you."

I had no idea what she was talking about, but I was glad to see that she wasn't angry with me as she continued.

"He was a good man, he deserved more than an old pine box. You've got jewels in your heavenly crown, girl, that's for sure."

She pulled away, sobbed into her hanky, and went back to her seat.

Utterly confused, I headed down the aisle, relieved to see a wheelchair rolling through the doorway at that moment. I recognized the chair but not the man in it, for this guy was nicely dressed in a crisp shirt and tie, his hair cut short and his face shaven clean, the cheeks pale and soft-looking where the beard had been.

"Uncle Holt?" I said, my eyes growing wide. With the beard gone, I could definitely see the strong Fairmont resemblance. He was almost as handsome as his brother, though Holt's features were softer somehow, the angle of his jaw less severe. "You look amazing."

"Thanks. I decided to go al fresco for a change," he said with a wink, stroking his naked chin.

He rolled his chair to the outer aisle of the back row and I sat in the seat next to him, telling him about Deena's strange words just now. Rather than puzzle over them, however, he merely smiled. After a moment, one of the funeral home employees came over and spoke softly to him.

"At first, she just about blew a gasket," the employee said, "but when we assured her it had been covered by an anonymous donor, she calmed down and started crying with joy."

The man handed Holt a piece of paper, which he discreetly took and slid into his pocket, thanking him for his help.

The guy patted Holt on the shoulder and walked away. I sat there for a moment, my mind rolling around the possibilities of what I had just overheard. Finally, curiosity overcame my manners.

"What's going on? What's on that paper?"

The corner of it was sticking out of his pocket and on a hunch I reached for it before he could stop me. Unfolding it, I saw that it was a receipt from the funeral home, just as I had suspected, for more than eight thousand dollars.

"What did you do?"

"Don't be nosy," he replied, grabbing back the receipt and stuffing it into his pocket. "I simply righted a wrong. At yesterday's viewing, Willy was in a cheap-looking, bargain-basement wooden casket. I knew my parents wouldn't have stood for that, so I took care of it. That's all."

"You upgraded him," I said, looking up front toward the beautiful silver-and-gold casket that sat there surrounded by flowers. I realized that Deena had made the wrong assumption, thinking that I had been the one to do such a kindness. "And I got the credit for it. Cool."

"You behave yourself, miss. This is a somber occasion."

With a twinkle in his eye, he jutted out his chin and studiously directed his gaze forward.

"Hard to behave when I'm sitting next to a modern-day Santa Claus."

"Hey, I shaved the beard."

"I'm not talking about looks; I'm talking about actions. For what it's worth, if you're feeling generous I'd like a pony and a big box of macaroons."

"Nosy young ladies get only coal."

A woman in front of us turned around and glared, so with a giggle I managed to remain silent. A few minutes later, my father appeared, greeted his brother with an awkward embrace, and then sat down next to me on the other side. Looking around, I also noticed a distinct police presence in the room, and I was reminded this was a funeral for a man who had been murdered as he lay dying. With a surge of emotion, I wondered if it had been my presence at Willy's bedside that had prompted the killer to act. What "terrible thing" had Willy done that required my forgiveness? What secrets had he been about to spill? With him dead and gone, I realized that I may never know.

The service started soon after, a somber, religious affair with a lot of standing and sitting and kneeling, not to mention the sickly sweet smell of incense and candles. I wondered what my service would be like when I died, and with that sobering thought I grew quite still, thinking about the man to my right and his rock-solid faith.

He'd said yesterday that buying into God meant accepting the whole package. Sadly, I realized, I wasn't even sure what that whole package was. I knew it had something to do with Jesus dying on a cross and then rising again a few days later. Beyond that, I wasn't sure what becoming a Christian even involved.

Once the service ended, we shifted over to the church cemetery for the final piece, which was brief. When it was over, they passed out flowers and invited each of us to place them on the casket. My father, uncle, and I got in the line and slowly filed forward, waiting our turn.

As I stood there facing the casket and laid the carnation atop it, I couldn't help but feel a surge of emotion about the man inside. He had died with some important truth on his lips, unspoken. As sick as he had been, and as imminent as his natural death was, someone had done the unspeakable by hurrying that death along. I tilted my head down in a gesture of respect and then turned and walked away. When I lifted my head my eyes met those of the detective who stood off in the distance, observing the proceedings. Whom did he really suspect?

More importantly, whom *should* he suspect?

A buffet lunch was being served back at the church in the fellowship hall, and though I didn't really want to go, I felt that attending would be the polite thing to do. There, I ate some of the light fare and stood around making small talk with Holt, my father, Lisa, Charles Benochet, and Livvy. When I asked Livvy more about the museum where she volunteered, she said it was only two blocks away from where we stood and that she'd be happy to walk over with me if I wanted to go right now.

That sounded good to me. Before we left, I told Lisa that I was going to run to the museum with Livvy and catch a ride home with her. In turn, Lisa offered to stop at the grocery store and pick up some food to replace everything of Deena's back at the house.

"I'm throwing it all out," she said, casting a hateful look toward Deena, who was sitting in chair against the wall, surrounded by fellow mourners. "I don't trust her."

Slipping her some cash, I asked if she could also pick up some beef or salmon steaks while she was there, if she didn't mind, as I had invited my uncle to have dinner with us tonight. I knew there was a grill on the patio outside of Willy's room, and I thought I might roll it out from under the crime scene tape and around to the back door where I could broil some steaks. Meat was one of the few things I knew how to cook well, thanks to a restaurant job I'd held during my college years that had taught me to man a grill but, sadly, little else in the kitchen.

"You got it. Sounds good."

Lisa offered to handle the preparation of the rest of the meal, including side dishes and dessert, which I gratefully accepted, thinking that if she knew how awful my cooking was, she would know what a favor she was doing for us.

Livvy and I gave Deena some final words and a hug, though I didn't have the opportunity to clear up her misconception about the casket just then. Outside, it was boiling hot, but the two blocks were short and Livvy didn't even break a sweat. When we reached the museum, she took me inside and introduced me to her fellow volunteers, gave me a quick tour, and then led me to the reference book section. As it wasn't specifically a Cajun museum but one that encompassed a variety of Louisiana cultures, there wasn't a whole lot there that might be of use to me. Still, I found several large books that seemed promising, and even though they were reference materials, Livvy let me take them out as long as I promised to bring them back the next day.

As she wrote up the checkout slip, I asked the other volunteers if they had ever heard of a Cajun myth about a bell.

"Somebody else was asking about that," one of them said. "Just a few weeks ago. Only they used a French term."

"*Chucotement du bayou de l'angelus?*"

"Yeah, that was it. They said it had something to do with the Great Expulsion, some old Cajun story about a whole town sneaking out some treasure right under the nose of the British soldiers."

I asked her to describe the patron who had been asking, but the girl simply shook her head.

"Never saw her. We just talked about it on the phone. She wanted more information, but we didn't have anything, so I suggested that she try the big Cajun museum in St. Martinville. They got everything over there."

I tried not to look as stunned, excited, and frantic as I felt. Forcing my voice into normal tones, I inquired about that museum. She gave me a brochure for it but said that, unfortunately, it was too far away to make it there before closing today.

"Thanks, then, maybe I'll go there tomorrow," I said, and then I gathered up the books Livvy had checked out to me, headed out the door, and hit the pavement, walking twice as fast as I had coming in. My mind was bouncing around between thoughts about the identity of the person who had called, the description this girl gave me of the myth, and the potential resource of the Cajun museum.

"Are you okay?" Livvy asked, racing to catch up.

"Sorry. I'm just excited. This is the first time I've heard that there's a whole museum dedicated just to the Cajuns. Why didn't you ever tell me?"

"I don't know, I guess it didn't cross my mind." After a few more strides, she spoke again. "You sure are takin' all this genealogy research seriously."

If she only knew.

Slowing my gait, I tried to relax, to come up with a reason for my intensity.

"My mother and s-sister died when I was young," I said finally, stumbling over the word "sister" as I realized I had never quite put it that way before. "I think that researching my roots gives me a way to reconnect with them and with the rest of my family."

That explanation seemed to satisfy her. She shared a bit about what it had been like to grow up as one of five sisters, and we quickly covered the two blocks as she chatted the rest of the way.

Nearing the parking lot at the church, I saw that only three cars remained: Livvy's black Volvo, Uncle Holt's handicapped van, and one more vehicle I didn't recognize, a champagne-colored Lincoln. As we moved closer, my heart stuck in my throat, for I recognized the woman who was standing there in the parking lot talking with Holt.

It was AJ, who must have made plans to fly down here the moment she got my message and learned that I had already come.

THIRTY-TWO

Patience and abnegation of self, and devotion to others,
This was the lesson a life of trial and sorrow had taught here.

AJ acted perfectly normal and friendly as I greeted her with a hug and introduced her to Livvy. It was only after Livvy had gotten in her car and driven away that AJ's expression darkened.

"Holt's been filling me in," she said, glancing toward him. "You and I have a lot to talk about."

"I guess we do," I replied, knowing he must have given her the basic facts about Willy's death and the involvement of the police. I wondered if he'd also shared the news that I had found and read all of her letters to my grandparents.

"You just got to town?"

"Yes. I flew to New Orleans this morning and rented a car."

We both looked at the car, as if it were the most fascinating thing to come along in a while, the air nearly crackling between us. I wasn't sure how to act, because I wasn't sure how I was feeling about her right now, and I certainly had no idea how she was feeling about me. Was she angry? Scared? Concerned? All of the above?

"Well, I'd better head out," Holt said, obviously sensing the tension.

"I'll see y'all tonight at six, 'less I hear otherwise. Hope you don't mind, but I mentioned dinner to your dad and he's coming too."

"Sure. The more, the merrier," I lied.

AJ offered to help him get into his van, but he waved her off and said he had it under control. Sure enough, we watched as he opened up the sliding side door and pushed a button so that a small elevator began lowering to the ground.

"I guess you and I should head out to the house?" I asked her, reaching for the car door.

"Eventually. There's somewhere I want to take you first. You want to know the truth? Fine. I'll show you some truth."

I got into her deluxe rental and waited as she started the car. Holt was just getting himself situated as we pulled out, and I glanced his way to give a wave, only to catch him looking longingly in our direction. Quickly, I turned to see AJ, and I realized that the look he'd been giving her was mutual. She was staring back at him with some emotion I didn't recognize on her face.

"He looks good, don't you think?" she asked as we pulled out of the parking lot onto the tree-lined street. "Older, of course, but still quite handsome, as always."

"I wouldn't know. I only just met him, remember?"

She nodded and continued driving in silence, heading toward a part of town that I had not yet ventured into.

"He said you were a little upset about that."

"There's an understatement if I ever heard one," I said, surprised at the anger suddenly boiling up inside my chest.

Again, she simply nodded and kept driving.

"There's one thing you need to know, Miranda, about your ties to the people down here."

"Ties? Or *lack* of ties, you mean?"

"Whatever," she replied. "I know you don't want to hear this, but I had my reasons. Good reasons. I'm sorry you lost an uncle in the process, but if you had been in my shoes you would have done the same."

"And here we go again, as Janet explains why everything she has ever done was purely for my own good."

"Not everything," she replied, glancing at me. "Not Holt."

"What do you mean?"

She put on a blinker and turned into a neighborhood filled with small houses and scraggly lawns. The farther we went down the street, the scragglier it got.

"Where are we going?"

"You'll see in a minute."

"What do you mean by 'not Holt'?"

She placed a high-heeled foot on the brake, slowing to cross over some railroad tracks.

"I kept your grandparents out of your life for your sake. I kept Holt out of your life for mine. I'm sorry if that cost you an important relationship, but tough. A person can only handle so much."

I looked out of the window as she slowed even more, finally coming to a stop in front of a ramshackle home so small it couldn't have held more than two or three tiny rooms, total. A busted chain-link fence surrounded the overgrown yard. In the front window, what looked like a bed sheet tacked up behind cracked glass was pulled away from the window, and a beady pair of eyes looked out at us, though I couldn't tell if they belonged to man or woman.

"Take a good look," AJ said, "because I'd better get moving again soon."

"Where are we?" I asked, studying the creepy house and yard, hoping someone didn't pull a gun out soon and start shooting. From the backyard a mangy dog was barking furiously, throwing himself against the gate.

"Home sweet home," Janet said. "My home. Yasmine's home."

I didn't reply but merely looked at her in alarm.

"It was just a rental," she continued. "Lord knows how many people have lived there since my dad died and my mom moved up to Ruston twenty years ago. But from the time I was small until I left home at seventeen, this was where we lived. And yes, it was just as bad then as it is now."

I knew that AJ and my mother had come from modest beginnings. I hadn't realized those beginnings were quite this modest. Our fancy car was starting to attract attention, curtains parting up and down the street and two kids stopping short on their bikes just to stare.

"Start moving," I told AJ. "I get the point."

"Do you, though?" Janet asked as she put the car in gear and slowly pulled out. "Can you imagine the life we lived here, all four of us squeezed into that one horrid little house, my father's body slowly degenerating from Parkinson's disease? My poor mother had it worse than any of us, caring for two kids and an invalid husband, working full time on an assembly line to bring in enough money to feed us, and then once she got home having to cook and clean and help us with our homework and empty my father's bags and feed him his supper like he was a baby. That was our life, Miranda. That's how I grew up."

"I'm sorry, AJ," I said softly. "I didn't know it was quite that bad."

She turned out of the neighborhood and back onto a main street.

"As soon as your mother and I were old enough, we had to go out and get jobs too. One year, we both worked the counter at an ice-cream parlor across town. Most of the teenagers who hung out there went to St. James, the private school nearby, so they weren't fully aware of our situation. That whole summer we were simply the Greene sisters and treated like part of the crowd, even if the two of us were behind the counter rather than in front. Yasmine set her eye on one guy who came in all the time: the rich and handsome Richard Fairmont. She knew all the tricks for reeling him in, and she went at it full steam ahead. She didn't love him, but she liked him okay, and he was smitten with her. He was going to be her ticket out."

I wasn't sure that I wanted to hear all of this, but AJ kept talking.

"As it happens, I had a major crush on Holt. He wasn't quite as good looking as Richard, but he was sweeter, a real heartbreaker. I was too young for him, though, so he barely even noticed me. Yasmine knew I liked him, and she used to spin dreams on our way home on the bus, describing the lives we would live as the beautiful Greene sisters married to the wealthy Fairmont brothers."

AJ glanced at me and continued.

"When Holt got shipped off to Vietnam, I cried for two weeks straight.

He missed his brother's wedding six months later, where he would have been best man to my maid of honor. If he'd been there, he might finally have noticed me. I had hit a tad of a growth spurt, shall we say, and a lot of guys were starting to pay attention. I didn't return their affections, though. I was waiting for my conquering hero."

She turned onto a road I recognized and began to head back toward town.

"When Holt Fairmont finally made it back home from the war, he was paralyzed from the waist down."

I looked at AJ's face, which was now shiny from tears.

"I still loved him, so I started visiting Yasmine at Twin Oaks almost every day, mostly as an excuse to spend time with Holt. After a few weeks, he started to fall for me too, but it wasn't an easy time for either of us. He was bitter and hopeless and not at all the guy he had been before he went away. Worse, every time I tried to picture our fantasy future together, all I could see was my mother and what her life had been like, married to a man who was handicapped and bound to a wheelchair. I'm not proud, Miranda, but I couldn't handle it. I tried, but finally when I realized that he was getting serious about me, I got scared and I ran. People had been saying I was pretty enough to be a model, so I took all my savings and went off to New York City."

This part of the story I already knew, how she soon realized that modeling didn't interest her—but that working for a modeling agency did. She became a receptionist and worked her way up to a position as a director in the same company where she still worked today.

"Your mom got pregnant pretty soon after I went away," AJ said, her eyes looking glassy and cold, "which was really hard for me, considering that I had always thought we would live near each other and raise our kids together."

I knew the next part of the story too, how my mother had seized her last bit of freedom before she was too pregnant to travel, coming up to visit her sister AJ in the big city. She took the train from New Orleans and had begun to bleed somewhere around New Jersey. By the time she got to New York, doctors there took one look and put her on complete bed rest for the remainder of the pregnancy. That's when they learned that she was carrying twins.

"Your father, he never came up once to see her, not even when you were b—" She stopped her story to correct it just a bit. "Not even when you and Cassandra were born. When y'all were finally cleared to travel back home, I came down too, just to help out on the airplane with the babies, though I couldn't stay for long. I saw Holt only once during that visit, and he was hopped up on drugs, acting crazy. He almost dropped little Cassandra on her head. Your poor mother, here she had a husband she couldn't stand, an addict of a brother-in-law, two babies to raise, and a mother- and father-in-law who ruled with an iron fist and lived right downstairs. It was not a happy time."

"Doesn't sound like it."

"After a few false starts, at least she found some good help. And Yasmine was a great mom. She was used to mothering, because she had mothered me for so many years. It nearly broke my heart to leave y'all here and go back to the city. I never felt so alone."

We made a turn and I realized that she had taken a back way around to Serein Highway.

"Flash forward five years," I said softly, still hoping she would get to the point before we reached Twin Oaks.

"Five years later your mother called and told me that Cassandra had died in a horrible accident. She was nearly out of her mind with grief."

"My father told me all about it," I said. "How Cassandra died, I mean."

"Or his version, at least. Your mother had a different story."

I looked at Janet in alarm.

"What do you mean?"

"What I mean is that I'm not at all sure how your sister really died. The family had their neat, sad little tale, but I didn't buy it. On the phone, all your mom told me was that there was 'more to it' than anyone was saying. I thought I would find out the full story once I got down here for the funeral. But by then Yasmine was so drugged up on tranquilizers she could barely get out a coherent sentence, much less tell me what was really going on.

Once we got through the funeral, I was going to take her away for a while, maybe get a place over in Biloxi where we could just rest at the beach and she could try and recover from the shock of losing her child. But she killed herself before I ever had that chance. I never learned the full story."

AJ put on her blinker, slowing as we neared the entrance gates.

"In your letters to my grandparents, in the last one, you said you were forgiving them. Forgiving them for what?"

"For covering up the truth, whatever it was. For closing ranks. For making me cut a deal just so I could take you away and try to give you a more normal life."

"If they were so strong willed, then why did they let me go?"

"Because they knew I knew something. I promised them my silence in exchange for custody and those monthly letters in exchange for money to help raise you. It actually worked out well for all involved, in the long run at least. I got a daughter. They got to protect their family name. You got someone to raise you who actually cared more about you than about appearances or their own selfish interests, which is what you would have had if I had left you here to be raised by them. Even your father made out okay, moving out West and starting a new life. The Fairmonts restructured their entire will so that their sons got their cut early and you would eventually receive the house and land. And then there was old Willy, who had worked so hard and faithfully for so many years. They gave him a life estate, as you know. And that's how you ended up here now, the owner of a home that probably took you by surprise, as it was more magnificent than I had ever led you to believe."

"You can say that again."

"I didn't want you to know, because I didn't want you to come."

She reached the end of the driveway, but rather than turn off her car, we just sat there for a while, some of my questions now answered, others still rolling around in my mind.

"But why?" I pressed. "Why didn't you want me to have anything to do with them? Despite their faults they were still my grandparents."

"They were hiding something, Miranda, something big. They didn't deserve to know you. Worse, they twisted things around so that somehow

Yasmine was the one who came out looking bad in all of this—stupid, weak, nutty wrong-side-of-the-tracks Yasmine, who was such a basket case that eventually she took her own life. I didn't want you to ever have that picture of your mother. She was nothing of the sort. She was smart and funny and ambitious and kind, and if she killed herself, she had to have had a pretty darn good reason. I just didn't want them to poison you against her."

I put my hand on the latch but didn't open the door, still struggling to understand.

"Bottom line, I didn't trust them one bit," she said finally. "Not for a minute. I was afraid if I gave them an inch, they'd try to find a way to take a mile. It was easier, safer, and just plain smarter to keep you apart. I'm sorry you didn't know them, Miranda, but trust me, theirs was the greater loss. They never knew you, and that was the price they paid for my silence."

Nodding, I opened the door and started to climb out, then I stopped.

"And Holt?" I asked. "Why did you keep me from him?"

She was silent for a long time.

"Because I loved him. It nearly killed me to get over him. I'm sorry, Miranda, but for my own sake, it was just too difficult to let him back in my life."

THIRTY-THREE

Talk not of wasted affection, affection never was wasted;
If it enrich not the heart of another, its waters, returning
Back to their springs, like the rain, shall fill them full of refreshment;
That which the fountain sends forth returns again to the fountain.
Patience; accomplish thy labor; accomplish thy work of affection!

The air now cleared between us, I carried AJ's bags from her trunk up to the bedroom just down the hall a bit from mine. As she settled in, I changed into more casual clothes and then took out the brochure for the Cajun museum to study it more closely. I opened it up and one of the pictures immediately caught my eye: It was a painting of an Acadian village, the design of the wood-and-thatch house in the background looking very similar to the house in my grandmother's mural. The artist's painting style was different, of course, but the subject matter seemed identical. Was it possible that I had been right about the mural, that my grandmother had painted scenes on those walls that told a story?

I brought the brochure into the room and held it up to compare. Sure enough, these houses were from the same era, of the same construction.

Furiously, I went back to work. By the time AJ joined me, I had managed to reveal several more chunks of the scene, mostly sky but also what looked like a person over on the left. Eager to make some real progress, whenever I reached a particularly stubborn area that would need more time, I simply picked up and started again a few inches over, trying to remove the easiest parts first.

While I carefully chiseled away, AJ sat nearby and pored over the books I had picked up at the museum today, searching for something about a bell. I decided to tell her most of the things Willy had said on his deathbed, only because she already knew about my tattoo and therefore I wasn't exactly breaking my oath. Unfortunately, once I finished the story, she couldn't make any more sense out of it than Lisa and I had.

"But this is interesting," she said, holding one finger on a page as she looked up. "Do you know how *chucotement du bayou* translates?"

"How?"

"It means 'whisper of the bayou.' Isn't that lovely? A myth that gets passed along among the Cajuns, person to person, is a whisper of the bayou."

A whisper of the bayou. I thought about that, about how the gentle breezes rustled through the reeds along the waterway, a sound that was indeed similar to hundreds of whispering voices.

"I just wished we knew what our whisper was, the one that would make sense of all this," I said.

Then I went back to work. Soon, I had managed to uncover a young man wearing a tricornered hat and carrying some sort of handle in his fist. I took a break to shake out my arms, feeling frustrated and tired.

Suddenly, AJ looked up and gasped.

"What is it? Did you find it?"

"No, she said, standing. "You did."

She walked forward, holding out one hand until she reached the wall, her finger touching the foot of the young man. In the shadows, on the bottom of his bare foot, was a tattoo of the Cajun cross inside the shape of a bell. I had been so consumed with removing the paint that I hadn't even noticed it.

"What's he doing here, in this scene?" AJ demanded.

I stepped back to see it in context. At this point, all we could tell was that the young man I had uncovered was walking barefoot on a path through what looked like woods. The item in his left hand was obscured, so I concentrated my efforts there, until I revealed what he was holding: a shovel.

"He was burying something," AJ said. "Work this direction."

My energy renewed, I began scraping down the path until I came across a mound of dirt. It was obvious that he had come from there, having just buried something, for his footprints led the way down the path.

I was so frustrated at the slow tediousness of this task, but I knew if I tried to go any faster, I would damage the painting hidden underneath. Tired of my complaints, AJ asked if there wasn't some chemical that would do the job, some solvent or paint remover, but I told her that we didn't dare try, because the mural had no protection to it, not even a coating of varnish.

"Lucky for us, Willy used enamel to cover the acrylic instead of latex. At least enamel peels off."

"What's that up there?" AJ asked, pointing toward the top of the wall. "It looks like a letter."

I hadn't been working all the way to the ceiling, because I assumed it merely showed more sky. I slid over a table and climbed on top, and carefully scraped until I revealed a few letters. Working to the right and to the left, I tried to figure out what that word was, until finally I uncovered an accent mark and realized that it was in French: *réciter*. Calling Lisa up from the kitchen where she was just unloading groceries, I brought her into the room and showed her the word and the young man's tattoo. Her eyes blazed with sudden interest, as if I just may have uncovered the truth we'd been searching for.

"*Réciter*," she said. "That means recite. Recite! Work to the left, Miranda. What's the word just before that one?"

Using one of the putty knives, I carefully scraped backwards until I had uncovered the two previous words, *Il devra*.

"Go the other way," Lisa said, nearly bouncing up and down with excitement.

I worked as fast as I could, eventually needing to hop down from the table, push it toward the right, and climb back up again. Finally, when I reached a period, I stopped, my arms throbbing. My efforts had revealed a full sentence: *Il devra réciter ce serment et le garder toujours en mémoire.*

"What does it mean?" I asked, knowing it sounded so familiar.

"'He must recite this oath and remember it always.'" I looked at Lisa, who was crying. "You found it, Miranda! You found *Le Serment.*"

I climbed down from the table and we hugged each other, relief flooding my veins. That was it! That was why Willy had yelled at his beloved Ya Ya and was banished from this floor. Because in her senility, she had insisted on painting out the secret that she had kept inside her entire life.

If Lisa had her way, we would take an electric sander to the wall and plow down the line, uncovering the rest as fast as possible. I had to argue with her to make her calm down, and though I was irritated at her impatience, I had to remind myself that I was used to working at a snail's pace because this was my job. This type of thing was what I did regularly for a living.

I offered to let her choose which she would rather see me uncover next: the rest of the words or the rest of the pictures.

"I say, keep going with the words for now," she replied. "But go in that direction. We already know what it says before this. Now we need to see what the rest of it says."

Too impatient to watch, she finally excused herself to go back to the kitchen to get dinner started. Once in a while, she would pop in and translate what I had uncovered. When I ran out of wall space in that room, I had to go on a bit of a treasure hunt to find where it picked up next. Moving to the various places Deena had shown me, I was able to keep finding the trail. I wasn't sure how I would know when I had reached the end. Eventually, however, I gave up, convinced that though there were more pictures, I had exhausted all of the words.

I called Lisa up one last time and asked her to read and translate as she went. I stood with pen and paper and wrote down what she said, then when she was finished, I read all of the words out loud, in English, the second half of the oath:

"In time of great danger, I must reveal the location of the angelus and present it to all Acadians whose ancestors were born in the village of Colline d'Or. The angelus belongs to each of us, its gold has come from each of us, and to each of us it will return, to serve as our protection and to guarantee that we will never again be forced to leave our homeland. Never again will we suffer from a great expulsion."

I lowered the paper and looked from Lisa to AJ.

"Do you think that's it? That's the whole oath?"

Lisa chewed a nail, her eyes scanning the wall.

"The pictures," she said. "You have to keep going now with the pictures."

Wearily, I set down the pad and tried to make sense of what it said. My eyes kept going back to one phrase: *The angelus belongs to each of us, its gold has come from each of us, and to each of us it will return.* Was it possible that these people from Colline d'Or, aka the Hills of Gold, had somehow combined their wealth to buy a valuable bell? Why a bell of all things?

"Hello?" a man's voice called out from downstairs.

Startled, I looked at my watch to see that it was six o'clock on the dot.

"Anybody home?" Holt called out. "Something sure smells good in here."

"We're upstairs. Be there in just a minute."

"Take your time."

In a mad shuffle, I realized that my father could be showing up any minute as well—and the stairs would provide no boundary against him. Soon, he would see the oath that we had uncovered, something that I felt we should keep from him if at all possible.

"I think you're worrying about nothing," AJ said after listening to me suggest ways we could cover it up. "This is Richard we're talking about. If we don't act like it's any big deal, he won't know. He was always bored by his mother's art anyway. Just tell him you're uncovering it because you're interested in studying her painting style."

Lisa didn't seem quite as certain, but finally she agreed. Short of repainting what we had uncovered, there didn't seem to be any way to hide it that wouldn't call attention to it.

I asked Lisa to go downstairs and make Holt feel welcome, assuring her I would be down in a minute to start the grill going for the steaks. After she left, I asked AJ if she was going to be able to get through dinner.

"Get through it? What do you mean?"

"Considering your history with Holt and all."

She brushed me off with a wave of her hand.

"So much water under the bridge," she said. "We're just a pair of old fogeys by now. It's no big deal. Really."

Of course, her statement was followed by a long visit to the mirror and lots of bottles, tubes, and jars. While she fixed herself up, I ran a brush through my hair and pinned it back up and then went down to greet my guest and take in the heavenly smells of the kitchen myself.

"I have something for you," Holt said as Lisa disappeared into the pantry. I was trying to appear as if I was relaxed rather than dying to get upstairs and get back to work. "But please don't think I'm trying to push anything on you. I wasn't sure if you had one, but this is a nice translation, very easy to understand if you haven't ever really read the Bible before."

He held out a box and I took it from him, opening it up to see a Bible with a snazzy two-tone leather cover.

"You bought this for me? Thank you, Holt."

"Ah, I was in town anyway. Not to mention, I couldn't find any macaroons or a pony."

I laughed, surprised at how modern Bibles had become since the last time I paid any attention.

"Actually, I have some questions about Psalm 141," I said, handing the Bible back to him. "Could you take a look at it?"

"Sure," Holt replied, taking it from me and quickly finding the passage. He read to himself, one finger leading his eyes down the page. "What did you want to know?"

"Let's walk as we talk."

Together, we went out the door, with him holding the Bible and me pushing his wheelchair. We went up the driveway alongside the house, in the direction of the bayou, as Holt told me what he could about the passage. Though his discourse was interesting, I didn't hear him say anything that seemed significant to my search. Basically, the psalm was a lament written by David, asking God to hear his prayer, to keep him in line, and to deliver him from his enemies. What that had to do with finding the angelus, I could not imagine.

"Does this passage have some significance to you?" Holt asked when he was finished, closing the book on his lap so that he could take over the rolling of his own chair.

"When I was at the boudin festival I overheard that last line, 'Let the wicked fall into their own nets,' and I was trying to figure out if it had some significance beyond what's written there on the page."

"Ah, well, everything in this book has significance for every part of our lives."

Not wanting him to launch into a sermon, I changed the subject, asking Holt about all of the various out buildings and what purposes they had served back when this was a working farm. He couldn't identify every one, but he named the ones that he could. He said that the tallest one there by the water had been for sugar storage and loading, from what he could recall. I nodded, thinking that was the one that had given me such an odd feeling of attraction and danger when I got close to it.

When we reached the end of the house, I told him to wait there while I crossed the lawn to go to the patio outside Willy's door and grab the grill.

"You're kidding, right?" he said.

"No, why?"

"I'm sure the grill was seized by the police. Impounded as evidence."

He gestured toward the patio and I turned to look, surprised to see that there was no grill to be found.

"I don't understand," I said.

He seemed to think for a moment, his eyebrows dipping low over his eyes.

"I guess they didn't tell you the details of Willy's murder?"

I shook my head, eyes wide.

"No, those cops didn't want to talk to me at all. Do you know more about it? Do you know what really happened?"

"I know some," he said, and we turned and walked back toward the house as he explained. He said that he'd been chatting with friends on the force, who told him that Willy's murder had essentially been death by lighter fluid.

"*Lighter fluid?*"

"That's why they think it wasn't all that premeditated. Whoever killed him simply reached under the grill outside his door there and grabbed the can of lighter fluid, used it to fill up the humidifier, and then put back the little bit that was left when they were done."

"That's how he died? Breathing in the fumes of lighter fluid?"

"Yeah, they said his lungs were so full of froth that the coroner knew right away there was something fishy about his death."

My mind reeled with the thought of poor Willy, struggling to breathe with the very mechanism that had been altered to kill him!

"So what's the DNA that they have? Why did they take samples from all of us?"

"Lucky for them, two cops checked out that grill together. One leaned down to grab the bottle of lighter fluid and the other goes, 'Watch out, Bubba, you're gonna bump your head on that piece of metal hanging down.' The other guy freezes and pulls his head out real slowly like, because he doesn't want to get hurt. He looks at the metal and says, 'Oops, looks like somebody else beat me to it.'"

"The killer," I said as we reached the back door.

"Yes. Judging by the freshness of the evidence there, the cops theorize that whoever killed Willy banged their head pretty badly, either when they grabbed the lighter fluid or when they put it back. The police were able to get a good little chunk of scalp tissue, some blood, and even several hairs. That's why they tested everybody for DNA. If they can find a match, they will have zeroed in on whoever reached for that lighter fluid."

"And that's why they insisted on examining my head," I mused, comforted that they really hadn't been looking for my stupid tattoo.

I opened the door and we went inside, now faced with the question of how to cook steaks without a grill. Shaking her head, Lisa said not to worry, there was a grill outside of Willy's room that we could use. Holt glanced at me, his expression grim, and then he explained to her everything he'd just told me.

She seemed very upset by what he told her, more than I would have expected, and finally I decided that was because she was the one who had put the mask on Willy, so theoretically she had been part of the cause of his death. Hoping to calm her down, I focused on the food, asking what we should do about the meat. With tears rolling down her dark face, she busied herself with broiling the gorgeous steaks in the oven, and soon the kitchen was filled with the delicious, sizzling smell of roasting beef. As she pulled the last dish from the oven, she set it on top of the stove and handed me the potholders.

"You have to take it from here," she sobbed, and then she grabbed her car keys and ran out the door.

I went after her, stopping her just as she climbed into her little red car.

"Lisa, wait!" I said. "Are you okay?"

She was crying in earnest now, deep heaving sobs that rolled up from her chest.

"I just have to be alone for a while," she sobbed. "I have to think."

I hesitated, not at all sure she should be driving in such a state.

"Miranda, please let me go. I'm all right. I need a good cry, and I'd rather not fall apart with all of these people here."

I reluctantly stepped back and let her pass, watching her car speed down the driveway and out of view around the trees.

Back inside, I tried to pick up the pieces of our little dinner party. All that was left was to get the food on the table. I knew that Lisa had planned for us to eat in the dining room, which seemed an odd choice to me since we had to make a big loop through the parlor, entryway, and living room just to get to it.

"No you don't," Holt said. Rolling his chair toward the door to the pantry, he flung it open, rolled inside, and then reached for a latch on the back wall—which turned out to be not a wall at all but a door. He slid the door open to reveal the dining room right there on the other side, just steps away from the kitchen. Amazed at the clever workings of this old house, I walked through, back and forth, several times, carrying all of the food to the table.

My father showed up just in time to eat, putting a damper on a gathering that had already turned quite somber with the exit of Lisa. He had brought along a bottle of wine, though he drank most of it himself. Halfway through the bottle, he grew a little more loquacious, though I could tell that he didn't really want to be there—either that, or he knew we didn't want him there.

Holt, on the other hand, was the very picture of charm. When AJ finally came downstairs, she looked lovely, her makeup and hair simply perfect, her outfit filmy and soft and vaguely sexy. She seemed nervous and self-conscious but also flirty, and I realized with a start that this was the first time I had ever observed her acting this way with a man. I wasn't sure what that was about, but I found it kind of cute. Old fogey or not, having Holt here was really rattling her cage.

During the meal, trying to lay the groundwork with my father, I brought up the subject of my efforts to uncover my grandmother's hidden paintings upstairs. As AJ had predicted, he asked no questions and didn't seem interested at all. Poor Holt was curious about them but in no position to get up there and take a look. I made a vague promise to snap some photos once I was finished so that he could see them that way. I knew that was a promise I might have to forget or at least put off for a while, depending on what the rest of the murals revealed.

Considering the dynamics of the group, conversation flowed along rather well. At one point, Holt and I got to laughing about something, and when I glanced at AJ, I could see a change coming over her face. Her smile dimmed somewhat and eventually disappeared all together. Before we even served dessert, she excused herself, and then she headed upstairs, putting a hand to her mouth to hold in a sob before she was even out of the room.

I looked at Holt, who seemed terribly disappointed.

"Do you think I said something wrong?" he asked me.

I shook my head.

"I think she's feeling guilty," I whispered. "For all those lost years. Seeing how well you and I get along and everything."

Of course, I thought with my own surge of guilt, I had probably been overdoing it a little tonight, trying to show off in front of my father. It was pathetic, but I just wanted Richard Fairmont to see that his daughter could be interesting and entertaining and very much worth spending time with if he'd ever just bother to try.

Except for steaks that would have been tastier from a grill, the meal was wonderful. We went ahead and moved along to the dessert without AJ, a light and heavenly bread pudding with a rum raisin sauce.

When we were finished, the men complained about having eaten too much and I knew that was true of me as well. While they sat there and talked, I stood and began clearing off the table. Now that dinner was over, I was embarrassed to admit that I wanted to go upstairs and get back to work, as there was a painting up there with my name on it. Still, I didn't want to be rude. In the kitchen, as I loaded the dishwasher, I dialed Lisa's cell phone, just to check and make sure she was okay.

Wherever she was, it was noisy, the music and clanking glasses in the background making me think perhaps she had gone to a bar. We talked for only a minute, but she sounded much better, saying that she had run into some friends who had taken her out for a bite to eat. When she said not to wait up for her, I reminded her of my sighting of Jimmy Smith yesterday and said that she shouldn't be coming back to the house late at night alone, just in case it hadn't been a dream.

"Don't worry about me, Miranda," she said. "I'll be fine."

I was just hanging up from our call when voices began to rise from the dining room. From the sound of things and the occasional mention of my name, I realized that my father and Holt were having an argument—and that it had something to do with me.

I tried to listen by hovering in the pantry, but their voices were too muffled to make out half of their words. Finally, I opened the dining room door and leaned in to ask if anyone wanted coffee. They both declined, but my father pushed out his chair and said that I would need to excuse the two of them. They were going over to Holt's house where they could continue their "discussion."

"If you want some privacy," I said, hating myself even as I said it, "you're welcome to go in the library. I need to get on to bed anyway. I'm pretty tired after such an emotional day."

They bid me good night, Holt thanking me for a wonderful dinner. Realizing my father intended on spending the night here, I explained where Lisa, AJ, and I were all sleeping and said he could feel free to choose between whatever bedrooms were left.

"I'll just stay in my old room on the third floor," he told me, and then I again said good night and headed upstairs. As much as I hadn't wanted my father here for dinner, I was glad he'd be spending the night. I hated to be a big chicken, but with all that was going on, it was comforting to know that there would be a man in the house in case Jimmy made another appearance.

As soon as I was sure the two men had relocated to the library, I made my way back downstairs to the laundry room. Quietly, I slipped inside and listened to a conversation between the two men that came through the vent so clearly it was as though I were listening to it on the radio.

"...your motives," Holt was saying. "You might be fooling everyone else, Richard, but not me. Willy was nothing to you, less than nothing. Why are you really here?"

They argued back and forth for a while, Holt insisting that my dad had an ulterior motive for having come to town this week, my dad defending himself by acting insulted that Holt could even insinuate such a thing. Finally, however, Holt wore him down by spelling out his suspicions.

"I know you, Richard. You're going to try and weasel your way back into this house," Holt said. "But that's wrong. Mom and Dad gave you your share years ago. That was your deal."

"That was the deal at that time, yes. They're dead now. It's time to come back and establish myself and my family in the home that is rightly mine."

"Rightly yours? Richard, they left it to Miranda. Their will is ironclad solid. It's a good document. You could never challenge it and win."

There was a long silence during which I couldn't imagine what was going on. I had a feeling that my father was trying to decide how much to say to his brother about his intentions.

"I'm not trying to rip you off, Holt. I hope you know that. Once I have the will overturned, we'll split things right down the middle. I want the house, but I'll be happy to give you the equal value in more land. I only want to be fair."

"Fair? Fair is leaving Miranda alone so she can do whatever she wants with the house and land her grandparents left to her. Not to you, to her."

I could hear the clomping of footsteps, and I realized that my father was pacing.

"There's just one thing wrong with that line of thinking," my father said. "My parents left this place to their granddaughter."

"So?"

"Miranda isn't their granddaughter."

"What? What are you—"

"I've never told anyone this before now, but it'll all come out soon anyway. I'm sterile, Holt. I always have been, since I had the mumps at thirteen. The doctors told me then that I might be sterile, so when Yasmine was trying to get pregnant and she couldn't conceive, I slipped off to Baton Rouge and had a sperm count done. A few months later, when she announced that she was finally pregnant, I knew she'd been having an affair. The truth is, there's literally no way I could have fathered those children. Miranda and Cassandra were not mine."

THIRTY-FOUR

So, at the hoof-beats of fate, with sad forebodings of evil,
Shrinks and closes the heart, ere the stroke of doom has attained it.

 My knees weak, I leaned back against the washer and slowly slid myself to the floor.

"Richard, that's ridiculous! Don't you see the family resemblance? She looks just like Mother!"

"Coincidence," my father replied. "Who knows who Yasmine was sleeping with? It could have been someone with similar features. All I know is that the person who impregnated her wasn't me. And I know it wasn't you, Holt, because you were...well, you were a paraplegic by then."

"As if I would have slept with my own brother's wife!" Holt shouted angrily.

"Not so loud," my father hissed. "Regardless, if it wasn't me and it wasn't you, then I don't care who it was, Miranda is not a Fairmont."

I could hear a roaring begin inside my head, like a seismic shift of the brain.

"What did Yasmine say about all of this?"

There was a long silence, and I only wished I could see as well as hear the two of them.

"You didn't tell her, did you?" Holt asked finally. "You never said a word."

"She pretended that the babies were mine. I let her pretend."

"But why? Just so you wouldn't have to admit that you were sterile?"

Again, there was a long silence and then my father spoke.

"Janet knows I wasn't the father of those children," he said. "Why else do you think she snatched up her niece and carted her away from here as fast as she could? To hide the truth, that's why, the truth that her dead sister's remaining child wasn't a Fairmont. The whole time that Benochet was putting together Mom and Dad's elaborate custody arrangements, changing their will, setting up their payment system, Janet must have been laughing all the way to the bank."

Could any of what he said be true? Could AJ have let me base everything I knew about myself and my parents on a lie? Was I really not a Fairmont?

I was ready to run upstairs and throw open AJ's door and demand to know the truth. But then the men were talking again, and I needed to listen.

"Why now, Richard?" Holt asked. "Why now, after all this time?"

"Willy's dead," my father replied. "I need to clear this up before Miranda sells off something that shouldn't even be hers."

"But you know how these things go. This could drag through the courts for years. If you really wanted to challenge the will, you should have done it sooner, like right after Mom died."

"Maybe."

"So why didn't you?"

My father rattled off some elaborate story about Willy and his faithfulness to the family and wanting to let him reap the rewards of his long labors, but it didn't seem to ring true with Holt, nor with me. In any event, their conversation soon drew to a close. When I heard them move outside so that Holt could get in his car and my father could retrieve his suitcase, I dashed through the darkened parlor to the stairs and up to my room.

I stood there with my back to the door until I heard my father come up the same stairs, go around to the next flight and up to the room above mine. There were footsteps over my head for a little while and then the creaking of bed springs as he climbed in, and then all was still.

Quietly, I went to AJ's room and tapped on her door, pushing it open to see that she was sound asleep in the dark, one arm flung over her eyes. As I listened to her gentle breathing, I could hear my father's bed creaking somewhere above us as he turned over, and I realized that the acoustics of this old house made it a bad place for the conversation AJ and I needed to have. Even if she and I whispered, the things we needed to talk about might be overheard by the man who was sleeping right upstairs.

Closing her door, I decided we would talk in the morning when we could go outside and take a walk or something, far from any listening ears. If my father really was going to challenge his parents' will and my inheritance, then I needed to know the truth, the real truth. No more lies.

Far too agitated to sleep, I returned to the mural and went back to work. Lost in the repetitive motions of what I was doing, I wasn't sure how much time had passed before I heard the crunch of a car in the driveway. Startled, I dropped my tools and ran to the window to see Lisa's little Honda rolling around the side of the house. Worried for her safety, I rushed down the hall to the back bathroom, just to watch over her until she got inside and locked the door behind her. From the window there, I could see her getting out of the car, but rather than racing into the house, she took her time, fiddling with her keys, and even pausing to readjust the headband in her hair.

I was about to tap on the glass and tell her to get herself inside when she finally reached the door, though still in no hurry. I could hear her key in the lock and the door open and shut, and then the outside light clicked off and all was still.

All except for the light that flashed somewhere up high in the trees, off in the distance.

I raced down the hall to meet Lisa just as she appeared at the top of the stairs. Holding one finger to my mouth, I led her to the bathroom and pointed toward the source of the light.

"Just watch, out this window. Tell me what you see."

She did as I asked, but nothing happened for the next several moments.

"What am I looking for?"

"A light. High up in the trees. I've seen it there before."

Together we waited, but it did not flash again. Finally, Lisa turned from the window, assuring me that there was a radio tower in that general direction, not to mention an airport, either of which could have been the source of that light.

"Either way, I don't know how you have the nerve to stand around outside in the middle of the night like this. It's just not smart."

Competing emotions seemed to pass across Lisa's features until finally she just looked chagrined.

"I guess I wasn't thinking," she said. "I'm so tired, and it's been a tough night."

"Are you feeling better?"

"Yeah," she replied, pulling off her watch and rings and earrings. "Sorry for ruining your dinner party."

I assured her that she had done nothing of the kind, that I was just sad she hadn't been there to see everyone enjoying her delicious food.

"We all ate way too much."

Lisa kicked off her shoes.

"Oh, I forgot to tell you, I talked to Mike. So far, everything he's tested for has come back negative. Looks like it really was plain old food poisoning."

"Does that mean you and Deena can make up and be friends again?" I asked, watching as she bent down to pick up her shoes.

"Were we ever really friends?" she asked, holding them wearily over her shoulder. "Housemates, yes. Sharing in the care of Willy, yes. Friends, not really."

With that, she headed off to bed and I went back to work. Lost in a haze of thought, I kept at it for hours.

By three a.m., my hands were throbbing and my arms were so tired I could barely lift them. Except for a few large, difficult patches that I'd had to leave alone for now, I had managed to remove the enamel paint from all four walls of this room. Tomorrow, I would tackle the hallway and the other rooms, but for now, this was the most I could do. Gathering my tools, I placed them in the cabinet and then brushed off my pants, crossed the room, and turned, to take in all that I had revealed.

The mural was not a continuous, circular one, despite the fact that it went all the way around the room. Instead, I could tell from the elaborate gold-colored scrollwork that periodically separated the scenes, this painting had a beginning and progressed along from there, telling a story as it went, almost like a big, gorgeous comic strip.

That first panel, to the right of the door, showed a group of people in colonial-type dress, gathered in what looked like a town hall, listening as a man wearing similar clothing stood at the center and spoke. Around the fringes of the scene, several women were crying and one man stood with his head somberly bowed.

In the next panel, the same people were in the streets of a quaint little town, the buildings there hewn from rough logs. Two men were carrying a large white sack, and the townspeople were running toward that sack, tossing in a variety of items, each of them gold: gold candlesticks, gold necklaces, gold nuggets. At the end of the street, in the direction that the men were going, was a store with an anvil out front, no doubt the blacksmith shop. In the background, further down the road behind them, was a church, a tall building with a wooden bell tower and a cross on top.

Pulse surging, I moved on to the next wall, and as I looked at it my skin raised up in goose bumps: Inside the blacksmith shop, as several of the townsfolk looked on, two muscular, sweating men poured what looked like molten gold into a black mold.

In the next panel, covering the third wall, those same men were doing something else in the shop. Part of that picture was covered by one of the stubborn areas of enamel, so I grabbed the sandpaper from the cabinet and risked harming the tableau as I carefully sanded down to the acrylic underneath. Brushing the dust away, I could see that the men were holding paintbrushes, applying gray paint to the shiny gold, curved surface of what I simply knew must be a bell. With a gasp I understood: They had forged a bell from pure gold and were camouflaging it!

The next scene, on the fourth wall, was particularly heartbreaking, a line of people being marched from their village by red-coated British soldiers on horseback. Off to the right, near the switch plate, were the two dogs that I had uncovered when I first began. At the very center of the wall, at the head of their procession, was a priest wearing a white robe and carrying a scepter on top of which was a cross—the same cross of my tattoo. Behind the priest, four men shouldered the load of a heavy wooden box affixed with carrying poles. That box, just about the size and shape to hold a large bell, was obviously made of wood, and its lid had been carved with the now-familiar image of the cross inside a bell.

My mind raced, remembering what I had read about Colline d'Or, that it was the only village where no one had tried to escape. Now I knew why. Pretending to be pious by claiming peace and nonviolence, they must have convinced the soldiers to let them cart off their most precious religious memento, what they had claimed was the simple iron bell from their church's bell tower. Sure enough, far behind the marching group, sat the church, its tower now empty, its eaves on fire.

Off to the left, two young men were emerging from the woods to join the procession. Behind them, further down the path from which they had come, was a newly disturbed mound of dirt, obviously the burial place of the real church bell, the one made not of gold but simply of iron.

The citizens of Colline d'Or had managed to smuggle out their most valuable possession—their gold—right under the noses of the British soldiers. Judging by the tattoos on the boys' feet and the oath that had now been revealed in full, I had to guess that when the citizens of that village made the choice to pool their gold, they decided to stick together and use that gold as their insurance policy for their future. Once they finally settled in Louisiana and the years continued to pass, the two appointed guardians of the bell had been charged with making sure that it remained hidden and protected but ready at a moment's notice, just in case they had to use it, as the oath said, "to serve as our protection and to guarantee that we will never again be forced to leave our homeland."

Fortunately for them, that fear had never come to pass. Louisiana had been sincere in its welcome, the region safe, the land bountiful. In the generations since, the descendants of this village had scattered far and wide, many of them not even aware that the legend their grandparents and great-grandparents told of the golden bell wasn't legend at all—as so many other Cajun tales were—but was in fact true.

I closed my eyes, picturing Willy before he died, exclaiming in French about the story of the bell: "*L'angelus!*" he had cried from his bed. "Is not a *chucotement de bayou* at all! Is *la vérité!* And I am the last surviving *gardien.*" The bell was not a myth at all, he had said, it was true. And he was the last surviving guardian.

The duty of hiding and guarding the bell had been passed down through the generations of the descendants of Colline d'Or, ultimately to Willy and my grandmother, finally landing squarely at the feet of Lisa and me.

She and I were the new guardians of the angelus.

My mind reeling, I simply paced around the room, taking that in. No wonder Willy and Portia had tattooed my head. They must have done it when they knew for sure that I would be moving away for good, as insurance that one day I would return when summoned. A tattoo to the head would have hurt a lot, so I had a feeling that they had either drugged me and done it as I slept or simply taken advantage of my wordless, traumatized stupor and done it while I was awake. I sincerely hoped it was not the latter. I couldn't imagine that two adults would be that cruel, even if their motives were noble. No doubt, most other *gardiens* in the past had gotten their tattoo voluntarily and after the fact, once they were an adult and understood the responsibility, not before.

Willy's summoning of me all these years later was finally understandable in its full magnitude. With Portia dead and her replacement dead—the stubborn fellow who had been killed on his boat during Katrina—the only surviving person who knew that the myth was true, and more importantly knew where the bell was hidden, was Willy. He was determined not to die until he gave us the oath and then revealed the hiding place. Someone else, however, had had other plans.

Willy's life had been cut short before he finished saying all that he had to say. Obviously someone else knew where the bell was—or at least knew that it existed—and they were willing to kill in order to keep that secret for themselves. I wondered what that bell would be worth today. More than likely, its value as a historical artifact would be even greater than its value as a big honkin' load of gold: In short, it would be priceless.

Already, one man had been killed for it.

Who else could the killer be but Jimmy Smith? Obviously, he knew something, why else would he have come into my office under false pretenses just to show me the symbol and gauge my reaction? No wonder he had rushed off, saying he'd come back later: He was hoping that in the meantime I might remember where I had seen that symbol before. He must have thought that I knew more than I did. Having already placed a bug in my telephone a few days before, he probably hoped to catch me discussing it on the phone and steal that information for himself.

I didn't even look at my watch as I headed toward Lisa's room. Regardless of the hour, I needed to wake her up, to tell her all that I had discovered. I tapped on her door softly, not wanting to also wake my father who was slumbering overhead. Tapping again, I pushed the door open to see the bed, but the bed was empty.

"Lisa?" I whispered, the sounds of rustling coming from further inside.

Pushing the door open more, I saw that Lisa was awake and out of bed, though still in her nightgown. She was standing at the open door to the balcony, her hands clawing violently against Jimmy Smith.

He in turn was facing her, his white hands wrapped tightly around her dark brown throat.

THIRTY-FIVE

A secret,
Subtile sense crept in of pain and indefinite terror,
As the cold, poisonous snake creeps into the nest of the swallow.
It was no earthly fear. A breath from the region of spirits
Seemed to float in the air of night

I screamed.

I screamed so loudly they probably heard me all the way to Little Tara. In an instant, my father was pounding down the stairs, Jimmy Smith was gone, and Lisa was collapsing onto the bed, gasping for air.

I ran to the open door and looked out to see the intruder now running away in the moonlight across the lawn and then straight down the driveway toward the road. Lisa was making so much noise that I hesitated, but then AJ was there to take care of Lisa so I moved on outside.

Out at the balcony railing, I dashed around the perimeter and finally spotted what I was looking for: a climbing rope with a hook on the top and thick knots all the way down about every two feet. My father burst onto the balcony as well, and when I showed it to him and told him what happened, he immediately went to the phone and called the police.

While we waited for them to arrive, I asked my father to go downstairs and be ready to greet the cops at the door. Once he left, I whispered to

AJ that I needed her to go down there too and make sure he wasn't eaves-dropping, because Lisa and I had to talk about what we could and could not tell the police about the intruder—a conversation that I absolutely didn't want my father listening in on. AJ readily agreed. As she turned to go, I noticed that her eyes were puffy, as if she had cried herself to sleep.

Once we were alone, Lisa repeated what she'd been saying since she found her voice and could talk. According to her, had I not come into her room when I did, she would be dead now. She said that she had been awakened only moments before by a knock at that outside door. Since the last person to knock on that door was me, in her half-asleep state, she had just assumed it was me again.

"I know it was so stupid," Lisa cried, her face in her hands, "but I didn't even look outside! I just opened the door and there he was and the next thing I knew, he was choking me."

I didn't say "I told you so" for her nonchalance in the face of danger. I was just glad I had gotten there when I did—and I hoped she had finally learned her lesson and would be more cautious in the future.

The hardest part for both of us, I told her as she tried to calm down, was going to be finding a way to answer the police's questions without revealing anything about the myth of the angelus or the symbol of the bell—for that was obviously what had brought this man here in the first place. I didn't know why he wanted Lisa to die, but I knew we couldn't tell the cops everything right now. In the end, we agreed to stick with a limited version of the truth.

Lisa went to the bathroom to compose herself, not even yet aware of what I had uncovered with my night's work. I planned to save that huge news until after the police were gone. In the meantime, as we all waited for them to come, I went to the room with the paintings, turned off the light, and closed the door. Then I went to the other sitting room and crossed to the window in the dark. Pulling back the curtain, I looked out into the night, watching for the arrival of the police, wondering where Jimmy Smith had gone when he once again ran from here.

I looked out at the dark night, a light mist hovering near the ground.

The moon was exactly half full, and it cast an eerie glow to the whole landscape down below. I tilted my forehead against the window, letting its coolness calm me. My own face reflected back at me, but suddenly it wasn't the face of a thirty-two-year-old woman.

It was the face of a five-year-old girl.

My heart began pounding, but this time instead of grasping for the memory so hard that I would chase it away, I forced myself to relax and simply let it come.

It was night.

It was an upstairs window.

I was looking outside at someone walking across the yard in the moonlight.

Who was it?

Was it Willy?

The picture in my mind grew fuzzy, and in one moment it *was* Willy— Willy with a shovel in his hands—but in the next moment it was two people, their arms held tightly around each other as they walked. Then I saw Willy again, still with the shovel, still alone. Digging.

Whatever I was remembering was no ordinary scene. I pressed my hands against the glass and saw my arms begin trembling. I felt the urge to run out into the night and do something, anything. I felt horrified. For some reason I wanted to go up high. Higher.

I didn't know what that meant, but I could see stairs, metal stairs with no backing to them, so that as I walked, I had to look straight ahead so I couldn't see how far up from the ground I was.

"Miranda? Are you okay?" Lisa rasped.

"I'm having a memory," I said as evenly as I could. "I'm trying not to lose it."

Understanding my situation, she didn't speak again, but it was too late; my concentration had already been broken. I stepped backward and took a deep breath and hoped that soon, maybe once the police were gone, I might be able to get to that place of remembering again.

"Sorry about that," I said to Lisa, who was standing there in her robe looking calmer than she had a few minutes ago. "I was just standing here looking outside and I had this flashback to the sight of Willy out there with a shovel."

"A shovel? In the middle of the night?"

I studied her eager face, took one more quick look out the window, and made my decision.

"I have something huge to show you," I said. "Do you want to see now or after the police are gone?"

"They're not here yet. Show me now."

Taking Lisa by the hand, I led her to the room with the mural. Talking quickly, I moved from wall to wall, pointing out the story as I saw it taking place. When I was finished, I saw that her eyes were glistening with excitement, her terror at being choked already forgotten in this moment.

"We have to do the rest of the walls out there," she said. "One of them must show where Willy hid the bell."

"I know," I replied. "But even if the walls don't give us that particular bit of information, I think it might be stored somewhere in my brain anyway, the knowledge of where Willy was digging."

We heard voices from downstairs, so we turned off the light, shut the door, and went to Lisa's room. We were just sitting down on the bed when my father and AJ came walking up, accompanied by two policemen. I could see lights flashing outside, lots of red flashing lights.

For a small town, Oak Knoll sure had a variety of responders on the police department. First there had been Bubba, the guy who came to check out my report of animal abuse. Then there were the two detectives who had examined my scalp. I had been so out of it at the time that I hadn't really formed an opinion about them or about their competency, though thankfully the two goofballs who had been guarding the crime scene were not around tonight.

This time, two female cops greeted us, and they were obviously in charge this time. They were there a good while, questioning Lisa, gathering evidence from outside, interviewing the rest of us. Again, I couldn't shake that feeling that they viewed us primarily as suspects, not victims. They seemed particularly unimpressed with the markings left on Lisa's neck, one of the cops even commenting that she'd seen a lot worse. That made me angry, that they would challenge the veracity of our claims based on how bruised Lisa was—or wasn't, as the case may be. Because he had grabbed her seconds before I opened the door and scared him off, there probably hadn't been enough time to cause significant bruising anyway.

I told the policewomen that I had already given the detective a sketch of the man that morning, and they said they would use it to put out an APB. Hopefully someone would spot him soon and they could bring him in. By the time they were finished questioning me, the sun was about to come up. I wanted to return to my work on the mural, but they were still here, talking to my father for his version of things. Realizing that I had never gone to bed for the night, I stretched out on the top of my covers, just trying to rest my eyes until the police were gone and I could get back to work. As I drifted off to sleep, I could at least be comforted by what one of the policewomen had told me, that they'd gotten back the lab report on the potentially poisonous food confiscated from Deena's kitchen, and it hadn't been positive for anything more lethal than spoiled beef. At best, she was guilty of being a cheapskate—not to mention a bad cook.

When I awoke, the sun was much higher in the sky, and I felt as though I had gotten some much-needed deep sleep. Sitting on the edge of the bed, I rubbed my eyes and looked at the clock to see that it was almost 11 a.m.

Embarrassed that I had slept so late, I straightened the covers and grabbed a change of clothes and some toiletries to take down the hall to the bathroom. As I opened my bedroom door, it was to the sound of a machine whirring. Confused, I followed the sound into the hall and down a bit, where Lisa was removing the outer layer of enamel over the mural—by using an electric sander!

"What are you doing?" I yelled, dropping my things to run forward and rip the plug from the wall.

"Oh hey, Miranda, big news," Lisa replied. "The police called a little while ago and the DNA reports came back. As it turns out, the DNA evidence found at Willy's crime scene was not a match for any of us that they tested. Not you, me, Deena, Charles, or his driver."

While I appreciated that news, it wasn't the most important thing on my mind at this moment.

"How could you do this?" I cried in dismay, the wall a series of vicious gouges and scars.

"Don't worry, I haven't come across anything important yet. So far, from what I can tell, they're just languishing inside a prison camp and then heading to America and getting settled here."

Heartbroken at the condition of the artwork, I stood and surveyed this part of my grandmother's mural. Though Lisa's progress with the sander had certainly moved faster than my diligent peeling had, the handheld device had also taken its toll on the artwork underneath. The images were still intact enough to follow the story, but in many places, the layers had been removed or scratched so severely that the acrylic had been obliterated. I studied the newly revealed panels of the mural through the scratches and blank spots, trying not to weep at the damage that had been done. This picture showed the Acadian refugees in various stages of illness, suffering, and even death. In one corner of the prisonlike setting was a carved wooden box with carrying handles, a dirty, ragged cloth draped over the top and three half-melted candles on top of that. Inside the box that was now serving as an ad hoc bedside table was, no doubt, the bell. The angelus.

I don't think I had realized how important this mural was to me—not as a clue to a mystery but as a work of art, as a link to my forebears—until that moment. Feeling as if she had sanded off my own skin, or sanded away my past, I simply sank to the floor and put my head in my hands. Further up the hall, Lisa remained silent and still, and I could only hope that she understood the true cost of her impatience.

"Why?" I asked finally, looking up at her. "Was it worth it?"

I expected to see guilt radiating from her face like a neon sign. Instead, the angle of her chin was defensive, and as I watched she returned to the wall outlet and plugged the sander back in.

"A man tried to kill me last night. We're out of time. We can't do it your way anymore."

She was about to turn the machine back on, but I jumped up and crossed to her, nearly trembling with rage.

"You may be the other *gardien* of the angelus," I said in a low, even voice, "but Twin Oaks is *my* house. This wall is *my* wall, and it represents more than a set of clues. It's one of the few connections I have to the family I lost. Do you even understand what you've done here?"

"Miranda, I—"

"Lisa, please. Just go."

With that, she put down the sander, walked back to her room, and shut the door.

THIRTY-SIX

Silent a moment they stood in speechless wonder, and then rose
Louder and ever louder a wail of sorrow and anger,
And, by one impulse moved, they madly rushed to the doorway.

I headed downstairs, my heart heavy, to see where everyone was. I could hear some sort of activity in the back of the house, and when I got there, I realized that Deena was there with a moving van, and two workmen were loading up her possessions. I was standing in the hallway talking to Deena, explaining who really paid for the upgrade to Willy's casket, when Lisa suddenly opened the door and brushed past, suitcase in hand.

"What are you doing?" I asked.

"You don't want me here. Fine. I'll leave."

I closed my eyes, pinching the bridge of my nose.

"I didn't mean you had to move out. I just meant for you to leave the mural alone."

She shook her head, tears filling her eyes.

"I know when I'm not wanted," she muttered.

Then she turned on her heel and simply left.

"Long live the queen," Deena snarled after her. "The drama queen."

In the distance, I could hear the back door open and close.

Deena returned to her packing, and I took a deep breath, shook off the unpleasantness of the confrontation with Lisa, and walked into the kitchen, where I found AJ quietly making sandwiches at the counter. Beautiful and perfectly put together as usual, she was dressed in an elegant gray blouse over black slacks, a hammered silver belt circling her narrow waist, with matching hammered silver earrings dangling from her ears like shiny twin icicles.

"Where's my father?" I asked her.

"I don't know, but when he left here, he was carrying his suitcase."

I considered that, wondering if he had left town without even saying goodbye—or if he was merely clearing out of my immediate vicinity before I was given notice that my right of inheritance was going to be challenged.

"Can I make you a sandwich?" AJ asked, waving vaguely toward the fixings in front of her. She seemed subdued—almost depressed—and for a moment I thought about our conversation several days before, when she warned me not to come here for the sake of my mental health. I was surprised to see that the same could have been said for her. She was not doing well, and I realized that for AJ this whole place represented, primarily, pain.

"No thanks, but we do need to talk," I said to her now, thinking of the conversation I'd heard last night between my father and his brother. Though I should have been angry with her, she was so downcast that I didn't have the heart to be all that mad, at least not yet.

"What is it?" she asked, spreading fat-free mayonnaise on a slice of whole wheat bread.

"Not here. Can you take a walk?"

"Give me just a second."

AJ finished making the last sandwich, wrapped it in plastic, and placed it in a paper bag along with a bag of chips and some soda. Satisfied, she wiped her hands on a nearby towel and followed me outside.

"This might not take long," I said as we made our way around the side of the big truck and then briskly walked toward the bayou. The longer I stayed around here, the more I was drawn to the cement bench there with its lovely view of the water. "I overheard a conversation last night I shouldn't have between my dad and Holt."

AJ looked at me, eyebrows raised.

"Sounds like my father is going to challenge my grandparents' will. He wants Twin Oaks for himself."

"Challenge the will?" she scoffed. "On what grounds?"

"Paternity. It seems he neglected to tell my mother he was sterile. Yet somehow she miraculously ended up pregnant anyway. Do you know anything about that?"

I said it all quickly to catch her off guard, and my ploy seemed to have worked. AJ blanched, frozen to the ground, her mouth practically agape. Unfortunately, at that moment Deena chose to emerge from the house, her packing finished, her time here done. I had no choice but to excuse myself from AJ to give Deena a final farewell, one of the workmen carrying the sack of sandwiches AJ had made. By the time the truck was lumbering down the driveway and I had returned to AJ on the bench, she had managed to collect her thoughts and recover from the shock of my words.

"How certain are you that this is his intention?" she asked me.

Before I could reply, another car appeared in the driveway. Standing, I watched as it parked by the house, the door opened, and Charles Benochet climbed out.

"Looks like we're about to find out," I replied.

AJ and I greeted Charles at the back door, and we all went inside together. There, sitting around the kitchen table, Charles informed us that he'd just learned Richard Fairmont was about to file suit against Miranda Fairmont Miller for the estate known as Twin Oaks, claiming that sterility prevented him from being the father of his wife's twin daughters and therefore the surviving daughter could not be the rightful heir to his parents' fortune. Charles explained to us how it was going to work, how DNA testing could settle the matter quickly, depending on the results. Finally, however, AJ interrupted him and said simply, "Bring him here."

"Excuse me?" Charles asked.

"Get him here, right now. Get Richard. I can stop this before it even starts. I can tell him exactly what it is he wants to know."

Charles and I looked at each other.

"You want my dad to come over now?" I asked.

"Yes," AJ replied. "I have something to say. It's time for the light to be shone on every dark corner of this family."

No matter how hard I tried, I couldn't get another word out of her. As Charles got on the phone trying to track down my father, I thought I might go crazy trying to figure out what she was about to say. To be polite and kill time, I offered to make Charles a sandwich and ended up eating one myself. Within twenty minutes, there was a knock at the door, and it opened to reveal my father with Holt behind him.

AJ was waiting in the living room, so Charles led the way there, my father falling behind, not even meeting my eyes.

"Are you taking his side in this?" I asked Holt softly as we brought up the rear.

"No way," he replied, rolling through the doorway. "I was with him when Benochet called, trying to talk some sense into him. I thought I might come along and help out if I could."

We entered the living room, AJ standing at the window, her back to us.

"Present and accounted for," my father said dryly. "What do you want to say, Janet?"

She spun around looking almost confident until she spotted Holt. That caused her to falter for a moment, but she seemed to regain her composure.

"I have to tell y'all something," she said, "and when I'm finished, more than likely three of the people in this room are going to hate me. Before I start, I ask only that you look at the actions of the past through the eyes of someone who was very young."

I exchanged glances with Holt and then Charles. My father kept his eyes on AJ, though I thought I could detect a smirk turning up the edges of his lips.

"You're right, Richard, you were not Miranda's father," AJ said. After a moment of stunned silence from the rest of us, she added, "That's because Yasmine was not the twins' mother. I was. I am. Miranda, I'm your natural mother."

In a flash, I wasn't sure if I was even in the room anymore. It felt more as though I were somewhere up around the ceiling, simply floating, wondering if I had heard correctly.

"How is that possible?" Charles demanded, as shocked as the rest of us.

"I found myself in trouble right about the same time my sister desperately wanted a baby and couldn't seem to get pregnant. She and I figured out a way to make things work out best for everyone, considering the situation. Put simply, she and I pulled off an elaborate deception."

Charles and Richard both had a lot to say, but mostly it came out like white noise to me. I was still lost somewhere up there around the ceiling, wondering what universe I had just wandered into.

"If you're her mother, then who's the father?" I heard Charles say.

At that, AJ turned and looked directly at Holt. Only then did I see the expression that had been on his face all along. He was a pale white, stricken with shock. My father also followed AJ's glance, but when he saw Holt's face, he jumped up from the couch.

"This is impossible!" he cried, looking from his brother to AJ. "Holt was back from the war by then. He was a paraplegic."

AJ didn't reply but merely kept her eyes on Holt.

"There are..." Holt said, struggling to get out words. "There are ways." He seemed unable to look at AJ or me or his brother, so he settled for Charles as he tried to explain. "I always knew pretty little Janet Greene had a big crush on me. When I came home like this, in this chair, I took advantage of her affections. I told her I needed to feel like a man again." He looked at Richard. "Sorry, brother, but it's not impossible."

Holt looked down at the floor and then back up at Charles.

"I thought that being with someone would make me feel better about myself," he continued, "but actually it made things worse. Janet was just so beautiful, so loving, so innocent. Afterwards, I was disgusted with myself for having taken advantage of her feelings. I know I wasn't kind. I was demanding and irritable and impossible to be with, probably trying to punish us both. That's why she left and ran away to New York. I have never blamed her for going."

"That's not why," AJ said, her voice breaking as she stepped toward Holt. "That's not why I left."

"Why then?" Holt asked, finally looking at her.

"Because I fell in love with you. I could see beyond all the meanness and frustration to the man you were inside. The problem was my life, my parents...I'm sorry, but I couldn't end up like my mother, chained forever to a man who might need me too much. So I ran away to the big city. Three months later I realized the shocking truth: I was pregnant."

She began pacing as she talked, describing the story for all of us.

"I had a friend who said she could get me an abortion, but I couldn't do that, I just couldn't. There weren't many other choices available to me though, because I knew that if Holt found out he would convince me to come back here, and I'd get stuck in the very situation I had run from. I considered adoption, but I just didn't think I could bear to give up a child and never know what happened to her."

My father sat again, momentarily silent.

"When I told Yasmine what was going on, she had a better idea. She wanted the baby for herself. She'd been trying to get pregnant for so long and couldn't. She planned it all out, she would pretend to be pregnant, she said, and when the time came she would come up for a visit with me and 'accidentally' have to stay until the baby was born. So that's what we did."

"How could the two of you pull off something as elaborate as all that?" I demanded. "No one in the family ever caught on?"

"Yasmine thought up all sorts of ways to keep her husband from getting too close, so he wouldn't realize that the bump under her clothes was fake. But once he learned she was pregnant, he didn't come near her again for at least a year, so it didn't matter. I felt terrible about the deception, but when I learned I was carrying twins, I knew it was the right thing to do. How could I raise twins as a single mother, all alone?"

"But the labor and delivery—" Charles cried.

"When it got close, Yasmine came up for a visit. When I went into labor, I used her insurance and checked into the hospital as Yasmine Fairmont. A few days later, Yasmine Fairmont came back out with her twin daughters. Because they were twins, they were tiny, so saying they were premature wasn't hard to believe. I recovered for another week or so, then she and I flew back down here together to get them settled. When I left, I knew I had done the right thing—even though it was the hardest thing I'd ever done."

We all remained where we were, the silence louder than any noise I had ever heard. I didn't even know what I was feeling, other than shock. Words bubbled out of my mouth unheeded.

"You've made me call you 'aunt' for thirty-two years!"

"I know, and I'm sorry. Never hearing my own children call me 'mommy' was one of the hardest parts of all. But at least it was a choice I had made. Poor Holt, you never got to hear the word 'daddy,' either, even though you were one. I made that decision for you. There's nothing I can say except that I'm so, so sorry."

Again, the room went silent. Holt's face was so drawn and pale that I was afraid he might actually pass out. Concerned, I scooted closer to him and put a hand on his arm.

My father's arm.

"Are you okay?" I asked.

From the corner of my eye, I could read AJ's body language, could see that she wanted to step forward and join us. I tilted my shoulder to indicate that she wasn't welcome right now; Holt and I were the injured parties here and she'd do best to leave us alone.

"Well, this sure was a fun little story," said the man I would have to begin thinking of as my Uncle Richard, rather than my father. "But now it's quite clear that the house is mine. The will left it to my child. Miranda is not my child; therefore, it is invalid."

Charles cleared his throat.

"Not so fast," he said, putting on his glasses and pulling a file from his briefcase. "I believe from the wording in the document that they make it very clear that Twin Oaks is to go to their granddaughter Miranda. It never refers to her as Richard's child, only as their grandchild. I seem to recall Xavier tinkering with the wording a bit so that there would be no question." He looked up at us, pulling off his glasses. "To be honest, I have to wonder if they knew all of this."

"No, they couldn't have," AJ said. "Yasmine never told a soul."

"How well did you know Portia?" Charles replied. "She was very sharp, very perceptive. Here you had two women living in the same house, one of them pretending to be pregnant? I'd put money on the fact that Portia figured out the truth and simply kept her mouth shut. Mothers-in-law know all sorts of things that husbands are too stupid to figure out."

Next to me, I could almost feel the anguish radiating out of Holt. I looked at him to see that he was even more pale and drawn than before.

"I, uh, I have to get out of here," he said.

He looked so lost, so shocked, but then his eyes finally focused in on me. Without saying a word, he reached up one hand and tenderly cupped it to my cheek. Through tears in both our eyes, the look we shared spoke volumes without saying a word.

Then he simply lowered his hands to the wheels of his chair, spun around, and rolled away. Moments later, I heard the back door close, and I turned to Charles in alarm.

"Charles, maybe you should—"

"I'll go see about Holt," he said, understanding my intention. "You folks excuse me."

He hurried out of the room, leaving the three of us there together. After an awkward silence, I spoke.

"Well, this is interesting. Ordinarily, I'd say I was sitting here with my father and my aunt. But as it turns out, I'm sitting here with my uncle and my mother. Gosh, but a few well-placed words sure can turn things upside down, can't they?"

"Sarcasm doesn't become you, darling," AJ scolded.

"A lifelong deception doesn't become you, either, *Mother.*"

I'd said the last word to sting, but when it hit its mark I felt a rush of pain flowing from my heart straight to hers. Yes, I had a right to be angry. But maybe I didn't have the right to lash out so fiercely. I thought of Holt and his reaction, and I respected his discretion and restraint. No doubt, he would go home and take out his frustrations on a big pot with a spoon or something, rather than causing verbal damage to someone who was important to him.

"I'll leave the two of you to hash this out," Richard said, standing up. "But trust me, this is not over yet."

With that, he strode from the room. I heard him reach the back door and throw it open, but suddenly I could not resist jumping up and running after him. I realized that my anger at AJ paled in comparison with my anger to this man who had pretended for more than thirty years to be my father, knowing all along that there was no way he could be. When I reached the back door, it was to see him just reaching his car, the vehicles of Holt and Charles both gone already.

"At least I finally understand," I said, blood pounding between my ears, "why you spent thirty-two years *ignoring* me."

Richard spun around as I came toward him.

"My whole life," I yelled, "making me feel like I was worth nothing, that I was less than nothing!"

I didn't know where my rage was coming from, but it was from somewhere deep inside, the inevitable release of a lifetime of built-up hurt and rejection.

"You knew you couldn't have children and yet you never said a word! You knew I wasn't yours but you never did a thing about it! Now here we are all these years later, after a lifetime of you making me feel like I was worth less than dirt. Well, you know who the dirt is? You are. *You are!*"

Unable to stop myself, I stepped forward with fists raised, trying to pound at him in my fury. As AJ stood nearby, yelling at me to stop, Richard caught me by the arms and held me off. In the struggle he had to turn his face away so that I couldn't scratch at his cheek, and in that position, his head bowed, I saw the cut on his scalp, a distinctly fresh scab right at the top of the back of his head.

THIRTY-SEVEN

As, when the air is serene in the sultry solstice of summer,
Suddenly gathers a storm, and the deadly sling of the hailstones
Beats down the farmer's corn in the field and shatters his windows,
Hiding the sun, and strewing the ground with thatch from the house-roofs,
Bellowing fly the herds, and seek to break their inclosures;
So on the hearts of the people descended the words of the speaker.

"Help! Miranda! Help!"

Before I could react to the sight of the cut on my father's head, I heard Lisa's voice, coming from somewhere beyond the garage. I stopped struggling and we all turned to look in the direction it had come from.

"Please! Help me!"

I didn't know what was going on or why Lisa was calling for me, but I didn't think she was just being a drama queen now. Richard, AJ, and I all took off after the voice, my mind spinning with the implications of the cut on my father's head. As we ran I was afraid we would find Lisa at the bottom of a well or bitten by a snake or half eaten by an alligator. Instead, as we rounded the corner of the canning shed, it was to find her being held at gunpoint there by Jimmy Smith, who had one arm clutched around her neck, the other with a gun barrel pressing against her head.

"There you are," he said to me, smiling eerily, the caterpillar on his lip glistening with sweat. "Took you long enough."

At that, two more men stepped out from the shadows of the building behind us, also with guns, essentially cutting off all escape routes and making us their prisoners.

"Who *are* you, Jimmy Smith?" I demanded. "What do you want?"

I glanced at the two men who stood behind us, guns raised, and with a shiver I knew they were the ones who had attacked me in the alley, looking for my tattoo.

"What do you think I want? The bell. Tell me where I can find it. "

I looked at AJ, who was stricken and pale, and Richard, who was merely confused. Then I looked back at Jimmy Smith, whose eyes were black and cold as onyx.

"Trust me. I would if I could. But I don't know where it is."

"Try, Miranda," Lisa whimpered. "Just last night you remembered something. You remembered seeing Willy outside with a shovel in the middle of the night."

"I don't know if I did or not," I said. "Besides, it was just a shred of a memory, just a trace of something bigger that made no sense at all."

Jimmy repositioned the gun against Lisa's face and pressed harder as tears filled her dark eyes.

"I think it's time for you to find that memory," he said. "Or the little spitfire here gets shot."

"No!" Lisa sobbed, her hands clutching powerlessly at his arm.

"Okay, okay," I said, my mind racing. "I'll try."

Richard was angry and frightened, demanding to know what was going on here. As AJ gave him an abbreviated version, I moved several feet away and closed my eyes, hands to my ears. I simply needed to think, to clear my brain and maybe, just maybe, bring back the memory that had almost resurfaced last night.

At first in my mind I listed the things that I had remembered: I had that feeling that I was up high but I wanted to go even higher, that the stairs had no backs and were frightening. I kept trying to imagine the view of this yard from the house upstairs, but it didn't work—until I realized that

I hadn't been looking down at this yard from the house, I'd been looking down from somewhere else, somewhere close by and just as tall.

"The building beside the water," I said suddenly. "That's where I was when I saw him, not the house."

I could see myself running there in the night, running across the lawn in my nightgown, my bare feet getting wet in the dewy grass.

"The tallest one?" Lisa asked.

When I nodded, her captor barked, "Then let's go there now."

We crossed the yard as a group. Jimmy dragging Lisa in front, AJ and Richard and I following behind being herded at gunpoint by the two goons. As we neared the building by the water, the one that towered over this part of the yard at three stories tall, I again felt that rush of danger and attraction. I knew that even if this quest did not lead us to the bell, it was still of some importance to my mind, to my past.

The door to the building wasn't locked, and it squeaked open on its hinges, the sound echoing against the walls inside. We stepped inside, and with a gasp I saw that the stairs from the first floor to the second were indeed metal stairs with no backs, the kind that you could see through to the ground while climbing.

"Move."

Prodded onward, we stepped inside, and though I know AJ was probably concerned about rats and Richard was no doubt looking for some way that he could get free and run, I was focused on the stairs that I knew I had taken at some point in my youth. Why would I have been out here in the middle of the night, just a little girl all by myself?

I began to lead the way, weaving past the refuse of this old agricultural building to get to the steps.

"It wasn't like this here," I said, looking around at the mess. "There were machines, all sorts of machines."

"My father sold off the equipment from this building years ago," Richard replied.

"How do we know the stairs are strong enough to hold?" AJ asked. "They're so old."

"I been living out here all week," Jimmy replied. "They're fine. Now go."

I climbed the steep stairs, stunned at the thought of this man being here all along, so close to where we were. Had he been watching us? Watching me? Coming out at night to peek in the windows of the house?

"The light!" I said suddenly, remembering the view from the upstairs window. "A light shining through the trees! That was you?"

"Yeah. Whatever. Hurry up."

When I reached the top of the stairs, I tried to look around not as a grown woman, but as a little girl in her nightgown in the middle of the night. Why hadn't I been scared? Why had I done this? Was this a good place or bad? I just didn't know.

The others reached the floor behind me as I strode quickly across the room to the front window, which was cracked but still intact. Our main gunman, though he held Lisa as leverage, was really interested only in me. With a strong hold on Lisa, he watched me and waited.

"Not high enough," I whispered as I stood at this window, looking out above the crack. "I couldn't see from here. I had to go higher that night."

From this floor to the next were not stairs but a ladder that led to what looked like a loft. The equipment was gone from up here too, leaving the sides of the loft completely unprotected. As I reached the top, I wanted to run across the room to the window to see out, but the floor was littered with limbs and leaves and pine straw, which I was afraid might also hide snakes or rats or raccoons. Looking up at the dark ceiling, I had no doubt bats were there as well.

"Keep going," Jimmy prodded.

Deciding I'd rather take my chances with a snake than a gun—though both could be fatal—I carefully picked my way through the rubble to the opening where the window used to be. There I stood and looked out over the yard, trying to imagine the scene by moonlight rather than sunlight.

Something wasn't right about the way things were laid out. Some buildings were missing, and others were in all the wrong places. Still, imagining the dark, moonlit landscape from this perspective, I suddenly knew without question that I had seen Willy Pedreaux digging in the ground directly below and in front of this window, right in the middle of the green, grassy lawn.

"Right there," I said, pointing. "About twenty feet back from that mag-nolia tree. That's where he was. That's where he dug that night."

As I made that statement, my mind was filled with an incredible sense of relief, which was followed immediately by regret and self-recrimination. I shouldn't have been so quick to tell them! Now we were all expendable, not to mention that now they would be able to find the angelus and steal it away while we were being held prisoner up here.

"Out in the middle of the yard?" Jimmy asked, seeming not only skepti-cal but angry as well.

"I thought you said he buried it under the canning shed," one of the goons blurted.

"Well, there ain't no canning shed right there, now is there?" Jimmy screamed in return.

"There used to be."

We all turned to look at Richard.

"The canning shed used to be right there," he continued. "It got blown over there by Katrina. Nobody ever bothered to have it moved back."

That seemed to be what Jimmy wanted to hear.

"That's been our mistake!" he said, the rage on his face turning to joy. "We had the correct building, all right, we just didn't know the building got moved. You, start digging. You, tie them up first."

One man left while the other forced us to sit on the floor in the middle of the room. He pulled out a roll of duct tape and used it bind our wrists and ankles together, first Richard, then AJ, then me. When he was finished, he headed down the ladder to join the other in the digging outside.

I glanced up at Jimmy, who was pointing the gun at Lisa but watch-ing out the window at the activity below. I tried to make eye contact with Lisa, but she looked nearly out of it, her eyes cast down toward the ground. My hope was that if the men outside actually struck gold, so to speak, the surprise of the moment would distract Jimmy enough that somehow we could take advantage of the moment and get ourselves free. Still, there was no play at my hands or ankles with this duct tape. Unless we had a knife or something else sharp to work with, we would never be able to get loose.

"What on earth could Willy have buried that was worth all of this?" Richard demanded suddenly. "He was just a poor Cajun caretaker."

I looked at AJ, but before we could think of an answer, Jimmy told us to be quiet.

Suddenly, from outside came a cheer and I knew they had found what they were looking for. A walkie-talkie crackled to life at Jimmy's waist.

"Yeah? Over."

"We've struck something. Over."

"Is it what we're looking for? Over."

"Give us a few. Still digging. Over."

My mind raced, wondering how we could ever turn the tide here before it was too late.

"Well?" Richard demanded, looking at me. "What on earth did Willy have that he buried in our yard?"

In a flash, I remembered the cut on my father's head, the one I had seen just a while ago near the house. It had disturbed me, but it wasn't until now, with him talking about Willy, that I realized why: According to the police, Willy's killer had cut his head on the barbeque grill when grabbing the lighter fluid!

Had Richard killed Willy?

He hadn't even been on the list of suspects, hadn't even been tested for DNA—because he hadn't arrived until after Willy was dead. Or at least that was how he had made things appear. In truth, who knew when he had flown in—or what he had been doing before we ever saw him here?

Could the man I had always thought was my father actually have killed someone?

Yes, I heard my own mind say. *He has killed before.*

I closed my eyes as the memories, old memories, chose to come flooding back.

I thought of my twin sister, Cass, so brave, too brave.

Brave enough to try and stop our parents from fighting again.

We were both crying, but she was the one who ran into the hall, begging them to stop. She was the one who was tugging on Mommy's robe, crying for them to quit it.

She was the one who got in the way when Daddy hit Mommy.

She was the one who fell—fell down the stairs.

The one whose neck broke when she hit the bottom.

I didn't tell. I never told anyone I saw. I just got back in my bed and waited for morning, when Cass would come back to our room and everything would be okay. Only she didn't come back.

It wasn't okay.

My eyes opened wide, staring at the man I had always thought of as my father.

He killed my sister! It may have been an accident, but it had happened in anger, as he struck at the woman I thought was my mother and hit my twin sister instead.

Could a man who killed once accidentally kill again on purpose?

Suddenly, I knew what I had been doing out here that night so long ago.

It wasn't much later, maybe three days, maybe a week. Again, my parents were fighting, but this time Cass wasn't around to try and make them stop. I was too scared to try, so I waited in my room, listening and hiding.

Then finally the fight ended and there was movement. I heard them leaving, heard both of my parents going down the stairs, leaving me there alone.

I was scared to be there alone without Cass to protect me.

So I followed.

Down the stairs, through the house, out to the yard, my mother so weak she could barely stand, my father strongly supporting her the whole way.

They kept walking into the night and I wanted to follow but I was scared, so scared that they would get mad at me if they saw me, scared my father would hit me the way he hit Cass and I would fall down dead too.

So I went to the big building instead, the sugar house. I loved it there, loved to look at the machinery, loved to see the fine powder of sugar on the floors. I raced up the scary stairs to the second floor window, where I could see them as they walked toward the garden. But they had disappeared behind the shed.

Quickly, I had climbed up the ladder to the third floor, raced to the big window, and looked out at the yard in the moonlight. From there, from so high, I could see better, I could see nearly everything: my parents behind the shed, still walking toward the garden. Then I saw Willy, who was digging with a shovel nearby, on the ground next to a blue tarp, in the place where a building was just about to be built. Why was he digging in the middle of the night?

He must have been doing something wrong, I thought, because when he saw my parents coming, he dropped that shovel and hid behind a tree. Soon, I couldn't see my parents anymore. Only Willy, still hiding. I waited, trying to decide what to do, when finally my father came back.

He came back alone.

He went to the house and I came down the ladder and then the stairs, not sure which way to go. Check on my mom? Follow my dad? Finally, I heard crying, so I went that way. The crying sound was coming from Willy. He was looking up at Mom, who was hanging from a tree. She wasn't moving.

She was dead.

I didn't want to get in trouble, so I went back to the house.

I went to my room.

I crawled into my bed.

I pretended I hadn't seen, hadn't heard, hadn't hurt.

I pretended so hard that soon I forgot completely.

THIRTY-EIGHT

Multitudinous echoes awoke and died in the distance,
Over the watery floor, and beneath the reverberant branches;
But not a voice replied; no answer came from the darkness;
And when the echoes had ceased, like a sense of pain was the silence.

I looked over at Richard, who was sweating profusely, chafing against the tape that bound his hands and wrists. Jimmy had dragged Lisa to the front window, where he stood watching the action on the ground far below.

"You killed Cass," I whispered incredulously. "I saw it. I saw it with my own eyes!"

AJ gasped, spinning to look at Richard in horror.

"You went to hit my mother," I said, my eyes on him but my mind vividly in the past, "and instead ended up knocking Cass down the stairs by mistake. You killed her. I saw you do it."

The man who was so handsome for his age, so tall and commanding, looked back at me, his expression one of exaggerated disdain.

"You're nuts, do you know that? No one would believe a ridiculous story like that."

Across the room, Jimmy's walkie-talkie crackled at his waist.

"All right. We got a good look. Over."

"Is it the bell? Over."

"Not even close. Looks like..."

"Looks like what? Over."

"Bones. Looks like old bones. A human skeleton. Over."

Bones! Just like the bone Tess found nearby, the one that we turned into the police. My stomach clenched in terror. Could someone who had lived here in the past have been some sort of serial killer? Were bodies buried everywhere out there? Or was there just one body, whoever it was, and the bone we found had come from the same source?

Again, the voice crackled to life.

"Looks like they were in a wooden box at some point, but the box is all busted up. Wait, there's something carved in the lid."

We waited and then the voice came through again.

"It's not carved exactly. It's like a handmade sign. The letters are burned in—you know, like with a woodburning kit?"

"Woodburning? Like they do in cub scouts? Over."

"Yeah, I wasn't never no cub scout. Over."

Jimmy rolled his eyes.

"What's it say? Over."

"Hold on. It says, 'Let us bury him here by the sea...when a happier season brings us again to our homes from the unknown land of our exile... then shall his sacred dust be piously laid in the churchyard.' What's that mean? Over."

Everyone was quiet for a moment, but my mind was racing. I knew that quote. It was from something I had read just recently, maybe *Evangeline*, the fictional poem set against the true backdrop of Cajun history. I tried to remember where it had come in the story and what it meant.

"Keep digging," Jimmy said finally. "Get those bones out of there and dig deeper. See if there's anything underneath. Over."

We all waited for what felt like an eternity until the voice crackled through again.

"Sorry, boss. Nothing under all those bones except dirt. Over."

Jimmy cursed loudly, kicking at some of the refuse for emphasis and sending several giant roaches scampering for cover. Still dragging Lisa, he marched furiously over to us and pointed the gun at my head.

"You lied," he hissed.

"I didn't lie. I said I had a memory of Willy digging in the middle of the night. I never said I saw him burying the bell."

He seemed to consider my words as the walkie-talkie crackled again at his waist.

"What do we do now, boss? Over."

Jimmy was silent for a moment, thinking, then he lifted it to his mouth, pushed the button, and spoke.

"Go get the equipment. We'll rip up the whole yard if we have to until we find it. Over."

I was hoping Jimmy would leave us to ourselves for a while as they embarked on the next part of their search. If he did, we just might be able to escape. Amid all of this rubble, surely there was something sharp we could use to cut ourselves free if we had some time unobserved.

"Liars have to die," Jimmy said, still holding the gun to my head.

AJ moaned and whimpered beside me, begging him to spare my life, but I wasn't going to beg. I wasn't going to cry. All these years of feeling disconnected and separate from everyone else in the world had prepared me for this moment. I looked up at him, oddly numb, and tried to reason with him instead.

"What makes you think it's buried here at all? Willy could have hidden that thing almost anywhere."

"Oh, it's here somewhere," he said. "That's why he got a life estate from your grandmother—so he could protect the angelus for as long as he lived."

"Fine, then," I replied, wondering how he knew that, "even if it's here somewhere, how do you know it's in the yard and not in the house? How do you know it's not behind the walls of this building or buried under the garage or bricked into a fireplace? There are too many places to look. You'd have to burn the whole house and every surrounding building down to find it—but you wouldn't dare, because a fire like that could damage the bell as well."

"Sorry," Jimmy replied smugly, "but I know some things you don't. Your tattoo has a code. Every *guardien* wears a tattoo in case something happens to them and the next *guardien* needs to find the bell. Just by where they placed it on your body, we know that the bell is buried underground, not hidden above. From the curve on the bottom of the bell, we know it's underneath some structure, not buried somewhere out in the open. And from the whirls of the cross, we even have an approximate latitude and longitude. Trust me, we're very close to getting our hands on it. "

All of that information—and I had been carrying it around on my head since I was a little girl? Unbelievable!

"We've got a backhoe waiting up the road. My guys will have it back here in fifteen or twenty minutes and start digging in every single place where each of these buildings used to stand. The bell had to have been buried underneath one of them. Eventually it'll turn up. In the meantime, I'm sorry to say, you're of no more use to us. Sadly, the world will learn tomorrow how you and your aunt were accidentally trapped up here in the sugar house when an old gasoline can ignited downstairs. How tragic that you both burned to death."

I glanced at Richard, wondering what fate Jimmy had in mind for him.

"You, however, might get a little reprieve," Jimmy added, poking a foot at Richard. "If I untie your legs and take you downstairs, can you show me every spot where a building used to stand before Katrina came and messed things all up?"

Richard looked at AJ and me and then back up at our captor.

"Yes, I remember where they all were. I'll show you if you promise to let me go."

"Of course," Jimmy replied, though I couldn't imagine that anyone there believed him.

Releasing the traumatized Lisa from his grasp, Jimmy handed her a pocketknife, instructing her to use it to cut Richard's feet free. She did as he instructed, her hands shaking so badly that I was afraid any moment she might accidentally cut into his skin too. I kept trying to catch her eye, to let her know somehow that as long as she was holding a knife, she had a chance to overpower Jimmy and help us all break free.

"I can't go down the ladder with my hands taped," Richard said, and reluctantly Jimmy had to admit that was true.

"Go ahead, Lisa. Cut his hands free too. But if you try anything stupid, mister, I will not hesitate to shoot you."

"I believe you."

I wasn't sure what it was about that moment that caused the situation to reframe itself in front of my eyes. Maybe it was the way Jimmy said Lisa's name, or the glance she gave him, or the simple mathematics of how many were going to die here and how many were supposed to live. What of Lisa? I understood why Jimmy was sparing Richard for now, but why wasn't Lisa going to be a victim of the same "accidental" fire that he intended to use to kill me and AJ? Lisa wasn't going to die, I suddenly realized, because Lisa was in on this with Jimmy.

Lisa, the actress.

Lisa, the girl who had grown up in Cajun country and had probably been hearing that particular myth her whole life.

Lisa, who took a job here with Willy and somehow found out that the myth was true—and that he was the *gardien*.

Lisa, the voice of the woman who called the museum to learn more about the myth of the angelus.

Lisa, the one who had managed to find out a lot but still hadn't quite found that hiding place.

At the moment that Richard's hands were free, I knew I had to do something.

"Grab Lisa!" I yelled to him. "She's in on it with him!"

Fortunately, Richard moved fast, reacting almost instantly to my words. He had probably been planning to make some sort of move as soon as his hands were loose anyway, but the news I supplied allowed him to make that move count. In one strong swoop, he managed to twist Lisa's arm behind her back, grab the knife from her hand, and point it at her throat.

It was a standoff, Jimmy with the gun and Richard with the knife held at Lisa. Neither man would budge, and so finally Jimmy pointed his gun at my head.

"If you hurt her, I'll shoot Miranda."

What Jimmy didn't realize was that by shooting me, he'd actually be doing Richard a favor! My mind raced as I considered the situation. Next to me, AJ had found a small stick in the rubble, and she was trying to use it to cut the tape that bound her hands behind her back. I wasn't sure if her efforts could work, but I needed to provide a distraction, just in case.

"Hey, Jimmy, I just figured out how you managed to fake such a convincing Long Island accent," I said.

"What are you talking about?"

"That's not a Long Island accent," AJ corrected. "That's downtown New Orleans. They sound the same."

"That confirms it then. His name's not really Jimmy, it's Junior. Jimmy is Junior. Lisa's husband."

AJ stared from one to the other, incredulous.

I felt stupid that I hadn't made the connection before now, though I knew why I hadn't: Lisa's husband was a Creole, and Jimmy Smith's skin was white. I had forgotten that skin tones of Creoles varied widely.

"Shame on you, Lisa," I scolded. "You knew way more about the angelus than you let on. You knew enough to send your husband up to Manhattan to come after me."

No one replied, so I continued.

"Let me guess how it went. I wasn't responding to Willy's letters, so you had to do something. You bought a cheap painting, added the symbol, and then brought it to me to get a feel for whether I knew where the bell was buried or not."

"Yeah, yeah," Jimmy said, cutting me off, switching his voice to a high tone as he imitated me. "'I know I've seen it somewhere, I just can't remember where. I'm sure it'll come to me.' I had my guys search you to be sure. There it was, right there on your head. You're a slick one. The next thing I know, Lisa tells me you skipped town and popped up here."

"Where Lisa has been playing me all along, just waiting for me to figure out the things the two of you couldn't."

"You're a smart girl, Miranda. It was worth a try."

I shook my head, wishing I could think of a way to end this tragic standoff. AJ's efforts with the stick had not worked after all. I spoke again.

"Even if you find it, you'll never be able to sell that bell. It's a priceless historical artifact."

"News flash for you, babe, we already have a buyer. Did you really think I was an offshore oil worker? I'm in the import-export business. I've got several interested parties, mostly private collectors. Trust me, the price on this bell is more than you could fathom. Now we just have to get all of you out of the way so we can find it ourselves and get out of here. So how 'bout it, mister? How 'bout you let my wife go and we'll cut you in, give you a piece of the pie."

Much to my shock, rather than speaking, Richard simply pressed the knife into Lisa's neck until he pierced the skin. Held tightly in his grasp, she began to cry, though her tears were for real this time. With a sickening grip in the pit of my stomach, I realized that by telling Richard about Lisa I may have taken us all from the proverbial frying pan into the fire.

"If she's his wife," AJ demanded of me suddenly, "why was he choking her last night?"

I thought for a moment and then ventured a guess.

"He wasn't choking her. He was kissing her goodnight. Then they heard the door open and had just a second to cover for it."

"Lucky for us that I'm a quick thinker and she's a good actress," Jimmy said.

Richard pushed the knife deeper as Lisa choked and gasped.

"Stop it, man, or I really will shoot her," Jimmy said, the *her* being *me*.

"Go ahead, I don't care," Richard replied. "I just want out of here. You people can do whatever you want to each other."

Somehow, I had a feeling that he really meant it.

"Fine," Jimmy said, hearing the truth in Richard's voice as well. "Leave."

"Put down the gun and your walkie-talkie first," Richard instructed. "If you do that, I'll let your wife go."

To my surprise, Jimmy did as he said, placing both items on the dirty floor in front of him.

"Kick the gun over toward those leaves."

With great reluctance, Jimmy kicked his gun, sending it skittering noisily across the floor and into a massive pile of rubble.

"Now kick the walkie-talkie this way."

Jimmy gave it a kick but it slid only halfway to Richard, coming to a stop about five feet from the ladder.

"Kick it again," Richard said.

Jimmy did as instructed, though he grumbled as went. At the same time, Richard dragged Lisa with him toward the ladder and then let her go as soon as he had reached it. Sobbing and clutching at her bleeding neck, she flew into the arms of her husband straight ahead of her.

Richard's next move took us all by surprise.

Before anyone could stop him, he jumped forward with a twist and rammed his body against the couple, knocking them off balance. In a flash, they both tumbled over the side of the loft and went crashing to the ground one floor below.

THIRTY-NINE

Swiftly they followed the flight of him who was speeding before them,
Blown by the blast of fate like a dead leaf over the desert.

Smoothing his clothes and hair, Richard stepped closer to the edge and looked down, obviously pleased with what he saw. There were no sounds coming up from down there, and I didn't know if that meant that Jimmy and Lisa were both dead or just injured. Standing up straight, Richard looked at us without expression, calmly folded up the knife, and slipped it into his pocket.

Then, ignoring us, he crossed the room toward the general direction of the gun.

"And so you kill again," I said, as he clearly had no intention of letting AJ and me go free.

"The first time was an accident, a horrible accident," he said, kneeling to search through the rubble. "Cass was in the wrong place at the wrong time. She shouldn't have been butting into something that wasn't any of her business."

"She was a little girl," AJ cried. "Her parents were fighting and she was scared."

"Yeah, you sound just like your sister. Yasmine wanted to tell the police exactly what happened, how I went to hit her and accidentally knocked

Cassandra down the stairs instead. I talked her out of it, but then you showed up for the funeral, and I knew she'd tell you sooner or later." Looking at me, he added scornfully, "Yasmine and Janet shared everything. Even their own children, as it turns out."

AJ bristled at his cutting remark.

"At first I just kept Yasmine sedated," he continued, still rooting through the debris. "I told everyone she was completely unhinged, on the verge of a breakdown so that nobody would believe her babble. But even in her haze, I knew she wasn't going to stay silent forever. So I did what I had to do. The night after Cassandra's funeral, I brought Yasmine outside to the garden and helped her commit suicide. She wanted to anyway, you know. I just speeded things along."

"She was grieving the death of her child," AJ said. "Of course she wanted to die. That doesn't mean she would have taken her own life for real."

He continued his search for the gun, ignoring her remark.

"Obviously, Willy saw you out there that night. He saw what you did," I said, discreetly looking around for something sharp to cut ourselves loose while he was so distracted. "Why didn't he go to the police?"

Richard continued digging, clicking his tongue.

"Good question," he said. "Until all of this excitement here today, I always wondered that myself. Family loyalty? Some deep sense of Cajun justice? As blackmail so he could get a mention in the will? I was never sure of the real motive behind that man's silence. All I knew was that instead of going to the police, he took the information to my parents, who handled everything without involving the authorities. And handle it they did, telling me I had to leave this place and never return, giving me just enough money so that I wouldn't end up homeless, signing my rightful inheritance over to a little girl who wasn't even my own child..."

He flashed a look of pure hatred our way, though I wasn't sure if it was directed at AJ or me—or both.

"Sit still!" he boomed, having caught both me and AJ discreetly rooting through the nearby rubble with our feet. "Not another move."

We sat there, frozen, and after a moment he returned to his search, pushing more rubble aside in his attempt to find the gun.

"I guess my parents figured that with one son a murderer and the other a drunk who'd probably be dead before they were, the only relative left who deserved to inherit the bulk of their fortune was you, Miranda."

"You murdered their grandchild and their daughter-in-law," I replied sharply, "and they allowed you to walk away from here free and clear? They actually thought that taking away your precious inheritance was punishment enough?"

"You think it's been easy for me, getting cut off and kicked out and having to start over somewhere else?"

"You made out okay," I said, thinking of his wife and stepchildren and rambling faux stucco house complete with pool. Shockingly, depending on how all of this played out, he might just slip right back into that life without any of them ever realizing that they were sharing their home with a murderer.

"What do you know of my life? You're a stranger to me."

I didn't justify his comment with a reply. Beside me, I could feel AJ shifting, and as I glanced at her, I realized what she was doing. She was rubbing her shoulder to her ear, trying to knock loose one long, silver earring. Even though I didn't think she'd be able to get it loose by herself, it was a good idea. Though not exactly sharp, the metal might be the right shape to break through the duct tape—provided we had enough time before Richard found that gun and shot us both dead.

Scooting forward, I rested my head on her shoulder, innocently keeping it there until he glanced in our direction. To him, we were merely mother and daughter, huddled together for comfort. When he returned to his rooting—more frustrated now—I tilted my head back and used my mouth to bite the earring back and pull it away from the front.

"Finally," Richard said, victoriously pulling the lost gun from the rubble and holding it up in the air.

As he did so, I discreetly spit the silver backing into the leaves and AJ shook her head in such a way that the heavy earring now slipped loose and dropped to the floor beside her.

The way we were sitting, she had a better chance of giving this a try than I did. Without a word between us, she struggled to pick up the earring while I prepared to run interference yet again.

"Why did you kill Willy?" I asked, watching as Richard cleaned the filthy gun with the bottom of his shirt. Beside me, AJ managed to get a grip on the earring and rub it against her bindings behind her.

"Because I was afraid he was finally going to spill the beans at the end of his life. I heard he was asking for you to come down, that he needed to tell you something. I figured that something was the truth about Yasmine. So I came here too. It wasn't easy getting into the house unseen. The man was never left alone. Then you showed up and I knew it was now or never."

"You were hiding in the bushes near the water."

"Came up the bayou by rowboat and spent an entire day hiding out there in the brush, just waiting for my chance. Originally, I was going to smother him with his own pillow, but then I saw the lighter fluid just outside his door and thought that might be a better idea, that his death would be far less suspicious if it happened right in front of everybody rather than while he was alone. I just didn't expect to cut my head when I put the lighter fluid back."

I glanced down at AJ's hand, thrilled to realize that she was making some progress with the earring. Unfortunately, Richard finished cleaning off the gun at that moment.

"You know," he said as he examined the weapon more closely, "when Willy told my parents what he saw that night in the garden, he said that he'd been out there taking a late night walk and smoking a cigarette. Now that I've been learning about all of this bell business here today, I realize that Willy was lying, that he'd had his own secret to hide about that night too. That's why he went to my parents instead of the police, so that he could get rid of me without his own secret being revealed."

"Do you know whose bones the men found out there today?" I asked, wondering if Willy had also been a killer, if he had been up to something far more sinister that night than burying a bell—such as burying a victim. Willy even said that he had done something terrible, that he needed my forgiveness.

"No, but I have a theory. I've been listening to all of this, thinking you people are so convinced that the angelus is a bell. I'm thinking maybe the angelus was a person. Willy buried a person under the canning shed. This Jimmy or Junior or whoever he is who came here today to find some big valuable treasure, but he didn't realize that he'd already found what he'd been looking for. Only the angelus wasn't a bell, it was a body."

Could that be true? Could the angelus be someone's remains? If so, at least that would explain what Willy had been doing out there that night. Maybe the bones dated back several centuries and they were the treasure that I had sworn an oath to protect. It made a certain amount of sense, until I remembered my grandmother's mural that I had uncovered upstairs. In that mural, there had clearly been a bell—forged from gold, carried out in the expulsion, kept safely hidden ever since.

"You're probably right," I said, now aware that nothing could be gained from telling him he was way off base. "But even so those bones might be valuable. With my training, I could help you excavate them, get them evaluated, and maybe even find a buyer. Depending on who or what they are, they could be worth a fortune. If people have been guarding them since the mid-seventeen hundreds, they could even be the secret remains of Columbus or Pocahontas or something."

I couldn't chance another glance at AJ's hands, but from the subtle movements of her shoulders, I had a feeling she was close to breaking free.

"Yeah, or maybe Amelia Earhart or Al Capone. Whatever. I don't need to bother with all that. I'm about to inherit a great big house along with a nice stretch of bayou front property. Besides, you can't help me out with that anyway because you'll be dead."

With that, he raised the gun and pointed it straight at me. Refusing to cower, I jutted out my chin and stared back at him defiantly.

"If you shoot me," I said, "the police will know for a fact this was murder. Shouldn't you try to make it look like an accident?"

"Oh, I am," Richard replied, surprising me by lowering the gun and then tucking it into his waistband. Then he crossed to the ladder and climbed on, pausing before he headed down. "Funny, isn't it Miranda?

You saw everything that happened that night, but then you got all wacky on us and forgot about it anyway."

"Lucky for me," I replied, "or else you'd have killed me long before now."

His only response was to give us a final smirk and climb down the ladder. My hope was that either Jimmy or Lisa had managed to survive their fall and were waiting at the bottom to ambush him. There were no sounds of a struggle, however, just the echo of Richard reaching the bottom and then wrenching the ladder loose from its rusty moorings.

"That's just to slow you down in case that ridiculous earring trick actually works and you manage to cut yourselves free," he called up to us.

AJ and I looked at each other and then I looked down at her bindings, which were nearly severed in half. She worked more quickly, continuing to saw away with the silver as we tried to figure out what Richard was doing down below. From the sound of things, he had continued on down the stairs to the first floor, though he hadn't yet left the building.

When she finally got herself free, AJ frantically went to work on the tape around my wrists. This time it went much faster, of course, and soon she handed over the earring so I could cut my feet loose while she took out the other earring to do the same for herself. We were half finished when the smell finally reached us, the strong, distinct odor of gasoline.

"He's going to burn the place down," I hissed.

We kept working, and once we were both completely free, we crawled to the edge of the loft and looked over the side. To her credit, AJ didn't gasp, though I knew we both wanted to. Jimmy was the only one still alive, but he was terribly injured. It looked as though he was crying, one hand touching his wife's lifeless face. The other hand was grasping at his chest, and then I realized that he was trying to remove something from his front shirt pocket.

Through the open stairwell, we could see Richard on the bottom floor, still sprinkling gas from a can onto the trash and leaves and papers that were spread around down there. Before he was finished, Jimmy managed to roll over and with one big push slide himself toward the stairs. Then before we could stop him, he held out the item he had retrieved from his pocket: a pack of matches, which he lit and tossed down at Richard.

In an instant and intense explosion, Richard was gone. Directly below us, Jimmy simply rolled onto his back and closed his eyes, ready to sacrifice himself for the sake of avenging his beloved wife's death.

I wasn't ready to sacrifice either myself or AJ. Unable to do anything to help out below, I ran toward the open window, hoping to find handholds that we could use to climb down outside. There was nothing of the kind anywhere in sight.

Frantic, I returned to the place in the railing where the ladder had been. Empty now, there was no way to get ourselves down to the next floor even if we wanted to descend toward the fire, nothing that we could climb or slide down at all. Even up here on the third floor, the heat from the fire below was astonishing, the smoke burning our eyes and clouding our vision.

"We're going to have to jump," AJ said, eyeing the distance between us and the grassy ground below. "We have no choice."

"That'll kill us, AJ. It's just too far."

"What if we tied our clothes together and climbed down them like a rope?"

"There's not enough. We'd still be badly hurt when we hit bottom."

I caught sight of a movement in the distance, and after a moment I realized I was seeing a big truck pulling up the driveway. Hope filled my heart for only an instant, until it got closer and I saw that the truck held a large piece of construction equipment; it was Jimmy's two goons, finally returning with the backhoe.

They didn't stick around for long. Obviously spotting the burning building, they used the front loop around the fountain to make a U-turn, rumbling away much more quickly than they had come.

We really were alone.

We really were going to die.

"If only there were an opening on the other side of the building," AJ cried. "If we could jump out that way, we'd land in the water."

I inhaled deeply, looking at her.

"There is, AJ," I gasped. "I know there is."

Running across the hot floor, the heat of the encroaching fire licking at our heels, I raised my hands in front of me, remembering what it was that my sister and I had loved about this building. Our grandfather had let us come up here with him sometimes, whenever the loft storage had been newly emptied of its bounty. As he supervised the workmen sweeping up the last traces of sugar from the floor, he would let us peek down the long loading tube that hung out over the bayou, the one that the sugar was poured through for filling the containers on the boats. If he was in a really good mood, he would even have let us bring up handfuls of pecans gathered from the ground outside, and we would take turns rolling the pecans down the tube and listening as they splashed into the water far below.

"It's here," I cried, running my hands over the irregular surface of the wood-and-steel outer wall. "I *know* it is. Look for a door."

The ground under my feet was hot, so hot that I knew any moment it was going to burst into flame and swallow us down whole. As it was, the fire was now raging so fiercely underneath us that I couldn't understand why the entire structure hadn't begun to buckle.

"There!" AJ yelled, spotting a handle alongside a beam.

Together we gripped it and pulled, and with a mighty creaking groan the metal covering swung open to reveal the loading tube. Like a giant blow drier, a burst of hot air shot from the tube and slammed into our faces.

Ignoring the heat, I looked down the tube to where it ended, the bayou sparkling in the distance below.

The tube might not be sturdy after all these years. Even if it was, the flames might catch up to us when we were halfway down. Even if we made it to the water without the tube collapsing or burning, the bayou might be so shallow that we would break both of our necks on impact.

Still, we had no other choice.

"Just a second," AJ said and before I could stop her she turned and ran through the thick smoke to the edge of the loft and looked over. She ran back to me twice as fast, her face reflecting the horror she had just seen, saying "Go, go, go! It's too late. They're all dead."

As if to punctuate her words, the wooden edge of the loft sprung up into glorious orange flames. Now we *really* had no choice.

At least the tube was wide enough for us to go down it together. We climbed in and wrapped our arms around each other and pushed off, leaving our stomachs behind as our bodies plummeted in a steep angle toward the water. We both screamed all the way down, locked together in a death grip, eyes shut tight, awaiting the jolt of either death or life.

Finally, we felt the tubing disappear from under us and then we were airborne, flying through the sky in slow motion until we crashed into the black bayou, its deep waters sucking us in and pulling us down to the muddy bottom. With a mighty push, it released us again, popping us both toward the surface, our eyes wide open now, our lungs screaming for air, our hands still clenched together.

We had made it.

We had survived, my mother and I.

FORTY

Whither my heart has gone, there follows my hand, and not elsewhere.
For when the heart goes before, like a lamp, and illumines the pathway,
Many things are made clear, that else lie hidden in darkness.

As always, AJ processed herself through the aftermath of the trauma differently than I did. When I went looking for her the next morning, I found her sitting on the front porch swing, staring out across the green, shady lawn and weeping into a lace handkerchief. She'd been so brave as we managed to escape the burning building, float down the bayou to the beach at Little Tara next door, and climb out to get help. But even as Livvy and Big Daddy and Melanie and Scarlett had buzzed around us with towels and blankets and hot tea and kind words while we waited for the police and fire departments to arrive, AJ had finally broken down and sobbed.

She continued to cry all through her statement to the police. She did manage to pull herself together at the hospital where we were both treated for smoke inhalation, minor abrasions, lacerations, and, for her, a sprained wrist acquired during our ride down the tube. At Livvy's insistence, we spent the night at Little Tara, where we had been lovingly pampered and made to feel safe. But this morning, when AJ and I had returned to Twin Oaks, she had burst into fresh tears the moment she caught sight of the smoldering building by the water. The estate had still been crawling with authorities as well as reporters, so I had ushered AJ into the house where she could deal with her emotions in private and I could go upstairs to be by myself for a while.

Now here she was just two hours later, sitting on the porch and crying again. At least the reporters that remained were all around back and hadn't realized we were out here. Personally, I hadn't even felt the urge to shed a single tear. As usual, my emotions had receded somewhere deep inside, though this time I was determined not to let them disappear in there completely.

"Coffee?" I asked, handing her a cup fixed just the way she liked it.

She took it from me with a sad smile, motioning for me to sit next to her. I did, grateful for the comfort of her presence, even if it did include a little waterworks. There were details to discuss, so many details, but for now we just sat there, side by side, and rocked. I asked if she had heard from Holt, and she said no.

Last night he and Charles had stopped by Little Tara just to update us on the police activity at Twin Oaks and to make sure we were both okay. That visit had been brief and strained, with Holt speaking almost exclusively to me, unwilling even to look AJ in the eye. As soon as they left, she had gone up to bed, and I had to wonder at this point if her tears were less about processing the general trauma of what had happened to us and more about the pain of lost love, not to mention the guilt of what she had done to him by withholding the truth for so many years.

Strangely, I wasn't all that angry with her myself, despite the fact that she had forced us to live a charade of aunt and niece since the day I was born. Though I wished she had acted differently from the beginning, I could also understand the youthful fears that had driven those original decisions. In a sense, I couldn't help but feel that she had already been punished enough—by losing one child in death, by living such a tremendous lie, by hearing her own children address her as aunt.

"I'll probably never call you 'Mommy,'" I said to her now as we sat there on the swing, "but I want you to know that I forgive you. As much as anyone can forgive something like that, I mean."

That sent her into more sobs, and I put an arm around her and pulled her close, wishing for a moment that I could cry that hard too.

Once her tears had subsided somewhat, she began to talk about Yasmine, about their childhood together, about the incredibly strong bond that they had shared, about the astonishing deception they had managed to pull off. As AJ talked, I remembered with a start that *I* had had a sister too: my sister Cass, my mirror image, my deepest loss.

We were silent again, each of us occupied by our own thoughts, when a car came slowly up the driveway. Thinking it was another reporter, AJ said that sooner or later we were going to have to talk to them. They had so many questions—about the deaths of Jimmy and Lisa and Richard, about the capture of the two goons by the police twenty miles out of town, about the whole angelus-bones-Cajun myth thing, which was still totally up in the air and garnering more and more attention from the media. In my statement to the police, I'd had no choice but to tell them everything, and that information had been leaked to the press.

Some *gardien* I had turned out to be.

"I'll wait until after we find out more about the bones," I said. "Then, if they really do turn out to be something important, I'll have a better idea of what I should say."

The car continued up the driveway, but as it drew closer, my heart moved into my throat. There, behind the wheel, was my husband.

Nathan.

So much for not crying. Suddenly, deep heaving sobs rose up from my chest as I jumped up from the swing and ran. I ran across the grass toward the car he was climbing out of. I ran into his arms.

I never held on to anyone so tightly.

I never needed anyone so mightily.

I had never missed anyone so badly.

He must have thought I was crazy. As I gripped him with every shred of strength I possessed, he held on to me strongly in return, burying his face into my hair, whispering gentle words of love. I don't know how long we remained there like that, but at one point I could hear the sound of excited voices as the reporters spotted us and the click of cameras as they photographed us and then the scolding tones of a policeman as he ushered all of them away. Finally, I felt Nathan pull back a bit. Quietly, he suggested that we go to some place more private where we could talk.

Taking him by the hand, I led him around the far side of the house, past the police barricade, and down to the stone bench, which was now in an area protected from reporters. Though we had passed several cops on the way, none were near us now. We sat on the bench, and as Nathan seemed to be taking in the beauty around him, I moved even closer into his muscular embrace, wishing he could hold me forever and ever.

How had I ever risked what we shared by keeping myself so distant from him? Though I would probably always have to fight that tendency within myself, what I wanted most now was closeness and sharing. Even if I ended up having to go into counseling for a while, to work through all that I had learned on this trip, I knew that our estrangement was officially over. All that remained was to tell him so—and then prove it to him day after day after day.

Nathan already knew everything that had happened here, thanks to a marathon telephone call we'd shared last night before I went to bed. Our plan had been for him to fly to Houston to pick up Tess today and then bring her with him here to join me at Twin Oaks tomorrow. As he explained now, however, he'd made an impulsive, last-minute change at the airport early this morning, canceling the flight to Texas and booking one to Louisiana instead. He said he couldn't wait one more minute to be with me and that of course his parents hadn't minded the switch at all as it bought them more time with their granddaughter.

"I just needed to be with you," he said. "I couldn't bear to be apart any longer."

I sat up and looked him in the eye and told him that I felt exactly the same. I told him that I wasn't sure how or when or where it had happened, but somewhere amid all this drama, I had broken down that Plexiglas wall and found myself ready to let him in. All the way in.

"Plexiglass wall?"

"Long story," I said, tears filling my eyes. "It doesn't matter. I don't want what we had before, Nathan. I want to be close. I want that same bond you want. I want to be united."

At that, his eyes filled with tears as well.

"You have no idea how long I have waited to hear you say those words," he whispered, reaching up with both hands to grip the sides of my face.

Leaning forward, Nathan brought his lips to mine, the heat of his mouth seared with passion and promise. I kissed him back deeply, wishing we could become one person instead of two, one single-but-incredibly-strong entity, a cord of three strands.

"I have to tell you something important," he said as we pulled apart. "Something I couldn't explain over the phone."

"What is it?"

Slowly, gently, my husband explained to me that while we were apart one thing in his life had drastically changed.

"It's all been so amazing, but it's hard to explain," he said earnestly. "It started Sunday morning at that service, which didn't go exactly as I had expected. There I was, representing our big fancy firm, looking around at this magnificent structure we had designed, and all the preacher could talk about was how none of it was of any real or lasting importance. I was so offended by his words that I waited until after the service and confronted him about it."

Not being a very confrontational guy, I knew that Nathan must have been extremely upset to do that.

"The preacher said he appreciated my candor, and he invited me to join him in his study for lunch. I ended up staying there and talking to him for almost three hours."

"Wow."

"Yeah. You know how he's been trying to share his Christian faith with me in subtle ways for months throughout this entire project. Once he finally got the opportunity to say everything he wanted to say, it all began to make sense. Our conversation left me with a lot to think about, and by the next afternoon I was back there at his office again with about a hundred more questions." Nathan smiled, and there was something so peaceful, so otherworldly about that smile, that suddenly I realized he'd found what I had been searching for too, almost since the moment I had arrived here. "I realize now that the Holy Spirit had been working on me for a while. Late that afternoon I accepted Jesus Christ as my personal Lord and Savior. Now it's just like I had heard it would be. I'm a new person, Miranda. And even if this bothers you and even if you think I'm nuts, I'm going to show you that this change is a good one, good for both of us. To be honest, I've already started praying that eventually you'll make the same decision I did."

His speech complete, Nathan sat back, looking both nervous and settled at the same time. I knew that he was expecting me to protest or make fun or play it all down, but instead I took a deep breath and looked into his eyes, feeling kind of shy.

"This path you went down," I said awkwardly, "I think it's a path I might have started on too. At least, I've been thinking about God more and hearing about the Holy Spirit through talking to Holt. He even gave me a Bible."

At that moment, we were interrupted by the arrival of several police cars. We both stood and headed back to the house, where a full contingent of officials in suits were climbing out of their vehicles and posturing for the press.

"What's going on?" AJ asked me as she came out the back door. I just shrugged and pulled her close while we waited to find out.

"Miranda Miller?" one of the officials asked, stepping forward.

"Yes?"

"I'm with the Louisiana State Medical Examiner's office, here with the results of the bone analysis."

Nathan and I exchanged glances.

"Our office has determined that the single bone you found here the other day came from the same source as the rest of the bones discovered here last night."

I nodded, as that had been my thought too, that the first bone had become separated from the rest in the hurricane, but that they all belonged together.

"Of course, we will be conducting extensive tests on the whole lot, but at this point we do have a positive identification based on DNA analysis from that first bone."

"You have a name?" I asked. "You know whose bones they are?"

"Yes, ma'am," he said, going on to tell us that the DNA results showed a 99.92% accurate match to a known person. From his pocket, the man produced an envelope, which he held up and opened with all the drama of an awards ceremony. "The bones in question are those of Miranda Fairmont Miller. Young lady, I don't know who you are or what kind of scam you're trying to pull here, but you're under arrest for false impersonation, attempted theft, and possible murder."

If the scene hadn't been so ludicrous, it might have been terrifying. Suddenly, the reporters went wild, snapping pictures and asking questions as two uniformed cops headed toward me with handcuffs.

"This is insane!" I said, not knowing whether I should laugh or cry. "I'm not impersonating anybody. I *am* Miranda Fairmont Miller. Ask *her!* She's my mother!"

They didn't seem impressed by that, so I tried again, shouting to be heard over the cop who had begun to read me my rights.

"Ask Holt Fairmont!" I cried. "He's my father!"

That seemed to do the trick. The speech ceased right after I had the right to remain silent, and the cops on each side of me hesitated, turning back to look at the official in the suit for direction.

"If she's really Holt's daughter," one of the cops said, "then I'm not going to arrest her. Can somebody go get him?"

"Look here," the official said, stepping closer. "These are official DNA test results."

Frantically I glanced from AJ to Nathan to Charles Benochet, who had arrived amid the melee and was making his way through the crowd.

"Wait!" Charles cried, stepping in to take charge. "Scooter, what are you doing?"

"Stay out of my way, Charles," the official said. "DNA doesn't lie."

"It doesn't always tell the whole story either, now, does it? Miranda Fairmont had a twin sister. Scooter, you know as well as I do that identical twins have identical DNA. Those aren't the bones of Miranda Fairmont. They must be the bones of her twin sister Cassandra Fairmont, who died many years ago."

Again, the reporters went nuts, but at least this time the cops let go of my arms.

All I could think of was my poor sister, who had been buried in an unmarked grave in the middle of the yard. My mind filled with the words of Psalm 141: *As one plows and breaks up the earth, so our bones have been scattered at the mouth of the grave.*

"I know where it is," I said softly. Then again, much louder, I repeated myself. "I know where it is."

"Where what is?" AJ called to me across the crowd, her expression distraught.

"The angelus," I said, my heart pounding, my eyes moving from her to Charles to Nathan. "I know where Willy hid it. I know what he needed me to forgive."

FORTY-ONE

All was ended now, the hope, and the fear, and the sorrow,
All the aching of heart, the restless, unsatisfied longing,
All the dull, deep pain, and constant anguish of patience!

Ten Days Later

Despite the somber setting of the cemetery, the mood was light. The judge had not granted our petition to prevent the press or the general public from attending this event, though we had been allowed to keep them outside of the family cemetery gates. The small cemetery was still packed with invited guests, but the turnout beyond the gates had been incredible, with news vans and cars lining the road and the near-constant whir and snap of cameras going behind us. I could only hope that when we reconvened here tomorrow for Cass's private re-interment ceremony that the hoopla would have died down so that we could lay my sister's bones to rest in peace.

I couldn't believe it had taken almost ten days to clear up the legalities of opening this grave. In that amount of time, as Charles worked our various petitions through the Louisiana courts, the story had continued to splash all over the media, putting Nathan and me in the amusing position of having to hire a publicist just to keep from being tailed by paparazzi. To appease the press, we had already appeared on several talk shows, but when Oprah asked me to show the back of my head to the camera, a trend was born: Now all over the country, people were shaving small squares in their hair and having their scalps tattooed.

With the wheels turning on many fronts, Nathan and I had made a number of important decisions and arrangements about the angelus, depending on what might happen here. Regardless of today's outcome, however, we had also taken care of some personal matters as well. With regards to Twin Oaks, as much as we loved it, we simply couldn't afford to keep the estate for ourselves, as the maintenance costs alone would be prohibitive. We had, however, decided to parcel off and retain several waterfront acres on which we would be building a modest vacation home perfect for long visits to Louisiana.

The rest of Twin Oaks would be sold intact, and judging by the offers that were already coming in, our windfall was going to be significant. Before Twin Oaks could be sold, however, there was an important task to be performed, one that was already underway, the careful extraction of the walls that held my grandmother's paintings. The mural was being removed intact and would be reconstructed in its entirety at the Louisiana Museum of Art and Culture—an acquisition for which Livvy West Kroft was receiving an enormous amount of acclaim in all the right circles. Today, if the angelus really was hidden inside my sister's grave as we suspected, then it would become a part of the exhibit as well, a priceless artifact that now belonged, as it always had, to the Cajun descendants of the Nova Scotian village of Colline d'Or. As the sole living *gardien* of the angelus, I was fulfilling the duty I had sworn to uphold—to guard it with my life and keep it safe from harm—by handing it over on a permanent loan to the Louisiana Department of Antiquities, who was going to work with the museum to create a state-of-the-art security system for its display.

Most of the experts we had consulted agreed that the safest place to keep the bell would be in plain-but-well-guarded sight under the auspices of state and local authorities, combined with several well-heeled private interests and an advisory board made up of various officials, representatives of the Cajun community, myself, and whatever descendant of Colline d'Or that I chose to become the second *gardien* to replace Lisa. Eventually, the exhibit would tour, as the display was wanted by museums across the country and throughout Nova Scotia and France. As its official protector, I hoped to be involved with that tour on many levels—something I should be able to do now that I had resigned from my full-time job as a senior preparator at the museum and was converting my position to that of a part-time restoration consultant.

I would also be free to spend more time focusing on my husband and daughter, not to mention any new little Millers that might come along now that we had decided it was time to try and give Tess a sibling. Someday I might choose to return to full-time museum work, but for now this was the right choice for us. The day I finally made the decision to do so, I felt a great peace about it and I knew deep in my heart that it was God's will.

In fact, God's plan for me was something I was learning about daily. Though the church in Connecticut that Nathan helped design was too far away from Manhattan for us to attend regularly, the preacher there had hooked us up with a dynamic guy who pastored a church in the city, and we were already enrolled in "new Christian" classes there. Though we had both been Christians less than two weeks, we were already seeing the change in almost every area of our lives, from how we ordered our priorities to how we conducted our affairs to how we related to each other. I couldn't believe that this life—this fulfilled, peaceful, forgiven life—had been available to me all along, and all I had had to do to receive it was ask.

Nathan and I were excited that Tess seemed to love her new Sunday school class, and already, AJ had agreed to go to services with us as well. Lately I had begun to sense in her the same hunger that had led me to fall on my knees late at night one week ago in the presence of God and my sweet husband and ask Jesus to come into my heart.

My heart had been renewed and restored, not just by the love of Christ that now filled it, but by the entire experience of facing my hidden past and unearthing every secret there. For the very first time in my life, I felt true peace and purpose.

The only question that now remained was whether Willy Pedreaux really had done as I suspected. My theory was that Willy and Ya Ya had been planning to bury the bell in the yard underneath the exact place where a small building, the canning shed, was about to be erected under Willy's supervision. Though that would have made a perfectly good hiding place for the bell, he wanted to follow his oath to the letter and find some place that was more accessible. When Cassandra died unexpectedly, Willy had seized the opportunity to house the bell in a location that was completely hidden but also very accessible: her above-ground tomb. As I saw it, the night after the funeral, Willy had come here to the cemetery and removed my sister's tiny body from her casket, putting in its place the angelus. Then he had laid Cass to rest in a simple pine box, one whose top he had etched with a verse from *Evangeline*, simply to proclaim that this was but a temporary resting place. That night he had buried the box in the exact spot where he told Ya Ya he was burying the bell. That was the secret that Willy said she and my grandfather would have learned in heaven, that her fellow *gardien* had desecrated their granddaughter's grave in order to better fulfill the dictates of *Le Serment* and protect the angelus. No wonder he wanted forgiveness.

"Looks like they're ready," Nathan said, taking me by the elbow as we moved forward.

Surrounding Nathan and AJ and me were a handful of state and museum officials, my father, Holt, and several delightful Louisiana cousins that I was just starting to get to know, Charles Benochet and his wife, and Livvy West Kroft and her husband, Big Daddy. There were also as many descendants of Colline d'Or that could make it on such short notice, including the mother of the Guidry boys who had died in Katrina and the old man who had warned me to be careful at the festival and then had given me the Bible verse that had helped lead me to this place. Deena had declined our invitation to come, saying that she was just getting settled in a retirement home in Florida with her sister, but she wished us all the best. Nathan and I had opted to leave Tess back at the house with Melanie and Scarlett gladly serving as her babysitters.

Now, with the soft whir of a special drill, two workmen removed the bolts from the end of the tomb as we all watched in somber anticipation. As they took off the end cap and pulled out the casket to the rough scraping sound of cement against stone, I thought of poor misguided Lisa, who had

336 MINDY STARNS CLARK

let greed get in the way of a much more important calling. I remembered the words of the psalm, *Let the wicked fall into their own nets, while I pass by in safety,* and I knew that that was what she and her husband and Richard had done. They had fallen into their own nets.

"Ms. Greene, Ms. Miller," the official said, addressing AJ and me, "we're going to open the casket now. As Cassandra's mother and sister, you may want to avert your eyes, just in case."

"Holt too—he's the father," AJ said, looking longingly toward the man who had kept himself slightly apart and was watching the proceedings from his wheelchair at the end of the row. Holt did not respond but continued to stare at the tomb, so finally AJ braced herself for this moment without him, turning her face against Nathan's strong shoulder. I, on the other hand, was not afraid to see what waited inside. I knew what was in there. As they slowly raised the lid, I saw that I was right.

It was a bell, solid and heavy, dented and dirty, and made of pure, sparkling gold—the same gold that had been forged by the citizens of Colline d'Or in 1755 into the shape of a bell, so that they could carry it out of their small Nova Scotian village right under the noses of their British captors.

The scene around us erupted into pandemonium, and in the midst of the confusion, the throng of reporters moved closer, jostling for attention just outside the cemetery gates. They kept calling out our names, shouting questions, but I tuned them all out the moment AJ gripped me fiercely by the hand.

"He waved for me to come over there. Come with me," AJ whispered.

Together, she and I extracted ourselves from the throng that was crowding around the casket and walked toward Holt. For the first time since we had all sat in the living room and listened to AJ's revelations about what she had done, Holt was actually looking her in the eye. As we reached him, AJ released my hand and knelt down so that the two of them were on the same level. Not wanting to intrude, I stepped back a bit and placed a comforting hand on my father's shoulder.

"Will you ever find it in your heart to forgive me?" AJ asked him, tears streaming from her eyes.

"Only if you forgive me too," he replied.

With a gasp, AJ put a hand to her mouth and simply looked at him.

"I'm sorry I put you through so much in the last ten days," Holt said. "I just had to work this through, to think and to pray. I do forgive you, Janet. I also...I, uh, I still love you."

"Oh, Holt." Smiling through her tears, Janet reached up one hand to stroke his weathered cheek. "Do you think we could have another chance? That we could start over?"

"Does that mean you love me too?"

"Yes, Holt. *Yes.* I never stopped loving you."

As they hugged and then kissed, I stepped away to give them some privacy, searching the crowd for my own true love. Nathan was watching and waiting from a distance, and when he saw my face he came and took my hand.

"Let's get out of here."

We braved the gauntlet of reporters, ignoring their shouted questions until one of them stepped directly in front of us, blocking our way.

"What will you do now about your sister's bones?" she demanded, thrusting her microphone at my face.

Irritated at her insensitivity, Nathan answered the question for me, saying that soon we would be having a small, private ceremony, so that Cassandra Lynn Fairmont could be laid to rest in her rightful burial place in the family cemetery.

"What will the two of you do next?" the reporter prodded. "Will you be going home to New York?"

Nathan looked at me, and I turned to take it all in: The friends and family that surrounded us, the buried ancestors who had come before us, the incredible beauty of the green earth, the moss-laden trees, and the black, life-giving water of the bayou.

The water that flowed through my veins.

"Yes," I said, nodding. "We'll go home. But this place will always be home for us too."

ABOUT THE AUTHOR

Whispers of the Bayou is Mindy's ninth novel for Harvest House Publishers. Previous books include the Million Dollar Mysteries and The Smart Chick Mystery series, which includes *The Trouble with Tulip*, *Blind Dates Can Be Murder*, and *Elementary, My Dear Watkins*.

She is also the author of the nonfiction guide *The House That Cleans Itself* as well as numerous plays and musicals. A popular speaker and former stand-up comedian, Mindy lives with her husband and two daughters near Valley Forge, Pennsylvania.

In any story, where facts are used to mold and shape fiction, sometimes it becomes hard for readers to tell the two apart, particularly when learning about a history or culture that isn't overly familiar. For more information and to find out which elements of this story are fictional and which are based on fact, visit Mindy's website at:

www.mindystarnsclark.com.

Discover the Smart Chick Mysteries

by Mindy Starns Clark

The Trouble with Tulip

Josephine Tulip is most definitely a smart chick, a twenty-first-century female MacGyver who writes a helpful-hints column and solves mysteries in her spare time. Her best friend, Danny, is a talented photographer who longs to succeed in his career...perhaps a cover photo on *National Geographic*?

When Jo's neighbor is accused of murder, Jo realizes the police have the wrong suspect. As she and Danny analyze clues, follow up on leads, and fall in and out of trouble, she recovers from a broken heart, and he discovers that he has feelings for her. Will Danny have the courage to reveal them, or will he continue to hide them behind a facade of friendship?

Blind Dates Can Be Murder

Blind dates give everyone the shivers...with or without a murder attached to them. Jo Tulip is a sassy single woman full of household hints and handy advice for every situation. Her first romantic outing in months is a blind date—okay, the Hall of Fame of Awful Blind Dates—but things go from bad to worse when the date drops dead and Jo finds herself smack in the middle of a murder investigation.

With the help of her best friend, Danny, and faith in God, Jo attempts to solve one exciting mystery while facing another: Why is love always so complicated?

Elementary, My Dear Watkins

When someone tries to push Jo Tulip in front of a New York train, her ex-fiancé, Bradford, suffers an injury while saving her—and the unintentional sleuth is thrown onto the tracks of a very personal mystery.

Jo's boyfriend, Danny Watkins, is away in Paris, so she begins a solo investigation of her near-murder. What secret was Bradford about to share before he took the fall? And when Jo uncovers clues tied to Europe, can she and Danny work together in time to save her life?

The Million Dollar Mysteries
Mindy Starns Clark

Attorney Callie Webber investigates nonprofit organizations for the J.O.S.H.U.A. Foundation, giving the best of them grants ranging up to a million dollars. In each book, Callie comes across a mystery she must solve using her skills as a former private investigator. A young widow, Callie finds strength in her faith in God and joy in her relationship with her employer, Tom.

A Penny for Your Thoughts

Just like that, Callie finds herself looking into the sudden death of an old family friend of her employer. But it seems the family has some secrets they would rather not have uncovered. Almost immediately Callie realizes she has put herself in serious danger. Her only hope is that God will use her investigative skills to discover the identity of the killer before she becomes the next victim.

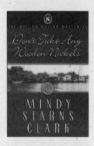

Don't Take Any Wooden Nickels

Just like that, Callie finds herself helping a young woman coming out of drug rehab and into the workforce...who's suddenly charged with murder. What appears to be routine, though, explodes into international intrigue and deadly deception. A series of heart-pounding events lands her disastrously in the hands of the killer, where Callie finds she has less than a moment for a whispered prayer. Will help arrive in time to save her?

A Dime a Dozen

Just like that, Callie finds herself involved in the life of a young wife and mother whose husband has disappeared. But in the search for him, a body is discovered, which puts Callie's job on hold and her new romance with her mysterious boss in peril. Trusting in God, she forges steadily ahead through a mire of clues that lead her deeper and deeper into danger.

A Quarter for a Kiss

Just like that, Callie finds herself on her way to the beautiful Virgin Islands. Her friend and mentor, Eli Gold, has been shot. This unusual—and very dangerous—assignment sends Callie and her boss, Tom, on an adventure together to solve the mystery surrounding the shooting. Though Callie's faith in God is sure, will her faith in Tom survive their visit to the island of St. John?

The Buck Stops Here

Just like that, Callie finds herself in the middle of an intense investigation of a millionaire philanthropist and NSA agent—Tom Bennett, her boss and the man she hopes to marry. Callie overhears a conversation in which her boss implicates himself in her late husband's fatal accident, but Tom's association with the NSA prevents him from answering her questions. Callie must have answers. With God's help she embarks on an investigation that leads to a conclusion beyond her wildest dreams.